All rights reserved. No part of this book may be used or reproduced by any means, graphic, electronic or mechanical, including, photocopying, recording, taping or by an information storage retrieval system without the written permission of the authors or publisher except in the event of quotes embodied in articles and reviews.

The work is a work of fiction. All of the characters, names, incidents, organizations, and dialogue in this novel are either the products of the author's imagination or are used fictitiously.

Copyright © 2011. All rights reserved.

The views expressed in this work are solely those of the authors and do not necessarily reflect the views of the publisher, and the publisher herby disclaims any responsibility for them.

Printed in the United States of America
Dark Chocolate Publishing
Reprint 2016 Kirabaco Publishing

DARK CHOCOLATE PUBLISHING PRESENTS

CROSSROADS: THE ANTHOLOGY
Stories of Love, Lust, Revenge, and Murder

WEDNESDAY'S CUSTOMER
KR Bankston

FOR ONE NIGHT
Elizabeth LaShaun

THE PREREQUISITES OF PERDITION
Keith K. Williams

IN DESPERATION
DK Gaston

LIBERATION IS NOT A GIFT BESTOWED UPON US
FROM OUR OPPRESSOR.
IT IS TAKEN AND OWNED BY THE DECISION THAT
NO ONE CAN KEEP THEM FROM IT.

For too long we've watched silently as we've been violated by our government at every turn. The rights and needs of the poor, minorities, and women have been ignored and trampled upon. It's time to stand up and say no. You have the power to make a difference and it is as simple as casting a ballot in your local, state, and federal elections.

If you haven't registered to vote, you may do so in the following ways:
- Contact your Secretary of State and request a voter registration form by mail
- Register at your Public Library
- Register at the DMV when you renew your license
- Register when you renew your TANF/Food Stamp benefits

Registering to vote doesn't automatically sentence you to jury duty. If you get a jury summons, don't avoid it! We need rational voices to keep our men and women from behind bars! **Convicted felons are not barred from registering!** States such as Rhode Island, South Carolina and Utah automatically restore your voting rights upon completion of your sentence. Check your state laws for complete information on restoring your voting rights if you've been convicted of a felony.

To Report Voter Issues: call the Civil Rights Division toll-free at (800) 253-3931, or contact them by mail at:
Chief, Voting Section
Civil Rights Division Room 7254 – NWB
Department of Justice
950 Pennsylvania Ave., N.W.
Washington, DC 20530

Your right to vote was secured through blood, sweat, and tears. Exercise it to the fullest without relenting. Social change and justice for people of color is not optional: it is mandatory. Make them know this by registering your voting voice today!

WEDNESDAY'S CUSTOMER

KR Bankston

For all the 'dream believers' who never stop moving forward and for all my 'dream realizes' who came together and made this project happen. Much love to all of you, taking the world by storm one reader at a time.

Wednesday's Customer   KR Bankston

Jasmine saw him walk inside and immediately smoothed her uniform, putting on her best smile. He came every Wednesday without fail, at 10:15AM sharp. As always, he was impeccably dressed, clean shaven and smelling divine. *That man is too sexy,* Jasmine thought lustily taking him in as he sat in her section and she made her way to his table to take his order.

"Good morning," she greeted pleasantly, smiling her most persuasive smile.

"Hi," the man returned asking for his usual breakfast selection.

    Jasmine knew it by heart, but she still went through the motions, just in case.

"Sure, I'll have that out to you in a few minutes."

Smiling again and walking away, she prayed he was watching her butt as she switched it extra hard just for him. Jasmine turned in the order and set about getting the coffee and juice he asked for. She was a bit frustrated at the moment. She just could not seem to garner his attention. No matter what ploy she tried, or what hints she threw, he was unmoved. *Damn, please tell me he is not gay,* she panicked slightly as the thought began to take hold.

    Shaking her head to clear the feelings and once again putting on her award winning smile, she headed to his table, dropping off his drinks and leaving to retrieve the cream he requested. She ended up having to go out into the walk-in cooler and retrieve the cream since her shift mate had not bothered to refill the bin inside.

"Here you are," Jasmine told him smiling once more. "I had to go get some from the cooler, we were out up front," she told him apologetically.

"It's fine, really," he replied smiling at her.

    Jasmine thought she would melt from the sexy smile. He owned perfect white teeth, and the dimples in his cheeks definitely did not hurt. *Total damned package,* she fancied once more recalling his six foot plus frame, bulging biceps with sculpted chest and abs. His jeans made his defined thighs and butt look like something straight out of a fitness magazine. Jasmine loved summer. Especially looking at Mr. Wednesday in the form fitting tee he was wearing. She smiled internally of the nickname. It was what she took to calling him once his pattern was established some two months ago. She still was yet to work up the nerve to ask his real name. Sighing lightly, she again put on her game face as the cook called out order up and she headed over to his table one more time.

Chapter One

Elijah regarded the woman as she walked away. He observed her far more than she ever realized. She was sexy to him; thick build, shapely hips and butt, smooth chocolate cocoa butter skin. She possessed beautiful eyes that danced when she smiled and he loved the natural curl to her hair. He also knew she had a crush on him. *Bet she feels really good inside,* he smiled slightly. Glancing around the diner and changing his thought, Elijah took in the place again. He came because he loved the quick paced atmosphere. The place seemed to always be buzzing with people coming and going. His glance briefly rested on another patron in the diner he was observing off and on for a little while. The man seemed restless today. Normally there was a woman and kids that held his attention as he ate breakfast. Today he sat unrequited. Elijah knew from casual eavesdropping between the waitresses his name was Nash; vaguely wondering what his story was as he sipped his coffee.

Obviously he was interested in the woman, perhaps plotting to make his move today; but he was stood up, Elijah's mind told him, bringing a slight chuckle, as he began to once again enjoy his surroundings. The diner was indeed state of the art with just a touch of throwback appeal he noted. The antique style jukebox in the corner seemed just as at home with the contemporary fixtures and furnishings as if it were designed today. He liked the energizing green of the walls and the offsetting white trim. The chairs were the same deep evergreen with white backs and legs. The tables an interlocking pattern of diamond shapes with the same accenting colors. He looked the waitress over once more, *Jasmine,* he recalled her name tag. Sighing marginally Elijah rose and headed out of the diner, leaving his usual five dollar tip.

Stepping out in the warmth of the spring day, Elijah turned right and headed up toward Swan Park. It was named after some rich benefactor or other who left millions to the parks and recreations department. *I could sure as hell think of something better to invest my money in, dead or not,* Elijah surmised frowning slightly. Taking his time as he walked, he observed each person or establishment he passed along the way. He smiled seeing the young man and woman standing at the entrance to the alley he was passing. He could tell the young man was trying to get inside the

1

woman and she was playing hard to get for the moment. *Weak ass rap, blue ass balls,* Elijah observed the young man and continued his journey. Stopping at the tobacco shop he came upon, he went inside. He inhaled all the different tobacco's loving the scent of them. Stepping to the counter Elijah asked for three Montecristo's. The cigars were handmade in the Dominican Republic, accounting for their expensive price tag. Elijah loved them though, finding them to be a slow burning cigar loaded with rich, complex flavors.

Garnering his purchase he headed back into the day, his destination less than a block away. Checking the Rolex Cellini Classic on his wrist, Elijah smiled a tad and crossed the street with the light heading for the entrance of the park. He entered and found a bench, sitting down enjoying the shade of the huge Oak that towered above his head. He watched a couple of free spirits playing Frisbee with their dogs and the housewives out strolling with their babies, conversing freely with each other. He saw the man walk by but did not react. Elijah continued watching the park participants for the next fifteen minutes before glancing to his right and seeing the package. Picking up the small brown bag, he opened it removing the breadcrumbs and beginning to spread them for the gathering geese.

Moving the crumbs around in the bag, he discovered the small slip of paper, a single name contained. Turning the slip over he read the dollar amount listed and smirked. Folding the paper and putting it into his pocket, Elijah continued to feed the geese until the bag was empty. Rising, he brushed the crumbs from his lap and headed toward his converted loft apartment. Elijah Bower was a man who lived a charmed life; a man who enjoyed the finer things in life. A man who changed women like he changed his clothes; a man who, for a price, would eliminate any breathing human being whose name you wrote on a piece of paper.

*****

Montgomery Southby was a man with an agenda. He was currently serving as Alderman for District 19, the poorest and most crime riddled area in the city. Montgomery held far bigger plans however and he was not going to let a little thing like moral consciences cloud his vision. He currently was working with a major developer on leveling some of the older buildings in his district to make room for a new high rise condominium project, complete with specialty shops and restaurants attached. It was a winning situation to revitalize, bring jobs, and money, into the torn district. Problem was it would also displace almost 200 poor families from the housing projects that occupied the choice property. *Lazy asses should have done something more with their lives than sell dope and make babies,* he condescendingly surmised.

Montgomery despised the black half of his heritage, although come election time he used it to his full advantage, making sure he got all their votes to keep him in office. He would not need them once he pulled off this development coup d'état however. Montgomery knew a project of this magnitude would make millions for his political allies. It would secure his campaign funding from the developer, contractors, and other wealthy investors. Yes, Montgomery was going to be the wealthy and powerful politician he always dreamed of being and no low income, classless, dredges of society were going to stand in the way of it.

"Hi darling," Delia Southby greeted her husband.

He smiled seeing her enter the stately mansion they resided in and kissed her cheek softly as he hugged her. Montgomery looked his wife over, smiling appreciatively at her conservatively classic dress. Delia was seventeen years his junior at 30 years old, but she was the perfect political wife. She stayed in her place, only speaking on issues approved by her husband or his staff. She was mulatoo as was he, taking more of her coloring and features from the white side of her family, which was what drew Montgomery to her in the beginning. He could not marry a full blooded white woman, knowing that would always be a point of contention with some of his older constituents. But he refused to date or marry a full blooded black woman either.

Montgomery hated the fake hair and colored contacts they wore. He hated the smell of the chemicals they used to perm or bleach their hair. They were all loud and bossy with horrible attitudes and too much mouth. Delia was definitely a welcomed breath of fresh air, with her natural blonde hair and green eyes. The only slight imperfection was her broad nose, but Montgomery paid for the rhinoplasty early in their marriage and she was perfect now.

"We have that cocktail function at the ballroom tonight," Delia told him as she began walking up the stairs toward their bedroom.

"Yes, I know honey, I am on my way up now," Montgomery told her, taking in her sexy butt as she walked, his erection growing as he climbed the stairs hoping there was time for a quickie.

Wednesday's Customer   KR Bankston

Elijah was watching his erection slide in and out of Sage as he banged her hard. He loved the way her butt shook when he hit it hard with his thrust. She was moaning and writhing, throwing her sex to him as he eagerly took it. The sweat was rolling down his pecs onto the barreled stomach, the heat from their connection drenching them both.

"Fuck me Elijah, yeah, just like that," Sage yelled, groaning loudly as he complied with her request, going deeper and faster.

"I'm about to cum baby, yeah, Elijah, damn," she moaned as her body shook and the rush came from her coating him with a thick layer of her delight.

Elijah smiled and continued his journey, holding her hips even tighter as he pushed his ten inches all the way inside.

"Ohhh," Sage moaned as he hit her spot and she felt it in her stomach.

Quickly flipping her over, Elijah took both legs and put them behind her head going for the kill. Sage was screaming her pleasure as he banged her hard, his balls slapping her butt with each thrust.

"Mmph," Elijah mumbled as he came hard and spilled his finish into the condom he wore.

He was breathing heavily, finally releasing her legs and letting them fall on the bed as he removed himself carefully from her, rising and disposing of the condom. Walking back into the room moments later he addressed her.

"You need to be out," Elijah told her calmly as Sage opened her eyes and regarded him.

"You have business," she asked, rising and grabbing her clothing.

"Yes," he replied simply.

Sage grunted, but said nothing more as she began to dress. He knew she was not offended. They had an arrangement and it worked out well for both of them. Elijah screwed her on Wednesdays; never any other day of the week, just that one. They got together and enjoyed mind blowing sex. Sage was a print model and she was in a committed relationship with her agent. The problem was his sex left her horny and irritable. That is where Elijah came in. They met at a party a few months back and exchanged numbers. After talking and each agreeing to the arrangement, they began having sex regularly.

"I'll see you next Wednesday," Sage told him sweetly, kissing his cheek gently, as she grabbed her keys and headed out of the door. Elijah locked the door after she left and headed to the shower. He had business to take care of tonight. There was a party at the capital and he needed to go shadow his target. *"What exactly do you do,"* Allison asked as they lay together, her in his arms. *"Personal contracts,"* Elijah answered evasively. *"What kind of contracts,"* she asked again, stroking his chest gently. *"Baby, it's not important, okay,"* he tried as she frowned slightly but let the subject go. Elijah exhaled deeply as he showered and the memory left him.

Allison was the past and he made it his business to never dwell on the past. *Well Alderman Southby you better enjoy your last few days on earth,* Elijah instead alleged, chuckling as he exited the shower and went into his bedroom to dress. He wore the custom tailored tuxedo acquired a couple of weeks ago, adding the diamond cufflinks, watch, and two carat stud to his ear. Adding his favorite cologne, Elijah checked his reflection in the mirror smiling at what he saw.

"Time to go start earning your paper," he mumbled, grabbing the keys to his Porsche and heading out the door, destination, the Princess Imperial.

Chapter Two

Delia smiled slightly taking in the strikingly handsome man entering the ballroom. Tonight's party was being hosted by Clayton Tyler, one of Montgomery's allies and strongest supporters. He held great flair for corralling money and influence in one room and tonight was no exception as Delia once again took in the exquisite grand ballroom of the Princess Imperial hotel.

She loved the double stairway, perfect for regal entrances on either side. It boasted two floors, with a studded balcony so one could gaze upon guests and still be encompassed in the entire presentation. The crème silk draperies that adorned the archways and windows were at full attention, billowing softly from the continuous hum of the central air system, tied back with exquisitely hand tapered, gold marbled, rope ties. Looking again for the handsome stranger, Delia found him conversing with another attendee, drink in hand.

Who might you be, she questioned glancing quickly around to ensure neither Montgomery nor any of his cronies noticed the object of her attention. Her husband was extremely jealous. *As well he should be*, Delia pondered once again. Montgomery was generous to a fault and for that she loved him, but their sex life was another matter entirely. Her husband shared a myriad of hang-ups when it came to making love, leaving her for the most part, frustrated on a daily basis. Delia began sharing clandestine meetings with several men over the years just to fulfill her burning desire. *He looks like a wonderful candidate*, she lusted, her thong moist just from looking at him. She breathed lightly and began to plot how she would meet him. Delia needed to be extremely discreet. Montgomery would already blow a fuse if he found out she cheated on him. He would kill her if he found out she cheated on him with every beautiful black man she could find.

*****

Elijah was still conversing with the buxom blonde who was flirting shamelessly with him. As she talked he took in the entire room, finding both his target and his wife. Elijah did not miss the once over she gave him or the lust in her eyes as she watched him. *That should make things so much easier*, he plotted as the blonde shifted her hand to the other hip, tossing her hair back and beginning with yet another story Elijah wasn't listening too. He often talked to the white women present when he went to a party. It kept him focused since he had absolutely no desire to bed them. Sisters on the other hand, all the sexy sensuality they exuded would have him hard and ready to take them down at a moment's notice.

Returning his attention to Bianca, the woman talking, Elijah actually joined in the conversation, continually watching both Montgomery and Delia. Seeing his chance, Elijah politely excused himself as Bianca pouted making him promise to give her his number before he left. He chuckled, making her the empty promise, and left headed toward the ladies room. Making sure he timed it just right, Elijah saw Delia leaving the room and began walking, intentionally looking at his phone, bumping into her.

"I am so sorry," Elijah apologized smoothly, watching the smile grace her face.

"It's quite all right," Delia told him.

She could not have prepared herself for the electric shock that coursed through her when their bodies touched. *Oh my god, I bet the sex will be incredible,* she fancied her breathing becoming slightly uneven.

"I'm Elijah Bower," he told her honestly, extending his hand.

Delia quickly took the outstretched hand and told him her name.

"You are Alderman Southby's wife," Elijah asked as he looked her over and made sure she knew it.

"Yes," she answered calmly, jumping up and down inside knowing he was interested.

"The Alderman is a fortunate man," he complimented as Delia blushed.

"Thank you," she replied as Elijah smiled again.

He is gorgeous, she continued to think, unconsciously licking her lips. Elijah saw the gesture and moved in for the kill.

"You really should not tease me like that," he told her, audible only between the two of them.

Delia smiled again. "I don't have to be teasing."

Elijah slowly looked her over again and returned to her eyes.

"I'm rock hard right now," he told her seductively.

Delia bit her bottom lip and moaned silently.

"There is a room upstairs end of the hallway, on the left side," Elijah began again. "Housekeeping, so no one ever goes in there," he added, winking and speaking one last time.

Wednesday's Customer   KR Bankston

"I'll wait 10 minutes, but no more," he told her walking away and leaving the ball in her court.

Elijah wasn't worried. He knew she would come. Just as he suspected, Montgomery was not laying the pipe at home and she was needy. *Damn, hafta think of somebody else to fuck this pale bitch,* he brooded, stealthily making his way to the room. The woman was absolutely unattractive to him, but as usual, he would do what he must and accomplish his goal. Arriving, he let himself in and turned on the small table lamp glancing at his watch. Five minutes later Elijah heard the knob turning and smiled. *Works every time,* he observed as Delia walked into the room and returned the smile still sitting on his face.

*****

Montgomery was looking for his wife. He remained caught up most of the evening with Clayton, talking business and strategies for removing the undesirable element out of the neighborhood, making way for the renewal, and of course the feeding of their campaign coffers. Thinking of the political and financial coop they were about to pull off filled him with an innate sense of accomplishment. Right now however he needed Delia by his side. They were getting ready to be seated for dinner and presentations. *Where the hell has she gotten off too,* Montgomery wondered. He knew she was probably bored out of her mind with all the stuffy over-the-hill wives present, more than likely finding some quiet balcony to stand and observe the night sky.

Montgomery loved his wife's quiet demeanor. It was a refreshing change from most of the wives he knew, Clayton's being no exception. The woman was loud and brash, normally drinking too much and making a fool of herself. Sighing softly, Montgomery motioned one of the servers over describing his wife and asking if he noticed her. The server told him he had not, but offered to go and look around. Smiling Montgomery thanked him. That much solved, he returned his attention to the room, noticing that Clayton was vying for his attention.

Pasting on a new smile, Montgomery grabbed another glass of champagne and headed to where the man was standing.

"Montgomery, this is Ronnie Glazer," Clayton introduced the two men. "Ronnie owns Glazer Construction Conglomerates," he added as Montgomery nodded knowingly.

This was one of three contractors vying for the renewal project. He already knew the contract would go to the one that greased

Clayton's pocket best. Montgomery was not upset; he just wanted his own cut of the pie as well.

"Nice to meet you Mr. Glazer," Montgomery returned amiably.

"Please call me Ronnie," the tall lean rustic looking man replied.

Montgomery smiled and acquiesced. The three began to chat when Clayton's aide walked over to them informing the Representative there was an urgent call. Once they were alone, Ronnie wasted no time getting down to business.

"I want those contracts Alderman," he told Montgomery plainly. "I know what it will take dealing with Clayton," he went on calmly. "What I don't know is what it's going to take to get the okay from you?"

"I like your bluntness," Montgomery replied. "So I will be just as blunt, it will take at least half a million to keep my affections," he told Ronnie, watching his reaction.

The man didn't flinch, simply smiling slightly and telling Montgomery he understood completely.

*****

Elijah sipped his cognac and continued to watch the two couples. He sighed lightly thinking of the tryst with Alderman Southby's wife a few moments earlier. *She has definitely done this shit before*, he concluded watching her calm demeanor, continuing her interactions and conversations as if nothing ever happened. Thinking of the sex made him frown a tad. Elijah hated her body, hated how pale and pasty she was. When she undressed, he fought hard not to frown. She had small breasts with pert pink nipples. Her skin was so translucent you could see every vein network encased. *Then she had the nerve to get them enlarged, so they must have been a double A cup before*, Elijah thought of the barely B's Delia showcased now. She tried to kiss him and Elijah smoothly dipped and kissed her neck and chest instead. He would screw her, but he was not going to kiss her and he certainly was not going to eat her out.

Delia was aggressive, her hands everywhere on his body. Normally he would have been completely turned on by the actions, but Elijah found himself utterly repulsed by the woman. She was not sexy to him at all. He forced his thoughts to Sage and their earlier session, finally bringing life to his member so he could sex the obviously desperate woman. After fingering her to saturation, Elijah pulled the extra large magnum from his pocket.

Delia again took charge, removing the latex from the package. Instead of putting it on immediately however; she took the opportunity to suck his erection, almost causing him to go flaccid again.

Instead Elijah closed his eyes and imagined Reesa, his Thursday chick, was the one trying to suck him dry. Reesa was a sexy blue black beauty with a bald head and beautiful eyes. She was Ethiopian by origin and loved oral sex. They often spent more time tasting and enjoying each other than having actual intercourse. The ploy worked and Elijah found himself harder than he was in ages.

Delia noticed and smiled thinking she was responsible for the change. Finally rising and slipping the condom on, she sat back on the desk and opened her legs, allowing him full view of her sex. Elijah was not impressed, but remained silent. Instead, he pulled her up and turned her around, bending her over the desk and sliding deeply inside her. *I definitely don't want to look at the bitch while I fuck her,* he fumed beginning to slam into her with his full aura. Delia moaned deeply, biting her lip he could see, to keep from screaming. She came hard five minutes in, coating the condom with her release.

Elijah tuned her out, closing his eyes and letting his mind wander. To his surprise, Jasmine, the waitress at Morning Perk, came to his subconscious. He saw her chocolate skin in his mind; melon sized breasts in his mouth as he licked her purple nipples and sucked them gently. He saw his hands sliding down the small of her back, gripping her beautiful perfectly symmetric butt and squeezing hard. Elijah imagined her sex; wet and pliable to his hardness as he drove it inside her again and again. His pace increased as his daydream became more and more erotic and he soon came hard, groaning deeply and filling the condom. Coming back to himself, Elijah heard Delia softly sigh her satisfaction as he frowned, out of her sight, and removed himself and the condom from her.

Bitch is definitely sprung now, Elijah cockily thought. She begged for his number once they finished and he thanked her nonchalantly. He supplied her with the information she requested as she assured him she would be calling him soon. *She is going to make this very easy,* he once more plotted smiling, regarding the woman again. This time Elijah was going to make her invite him to their home. *What better place to kill this fool,* he surmised chuckling.

"Well there you are," Bianca gushed, finding him alone again. Elijah exhaled and returned her greeting, adding a fake smile as well.

"Did you miss me," he teased as she began to flirt anew and he once again tuned her out, thinking about his plans for tomorrow.

*****

Jasmine was trying to enjoy the movie but Damian wasn't making that easy. She only agreed to go out with him again after he called for the eighth time today. She knew he was trying to rekindle what they once shared, but Jasmine was done. She moved on, at least mentally.

"You smell good girl, damn," he whispered in the darkened theater, close to her ear.

Jasmine rolled her eyes in the darkness and said nothing. *I'm about 10 seconds from walking the hell out of here,* she groused as Damian finally calmed down and they continued to watch the big screen. Jasmine's mind was also on her regular Wednesday customer. *That man is so sexy,* she pined of the still nameless patron. She continually tried to talk herself into at least asking him that much information, but she was petrified. *What if he thinks you are an idiot,* her mind seized. Sighing lightly she dismissed the thoughts for now, still very much curious about his romantic status and if he ever considered her on that level.

The movie was excellent once Damian left her alone and allowed her to watch, Jasmine thought as they headed to her apartment. Arriving shortly, he got out and opened her door. This was not new. Damian was always a gentleman. The problem was he was a cheater and a liar, two things Jasmine could not stand.

"Can I come in for a minute," Damian asked hopefully.

She turned looking him in the eye.

"I don't think that is a good idea," Jasmine returned calmly.

"Jazzy, baby, don't be like that," Damian returned, using his pet name for her.

"Damian, look," she began when he leaned in and kissed her.

Jasmine could not lie and say she did not enjoy it. Her body definitely showed its approval, her nipples hardening almost instantly. She was with no other man since breaking up with Damian nearly a year ago.

"Baby, stop pushing me away," he pleaded quietly, noticing her body's reaction. "I'm so sorry for hurting you, for lying to you," Damian tried, hoping he was making progress.

"Just for a minute," Jasmine caved as he smiled.

She offered him something to drink and Damian asked for tea, knowing she always made a fresh pitcher daily. Jasmine brought him the drink, sitting on the opposite end of the couch and flipping on the TV.

"You seeing anyone," Damian asked casually.

From what his friends told him, Jasmine was not dating, but he wanted to be sure.

"Not right now," she answered honestly.

For whatever reason the only man she was attracted to since they ended was Mr. Wednesday and that attraction only happened a couple of months ago.

"Who are you seeing," she threw back as Damian smiled slightly and sat his glass down, turning to her.

"I wanna be seeing you," he told her smoothly.

Jasmine scoffed and continued to drink her tea.

"Why you being so hard, Jazzy," he asked, moving closer to her as they continued to sit.

"You know why," she returned hoping he did not push the issue.

"Baby, I told you that was a mistake, a stupid mistake on my part," Damian explained patiently.

He really did regret messing around on her. Jasmine was a good woman, and those were hard to find. He learned that the hard way in the four failed attempts at a relationship since she broke up with him.

"Whatever," Jasmine replied nonchalantly.

Damian decided talking was not going to help his cause right now, so he leaned in and kissed her again, this time pulling her to him and slipping his tongue in her mouth. Jasmine moaned softly without thinking, loving the taste of him. Damian continued to kiss her, laying her back on the couch, him atop her, grinding against her sex. His hands slid down her back and smoothly across her butt. Jasmine's breathing became ragged and uneven. She was on fire, needing a release in the worst way. *Don't screw Damian*, her mind shouted. Digging deep and finding her resolve, Jasmine pushed him off her.

"You need to leave," she told him standing and rearranging her clothing.

"Baby, Jazzy, don't do this," Damian told her, rising and stepping to her, trying to hold her again.

"Go now," she replied becoming irritated.

Sighing deeply he decided not to push. Damian knew Jasmine was scared to trust him again and he still had work to do.

"OK baby," he told her sweetly. "I can get you off if you want before I go, no strings," he offered knowing she ws as aroused as he.

"No Damian, I, um…," she stuttered and Damian moved in for the kill.

Pulling her to him and kissing her again, he removed her panties, finally pushing her back onto the sofa, opening her legs and burying his face between them.

"Mmm," Jasmine moaned as his tongue connected and she shivered with delight.

Damian pulled out every stop licking, slurping, drinking deeply as she came hard and her entire body trembled.

"Aaah, mmmm," Jasmine continued to purr as Damian's tongue brought her yet another wave of blissful delight. Seizing the opportunity, he freed his erection as he tasted her, carefully positioning himself on his knees, Damian smoothly slid inside her as Jasmine put her hands on his chest.

"No, Damian, stop," she told him as his mouth found hers again and he continued to thrust into her.

Her hands left his chest, sliding down to his butt, pulling him inside her. Damian was kissing her neck softly now, enjoying her warm wetness.

"Don't cum inside me Damian," Jasmine whispered.

He kissed her ear gently.

"I won't baby."

Keeping his word, Damian withdrew moments later as he came hard, his body quivering.

"Damn baby," he told her softly as they rose and headed to the bathroom to clean up.

Jasmine knew she opened a door that should have remained closed, but the orgasms were worth the price; for now.

Chapter Three

"How has your week been," Reesa asked as she rose and began to dress. They spent most of the morning into the afternoon pleasuring each other. Elijah loved Thursdays. It meant he could relax and enjoy being pampered for a while. Reesa was very much into control and he allowed her to have her fill while they were together. She gave him head in every conceivable position, allowing him to eat her at will or just close his eyes and enjoy her service. Of course, he delved inside her warm wet center at least three times today and eyeing her sexy chocolate skin as she dressed, his manhood began taking on yet another life.

"Mmm, darling, are you ready again," Reesa purred, noticing his erection.

"You make me like this," Elijah answered honestly as she smiled and told him to sit up.

Guiding him to the edge of the bed, Reesa assumed the position, eagerly mouthing his freestanding sex.

"You are so damn good, Reesa," he murmured honestly.

The woman was an artist when it came to giving head. She could definitely teach some classes.

Reesa's steady rhythm had him breathing hard, toes curling and thighs tensing as Elijah tried to hold back the monsoon he wanted to release in her mouth. He wanted to make it last, keep those soft lifts on his shaft and her wet tongue lapping greedily at the head.

"Reesa, girl, mmm," he moaned unable to resist any longer as the hot semen made its way up and out of the shaft into her waiting mouth.

She moaned slightly as she swallowed and Elijah noticed her hand as she fingered herself and obviously came hard simultaneously. Collapsing onto the bed he closed his eyes, hearing her chuckle and finish dressing.

"I'll see you next week darling," Reesa told him sweetly as Elijah opened his eyes and smiled back.

"Looking forward to it."

The Ebony goddess left him as Elijah grudgingly rose and headed for his shower. He supposed most people would consider him a whore, but Elijah loved sex, and the women he slept with loved sex. So what was the problem?

He chuckled as he showered recalling all his weekly trysts. Shanice was his Monday chick; she was the fairest of the group but he found her incredibly sexy with her doe eyes. Her skin wasn't pale; it was kissed with just enough sun to make her alluring. She was also the anal freak. No matter what else they did, Elijah knew where they would end up, he thought laughing at the pun. Katrina took care of Tuesday's, Sage on Wednesday's, Reesa was tantalizing Thursdays, and Tangela rounded out his week on Friday. Elijah laughed at his schedule noting that he gave himself the weekends off. That was his time to relax and unwind. He was not always out here like he was now, but Allison was a long time ago, Elijah mused frowning lightly and dismissing the thoughts.

Returning to his bedroom he picked up his secondary phone and saw a missed call from Delia Southby. *OK, time to get back to business,* Elijah alleged sighing deeply and calling her back.
"Hi there," she purred into the phone.
Elijah frowned and rolled his eyes before speaking.
"Hey beautiful," he threw out amiably.
"I was hoping I could see you today," she told him.
Elijah smiled knowingly.
"Hmph, glad to hear that," he told her. "I definitely want to spend some more time with you," he lied smoothly.
"When can we meet," Delia asked.
"I can come now if you are free," Elijah fished.
"Yes, I am alone. That will be fine," she told him.. "Park behind the guest house."
"There is an enclosed walkway you can use and not be seen. I will would meet you inside the guesthouse," Delia plotted.
"I can't wait," he lied again, hearing her giggle.
"Well hurry up then, sexy," Delia replied.
"Walking out now," Elijah told her.
Disconnecting he went to his closet and pushed back the false wall revealing the arsenal kept inside. Taking two .380's, .9mm, and a .25, he put them in his case and headed out to the Porsche. *Now which of my sexy beauties will I think of today when I screw this arctic ironing board,* he queried, chuckling at his thought and concentrating on the road.

*****

Montgomery loved Marqano's. The classy Greek restaurant was one of his favorite places. He was meeting Ronnie Glazer today to work out the terms of their deal. Of the three contractors vying for the multimillion dollar deal, Ronnie was by far the front runner. Montgomery was pretty sure he could enlist Ronnie's help in removing the unwanted residents.

"Hello Ronnie," he greeted the man as he walked up to the table. "I apologize for being late," Montgomery threw out amiably.

Ronnie assured him it wasn't an issue, handing him a menu. "Thanks," he replied opening it and beginning to peruse the offerings.

"Have you gentlemen decided or do you need a few moments more," the server asked coming back to their table. Montgomery and Ronnie gave their order and she promised their food quickly, walking away and leaving them alone once more.

"I don't believe in playing games Montgomery," Ronnie told him frankly. "Clayton is not ready to move forward and I am."

Montgomery smiled a tad understanding where Ronnie was headed with the conversation.

"I am more than ready, Ronnie," Montgomery told him honestly. "I think you and I can pull this off, even without Clayton."

Ronnie smiled at Montgomery's statement, liking what he was hearing.

"Fine, lets talk about the how," Ronnie told him, excited they were making progress.

"We need to get those squatters out of the projects first," Montgomery said flatly.

Ronnie was slightly surprised hearing the man speak that way. He was aware of Alderman Southby's African-American heritage. It seemed however, that the man wanted to distance himself from it.

"Well, as I told Clayton, let's offer them relocation," Ronnie began. Montgomery's mind was working as Ronnie explained his entire plan for getting the residents out without much of a ripple effect on the city's daily autonomy. He was also thinking about Clayton and how the man did not mention one word about Ronnie's offer. He was supposed to be his closest friend and ally; right now though, Montgomery was definitely rethinking his alliances.

"Tell me more about the relocation," Montgomery told him, reeling his mind in and paying attention once again.

Ronnie sipped his soft drink telling him about his ownership of 35 acres of real estate where they would build cheap subsidized housing for the current residents at a fraction of the cost of relocating them individually.

"Sounds like a winning proposition," Montgomery returned. Ronnie grunted telling him that the land was once a landfill and because of that everyone was hesitant to build there.

"Some concern about health hazards and such," Ronnie threw out wanting to gage Montgomery's reaction.

He shrugged.

"What do we care," he returned coldly. "As long as their welfare receiving, food stamp eating, drug dealing, baby having, habeas corpses are out of the projects and we can build our high-rise community, it can be built on top of a methane mine and I would not shed a tear," Montgomery told him evenly.

Ronnie frowned imperceptibly but said nothing more about the matter, choosing to move on.

"Don't worry," Montgomery told him, catching the slight frown. "I can sell it and make them think its Lincoln's promise of forty acres and a mule," he boasted.

"You pull that off and I will give you your price and half of Clayton's," Ronnie told him plainly.

"That is 750K in your pocket," he clarified as Montgomery smiled and asked what timeframe he had in mind.

*****

Jasmine was up early getting ready to head for Morning Perk. She heard Damian stirring and silently chided herself for first of all having sex with him, but then also for letting him stay the night. Exhaling lithely she headed into the kitchen to grab herself a quick breakfast. She seldom ate at the diner, since it was almost always already busy when she arrived. The slight buzzing vibration caught her attention and she turned to the counter seeing Damian's phone laying on it. Frowning, wondering who would be texting him this early, Jasmine picked it up. Normally she would have never invaded his privacy this way, but Damian proved to be untrustworthy on more than one occasion.

'I don't know what bitch you are out with but you better tell that hoe that you got a woman, and she don't play' the message read.

Jasmine found at least 15 others almost identical. Whoever the woman was she was texting almost non-stop for the past four hours. Putting the phone down and shaking her head, Jasmine returned to her task and made herself eggs and toast, with a side of bacon and a glass of orange juice.

Damian came into the kitchen just as she sat down to enjoy the offering, regarding her.

"Where's mine," he teased as Jasmine gave him a look, rolled her eyes and began to eat.

"That's messed up Jazzy," he continued to tease, picking up his phone.

Jasmine glanced up watching his expression as he saw the collection of messages.

"Guess you forgot to tell miss thang you were going out, hmm," she told him calmly.

Damian exhaled deeply knowing his explanation was going to fall on deaf ears, but trying anyway.

"It ain't like that Jazzy, for real," he began as she continued to eat wordlessly. "This is LaNeesa crazy ass, my ex."

Jasmine finished her breakfast, rising and washing her plate. Finishing her task she turned heading out of the kitchen, intending to walk by Damian when he grabbed her arm, stopping her.

"Jazzy, baby, please, I swear nothing is going on with us," he tried anew, looking into her eyes now. "She just does not want to hear it, so she does this drama anytime I do not call her back," Damian told her truthfully.

"Who you are seeing is none of my business Damian," Jasmine told him decisively. "You and I had sex last night, but that's all."

He was stung to hear her say the words. Damian was still madly in love with Jasmine. He knew he messed up cheating on her, and he was genuinely sorry.

He thought last night was a new beginning for them; that they would talk through their issues and slowly make their way back to what they used to be.

"Come on Jazzy," Damian told her, pulling her close and holding her. "You don't mean that baby," he pled softly.

"I have to go to work, Damian," Jasmine returned dryly.

Hurt, he let her go and she walked to the front door.

Stopping, she turned and gave him a look as Damian picked up his keys and walked to where she stood, door open, hand on the knob.

"I want you back Jazzy," he told her looking into her eyes once more. "I'm going to prove to you I have changed," he added as she again withheld comment and waited impatiently for him to walk out.

She closed the door behind them and locked it.

"I can give you a ride to work," Damian told her praying she would say yes.

"No thanks," Jasmine returned crisply. "I would rather walk," she told him turning her back and heading down the stairs.

Chapter Four

It was Wednesday again and Jasmine was hustling as usual. Morning Perk was even busier this morning for some reason. She glanced over her section, taking in her various patrons, eyes coming to rest on Damian, once again finding him watching her intently. Jasmine exhaled cavernously, turning her back and praying he would leave before Mr. Wednesday arrived. She did not want him to think she was not available and she knew if Damian even thought she was attracted to the man, he would go out of his way to be a nuisance. *Damn, I should have never ever slept with him,* Jasmine continued to brood as she took his order over and sat it before him.

"Do you need anything else," she asked politely, keeping everything strictly professional.

"I need you to believe me and give me another chance," Damian replied calmly, never losing eye contact.

"That will not happen," Jasmine told him crisply, frowning as she turned and walked away from the table.

Damian continued showing up at her house almost every day since the night they shared last week. This was the first time he appeared at the restaurant and Jasmine certainly hoped it was not the beginning of a trend for him. That night meant nothing to her. As mean spirited as it may have sounded, all she wanted was sexual tension relief and he provided that. The problem now however was how to make him believe she was not in love with him anymore and move on. Jasmine checked her other tables, refilling coffee and bringing various requested items before going to Damian's table and retrieving the empty plates. She hoped now that he was finished with his meal he would leave.

"Can I get you anything else," Jasmine asked once more praying he said no.

"I would like a coffee refill please," Damian returned still looking deeply into her eyes.

Sighing quietly, Jasmine left to retrieve the pot. *Please let him leave before Mr. Wednesday gets here,* she continued to pray returning with the pot and filling his cup. She finally made up her mind to at least ask the man his name today. Now with Damian being here, there was a defined crimp in her plans. Dismissing the thought and hoping for the best, Jasmine returned to her other tables and continued to serve her customers.

Wednesday's Customer   KR Bankston

Delia Southby had a full day planned today. She was headed to her Politician's Wives for Change brunch this morning, then it was off to yet another fundraiser for Montgomery, after that, late lunch at the country club with him. *Then I can finally see my sexy Adonis, Elijah,* she ruminated and smiled. Delia would be the first to admit the man completely infatuated her. She indulged in affairs before, and even great sex, but there was something about Elijah that made her want to completely let go and lose control. She fretted slightly thinking how he was still standoffish in some respects when they were together. Breathing deeply however she told herself she must understand his point of view, as she recalled their last conversation.

"*Why don't you ever kiss me,*" Delia asked, slightly hurt when Elijah once again turned his head and refused to meet her lips. "*Because it keeps things uncomplicated,*" he answered cryptically. "*What do you mean,*" she asked, giving him a look. Elijah sighed slightly before looking directly into her eyes. "*When you kiss someone, you exchange a part of your soul with them,*" he told her. "*You give them a small portion of your heart and you slowly begin to love them,*" Elijah patiently made his case. "*I am no fool,*" he began anew as Delia continued to look into his face and think to herself how handsome he was. "*You and I have great sex, but you will never leave your husband for me,*" he told her slightly irritated. "*And where would that leave me, after I have let the feelings I have for you become real and full blown,*" Elijah finished, waiting for an answer. "*I understand baby,*" Delia told him sweetly. "*Is that why you won't taste me either,*" she quizzed.
"*Yes,*" Elijah replied flatly. "*All right, I won't push,*" she told him as Elijah smiled and began arousing her to make love once more.

Delia was not angry and the fact that he did not kiss her or even taste her, did not take away from his skill. Elijah was damned good at what he did with his hands and his lips in other places, she thought and smiled once again.

"What are you over there thinking about," Montgomery asked, grinning as he watched her.

Delia hurriedly gathered her thoughts, reeling her mind back in as she regarded him.

"Nothing," she replied blushing as Montgomery laughed.

"Ohhh, our escapade hmm," he teased as Delia blushed deeper.

Truthfully the sex last night was no better than any other time; she was simply hornier than usual. She had not seen Elijah for the last three days and it was wearing on her.

You are getting far too attached, her mind told her as Montgomery walked over and took her in his arms, kissing her lips.

"I love you," he told her earnestly as Delia smiled slightly.

"I love you too."

Her mind immediately called her a filthy, lying, hypocrite and she just as quickly told her mind to shut the hell up. Montgomery began kissing her neck tenderly, his hands caressing her breasts.

"I will be quick," he pleaded in her ear, knowing she was on a time schedule.

"OK," Delia replied knowing he would be and needing his continued trust.

Montgomery kissed her passionately, laying her onto the bed, parting her legs and entering her as Delia sighed softly and began to go over her day's agenda once more in her head.

*****

Elijah sipped his juice continuing to watch Jasmine and the customer interact. *So who is this,* he queried of the man she was talking to. It was obvious the man was attracted to her, the question was, what she thought of him. Jasmine was being professional but Elijah could see the tension etched on her face. He was a bit dismayed at how deeply disturbed he was by the idea of the man being romantically attracted to the woman. *So, now what,* his mind threw out as Elijah sighed deeply and turned his attention to the newspaper in front of him. He read with interest the article on the construction of new affordable housing for the relocation of several families in the housing projects, conveniently in Alderman Southby's district. *I am sure that snake is getting a pretty penny from the kickbacks on this shit,* Elijah believed frowning slightly. He heaved a sigh thinking about the hit. He was almost ready. It took him almost a week, and too many sexual sessions with Delia to finally get inside their home and learn the layout.

Thinking about the Alderman's wife made Elijah exhaled again. He hated touching her, having sex with her, but he unfortunately needed her right now. Elijah smiled however recalling their conversation the other day when she finally asked him about kissing her. *She is disgusting,* he surmised finishing his juice. Once he owned the alarm code and the house key he planned to take from her, Elijah would never touch Delia Southby again. Glancing up he saw the man standing in front of Jasmine as she frowned, obviously not liking whatever he was saying. Elijah took the time to look her over once more, very much enjoying the view.

He understood the man's attempts to gain her attention. She was very beautiful woman. Elijah saw the man lean over and whisper something in her ear as Jasmine shook her head no. *Tough luck buddy*, Elijah thought and smiled as the man admitted defeat and finally left. Turning toward him, their eyes met and Jasmine smiled slightly coming over and asking if there was anything he needed.

Elijah regarded her silently for a few moments as she stood in front of him.

"May I have another juice?"

"Sure," she smiled.

Jasmine left and he continued to regard her and struggle within himself. *Why the hell am I jealous*, Elijah brooded, knowing very well the answer to his question. She returned shortly afterward and put the glass in front of him.

"Anything else," Jasmine asked sweetly.

"No, I'm fine for now," Elijah smiled.

She returned the gesture and left him alone as his mind continued to work. He was in no position to begin a relationship right now. His time was measured. There was nothing extra to give to anyone. *She is not going to push him away forever waiting on your time*, his mind again charged. Elijah did not know why he was even thinking about her that way. The last relationship he shared was a disaster. He promised himself never to repeat it. Why wasn't his heart listening? Jasmine returned to his table, check in hand and spoke once more.

"Are you sure there is nothing else I can get you?"

Elijah sat back in his chair and looked directly into her eyes.

"Your number," he said calmly, allowing his heart to have its way.

Jasmine blushed from the look, but complied with his request, writing it on a small piece of paper and giving it to him. Elijah took the paper and smiled marginally, rising and handing her the money for his check and her tip. Stepping close to her, he leaned near her ear and spoke.

"Thank you," Elijah told her softly. "My name is Elijah, Jasmine," he continued, hearing her breathing become erratic. "I will be calling you soon," he finished speaking, walking out of the restaurant that much established; a new agenda on his mind.

*****

Damian was not at all happy that Jasmine was still pushing him away. *Why the hell is she being so damned unreasonable*, he pondered becoming slightly irritated. Sighing heavily he pushed the feelings

Wednesday's Customer   KR Bankston

away. Damian knew he hurt Jasmine deeply with his betrayal and it was going to take some serious work on his part to make it better and her to forgive him fully.

"Damn LaNeesa surely isn't helping," he mumbled aloud of his ex and her constant calling and texting.

The woman was determined they would get together again and so far she managed to break up any other affiliation he made. *She is the reason Jasmine is pissed now,* Damian fumed. He was a changed man though. He did not cheat anymore and he definitely knew who and want he wanted now. The problem came however, in proving it to Jasmine and her accepting and believing it.

    Damian enjoyed his breakfast and her company this morning. Even if it was in a professional setting, time with Jasmine was time with Jasmine. He decided he would stop into the diner more often and see her. He also planned to step up his visits to the house. *I should be there when she gets off, give her a ride home,* he continued to plot. Damian was going to do everything he could to get Jasmine back. She meant the world to him and his heart wanted only her. *Maybe it is too late,* his mind told him as Damian scoffed at the idea. They just made love not seven days ago. Jasmine still cared for him, more than she would ever readily admit, but the feelings were there. Now all he needed to do was bring them out into the open and force her to admit she was only scared he would hurt her again. *But I won't,* Damian promised as walked down the hallway to his apartment, unlocking the door and going inside.

*****

    Elijah followed him casually as the man walked toward what he assumed was his apartment. He was not sure what he planned to do to the man, but Elijah liked being in control. He needed to know more about this guy, who he was to Jasmine, how long he knew her, if they shared history. He finally opened his mind to being with the woman and Elijah was not going to allow anyone or anything to interfere with that. He watched the man walk toward a small apartment building and enter the front door. Elijah toyed with following him up and perhaps having a conversation with him, but ultimately decided against it. Instead he leaned against the wall in front of the Auto body shop directly across the street, his mind still racing.

    He allowed his heart a moment to revel in the knowledge he and Jasmine would be going out soon. The woman was very special to him, even in his grudging stubbornness to admit it.

I am not going to be hurt again, Elijah thought angrily as Allison once more flashed in his minds eye. His subconscious told him that Jasmine was nothing like his former flame. She beheld a sweet honesty to her, almost to the point of naivety. Elijah found that very refreshing. Movement caught his eye and he saw the man reappear on the street once more. Giving him a few more moments to outdistance him slightly, Elijah once again followed. He was disappointed moments later when the man retrieved his car and drove down the street, leaving Elijah to wonder his destination. Loosing another breath he began walking back the way he came his mind still spiraling. Elijah needed some answers and quickly. He did not like being kept in the dark, especially when it came to the woman who right now held his heart.

Chapter Five

Look at this lying ass, slimy bastard, Jaheem thought as he sat and listened to Montgomery's spiel. Jaheem Andrews was the community activist for ML King Gardens, the housing project that Montgomery and his cronies wanted for their high-rise project. Jaheem or Jah, as everyone called him, knew both Montgomery and Clayton for years. They were both two slimy weasels together in his book. They would sell their own mother for the right price. *Especially Montgomery's self loathing ass,* he continued to brood as the man at the podium continued to tell the residents gathered how great an opportunity they were being given.

"You will have brand new residences, with great amenities," Montgomery told them. "A brand new playground for your children, state of the art tennis and swim will be available," he added as several of those gathered began to nod their approval, smiling and nudging their neighbors sitting in close proximity. Jaheem did not like what he was seeing. As soon as the question period began he had a few for Mr. Montgomery Southby.

Montgomery continued to drone on sounding like a used car salesman as Jaheem continued to fume. Noticing movement, he turned his head and saw Delia enter the room, plastic smile in place. *This fake hoe,* Jaheem fumed, watching the woman stop and playfully tease a couple of the small children in the isle as she walked toward the side of the podium. Jaheem sucked his teeth in disgust knowing the woman could give two damns less about anyone in this room that was not able to add more money to her platinum card limit. *I got something for that trick though,* Jaheem thought malevolently. He did a bit of investigating, needing some leverage to push Montgomery's hand and make him ditch the proposed project. *Bet he doesn't know his wife is screwing his so called mentor huh,* Jaheem smiled inwardly. He possessed the pictures to back up his claims too. It seemed that Delia and Clayton Tyler were carrying on a sexual affair for the past two plus years. The sound of applause broke his thought as Jaheem turned to find Montgomery sitting and the moderator returning.

"We will take a few questions at this point," the stoic woman threw out. "Alderman Southby has a busy schedule, so the questions should be brief," she added giving everyone a look.

Jaheem was not impressed. He rose immediately and opened his mouth, loving the irritated scowl present on both Montgomery and Clayton's faces.

"You say this new project is such a great thing for the residents of the Gardens," Jaheem began. "Then you will not mind sharing what the geological findings were for that particular tract of land, would you," he threw out knowing very well what the land was once been used for.

Clayton stood and approached the microphone.

"Really Jah," he began, trying to sound friendly. "Why would you deprive these wonderful people of an opportunity to have a new life, with new homes, and a new chance to make it," he accused as several of the residents grunted their agreement, turning and giving him a look.

Jaheem frowned slightly and told Clayton to answer the question.

"Sit down Jah, damn," one of the women threw out, sucking her teeth and rolling her eyes.

"Yeah, you always tryna ruin shit for us," yet another chimed in.

Clayton and Montgomery smiled slightly as the activist admitted defeat for the moment and returned to his seat fuming. The moderator returned to the stage and asked if there were any other questions. Receiving a few nonsensical ones pertaining to free cable, washers and dryers, the two men wrapped up the town hall meeting and smiling waved goodbye to everyone heading for their chauffeured car. *Smile now assholes, but I am going to get that last laugh, believe that,* Jaheem thought darkly, watching the two men leave, shaking his head at the ignorance of his own people.

*****

"That went exceptionally well," Clayton remarked, lighting the huge cigar and puffing away. Montgomery chuckled and told him he agreed.

"Darling, would you like to go to the country club with us or be dropped off," Montgomery asked his wife.

Clayton cast a sly glance her way as she smiled graciously and told him she would be fine at home. Turning to instruct the driver of her desire, Montgomery missed the look that passed between the two. Clayton's dark stare was filled with jealousy. Delia was denying him for almost a month now and he knew there must be someone new. Granted he knew their affair was wrong, Clayton fell hard for the beautiful woman his mentee was married too. Delia was sexy in every language to him. He loved her fair skin and silky blonde hair. Her body was toned and shapely. The inside of her love cave gripped him like a vice when he made love to her. Delia gave him an arrogant smirk, the plastic smile returning to her face when Montgomery turned around and began conversing with Clayton again.

Truthfully Delia's mind was on Elijah. She could not get enough of the stunning obsidian Adonis who turned her world upside down every time he sexed her. *I need to know more about him,* she fretted. Delia did not like how aloof Elijah continued to be with her. She was sprung and she wanted him to be the same way. Clayton was a decent lay, and he was definitely more powerful than Montgomery, but he was not Elijah. That man was a machine with a purpose; Delia continued to muse, becoming deeply aroused. She was going to call him as soon as Montgomery dropped her off. She needed a serious dose of hard core sex.

"I won't be late darling," Montgomery told her sweetly, breaking her thought bringing Delia back to the present.

She was shocked to see they arrived at the house and were in the driveway.

"All right," she returned sweetly. "Have a good day," she added kissing his lips softly, knowing it was pissing Clayton off.

"Tell Marissa hello for me, will you Clayton," Delia threw out further driving the stake into his heart.

Clayton managed to conjure up a smile and assure her he would, as his eyes bored into her own. Delia stepped out of the car as the driver opened the door, waving once more at Montgomery before turning and going inside, her cell phone already in her hand.

*****

Jasmine was about at her end with Damian. He was at her door constantly. He was her job almost as much. *He is going to make Elijah think there is something going on with us,* she thought angrily. Jasmine was still waiting on her dream man to call. Two days passed since he took her number. She was hoping they would connect this weekend; perhaps go out and get to know each other. Jasmine smiled again thinking about him finally making a move on Wednesday. *I never knew he paid attention to me,* she smiled happily again. She carried a good feeling about him. Elijah seemed like a very thoughtful man. He was refined but not flashy. *Please let him call today,* she thought as the knock came to her door and she sighed deeply knowing already it was Damian.

"Why are you here," Jasmine asked taking him in as he stood once again on her stoop.

"I thought maybe you would like to go to the park and relax a little," Damian tried.

"No, not really," Jasmine returned dryly wanting him to go away.

"What happened to you anyway," she asked curiously seeing the bruising to his face and noticing the slightly pained step.

"Someone jumped me," Damian told her, hoping to illicit sympathy.

Truthfully he and LaNeesa got into yet another violent confrontation.

"Why, what did you do," she asked as he sighed deeply and told her nothing.

"Can I at least come inside," Damian asked, noticing they were talking for the last 10 minutes and she still was yet to invit him into the apartment. Jasmine sighed deeply again.

"I don't see why," she replied still standing in the same spot.

"Jazzy, damn, why are you being so cold," Damian asked, hurt that she was treating him this way.

"Damian, you just do not seem to get it," she replied. "We had sex the other week, nothing more," Jasmine patiently explained. "I am not trying to be a bitch or anything, but I am not trying to get back into a relationship with you either."

Damian nodded thoughtfully, sighing deeply. "Can I come in and we honestly talk about that," he pleaded.

Jasmine rolled her eyes exasperated and finally moved aside allowing him entrance. Damian was praying with every step that he could convince her to give them another chance. He could hear in her tone that Jasmine was serious and for her it was the past, permanently. *I cannot let that happen,* Damian continued to think as she offered him something to drink and he graciously accepted, his mind still whirling as she left him alone and he tried to think of the best arguments known to man for them to once again be a couple.

*****

Elijah opened the door without asking who it was. It was Friday, so he was expecting Tangela to be on the other side. What he found instead shook his foundations.

"What are you doing here," he asked calmly, feeling anything but.

"Can I come in," Allison asked, never taking her eyes from his.

Shrugging, Elijah moved aside and allowed her entry. She took in the loft apartment, recalling what great taste her ex-lover had.

"What do you want Allison," Elijah asked again, getting directly to the point.

Her presence opened up the raw gaping wound to his psyche once again.

"Do you still hate me that much Elijah," Allison asked softly, finding his eyes once again.

"What do you want," he replied, jaw clenched, still angry.

Sighing deeply Allison shrugged and sat on the sofa, enjoying the feel of the black Italian leather against her skin.

"How long have you been screwing Delia Southby," she asked calmly as Elijah immediately tensed.

Allison being here was not a good sign as it were, but her knowing about his sexual activity with Delia was even worse.

"Elijah, I came here as a friend," Allison began again, garnering his attention once more. "I don't know what you are up too, but I know you well enough to know its business and not pleasure," she added, never taking her eyes from his.

Elijah held his tongue, admitting nothing. Allison sighed once again and sat back on the couch, her blazer falling open as Elijah scowled.

"I am sorry," she told him, immediately covering the gun and badge attached to her hip.

Allison Register was an FBI agent and she broke Elijah's heart in unimaginable ways when she left him nearly three years ago.

"Are you investigating her," Elijah finally asked.

He took her in again as she spoke. Allison was still absolutely beautiful to him. She kept herself in excellent shape, her curvaceous hips and butt turning him on, even now. Her hair was naturally curly and swept back from her face today, showcasing the beautiful soft brown eyes and pouty lips. Reeling his mind in, Elijah returned his attention to her words. He vowed he would never again allow Allison into the inner sanctum of his heart and he meant it. The small fact that she could put him in prison for the rest of his life played no small role in his decision.

"You know I cannot answer that," Allison told him calmly. "But please Elijah, whatever the assignment, pass on this one," she pled giving him yet another look.

She answered his question in that simple sentence. Elijah frowned slightly thinking how complicated things had become.

"Please Elijah, for me," Allison tried, giving him a beseeching look. As hard as she tried she just could not seem to rid her system of Elijah. He was like a recurring hit of acid. Every time she thought she was over him, her mind would take her on a new trip.

"Why would you care anyway," he returned petulantly.

"That's not fair," Allison returned quietly, the hurt apparent.

Elijah grunted but said nothing else. He understood, at least in theory, why they could not be together, but that did not stop the hurt he felt. The abandonment or betrayal when she walked out of his life and told him they could not see each other anymore. Elijah wanted to marry her, to have a future and children with her. All Allison wanted was to climb to the top of the FBI ladder and become director.

"OK, so you have done your civic duty," Elijah told her rising, giving her the cue.

Allison sighed deeply and rose also, following him to the door.

"Elijah please, don't do this," she pleaded once again praying he was hearing her.

The things she could not disclose to him were things that went far wider and deeper than any contract he accepted.

"Thanks for coming by Allison," he replied basically, opening the door and waiting for her to leave.

Allison shook her head in defeat and left, hearing the lock engage behind her.

31

Chapter Six

Jaheem sighed evenly looking at the remaining flyers lying on the table in front of him. He was out most of the morning trying to talk to the residents at The Gardens. He was trying to warn them that the bill of goods they were being sold was all a huge illusion and there were serious dangers present.

"Would you like a refill," Jasmine asked coming over to his table. Jaheem smiled at the young woman and told her yes as she smiled back and refilled his tea, leaving him alone once more. He liked coming to Morning Perk. The cafe always served delicious food and the service was excellent. He watched Jasmine wordlessly thinking what an attractive woman she was. Jaheem was glad to see she was still working. He patronized the establishment for a while and they had a high turnover rate, especially with the African American wait staff. *Too busy doing nothing with their lives*, he thought disappointed. The young woman also took his mind back to his earlier outing and the flyers.

Jaheem saw them coming and immediately put the flyers by his side. He was not going to try and give them one, already knowing the response. *"What you doing now, Jah,"* Tazzy inquired, hand on her hip. Her friend Quita was eyeing him equally as distastefully at the moment. Both women were young, extremely young, and already shared three children a piece from three different fathers. *"I'm just talking to people, Tazzy,"* Jaheem replied calmly. Truthfully he wanted to shake some sense into both of them to open their eyes and do something more with their lives than chase every dope boy and pipe dream they offered. They were not stupid by a long shot. Both women knew very well how to milk the system and survive. They were lazy and did not want to work hard to accomplish their goals, preferring to let everyone else take care of them. *"You need to stop trying to block everyone from getting this new housing,"* she threw out once again as Jaheem sighed deeply. *"We living in these rat infested, raggedy ass apartments and you think we ain't gonna jump at the chance to get a fresh new place,"* she accused as Quita grunted her agreement, rolling her eyes and neck as well.

"Tazzy, I'm just saying that what Alderman Southby is offering is not what he is trying to tell you it is," Jaheem began. *"I don't want to hear no more of your activist bullshit, Jah, for real, let it rest,"* Tazzy cut him off rudely. *Without another word she and Quita turned and walked away leaving him shaking his head.* Jasmine came and gingerly placed his check on the

table, shaking his thoughts and bringing Jaheem back to the present.

He sipped his tea and finished his meal checking out the patrons as he sat. His glance fell on Eddie, the supposed lawyer, who held court in the back booth of the restaurant. Jaheem considered the man nothing more than an ambulance chaser. He was sure at one time or other Eddie was probably quite the legal eagle. The man was obviously intelligent, having gone through law school and passed the bar exam, but somewhere along the line he gave up. At least that was Jaheem's estimation of the situation from the things he saw. As he thought, Jaheem saw another man join Eddie as the two began to converse. *Wonder what fraudulent lawsuit he is cooking up with this guy,* he continued to brood. He sighed deeply thinking of all the people in the housing projects Eddie could help if he just put his talents to good use for a change.

"Not unless there is a dollar in it for him," Jaheem murmured, wiping his hands and seeing the waitress as she passed his table once again.

"Jasmine," he called out as she turned and came back to his table. "Can I get the number six to go please?"

"Sure, let me put that in for you," she smiled.

Walking away once more Jaheem regarded her wishing he were 10 years younger. Glancing out of the window he saw the car pass with Clayton Tyler's picture, pitching his re-election. *Time to visit a certain Alderman,* Jaheem darkly deliberated as Jasmine brought his to go order and he paid her, smiling and telling her to have a nice day.

*****

"Where is your husband," Elijah asked calmly as he and Delia relaxed in the master bedroom.

"No worries darling," she purred softly, stroking his chiseled chest. "He won't be home any time soon to disturb us."

Elijah grunted but said nothing else. He accomplished what he set out to do, and that was to get inside the main house and learn the layout. Unfortunately sleeping with Delia was part of that package, but he sucked it up and dealt with it. Elijah was going to charm the alarm system information out of her before he left today. Then he would return in the next few days and fulfill his contract. *I should kill her ass too, just as a bonus,* he thought as the woman began kissing his neck again. Elijah was still repulsed every time she touched him, but again, he must play his role. His mind wandered and he thought back to Allison's visit a day ago. He was still furious that she showed up at his place; even angrier that she knew about him and Delia. *What the hell is the FBI up too,* Elijah wondered as Delia began sucking his member.

He reeled his mind in and instead turned his thoughts to Jasmine and their date tonight. He was going to show her a really good time. Elijah felt much more than an extremely strong attraction to the woman. She was, he decided at that moment, the one for eternalness. He thought of the perfect spot to take her and asked her if she visited a Latin club before. He smiled slightly thinking of her answer when he asked if she could salsa. *She is sweet,* he thought of Jasmine before picturing her sexy body devoid of clothing. His manhood immediately took on life and was standing at full attention.

"Mm, that's what I like to see," Delia purred once more as Elijah fought not to slap the hell out of her.

She was about to mount him raw when he stopped her.

"No," he said simply as she frowned.

"I will not get pregnant," she told him, wanting very much to feel Elijah's glory uncovered.

"No," he said simply again.

Delia surrendered and retrieved the condom, putting it on him before sitting on his erection and riding him hard.

Elijah closed his eyes refusing to look at the ghost riding his lap. He would not even let his mind entertain that it was Delia atop him. He instead pictured Jasmine and all the things he wanted to do to her once they made love. Just as he was slipping deeper into the fantasy, Allison screamed vividly into his minds eye. He saw one of their more violent sexual encounters complete with beating and strangulation. Allison was into some very dark and deviant sexual behaviors, but Elijah enjoyed the hell out of experimenting with her. His breathing became more and more erratic as he thought about her. Allison was really into the strangulation thing and she would beg him to choke her to orgasm.

Elijah was a bit leery the first couple times, but after the initial shock wore off, he found he enjoyed it as well. He vaguely heard Delia moan as his mind continued showing him Allison's beautiful face contorted in agony and ecstasy as he strangled her and thrust deeply into her. *"Elijah,"* Allison croaked. *"Yes,"* she *managed again as he held her fast. "Ohhhhh," she moaned loudly cuming hard.* Elijah exploded at the same moment as Delia groaned in delight.

34

He opened his eyes breathing hard, still holding the woman's hips tightly as she smiled down at him.

"That was spectacular as usual," she told him, getting off his lap as Elijah rose and headed to the bathroom.

Time to get back to business, he thought once more, alarm code on his mind as he walked back into the bedroom.

*****

Jasmine was excitedly looking forward to tonight. Finally, off from work she was headed straight to the mall. When Elijah told her about the Latin club and wanting to salsa, she knew a new dress was in order. *Got to have new shoes too,* she thought chuckling aloud and walking still toward the bus stop.

"You want a ride," the familiar voice called out.

Taking a huge breath Jasmine turned finding Damian slowly following her down the block.

"No Damian, I am fine," she returned.

She really was not in the mood at all today. Damian was not listening to her. They talked the other night and Jasmine iterated again and again that she only wanted to be his friend. While Damian said he understood and would respect her wishes, he obviously did not.

"Jazzy, it is not a date," he tried. "I'm just offering you a ride."

Turning to him once more, she stopped walking.

"Damian, thank you for the offer, but I am fine," Jasmine replied a lot calmer than she felt.

"OK, fine," he replied, raising his hands in surrender. "Would you like to get out later on," he asked immediately after.

"Thank you, but I have plans," Jasmine returned simply.

She could see the questions in his face, but thankfully he controlled himself and did not voice them.

"Well have a great day Jazzy," Damian said finally before pulling away and heading down the street.

Please let him catch a clue, Jasmine thought as she arrived at the bus stop and the bus arrived simultaneously. Boarding and paying her fare, Jasmine found a seat and relaxed. She thought about the date tonight once more, wondering if it would lead to anything long term. She really was not the type for quick flings. Jasmine liked committed relationships that were long term. She wanted to be married. Unlike some of her friends and even the women she worked with, Jasmine was not running around pretending that she did not want a lasting and legally binding commitment from a man. She felt that as a woman it was the respectable thing to do. She knew it was pretty old fashioned thinking, but that was how Jasmine felt. *I hope he is not a player or any of that craziness*, she thought sighing deeply as the bus stopped at the mall and she disembarked. Jasmine headed inside, the dress she wanted dancing in her minds eye.

She did not see Damian as he entered the mall almost right behind her, discreetly following her at a distance. Jasmine headed into the Boulevard and began looking at dresses. She found an electric purple offering that form fit from her breasts to her waist, then flared dramatically. It was tank strapped with a deep plunge neckline. *Perfect for showing off the girls*, Jasmine chuckled internally, heading to the dressing room to try it on. Damian watched her as she played with the dress, his eyes following her as she walked to the dressing room, the deep frown on his face as his mind whirled and he fumed knowing Jasmine had a date, and it was not with him.

*****

"Tell him I'm not here," Montgomery told his secretary as he held his phone.
His door opened 45 seconds later as Jaheem strolled inside.
"I tried to stop him Alderman," the woman was explaining, obviously flustered.
"It's okay," he replied simply as she nodded and left them alone.
"What do you want Jah," Montgomery threw out regarding the man in front of him with disdain.
Why anyone would want to throw away their lives trying to fight for the rights of the scourge of the earth that lived in ML King Gardens was beyond him.
"I want you to halt this damned project you and your boy Clayton are cramming down the people's throats," Jaheem replied point blank.
Montgomery scoffed before pulling out a cigar and lighting it.
"Jah, you seem to be out of touch with your people," he returned sarcastically.
"They are all on board for the project and their brand new homes," Montgomery told him calmly.
"I'm sure they are," Jaheem returned. "People who have never had anything of course would jump at a pipe dream like you are selling," he told the Alderman.

"I'm not twisting their arms, Jah," Montgomery returned. "We do not have to play the game in here," he went on. "It is just you and me and we both know those damned people do not give a shit about anything except their next government handout."

Jaheem was deeply offended by Montgomery's words as well as his condescending attitude.

"Not all of them are like that," he tried as Montgomery again scoffed.

"Half the women in the projects have 3 or more children, barely a high school education, and no prospects for either husbands or jobs," the Alderman spat.

"The men," he began contemptuously. "They are either drug dealers, thieves, pimps, or killers," Montgomery told Jaheem. "What we are presenting is the best thing that will probably ever happen to them in their lifetime," Montgomery arrogantly informed Jaheem.

"The best thing in their lives, really," Jaheem questioned incredulously. "Being moved into houses built on top of a landfill," he threw at Montgomery, the irritation evident.

The Alderman waved his hand in dismissal.

"More than they actually deserve," he returned haughtily.

Jaheem heard enough.

"Well that does not matter, because you are going to call a stop to the shit and they are going to stay where they are," Jaheem told him as Montgomery gave him a look.

"Then you're going to take that same money you were going to use to relocate them, to fix up the place they are in right now," he finished as Montgomery opened his mouth to speak.

"Be quiet," Jaheem told him rising. "I am leaving this with you," he said of the manila envelope he still held. "You look inside, then think about your project and ask yourself how much you are willing to actually pay to make it happen," Jaheem finished cryptically. Without another word he laid the envelope on Montgomery's desk and walked out of his office.

Chapter Seven

The club was live and Jasmine was having a fantastic time. *This is seriously fun,* she mused continuing to take in the club and the patrons. She slyly looked Elijah over once more. The man was incredibly fine. He was wearing all black; silk shirt and tailor fit pants. The ice in his ear, around his neck and wrist, brought life to the otherwise monotone ensemble. The only other hints of color in his outfit were the black and grey Kenneth Cole's he paired with it. Jasmine could not believe how much of a gentleman Elijah was. He opened doors for her, complimented her non-stop and he did not touch her without permission, even to hold her hand. She smiled slightly thinking of the electricity of his touch when he took her hand headed to the dance floor.

Jasmine was thankful now for her curiosity a year or so earlier when she signed up for the salsa lessons on a whim. She was proud to be able to keep up with Elijah and not make a total idiot of herself.

"Would you like another Sangria," Elijah asked breaking her thought.

"Sure, that will be fine," Jasmine replied as he smiled again.

Please let this be the real thing, she prayed silently. Elijah was so perfect in so many ways. He was an excellent conversationalist. He actually knew about art and sculpture, a couple other closely guarded secret interests Jasmine held. He traveled extensively and delighted in telling her about the various countries he visited.

"Why don't we leave and have a late dinner after you finish your wine," Elijah suggested leaning close to her ear so he would be heard above the music.

Jasmine was on fire praying she could hold out and not let him charm the clothes off her tonight.

"That would be great," she replied smoothly not betraying the smoldering fire burning deep inside her at the moment.

*****

Allison could not believe her luck. She came to Scorcher to enjoy the Latin rhythms, dance, and relax. It was also the one place she did not have to worry about slow dancing or love talk with Kevin, her date. Allison was no fool and she knew certain things were expected of her in order to climb the internal ladder she was perched upon. Kevin Whittington was already Special Agent and second assistant to the Jr. Director of the Bureau. He also sported a serious crush on her as Allison used it to her full advantage. He wasn't a bad looking man, but he wasn't cute either. He was rather normal; dark brown hair with green eyes and perfectly tanned skin. There was nothing that really just stood out about him. He treated her well enough and of course gave her the inside scoop on all the power plays and players. Allison of course slept with him. *Big mistake,* she regretted. Now Kevin convinced himself he was in love with her. She suspected he was more in love with the fact she was the first black woman he ever dated or slept with. He was constantly talking marriage, children and futures with her. Those were the last things on her mind right now, but he did not know that. So until he found out, or she obtained the position and favor she wanted, Allison would play along.

Kevin was oblivious as Allison once again regarded the couple seated on the other side of the room. She noticed him earlier as they danced and he took her breath away. Elijah was still so damned sexy too her. *Who is this woman,* she wondered not at all liking the way her ex was looking into the woman's eyes. Allison saw that look before, when it used to be directed at her. Elijah really cared about this woman and that pissed Allison all the way off. *Maybe I should investigate her a bit,* she fashioned jealously. The thought was quickly dismissed as she realized she did not have any idea who the woman was. Allison knew every one of Elijah's day of week chicks, but this one was new and she obviously meant something to him for him to be with her on the weekend. Allison continued to watch as they rose about to leave and Elijah put his arm around the woman's waist drawing her close and giving her a simple, sweet kiss on the cheek.

Bitch, Allison fumed furiously. Her mind immediately told her to swallow her pride and beg him for another chance. *I can't,* she thought sadly. Knowing what Elijah did and being who she was, Allison knew he was lost to her. It still did not stop the hurt or slow the jealousy as the couple walked out of the front door and her imagination took flight about what would transpire between them for the remainder of the evening.

*****

Damian watched the couple as the man opened the door and held while Jasmine got into the Porsche. Closing it, the man walked around to the driver's side and got in as well. *Who is this clown,* he fumed cranking his car and beginning to follow.

Wednesday's Customer   KR Bankston

Damian knew he was dead wrong, but he told himself that Jasmine would never know. *I gotta know what I a'm up against,* he continued to think. Taking in the car, Damian knew he was fighting an uphill battle. His simple Dodge Lancer was no match for the luxury vehicle. *Jazzy's not like that,* his mind piped up. Grunting Damian knew that much was true, but who could blame her for wanting something and someone better than the struggling she endured most of her life. Damian made decent money at the office where he worked in the IT department and he could provide them a good lifestyle if Jasmine would just entertain the idea of them being together again. His cell rang and he frowned deeply looking at the caller ID.

"What is it now LaNeesa," Damian asked tiredly.

"You need to come by the house and see me," she told him, her tone tense and angry.

"Why," he asked simply.

"Because we need to talk that's why," LaNeesa returned.

"I am not in the mood for anymore drama today LaNeesa, seriously," Damian returned.

        She continued to badger and cajole for the next ten minutes until he finally relented and told her he would come. Satisfied, LaNeesa disconnected and he was able to return his full attention to the couple now parked and entering the Chaparral. *Nice,* Damian grudgingly admitted of the exclusive steak house. Obviously this guy had money and it was going to be one hell of a struggle to keep up with him. *I've got too,* Damian thought again sighing deeply. He glanced at his phone seeing the time and decided he would head over to LaNeesa's. *I will swing by her house after I leave there,* Damian planned, praying silently that he did not see the Porsche parked outside when he did.

*****

"You are awfully distracted," Kevin commented as they drove home.

Allison complained of a headache to get him to leave the club.

"Sorry, just not feeling all that great," she told him honestly.

She was actually physically ill thinking of Elijah falling in love with another woman. *I've got to find out who she is,* Allison made up her mind. As unfair as she knew it was, she did not want him to love anyone else except her. *That is pretty hypocritical,* her mind condemned as Allison immediately dismissed the thought.

"Come on," Kevin told her sweetly as he turned off the ignition.

40

Wednesday's Customer   KR Bankston

She was dismayed to see they were at his house and not her own. Allison did not want to be bothered with him tonight, but what choice did she have. He was still the key to the lock on that glass ceiling she needed to get inside. Obediently following him inside, Kevin told her to go lie down and he would bring her something for the headache. He arrived moments later with the water and aspirin.

"Just lay back and relax baby," he told her once more, kissing her lips softly.

Allison managed a weak smile and said nothing more as she closed her eyes.

    Her mind was on overdrive behind the lids. She heard Kevin moving around but she did not open her eyes. Allison was still thinking about Elijah and the woman together. Her imagination was running rampant. She saw them together, naked, making love to one another. She heard Elijah telling the woman he loved her and he wanted to be with her always. Allison saw the woman smile and tell Elijah she loved him back. Overcome with anger and fear she sprang up in the bed startling Kevin who was about to lie down with her.

"Bad dream," he asked stroking her face gently.

"Yes," Allison replied honestly.

Smiling at her, Kevin climbed under the Seafoam green comforter, pulling Allison close and looking into her eyes.

"Let me make you forget," he told her huskily.

She almost opened her mouth and told him he was nowhere near qualified to do that, when she simply smiled and wrapped her arms around his neck. Kevin began kissing her lips his hand roaming her body. Allison forced the dark thoughts out of her mind about Elijah and the new woman, allowing her body to relax and enjoy the things Kevin was doing to her. *He is not Elijah*, her mind told her as Kevin entered her and began thrusting into her. Sighing deeply Allison began faking her orgasm once again, as she answered her minds accusation. *No one will ever be*, she thought sadly finishing the scripted response just as Kevin came and collapsed on top of her.

****

"Man you called me over here for more of this bullshit," Damian tersely told LaNeesa.

"Damian, it is not that crucial, I just wanted you to know," she replied calmly, handing him the piece of paper.

Fuck me, he screamed silently looking at the sheet seeing the positive pregnancy test results. He and LaNeesa were careful at least ninety-eight percent of the time. *Had to be that night I got high,* Damian thought as his heart broke. He wanted children; from Jasmine.

"So what do you wanna do about it," he asked, praying deep inside she wanted an abortion.

"You don't want it, so I could have an abortion I guess," she replied.

Damian almost smiled.

"I mean I think it would be for the best," he tried diplomatically.

LaNeesa grunted shortly but said nothing. Damian came over and sat down on the couch beside her, taking her hand and looking into her eyes.

"You and me are not even together anymore, LaNeesa," Damian tried. "It really would not be fair to the child."

She continued to regard him wordlessly before sighing deeply and speaking.

"Yeah, I knew you would want to throw it away," she told him angrily. "I am not having an abortion stupid," she threw out laughing now.

"This is your damned baby and you are going to step up and take care of it," LaNeesa told him nastily. "Now if miss thang that you are so busy chasing does not have a problem, shit, neither do I."

Damian was fighting hard to control his temper. He wanted to punch her with all that was in him. Sleeping with her was a disaster and now he was going to spend the rest of his life paying for it.

"Fine," Damian threw back, rising from his seat.

His temper was on overload.

"When you have the baby, and after the DNA test, then we will talk about child support," he spat bitterly.

LaNeesa's eyes narrowed as she walked right up in his face.

"Nah, you are gonna take care of me now," she told him. "I need to eat, to have a place to live, to go to the doctor and everything while I am pregnant," she continued calmly. "And since you were big enough man to stick your dick in me and bust your nut, you are gonna be big enough to take care of what you made while it is inside me as well as out," LaNeesa finished flatly, her look daring him to dispute her statement.

"You are such a bitch," Damian growled.

"Yeah, but I am the bitch carrying your baby," she told him turning and walking into the kitchen.

"Do you want something to eat," she asked without turning around.

Damian sighed deeply, frustrated beyond measure, but feeling fully defeated at the moment.

"Yeah," he said simply as she grunted and took out the hamburger meat preparing to make them sloppy joes.

*****

Jasmine was wrestling with whether to invite Elijah in or not when he dropped her off. She felt such a connection between them and it seemed the logical next step. Still she did not want him to think she was loose or easy. The trip seemed measurably shorter for some reason as they arrived at her apartment and pulled into the parking space. As he had all evening, Elijah got out and came around to her side opening and holding the door for her. Jasmine smiled and thanked him once more as they walked inside the foyer and headed for the elevator. She lived on the 5th floor. They chatted pleasantly on the ride up, and walking down the hallway Jasmine felt her pulse begin to race. *Are you or aren't you,* her mind pestered as they arrived at her door.

"Do you have an alarm system," Elijah asked.

Shaking her head, no, he grunted. Allowing her to open the door, he told her to stay put while he checked inside. Jasmine was again impressed with his thoughtfulness as she waited, hearing him walking around inside the unit. *Thank goodness I cleaned up and made my bed today,* she chuckled silently.

Elijah emerged a few moments later telling her everything looked fine.

"You really should invest in an alarm," he chided gently, standing once again on the outside of her apartment.

Jasmine began to walk inside, when he stopped her, touching her arm delicately. Turning she looked into his eyes and was once again mesmerized.

"Thank you for a wonderful evening," Elijah told her calmly. "I hope you had a good time and that we can see each other again soon," he fished.

"It is actually one of the best times I have enjoyed in years," Jasmine smiled.

"I am glad," he replied softly.

Elijah leaned in and kissed her lips.

"Good night Jasmine," he told her answering the uncertain question she entertained on the way home.

"Sleep tight," he added, turning and beginning to walk down the hallway.

"Elijah," Jasmine called out as he turned and regarded her, but did not come back toward her.

"Will you call and let me know you made it home safely," she probed, seeing the smile adorn his face.

"Yes," he said simply, turning once again and reaching the elevator. Jasmine smiled as she closed and locked the door, hugging herself tightly, thinking how much she was going to enjoy having Elijah in her life.

Chapter Eight

Montgomery's mind was on overload as he drove. There was enough going on without the new complications Jaheem presented upon his visit earlier this week. He was absolutely furious when the man came to his office demanding he stop the high rise project. *He has your ass in a vice, so now what,* Montgomery continued to brood. Delia placed him in a very precarious position. If he went forward with the project, there was no doubt in his mind Jaheem would leak the photos to every news agency and internet site in the state. His political career would be over before it even began. *Clayton's snake in the grass self,* he angrily thought of his mentor. Montgomery never suspected anything was amiss between the two. Sucking his teeth, he realized he had been played. That is exactly what they both wanted him to think, that nothing was going on. Sighing deeply Montgomery was still in thought as he pulled into the church parking lot. He really did not care for Pastor Richard Toplin, but the man was a powerful force in the community; even more powerful that Jaheem. Montgomery also knew Pastor Toplin held an agenda.

The good Pastor had political ambitions of his own, but he was trying to realize them vicariously through his son, Chad. Montgomery knew Pastor Toplin could not run for any office himself, not with his colored past of pimping and prostitution. He would have been laughed out of any forum he tried to compete within. With that in mind Montgomery watched the man try and groom his son into throwing his hat into the political arena. *Not working out so well,* Montgomery thought smiling a little. Chad did not have the stomach for politics and it showed. He was no threat and Montgomery always treated him amiably when they met for various social reasons. He put on his game face as he walked into the study where he was directed by the church secretary, greeting the man sitting behind the huge mahogany desk.
"How are you Pastor Toplin," Montgomery greeted the man.
"Good morning Alderman," Richard returned smiling slightly and shaking the man's hand.
"What brings you by this morning," he asked already knowing fully the man's intentions.

Montgomery wasted no time getting to his point as Richard listened intently.

"Hmm," he replied simply his mind still tumbling. "Do you plan to divorce her," he asked of Delia.

"Right now the scandal of a divorce would destroy not only my career but the high rise project that is so vital to the community," Montgomery told him.

"Yes," Richard replied. "I want to see the project completed myself," he replied having his own agenda for the new community.

"My problem now is how to deal with Jaheem," Montgomery told the Pastor honestly.

"I can take care of Jaheem," Richard replied without hesitation. "You need to get your wife and your supposed mentor in check however," he added giving the Alderman a new look.

"Yes, that is in the works for later today as a matter of fact," Montgomery replied evenly, the slight edge evident in his tone.

"Fine," Richard replied once more. "I will begin with my end and handling Jaheem," he went on. "You just make sure you handle your business and when this is said and done, you keep your promise to me."

His tone let Montgomery know that while he may have been a Pastor now, he never forgot the ways of the street.

"You have my word, Pastor Toplin," Montgomery returned as he rose to leave.

The two men shook hands once more as the Alderman left and the Pastor picked up his phone making two calls.

*****

Allison was smiling smugly as she waited for the agent to return with the information she requested. It was not difficult at all to procure the approval for surveillance on Elijah. After she explained that they needed to rule him out for any involvement other than adultery with Alderman Southby's wife, her superior agreed to a simple three-day surveillance and profile of everyone he interacted with. *Now let's hope he contacts miss thing,* she brooded silently. Allison had an appointment later this morning. She exhaled impatiently thinking of the abortion scheduled. Somehow Kevin managed to impregnate her. Allison wracked her mind trying to recall when the sex unprotected was unprotected. *Condom must have failed,* she concluded shrugging. She did not tell him anything about the pregnancy unwilling to deal with all the emotional trips she was sure he would put her through. *He would be trying to lock my ass down for real then,* Allison thought grunting slightly aloud.

"Good morning," Kevin greeted her cheerfully walking into her office.

"Hi," Allison returned amiably enough.

"What is on the table this morning," he asked, sipping his coffee and looking into her eyes.

Allison gave him a quick rundown of the operation and its progression as Kevin listened intently.

"So what is this appointment you have at 11:00AM," he asked out of the blue.

Allison was startled but tried to quickly cover.

"Doctor," she said simply hoping he would leave it there.

"Hmph," Kevin returned, still watching her intently. "Something wrong?"

"No, just a routine visit," Allison lied, immediately trying to change the subject.

"Wow, really," Kevin returned, unmoved and back on the original conversation. "Since when is an abortion considered a routine visit?"

Allison was determined not to let her face show the shock her mind felt. *How the hell does he know*, she catalogued silently.

"Kevin, I really do not want to get into this right now," she told him calmly.

He rose and walked over to her, taking in the beautiful woman in front of him. Kevin loved her and wanted nothing more than to spend his life with her. He was not stupid though. Allison was a climber and she set her sights on a far loftier perch than Special Assistant.

"Allison, this child is half mine," he told her as he stood before her. "Don't you think you could have at least told me about it, asked me if I wanted this," Kevin questioned his tone growing angrier.

Allison saw what was happening and not wanting it to escalate to shouting match, at least here in the office, asked him to step outside with her. Kevin only nodded, further allaying his anger with the situation. The two calmly turned and headed outside and away from the building. There was a park across the street and they headed there, finding a bench that was secluded by trees and shrubs. Sitting down Allison exhaled deeply before regarding Kevin and speaking.

"This is why I did not tell you," she explained calmly. "I do not want a scene Kevin, I do not want to fight with you."

Kevin chuckled bitterly at her statement and looked into her eyes once again.

"How many other babies have you thrown away Allison," he asked acidly.

She frowned before answering his question.

"So fuck, this really is routine to you huh," he replied in response to her admission of six abortions.

"It was a mistake," Allison told him, not rising to the insult, "I still do not even know how it happened considering we used a condom every time."

Kevin continued to watch her wordlessly trying desperately not to reach out and strangle her. He was absolutely livid that Allison held utterly no regard for the life inside her.

"Have the baby and give it to me," he told her as she gave him an incredulous look.

"Are you crazy," she spat before she could catch herself.

"No, I want my child, I do not want you to just flush it like shit in the toilet," Kevin growled.

Allison sucked her teeth and rose from the bench.

"This discussion is over," she told him coldly. "This is my body and I do not want this damned creature inside it any longer," she spat venomously.

"You are a complete bitch, you know that Allison," Kevin returned, standing as well now.

"So what," she fired off. "Thank you for the compliment, you mediocre bastard," Allison insulted.

Kevin was stung by the words, his face falling from the hurt.

"Let this be the end of us and this bullshit," she continued to rage, her temper at full throttle.

Allison was angry that she was forced to defend herself to a man she did not love; angry that she must spend $500.00 to get rid of his worthless seed. Angry that Elijah was with another woman and falling in love with her. Angry that she still had not heard a word on the position she applied for within the bureau and angry she was still working on penny ante babysitting gigs like Delia Southby when the big fish was her husband.

"Pay back is a bitch, bitch," Kevin spat acidly, pushing past her almost knocking her down as he stalked away and headed back toward the office.

Wednesday's Customer   KR Bankston

Allison took several deep breaths and got her poker face back in tact, turning now herself and headed back to the office. 11:00AM could not come soon enough.

*****

     Elijah sighed deeply as Katrina continued to give him head. Today was Tuesday, and it was her day. Katrina wasn't as skilled as Reesa, but she was good enough. They enjoyed a vigorous round of lovemaking already upon her arrival two hours ago. *What about Jasmine,* his mind threw at him just as Katrina put her sex in his face, prompting him to taste her. Elijah paused briefly, violently pushing the thought from his mind. He and Jasmine had nothing to do with the women he screwed during the week. They were strictly sex. No feelings, no attachments involved. That was the beauty of each arrangement.
"Mmm, Elijah," Katrina moaned bringing him all the way back to the present.
Whenever he and Jasmine became committed he would stop seeing the women. Elijah was a lot of things, but he was faithful. It was his one last stronghold on morality he supposed, given his profession. Katrina was flowing freely and his manhood was at full mast once again. She expertly placed the condom on him and went to her knees, butt up in the air, legs spread, inviting him to take her. Elijah needed no further prompting. He slid his hardened shaft deep inside her gushing wetness.
"Damn," he swore softly, slowly withdrawing and ramming her deeply upon his return.
"Hell yeah Elijah," Katrina moaned loving his movements.
He held her tightly his hand squeezing her breasts and twisting the nipple between his fingers.
"I'm cuming Elijah," she moaned as he saw the evidence on the condom once again sliding in and out of her.
     He smiled at her body's reaction and began sexing her for real. His pace and rhythm were melodic and consistent as Katrina moaned and writhed from his assault.
"So fucking good Elijah, shit, throw that dick boy," she groaned aloud, spreading her legs even wider wanting him to climb inside her.
Elijah stroked her long and deep, finding and hitting her g-spot with each thrust.
"Aaaah yeaaaaah," Katrina screamed coating him as yet another orgasm rocked her.

Elijah felt his own finish looming close and pushed her flat onto the mattress. He spread her legs to their full capacity, held onto the edge of the mattress and went harder and deeper than he ever went inside her.

"Elijah, mmm, oh my god, Elijah," Katrina moaned in ecstasy as he took complete control of her.

"You wanna cum again," he teased.

"Yeah Elijah, yeah," Katrina immediately replied.

"You love this dick," he asked getting closer and closer.

"You are my king, Elijah," Katrina moaned.

He liked when she began talking crazy. It let him know he was hitting her right.

"Grip me," he told her softly in her ear.

Katrina immediately complied, tightening her walls around him every time he plunged into her.

"Mmm, yeah that's it," Elijah murmured thrusting deeply once more and his body convulsing from the power of his own orgasmic release.

He carefully removed himself from her, rising and heading to the bathroom to remove the condom. She was dressing when he came back.

"You are leaving," he asked, giving her a look.

They normally spent the entire day together when she came over.

"I am sorry baby," Katrina told him, walking over and kissing his lips.

"I have a photo shoot today," she elaborated. "Riley will kick my ass if I am late again," Katrina added, chuckling slightly.

Elijah smiled.

"I understand."

"Thanks," she replied grabbing her purse. "I will see you next Tuesday," she told him sweetly as he held the door for her.

"I am looking forward to it," Elijah returned looking her over.

"And since you shortchanged me today, well, you know," he teased.

Katrina burst into laughter.

"I got you baby," she replied, giving him another short kiss as she waved and walked to the elevator.

Elijah closed the door still smiling and headed into the kitchen. He saw his phone on the counter and six missed calls. He picked it up and found exactly what he figured he would. Delia was blowing him up yet again. *OK, I gotta finish this bullshit by Friday,*

Elijah crossly entertained before tossing the phone on the counter. He picked up his personal cell and pushed a speed dial button.

"Hi," he greeted Jasmine softly.

Elijah smiled as she greeted him back and they began to talk. He disconnected some forty minutes later, his mind now better suited to deal with Delia and the resolve to end the affiliation, permanently.

Chapter Nine

"Things are progressing right on schedule," Ronnie was telling his partner on the phone. "I do not know how, but that damned Montgomery Southby has them all sold on the move."

He listened as his partner spoke before he once again joined the conversation. Dirk Swan was smiling as he listened to Ronnie tell him about the new politician in their pocket. He knew all about Montgomery and his antics. It was a bit unsettling to him how much the man loathed his own race, especially with Dirk himself being married to a black woman, but as long as he upheld his end of the business deal he did not let the man's personal tastes disturb him.

"Well Clayton really has not been nearly as helpful," he returned. "If we can get Southby in the state's house or senate, we will have a powerful ally," he told his partner.

Dirk again agreed. They needed leverage where it counted. Where they could get bills and referendums passed that suited and benefited them instead of the bloodsucking leeches always hiding behind helping the so called less fortunate.

Ronnie knew Montgomery was hungry and ambitious. He was also ruthless and seemed to have zero tolerance for his own people. Those were good things in Ronnie's book. He did not need yet another bleeding heart liberal in place worrying about the supposed poor of the community, who half the time, were personally responsible for their own situation. He built Glazer construction from nothing. If he could do it, so could they, he surmised missing some of the more obvious distinctions between himself and the people of whom he spoke.

"Yes, I' am meeting him again today," Ronnie once more informed his partner.

"That is great," Dirk replied. "How long before we see the benefits of our money invested," he added, his tone leaving no question about his impatience.

"Well with the way everything is going, we should have the losers out of the projects in about three weeks," he began. "After we get them moved over into the new slots, we can immediately get the demolition permit and take the buildings down," Ronnie told him, still doing the time math in his head. "We should have it cleared, foundations poured and construction begun in about 2 months," he finished.

Dirk, satisfied with the time estimation, told Ronnie to do what must be done to insure everything continued to stay on track, and disconnected. Dirk was glad that was taken care of. He had other pressing matters going on at the moment, the most important of which, what exactly his wife was up too with her early morning breakfasts at the Morning Perk. Ronnie's cell rang almost immediately after Dirk hung up and he glanced at the caller I.D., sighing deeply before answering.

"Hello," he spoke calmly.

"What is this bullshit you are trying to pull Ronnie," Clayton boomed into the phone.

Ronnie was expecting this call. He knew once the man found out his incentive was cut in half he would be furious.

"I am not pulling anything Clayton," Ronnie returned calmly. "I am simply compensating the man who has actually made things happen for this project, not just selling me a lot of empty promises and hot air."

"Montgomery is my fucking protégé, who the hell do you think taught him what he knows," Clayton continued to rage. "You think I am going to just quietly roll over and go away, while you two become bed buddies," he went on as Ronnie smiled, amused at his anger.

"You do not really have a choice now do you," Ronnie returned his tone all business. "You gonna turn him in, tell the officials what is really going on behind closed doors on this project," he continued to taunt. "Nah, Clayton, on this one you just lost out, that's all," Ronnie told him. "Maybe if we approach you again next time, you will actually do what you claim you could."

Clayton was still huffing and sputtering but Ronnie was oblivious. He was yesterday's news. Their new partner was Montgomery Southby and all the players in his organizational circles were going to make sure the Alderman attained bigger and richer heights as quickly as possible.

*****

Jasmine was still on cloud nine as she waited tables. Talking to Elijah earlier made her day. She was fully enamored with the man. He was incredible and much to her delight he seemed to return the deep feelings she felt herself developing toward him. She saw movement out of the corner of her eye and turned to find

Wednesday's Customer   KR Bankston

Damian entering the restaurant. Normally irritated by his presence, Jasmine did not flinch. Even as he sat in her section and began perusing the menu, she did not think anything of it. He was not around for a couple of days and Jasmine was beginning to grow hopeful that he accepted their arrangement of just being friends.

"Hi," she greeted walking up to the table.

"Hey Jazzy," Damian returned sweetly.

"Know what you are having," she asked as he nodded and gave her his order.

"OK, I will put this in and bring your juice right out," Jasmine told him.

"Okay," Damian again smiled slightly.

Hmm, that is odd, she thought making his juice. She knew him well enough to know when there was something going on with him. Jasmine battled with herself the entire time she made the juice and even on the walk back to his table, if she would inquire about his mood.

    Jasmine continued to ponder what she would do concerning Damian as she went to check on Eddie at the back table once again. He entertained yet another potential client sitting across from him, as she approached and filled their coffee cups.

"Hey Jasmine," Eddie called out as she was about to leave them.

"Yeah Eddie, what's up," she inquired amiably turning back to the two men.

"This is Justin, my client," he told her, introducing the man.

Jasmine immediately knew what was up as Eddie gave her a sly look.

"Hi Justin," Jasmine replied calmly.

The man returned the greeting giving her reference of interest from both his eyes and his tone. Jasmine sighed lightly as Eddie spoke again.

"How are things with you Jasmine," he tossed out giving her the opening she needed.

"I am good, just celebrated my third anniversary," she replied still calm and friendly.

"Oh really," Eddie replied as Justin frowned faintly.

"Yeah, she bought me a really nice jewelry set," Jasmine replied as Eddie fought to keep from laughing.

"Man, I cannot believe you and Daphne have been together that long," he replied, going with the flow and pulling a name out of the air.

Wednesday's Customer   KR Bankston

Justin was visibly repulsed Jasmine could tell from the look on his face.

"Mmhmm, true love," she chuckled, having accomplished her mission and left the men at the table once again talking over business.

She continued to smile as she gathered Damian's drink request. Eddie clued her to the game a long time ago when his clients first start meeting him in the diner. He told Jasmine that the men were so insistent upon meeting her he was unable to conduct business. So the two devised a scheme that would ensure Eddie got his clients full attention and Jasmine got them to leave her alone. There were three usual stories; she was married, or she had six kids and five baby daddies, or she was gay. Jasmine got the impression that neither husband, nor kids, would have deterred Justin, hence the gay pretense. Still smiling she headed over to Damian's table, glass in hand.

"Here you go," she told him amiably, putting the glass on the table.

"Thanks Jazzy," Damian returned.

"You OK Damian," she asked, her curiosity getting the better of her.

He sighed deeply before looking up at her again. The pain and sadness she saw in his eyes took her aback.

"Got some issues Jazzy, that's all," Damian replied.

Truthfully it was killing him sitting here looking at her, talking to her, and knowing that LaNeesa held his neck in a noose. Jasmine would never accept him having a child with another woman, especially after all the rhetoric he spouted about being with only her. *But it happened long before that night with us,* he tried to reason in his mind. Still Damian could not see Jasmine understanding; especially now that she was obviously already dating someone else.

"Well hopefully it will get better Damian," Jasmine returned sympathetically.

He smiled shortly once again and told her thank you, watching her longingly as she walked away. Damian put his head in his hands. He could not stand LaNeesa most times and now she was going to be tied to him for the rest of his life. *You shoulda never ever stuck your dick up inside that bitch,* he commiserated. *What you shoulda done was nut inside Jasmine the other night, idiot,* his mind once again accused. If she became pregnant Damian knew she would have come back to him and even if LaNeesa came later with tales of her own pregnancy, Jasmine would have stayed with him. *You are so stupid, missed that chance and you will never get it again,* his mind continued to berate.

"Jazzy, do you think maybe we could get together later, and just talk," he hurriedly clarified as she sat his food in front of him.

"Umm, what time," she asked hesitantly.

She could tell something was weighing heavily on him, and even though they were done romantically, Jasmine still cared about Damian as a friend.

"After you get off is fine," he replied, thankful she was even considering it.

"OK," she replied amiably.

"Thank you so much," he replied sincerely.

"No problem," she smiled.

"I will pick you up after your shift," Damian told her.

"Sure, that's fine," Jasmine told him and left him to enjoy his meal.

As he sat and ate, Damian plotted. He would suggest going back to her place and then he would pull out all the stops and seduce her again. *Not pulling the fuck out this time,* he thought darkly, his appetite returning as he contemplated his plan. Damian finished his meal and paid his check, reminding Jasmine he would be back in a few hours to pick her up. She smiled and told him okay, waving goodbye as he left. *Today you and I are getting back together, fuck LaNeesa and whoever this muthafucka is you are seeing,* Damian brooded silently watching her from his car. Smiling once more of his plans he started the car and headed out. There were a few things he needed to do before returning and picking up the woman he loved.

*****

"Why not," Elijah threw out managing to sound irritated. Quite the contrary he was thrilled when Delia called and told him they could not spend time today.

"My husband has informed me he needs my attention today," she returned irritably.

Elijah smiled, careful not to let it reach his voice.

"This is why I don't kiss you," he told her evenly.

"Darling, please do not be cross with me," Delia pleaded; terrified he would stop seeing her forever. "I promise you I will make it up to you," she told him.

Elijah saw his opportunity and pounced.

"I have a fantasy," he began, laying the trap.

Intrigued Delia asked him to elaborate. She was giggling by the end of it.
"Really," she asked still chuckling lightly.
"So will you do it," Elijah pushed.
"When," she returned and he smiled fully.
"Friday, late," he told her.
"I cannot believe I am saying yes to this," Delia replied.
"I want to give you all this dick while he lies upstairs asleep," Elijah told her. "It turns me on to know I am having his beautiful wife, right under his nose," he added as Delia again giggled.
"Mmmm, sounds sexy," she replied.
Elijah knew from her tone she was turned on.
"Give me the alarm code," he told her, moving in for the kill.
Delia immediately supplied the info, giving explicit instructions on the operation and location of the keypads.
"I cannot wait to see you Friday," Elijah whispered seductively.
"Mmm, I am already wet darling," Delia informed him, bringing a deep frown to his face.
"Well you better stay that way," he replied sounding jealous.
"I only let him when he begs," Delia told him, hoping she was reassuring him of her devotion to only him.
"Hmph," Elijah returned evenly as she again begged his understanding.
"I guess," he replied. "I may kiss you Friday," he added, hearing the smile in her voice as she told him she certainly hoped so.
"I shouldn't admit this to you Elijah," Delia began. "But I think I am falling in love with you."
Elijah laughed silently before speaking once again.
"I don't want to think about that," he told her. "I cannot have you, so…," he trailed off as she sighed deeply.
"Darling, I promise Friday will be so good," Delia vowed.
Elijah sulkily told her all right as he readied himself to disconnect.
"Call me at least," he told her, not really meaning it, but knowing she wanted to hear it.
"I promise darling," Delia told him sweetly, adding that she heard his car in the garage.
"Until Friday," she told him softly and disconnected.
Elijah smiled fully looking at the alarm code he put into his phone. Friday was definitely going to be a great day.

Wednesday's Customer   KR Bankston

Delia was not looking forward to whatever drama Montgomery was bringing her today. Truthfully she was actively reevaluating her entire life with the man since meeting Elijah. She was not like her husband. Montgomery hated his black ancestry, Delia simply felt disenfranchised from hers. All her life she was viewed as white by the African American community, but not quite white enough for the Caucasian community. She always loved black men. Not the passable mulattos like Montgomery, but real black men like Elijah and some of the others she dated and slept with in the past. *They could not take the pressure,* she thought sadly of the couple of true relationships during college. The guys were nice enough, but they folded when the pressure began to come, both from other black women who were angry they were dating what they perceived was a white woman, and from the white men, who felt they were just another threat to the preservation of the race. Montgomery was simply a means of escape when she met him. Delia was not an idiot either. She knew the main reason the man married her was absolutely because she looked every bit the white part. *I just want to be happy,* Delia thought sadly, wiping the errant tear, just as Montgomery entered the house walking into the study where she stood still gazing out of the window.

"Hello Delia," he greeted calmly.

Turning she regarded her husband. Whatever was going on must have been important for him to call her by her name. He seldom did that.

"Hello," she returned amiably, becoming slightly anxious from the look he was giving her.

"What's going on Montgomery," she asked getting directly to the point.

He exhaled evenly but said nothing, rising and making himself a drink. The bell rang and startled her. *Who is this,* Delia thought as Montgomery calmly walked toward the front door. He returned moments later, Clayton directly behind him.

"Would you like a drink," Montgomery asked his mentor.

Clayton declined, casting a quick glance at Delia, who returned a blank look having no more idea than he, why they were all here together. Montgomery returned to the lone leather highboy in the room and sat.

"What's so urgent, Montgomery," Clayton asked, his curiosity getting the better of him.

The anxiety he felt unfortunately filtered through his voice.

Again he said nothing as he reached inside his suit jacket, retrieving the photos. Montgomery unceremoniously dropped them onto the coffee table in front of them. The color drained from Clayton's face as he looked at the pictures. Delia remained silent, waiting on Montgomery's wrath to be unleashed.

"How long have you two been fucking over me, while you fuck each other," he asked acidly.

Clayton opened his mouth to speak, when Montgomery raised his hand and regarded his wife.

"You tell me," he said simply, his eyes smoldering as they looked into hers.

"Almost 18 months," she replied just as simply, not elaborating further.

"How fucked is that," he murmured almost to himself.

"Listen Montgomery," Clayton began before the man gave him a murderous look, silencing him.

"You and I will hash this shit out later," he told him angrily. "And you and I are going to definitely have a meeting of the minds," Montgomery continued looking at Delia. "Right now however, there are more important things to be handled," he told them both going on to explain his statement.

"This project is too important to let it be derailed because you two could not keep your hands off each other," he spat distastefully.

"So here is how this shit is going to play out," Montgomery began again as they both gave him their undivided attention. "Do you both understand," he asked at the end.

Clayton grudgingly acknowledged he did. He was promptly dismissed by Montgomery with one last admonishment to make sure he came clean with Marissa and that she equally went along with the plan. Alone finally he returned his attention to his wife.

"Your leash just got shortened," he told her coldly. "Your credit cards are cut off, you will not leave this house unless there is an appointed function I have authorized," Montgomery went on as Delia endured.

"There will be no divorce or separation," he began anew. "I'm taking you to Dr. Endison tomorrow for testing and removal of that IUD," he told her plainly. "You have put me off for years now about children, well that bullshit is over," Montgomery finished rising and walking over to her.

He slapped her hard, knocking her to the floor.

"As good as I have been to you, you nasty, trifling, cheating, bitch, I am going to be your personal devil in hell from here on end," he finished breathing hard as she continued to cower at his feet.

Done for the moment, Montgomery strode from the room as Delia broke and began to sob deeply.

*****

"Come on in and make yourself comfortable," Jasmine told Damian.

He smiled thanking her as he did what she instructed. She returned shortly afterward with their tea, sitting in the recliner adjacent to the couch where Damian sat.

"I don't bite, Jazzy."

"I am fine over here," she chuckled.

He was slightly annoyed but took a deep breath to push it away and continued talking to her. Damian fed Jasmine the contrived story he came up with earlier in the day about his job and his fear of losing his position. He told her falsehoods about office politics and the discrimination he felt being there.

"Have you talked to anyone, an attorney or maybe the EEOC," she asked trying to be genuinely helpful.

Damian sighed deeply for effect.

"You know how that goes Jazzy," he told her. "They would definitely find a way to get rid of me then."

She grunted slightly and sighed deeply nodding in agreement.

The knock at the door interrupted his next statement as Damian frowned. Jasmine rose and went to the door inquiring who was there. Smiling now she opened it, finding Elijah on the other side.

"Hi," she greeted him happily. "I didn't know you were coming by."

Jasmine quickly invited him inside. Elijah's smile left when he saw Damian sitting on the couch. The other man gave him a defiant look, pissing Elijah immediately off.

"I did not mean to intrude," he said simply, looking in Jasmine's eyes.

"It is not an intrusion," she told him honestly. "Damian is a friend, he just stopped by to talk," Jasmine explained.

Elijah could see the man carried more on his mind than talking and was glad he followed his mind and stopped in.

"You want some tea," Jasmine asked.

"I was actually coming to see if I could take you to dinner," Elijah answered.
Not having to be bothered with Delia today gave him an entire evening to himself.
"Yes, I would love that," Jasmine replied without hesitation.
Damian took the hint and rose from the couch.
"I will leave now and let you get ready," he told Jasmine sweetly.
She smiled and thanked him.
"I will keep you in my prayers Damian."
"Thanks Jazzy, that means a lot to me," Damian told her softly, looking right into her eyes.
Elijah was mentally preparing a midnight visit to the man after he dropped Jasmine off from dinner. *What is he really after*, he mused silently as Jasmine walked the man to the door closing it behind him.
"Give me 20 minutes," she asked as Elijah smiled and kissed her smoothly.
"Take your time," he replied calmly, sitting and taking the remote she offered.

He turned up the TV set as he methodically searched her home. The noise drowned out his movements as he shuffled papers and opened drawers. He found the picture in a drawer under the telephone table. *Just what I figured*, Elijah thought reading the back and knowing the two were a couple at some point. He could tell that for Jasmine it was over and she was genuine in her feelings of friendship. The man however held a far darker agenda and Elijah planned to show him the light tonight. Hearing her begin to come back into the living room, he returned to the couch, rising as she came into his line of sight.
"You look beautiful," Elijah told her honestly as Jasmine blushed and thanked him.
"Shall we," he asked, opening the door as she smiled and walked outside, locking it and taking his hand as they walked to the elevator together.

Chapter Ten

Kevin knocked lightly on the door hearing the reply before opening it and venturing inside.

"Kevin, good to see you," Perry greeted.

Perry Caldwell was the Deputy Director at the bureau.

"I was definitely glad to get your call, have a seat," the man told Kevin, all in one breath.

Smiling, he took the seat offered as well as the coffee and began to converse with his superior. They talked for the better part of forty minutes with both of them agreeing upon a decision.

"I should have the paperwork done by the afternoon," Kevin told Perry as he rose and the other man did likewise.

"That is fine Kevin," he told him walking him to the door.

"You are an excellent agent," Perry told him amiably. "Always been able to count on you and I definitely appreciate that kind of loyalty," he finished as Kevin again thanked him and left his office heading back to his own.

He was still smiling when he rounded the corner and ran into Allison. She rolled her eyes as he smirked and walked by her into his own office closing the door.

Allison was a bit taken aback by his demeanor. *What exactly is he up too*, she wondered as the office began to take on life. She saw people smiling and whispering excitedly.

"What is going on," she mumbled as the slight cramp hit her.

The abortion went off without a hitch and she returned to work for the rest of the day. She was heading to her own office, adjacent to Kevin's when she heard another of their colleagues speaking to him.

"Shit man, congratulations," Tyler told him.

"Thanks man," Kevin returned smiling broadly. "News travels fast as hell around here," he murmured as the man burst into laughter.

"You know everyone has been waiting for months now to know what was up," he replied cryptically.

What the hell, Allison wondered as her office phone rang and she walked over to it. Smiling, she lifted the handset seeing Perry Caldwell's name on her display.

"Hello Deputy Director Caldwell," she answered politely.

Perry returned her greeting asking her to come to his office. Smiling still Allison assured him she would be right up. *I sure hope this is what I think it is*, she mused leaving her office and heading for the elevator. Kevin watched her from the glass enclosed office having a pretty good idea where she was headed. He shook his head lightly and returned his attention to the paperwork on his desk and getting it completed.

*****

"Wait a minute," Marissa returned tersely. "What part of this bullshit am I supposed to understand, let alone go along with," she ranted furious with Clayton's admission and the position they now found themselves in.

"You and this tramp been bumping uglies for the last eighteen months, but me and Montgomery are supposed to be cool and understand that shit," Marissa asked again, still incredulous. "Clayton I have put up with a lot of crap from you over the years, but I still stuck by you through all of it," she told him as he sighed deeply.

"Oh stop acting like you are such a martyr," he returned finally fed up with her theatrics. "We have sex what, maybe twice a month and even then you act like you're doing me a favor," he spat bitterly.

"That's because you can't fuck," Marissa told him plainly as he rose from the chair and strode over to her.

"What," she threw out defiantly. "You put your hands on me the headlines will scream your obituary," Marissa informed him.

"All I want to know is that you are going to play your part," Clayton told her backing down.

"Why should I," she threw back as he sighed again.

"What is it going to cost me this time," he asked defeated.

Marissa rattled off a long list of things she wanted in exchange for her cooperation.

"Fine," Clayton told her at the end.

Satisfied she left him alone in the den heading upstairs to their bedroom, drink in hand.

He put his head in his hands wondering how the photos were obtained. *Did he hire someone to watch her*, he brooded of Montgomery and Delia. Clayton hoped the man did not hurt her. He only witnessed his protégé that angry once before. The ending was not pretty at all. They ended up paying the man almost 50K to keep quiet about the incident and not report it to the police. *He better not touch her like that*, he thought angrily not above violence himself if Montgomery hurt Delia.

Clayton finally admitted to himself that he was in love with the woman. She was perfect in his estimation; far better than Marissa and her borderline alcoholism. Delia made him feel 20 years younger. She did not complain about his lovemaking, reaching orgasm time and again when they were together. *I wish she would leave him*, Clayton thought. She talked about it from time to time but he knew she was scared. He was a bit leery himself. He still had his political career to consider. What would his constituents think? Clayton loosed a cavernous breath realizing they were all trapped in the same sparkling maze. His cell vibrated and he sighed again seeing the text from Montgomery. It was a simple message stating time and place. Knowing what was up Clayton rose and headed upstairs to shower and change, then head out to meet his protégé, settling their differences so they could conduct their business.

*****

Allison was livid as she rode the elevator. The door opened and she stepped onto the floor as more people gathered at Kevin's door. She frowned deeply seeing all the smiles and hearing all the well wishes. Managing to escape the melee, Allison retreated to her office and closed the door. She opened her desk drawer and retrieved the bottle of aspirin, immediately taking two. Her eyes fell on the .9mm that she kept inside the drawer, dark thoughts playing in her mind. Her door opened moments later and she looked up seeing Kevin entering. Sitting back in her chair she continued to regard him silently as he stood in front of her.

"I guess congratulations are in order," Allison told him sarcastically.

Kevin smirked again.

"Yeah, I would say they are," he replied calmly.

Allison rolled her eyes at him.

"You need to adjust your fucked up attitude," Kevin told her, no nonsense.

"If I don't," she replied defiantly.

"Then you can enjoy being unemployed Agent Register," he answered flatly.

"You certainly have already let your new position go to your head," she told him bitterly.

Kevin was the new SAC, or Special Agent in Charge, for the office of Congressional Affairs. It was the job Allison was awaiting word of.

"You said you were not even applying," she accused angrily.

"I wasn't," Kevin replied immediately.

"So what changed, why would you back stab me like that," Allison asked, the emotion in her voice.

"I figured one good fuck, deserved another, don't you agree," Kevin replied and she received her answer.

"All this because of the abortion," she asked softly.

"All this is because you played me," Kevin told her. "You played games with my heart, you used me, lied to me, all so you could get closer to Perry," he went on. "What was your plan after me setting up the interview, to suck your way into the position?"

Allison sighed deeply regarding him coldly once again.

"Well it's not an issue anymore now is it," she replied, not answering his accusation.

"No, its not," Kevin told her. "You should take the rest of the day off, get your mind right so you can come in and do your job in the morning," he directed.

Allison was absolutely furious. She was also impotent to do anything about it. Kevin was now her boss and since they were not sleeping together anymore she knew there would be no special favors. As angry as he was with her at the moment, Allison already knew she would get every dredge assignment he could find.

"Thank you sir," she replied smartly. "I will see you in the morning."

Allison made it to her car and inside before the reality hit her and she began to cry.

*****

Jaheem was enjoying his meal wondering when he would hear from Montgomery. *I know he has opened that package*, he supposed, sipping his tea. He was once again at Morning perk enjoying an early dinner. He missed Jasmine being here to serve him. She was such a pleasant young woman, always professional, courteous and friendly. His waitress this evening, while professional, lacked a lot of the social graces he enjoyed with Jasmine. *You are spoiled*, his mind chided. Jaheem smiled again thinking perhaps he was. He felt the slight vibration of his cell and pulled it from his pocket fully expecting to see the Alderman's name on the I.D. It was instead a specter from his past.

"Hello," Jaheem answered calmly trying to steady his breathing.

"How is it going Jah," the male voice asked.

"It's going," Jaheem replied as his mind continued to race.

"Glad to hear that," the man spoke once again. "You have time for an old friend?"

Jaheem's sense of dread grew.

"Umm when are you talking about," he hedged.

The last thing he wanted was to see this person again in the flesh.

"This evening would be good," the man replied still calm and even.

Jaheem agreed to meet the caller and they settled on a destination before disconnecting. His mind was still spiraling as his stomach did somersaults. *Why the hell are they calling now*, he thought, of his impending meeting tonight. Jaheem was to plugged into the community to get caught up in drama, and the person he was going to see tonight seemed to have drama attached to their hip. Sighing acutely, he pushed the thoughts aside deciding to wait until he actually met them and they talked before passing judgment of their motives. The waitress returned and refilled his tea, asking if he needed anything else before leaving him alone once more. *Come on Montgomery, do the right thing and call me,* Jaheem thought. He did not want to put the man's business in the streets, but to save his neighborhood he would. He did not want to see them swindled once again on a pipe dream that would quickly turn into a nightmare.

"I am looking for Jasmine," the woman told the cashier.

Jaheem looked up hearing the waitress's name.

"She is off," the cashier replied evenly.

The woman sucked her teeth rolling her neck before speaking again.

"So when the hell will she be back," LaNeesa asked.

She found Jasmine's number in Damian's phone the other night. She wanted to make sure that the woman knew she was with Damian now and they were having a child together.

"I am not allowed to give out that information," the cashier smartly told the woman, sick of her ghetto theatrics.

Jaheem sighed deeply as the woman called the cashier a foul name and walked out of the establishment. *This is why they think we are all a bunch of classless animals,* he mused, rising and paying his check. He prayed that Montgomery called soon and that this meeting did not turn into a nightmare tonight.

*****

Elijah walked Jasmine to her door and waited as she opened it.
"You coming in," she asked turning to him.
Smiling he followed her inside, closing the door behind him. He took a seat on her couch as she came and sat beside him. He liked her apartment. It was colorful but relaxing. The teals and greens were a nice blend Elijah thought finally turning his attention to the beautiful woman sitting next to him.
"You and him used to date," he asked calmly.
Jasmine told him they did.
"We broke up a year ago," she informed Elijah.
"Does he know that," he asked as Jasmine chuckled slightly.
"We went to the movies a few weeks ago, and…" she replied, shrugging at the end of her sentence.
"Mmph," Elijah grunted noncommittal.
"It's not like that with us, Elijah, seriously," Jasmine told him, hoping he believed her.
She was so caught up with him and the thought of him leaving her alone frightened her.
"Was he your first," he asked again catching her off guard.
Jasmine blushed, shaking her head yes.
"That's why he will not give up easily," Elijah explained.
She found his eyes as she began speaking once again.
"I don't feel that way about Damian anymore," Jasmine explained, putting a name to the face for him.
"I know," he replied softly.
She smiled, glad he believed her.
"What about you," Jasmine asked turning the tables.
"What about me," he returned giving away nothing.
"Who is in your life romantically," she asked playfully.
Elijah stroked her face gently assuring her he wasn't in a relationship with anyone.
"At least not yet," he added never taking his eyes from her.
Jasmine smiled slightly very much liking the statement made.
"I do not like games Jasmine," Elijah told her finally. "I want to be very upfront with you," he went on. "I'm extremely attracted to you and I would like to explore that attraction."

Jasmine swallowed hard, not trusting her voice but knowing she needed to speak.

"I would like that," she replied almost whispering.

Elijah smiled again, pulling her to him and kissing her deeply. Jasmine was wholly aroused as they kissed. His taste was delicious and his touch once again electric. Elijah held her tightly, stroking her back gently as they continued to kiss. The longer he kissed her, the harder she fell. When he finally ended the kiss and pulled away Jasmine was gone. She was his and at his mercy.

"So no more dating," Elijah told her calmly as she smiled.

"I only date you," she told him.

"No more visits from the ex," he added giving her another look.

"Okay," Jasmine replied.

Elijah grunted slightly nodding his head.

"The same applies to you," she told him returning the look he gave her moments earlier.

"Not a problem," he returned smoothly.

Elijah had no issue calling each of his daily beauties and telling them it was done.

"You are going to think this is very strange," Elijah told her as Jasmine frowned miniscule.

"I want you to work on trusting me, explicitly, no matter what," he told her as she continued to regard him curiously.

What is he trying to say, she wondered but said nothing.

"Will you try," he pried since she remained mute.

"Yes, I promise I will," Jasmine finally replied as Elijah smiled again and began kissing her one more time.

Chapter Eleven

Delia sighed softly as Montgomery came into the study where she sat. He was still deeply angry and she only spoke to him if he spoke first.

"Maria has been given the rest of the week off," he told her plainly, referring to the housekeeper.

"I expect everything to continue to run as usual," Montgomery added never taking his eyes off his wife.

He was still absolutely furious with her for the betrayal.

"I will see to it," Delia replied quietly.

Truthfully her mind was on overload trying to figure out how to escape the hell her life had become with Montgomery over the last few months. Meeting Elijah only intensified for her how very unhappy she truly was. Now with him on his one-man crusade to annihilate her self esteem and self worth, Delia knew she must get out.

"Come here," Montgomery called to her as she shook the thoughts and regarded him.

He was resting on the small sitting couch, pants at his ankles, erection at full mast. Swallowing the tears Delia rose and went to him, sinking to her knees and doing what he wanted. Montgomery smiled inside knowing how much she hated giving head. She told him it made her feel cheap and dirty. *Bet she did not mind giving it to Clayton,* his mind kicked in as he frowned and grew immediately angry.

Putting his hand on her head he pushed it further down his shaft gagging her. He did not stop even as he felt her distress, his anger wanting appeasement. He felt his orgasm looming and allowed her to pull back slightly. He still held her head in place however as his orgasm burst forth filling her mouth. Montgomery saw the disgusted frown come to her face as he forced her to swallow.

"Thanks tramp," he told her nastily pushing Delia away.

The tears streamed down her face as she slowly rose to her feet.

"Where the hell are you going," he inquired.

Stopping mid stride, Delia waited for him to once again speak so she could leave.

"I am not finished," he informed.

Wednesday's Customer

She spun around taking in his still hard member. *What the hell*, Delia thought. Montgomery normally came quickly and then only once. He was never known for stamina. He grinned malevolently at her, knowing she was at a loss to his still being erect. He picked up a sexual enhancement notion last night at the XXX-store.

"Strip," he told her without emotion.

Montgomery was going to enjoy every moment of punishing Delia. She betrayed him and broken his heart. He genuinely loved her. In his heart, there was absolutely nothing fake or political about that love. Now he simply wanted to avenge the hurt.

Delia complied and again awaited instruction. "Put this on," he told her holding the condom.

Again humiliated, she did what he instructed.

"Get on your knees," Montgomery barked, roughly pushing her down.

She steeled herself for his assault, feeling him get to his knees behind her. What he did however pushed the loud scream from her mouth without thought.

"Mmm, always wanted to fuck you in the ass," he told her chuckling as Delia began to sob.

He was hurting her in unimaginable ways with his wild thrusts.

"Shut up, you are messing up my nut," he told her crudely.

She closed her eyes tightly trying to block out the pain, beseeching God to hurriedly let it be over. It seemed her pleas fell on deaf ears however as Montgomery continued hurting her for the next thirty-five minutes, before slowing slightly and speaking in her ear.

"I think I will enjoy some of your pussy too," he whispered nastily. "Shit, everyone else has," he added pulling out and immediately entering her with the same condom.

Oh god, please, Delia prayed again knowing that he was trying to deliberately hurt her. Montgomery slammed unrelenting into his wife again and again for the next twenty minutes before coming hard and collapsing onto her back. Delia remained death still, not wanting to unleash anymore of his sadistic wrath.

"I will be home at 6:30, have dinner ready," Montgomery told her rising and pulling up his pants.

She continued to lay curled on the study floor in a fetal position, him standing over her.

"You know that saying, hell hath no fury like a woman scorned," he told her as he continued to regard her, eyes closed, silent. "Well they have nothing on a man with a broken heart," Montgomery finished and strode from the room slamming the front door as he left and Delia rose, running for the toilet, the bile making its way to her mouth.

*****

Jasmine was glad for a day off. She was headed over to Elijah's. He asked her to come by, promising her breakfast. He told her he wanted to talk and make some plans. *He is so wonderful,* she thought exiting the shower and beginning to lotion. Her mind began to torture her about being in such close proximity to the man and not sleeping with him. Jasmine could not lie. Elijah turned her on at such a deep level. He awakened feelings in her she did not know she possessed. *What is going on with me, I just got with the man, damn,* she told herself as she slipped on the teal and chocolate accented mini. The dress was sexy but not nasty. Jasmine felt pretty and feminine in it which lifted her spirits even more. She added the matching accessories and sprayed herself lightly with her favorite vanilla infused body spray. The knock at the door startled her since she was not expecting company.

"Who is it," Jasmine inquired, standing at the door now.
"It's me Jazzy," Damian returned.
A quick prayer and silent sigh, she opened the door, never moving from the jam.
"You look nice," he told her taking the woman in and wondering where she was going.
"What are you doing here Damian," she asked calmly.
Her mind was immediately recalling Elijah's admonishment.
"I was worried when you were not at work, so I came to check on you and make sure you were all right," he replied as she grunted.
"I am fine Damian," Jasmine returned. "I appreciate the concern though," she added trying to soften her reply somewhat.
"You know I love you Jazzy, of course I am going to check on you," he told her softly, looking into her eyes.
"Damian, seriously, let it go," Jasmine returned growing slightly irritated.
She could not let him mess up her new relationship. Elijah was a man she planned to have a long and happy future with.
"Where are you going," he finally asked his curiosity getting the better of him.
"I am having breakfast with my boyfriend," she replied, hoping the statement would shake Damian from the fantasy he was still living.

Hearing the words leave her lips Damian was furious. He reacted without thinking, slapping her hard, almost knocking her down.

"What the hell," Jasmine mumbled, shaking the cobwebs from her mind.

"I'm sorry Jazzy," he immediately tried as she pushed him away.

"Get the hell away from me, get away from my door," Jasmine screamed, tears coming now.

"Baby, wait, Jazzy, no, don't," Damian again tried as Jasmine began closing the door in his face.

He put his weight against it, pushing his way inside.

"Get out," she continued to scream running for her phone.

Damian grabbed her before she could dial for help, holding her tightly, immobile.

"Shh, baby, calm down, I am sorry," he repeated again and again still holding her.

Jasmine was terrified. All she wanted was Damian out of her apartment. Gathering her thoughts, she began to calm her breathing. She was going to have to use her common sense to get him out of her house and away from her.

"I am so sorry baby," Damian told her, kissing her cheek gently.

Seeing that she was not fighting him anymore, he released her. Jasmine would not look at him, so he tilted her face toward his own.

"I never meant to do that, I swear Jazzy," Damian told her honestly.

Hearing her say there was someone else in her life just pushed him over the edge.

"Please Damian, I have to leave," she told him trying to stay calm.

"Do you forgive me," he asked, searching her eyes for answers.

"Yes," Jasmine lied coolly.

Please let him believe me, she continued to think as Damian watched her wordlessly.

"Can I come by later and we really talk," he asked.

Jasmine would agree to anything if it would get him out of her house right now.

"OK," she replied softly as he smiled and began walking to the door.

"I will see you around 8:00PM , OK," Damian told her opening the door.

Jasmine again nodded as he smiled at her and finally left. Letting out the breath she held, she waited exactly ten minutes, washing her face and grabbing her keys heading out herself. She did not know what she was going to do about him coming back tonight, but Jasmine decided she definitely was not going to open the door.

*****

"What the fuck," Allison mumbled rising from bed. Someone was pounding loudly on the door interrupting her sleep. Grabbing her weapon from the nightstand she headed for the sound. Just as she stepped foot into her living room, all hell broke loose. Her heavy metal encased door splintered allowing entry to whomever stood on the other side.

"Freeze," the first agent screamed entering the penthouse apartment.

Allison's mind was not registering what was going on. *A raid, what, are you serious, what the fuck,* she continued to think as the S.W.A.T. agents descended from every angle.

"Drop the weapon ma'am," one of the officers screamed pointing his own at her.

Allison quickly found herself surrounded by black clad, heavily armed agents, all screaming simultaneously.

"Drop it, do it now," he screamed once more.

Utterly disoriented, she finally complied. The officers swarmed her, throwing her to the floor and cuffing her. Yanking her to a standing position once more the lead agent addressed her.

"Allison Register," he barked as she nodded in the affirmative. "We have a search warrant for this address," he informed as Allison's eyes narrowed.

"A warrant to search for what," she asked angrily.

The officer went on to tell her that they received tips that she was a major carrier and distributer for a local dope cartel. Allison sucked her teeth at how absurd the notion was and said nothing more. The officers began to methodically search the penthouse, finding all her FBI credentials in the process.

"Call her superior," the agent barked to another of his subordinates.

The man immediately scurried away to comply. The agent gave Allison a contemptuous look as they continued their search. Confident of her innocence, she simply relaxed in the chair where they'd placed her.

"Found it," an agent yelled as the lead agent turned to Allison giving her a smirk.

Wednesday's Customer   KR Bankston

Found what, she thought becoming nervous for the first time. *I don't have a damned thing here that is illegal*, she continued thinking before looking up and seeing both the lead agent and his partner return to the living room dropping the 4 kilo's of cocaine on her Italian marble coffee table.

"Guess you crossed the wrong people out there," the agent told her haughtily just as Kevin walked through the door.

"What kinda set up is this," Allison screamed.

The lead agent walked over to Kevin introducing himself as the two men exchanged handshakes.

"She was one of our best agents," Kevin said sadly addressing the agent who was commiserating with him.

"What the fuck are you trying to pull," Allison yelled again. "This is not my dope," she continued to yell.

Her mind was not processing what was going on around her. She could not, no, would not believe that she was looking at the end to her career as well as a long, long, stint in a federal prison.

"I want my attorney," she finally said, subdued.

Kevin asked for a few moments alone with her as a courtesy. The agent patted him on the back and told him it was fine. They left the two alone in the living room as they continued to search Allison's bedroom.

"Why," Allison asked simply and quietly, looking directly into his eyes.

"You should have played my game," Kevin told her, never denying he set her up. "I would have been good to you Allison, taken care of you, given you anything you wanted," he whispered, stroking her face gently.

"I am going to prison Kevin, how fair is that," she asked the tears escaping and rolling down her cheek.

"You chose that fate Allison," he informed still looking at her emotionless.

"I am going to give you a chance though," he told her.

"How," Allison asked.

She would do anything to escape prison. She knew her life as an FBI agent was over, but she did not want to be locked in a cage either.

"I am going to give you this key to the cuffs," he told her pressing the small metal object into her hands as they remained behind her back.

"Use it in the elevator when they are taking you down, then the first chance you get, run like hell and do not look back," Kevin told her.

Allison swallowed hard. That was a dangerous ploy but at the moment what choice did she really have.

"Go to the Stratford," he went on, referring to the hotel where they would meet during lunch to have sex.

"Our usual room," he went on, referring to room 117.

"I left clothes and money there for you," Kevin finished as Allison took a deep breath and let it out slowly.

The agents returned to the room as Kevin rose and stepped away without an answer from her.

"Let's catalog all this stuff and get it downtown," the lead agent spoke once again. "Does your office want a copy of all the reports," he asked Kevin.

The SAC nodded telling him yes.

"We will need it for her termination file," he added turning away from Allison and leaving the room.

*****

"How jacked up is this shit," Jaheem mumbled the unshed tears in his voice. His meeting last night was just what he thought it would be. His past once again found him and just like before, was forcing him to run away. He sighed deeply continuing to pack his few meager belongings into his beat up, outdated, Jetta as his mind replayed the night before like a bad movie. *"How's it going Jah," Malik asked, puffing the cigarette hanging between his lips like a limp strand of spaghetti. "What do you want," Jaheem replied, not at all wanting to be in the man's presence. "How you gonna greet an old friend like that," Malik returned his tone growing edgy. Jaheem sighed deeply gathering his thoughts and changing his tone. "Our business is done Malik, so I'm just a bit concerned you are here again," Jaheem explained. Malik grunted simply but said nothing else for a while. "You remember them streets we used to be in," he asked as Jaheem's heart sank. Malik aka Poison was a part of his past he would give any amount of money or restitution to erase. During the times they spent, Poison was the deadliest drug dealer in the hood. He made all the money and no one dared cross him for fear of ending up dead. Jaheem was not into dope, but he enjoyed hanging with Poison and by proxy the lifestyle the man lived. The beginning of his nightmare happened during one of Poison's famous block parties. There was plenty for everyone that night. Food, drugs, drinks, women, or whatever else you wanted to indulge. Poison told Jaheem to take whatever he* wanted, there was no limit. The only thing he wanted that night however was the pretty light skinned cutie from the neighborhood named Twyla.

    Everything was still cool and innocent when Jaheem talked her into coming upstairs with him at Poison's house. They entered the room and began to talk. Jaheem smoothly convinced the girl to let him kiss her, which of course led to him touching her. He was harder than steel and really wanted to have sex with her. Twyla was still a virgin though, and while she enjoyed the petting, did not want to take it any further. Jaheem was 19 years old, hardheaded, with raging hormones. His mind was not hearing anything about reason at that point or the no that kept ringing from her lips as he ripped her panties off and raped her. Twyla was crying hysterically, threatening to tell her father what Jaheem did. Terrified of being arrested he panicked. Poison walked in as Twyla finally stopping kicking and screaming, falling limp as Jaheem's hands at last left her neck. Never uttering a word, Poison collected the girl's body and took it away. Jaheem heard days later they found her body in the river and presumed she was attacked and thrown into the murky depths. They never talked about it, but Jaheem knew the dye was cast and the debt was owed.

    "You are standing in the way of progress Jah," Malik told him calmly. "What do you mean," he threw out, having a suspicion but wanting confirmation. Malik chuckled slightly telling him all about the housing project, the pictures he gave Alderman Southby, and his own instructions from Pastor Toplin. "You and me have no real beef, Jah," Malik told him. "But the good Pastor and me go back a ways and I owe him," he added as Jaheem nodded slightly. He never liked Pastor Richard Toplin. The man was a snake in every way as far as he was concerned. "There ain't no statues of limitations on murder, Jah," Malik said softly as Jaheem sighed deeply knowing he was defeated. "So what does he want," he asked Malik finally looking into his friend's eyes again. Malik gave him the answer, told him not to force his hand, and walked away leaving his friend devastated and his life once again shattered.

    Jaheem loaded the last box into the car. He felt like a complete fraud as he looked at the twenty thousand dollars that Malik was instructed to give him. *"He ain't trying to destroy you Jah, but you have overstayed your welcome," Malik spoke.* Cranking the Jetta and taking once last look at the city, Jaheem Andrews pulled away from the curb to once again find a place he could call home and begin his life yet another time.

Chapter Twelve

Jasmine was standing on the veranda enjoying the view. *This is breathtaking,* she thought of the ocean as it whispered quietly upon the shore with each progressive inland crash. She still could not believe she was here. Jasmine never traveled to Cozumel, Mexico. When Elijah asked her to go with him, she at first thought he was joking. She smiled again thinking of the last week. They flew out that Thursday when she went to visit him for breakfast. It seemed that Elijah had quite a bit on his mind besides talking that fateful morning. Jasmine hugged herself slightly, still smiling as she thought back on it. *"You're serious,"* she asked as Elijah chuckled and assured her he was. Taking her hand, he placed it on his chest, where she felt his heart beating. *"Jasmine, this part of me cares only for you,"* Elijah told her honestly. *"I need you to always believe that and trust me that I will never do anything to hurt you,"* he added as Jasmine melted. She could not describe the emotion she felt when he told her that. Elijah sensed her turmoil, leaning in and kissing her. He began softly kissing her neck after they parted, his breathing becoming uneven. *"Come with me,"* he told her rising and taking her hand. Jasmine followed without protest as Elijah took her into the master bedroom. She remembered quickly looking around and remarking to herself how beautiful the deep mahogany furnishings were. His room was done in a succession of cream, burnt orange and chocolates. Elijah pulled her to him kissing her again as he quickly removed her clothing. *"Elijah, wait, I um,"* Jasmine got out before he kissed her again.

"I know you are a virgin Jasmine, but I will not hurt you," he told her as she frowned slightly and opened her mouth to correct him. *"Shh,"* Elijah stopped her. *"You are my virgin,"* he clarified as she smiled and blushed. She helped him out of his own clothes, fighting hard not to stare at his magnificently sculpted body. Jasmine got a look at his growing erection, wondering if she would not indeed feel like a virgin when he went inside her. Elijah began kissing her again, admonishing her to relax and let him make love to her his way. *"Remember what I told you about trusting me,"* he asked as Jasmine again nodded yes. *"Do you,"* he threw out once again. *"Yes, without reservation,"* she returned as Elijah smiled and took her breast into his mouth. Jasmine moaned softly loving what he was doing with the nipple between his teeth. His other hand was between her legs massaging her clit gently as it began to harden and swell even more. Elijah slowly licked and kissed his way between her thighs, kissing each one tenderly as she breathed deeply, moaning lightly. He gently pulled back the hood hiding her clit, blowing gently on the exposed feminine erection, bringing a cry of delight from her. Elijah smiled

again as he saw her flow leaving her body saturating his sheets. Deciding he wanted to taste the nectar for himself, Elijah buried his tongue inside her opening as Jasmine reached her first orgasm.

He continued the pace, gently palming her breasts as he continued to lick and suck her juices. Putting his hands under her butt, Elijah pulled her even closer, his tongue reaching new depths inside her. Jasmine was ready to climb the walls as he brought her to yet another dizzying climax. She was still whimpering softly as Elijah kissed his way back up to her lips. "My sweet Jasmine," Elijah whispered in her ear as he carefully, slowly, slid inside her. Jasmine dug her nails into his back as he began to move in and out of her. Elijah loved the rhythmic sounds of her lubrication while they made love. The soft gushing was driving him wild, as was the extreme tightness of her walls. Even though he technically knew, Elijah truly felt he was her first and was consuming her for the first time. "Mmm," Jasmine murmured, becoming even wetter. Elijah couldn't believe how good it felt to be inside her. He never wanted to be without her again. He finally found a woman he could love and who would love him back, no questions or reservations. Jasmine felt his rhythm increasing; she felt his erection pulsating and knew he was close. She thought about telling him pull out, but he felt so good, and the orgasm completely destroyed her logical train of thought when it hit her again full force. Elijah felt her walls convulsing around him once more and pushed himself deeply inside her, his own eruption leaving him and depositing itself deeply inside her.

The sounds of people on the beach below broke her thought and brought her back to the present. Jasmine smiled again and headed inside to shower and dress. They were going sightseeing today. She glanced at her hand taking in the 5-carat diamond Elijah placed on it last night.

"I need to start planning," she mumbled of their wedding before quietly passing him still asleep and slipping into the bathroom, turning on the shower.

*****

He rose as soon as he heard her enter the bathroom. Elijah was a light sleeper. He felt her almost an hour earlier when she got up and walked outside. Jasmine was perfect and he loved her without question. Heading into the other bedroom of the suite he booted up his laptop. He had business to catch up on. He pulled the other briefcase he carried from under the bed, putting in the combination before opening the locks. The $250K was neatly packed inside. While they were out sightseeing he would stop by the bank and deposit it. Elijah already planted the cover story, telling Jasmine he needed to drop off paperwork and would not be long. He was taking her to the spa and leaving her for the hour it would take him to conduct the transfers. She was so sweet and true to her word, she trusted him. Elijah was well aware she was not on any birth control when he consumed her the first time they were together. He had a lot of lost time to make up for, wasting it with Allison and that dead end relationship. Jasmine becoming pregnant was not a concern at all.

Elijah saw he an email from one of his contacts. Opening it, he read with interest the information contained. 'Thought you would find this entertaining' the subject line stated. Frowning slightly, he clicked open and began reading the content. '**FBI Agent killed during daring escape attempt**' the headline read. Reading the story attached Elijah felt a slight sense of melancholy over Allison's death. *Ain't this some bullshit*, he thought irritably of her being involved in drug distribution. He thought of the times she chided him about his professional endeavors, all the while being dirty herself. Finishing that story, he went to the next headline. '**Alderman killed in domestic dispute**' Elijah actually chuckled aloud reading this story. Seemed that Delia finally got a backbone and killed the Alderman in a fit of rage after he beat her. He knew the woman would get off. She was a fantastic actress and the story she was spinning as he read the article, painted Montgomery Southby as a womanizer who loathed his own heritage, drank heavily, and constantly beat his wife. His former mentor and supposed best friend was leading the witch hunt, having recently filed for divorce from his own wife, whom he accused of having an ongoing affair with Alderman Southby.

"What a bunch of fucked up assholes," Elijah mumbled. '**Highrise project suspended due to allegations of misconduct**' Elijah smirked again reading the article. Seems Ronnie Glazer and his partner Dirk Swan were in a whole lot of trouble. Someone anonymously tipped off the EPA about the landfill underneath the new proposed housing development. There was one other small blurb at the bottom of the email. '**Damian King and LaNeesa Brooks, married in courthouse ceremony, yesterday morning.**' The final line read as Elijah sighed deeply shaking his head.

He left someone watching Damian, with instructions to kill him if he went near Jasmine's apartment that Thursday. He received the call right as she arrived and he told them to stay put for now. After making love to her and knowing she was leaving with him, Elijah called off the surveillance and the hit. Elijah thought about the fateful Thursday morning before Jasmine arrived when he found the briefcase and note outside his door. The hit had been cancelled and his fee delivered. He did not ask questions as he never got into the reasons for hits. That was a total waste of time in his book. Elijah simply did his job and expected his money.

Putting his laptop back to sleep and gathering the other case with the money, Elijah returned to their bedroom just as Jasmine exited, wrapped in a towel.

"Mm," he remarked looking her over.

"Don't even think about it," she teased.

The knock at the door startled them both.

"Did you order something," Elijah asked calmly, fully on guard however.

"Yes baby, I'm sorry I forgot to tell you," Jasmine replied, explaining she wanted orange juice.

Elijah smiled and headed to the door opening it and retrieving her request. There was also something for him the clerk quietly informed, slipping the small envelope discreetly into his hand. Elijah set the juice on the counter and kissed Jasmine's cheek as he left her alone heading back into the bedroom. He walked into the bathroom, closing and locking the door before opening the envelope and reading the note inside.

"What goes around comes around I guess," he murmured seeing Pastor Richard Toplin's name on the paper and Clayton Tyler's signature on the completed bank wire transfer.

Chuckling slightly, Elijah added it to the other slip, name contained, that already lay inside his briefcase. Business was definitely booming.

FOR ONE NIGHT

Elizabeth LaShaun

I would like to dedicate this story to everyone that supported me with my debut novel Inconvenient Love. I cannot say thank you enough and pray that I provide some form of entertainment, escape, and/or knowledge with my friends in my head and heart.

For One Night   Elizabeth LaShaun
Chapter One

The room was romantically decorated; the curtains red and black in color, preventing moonlight from entering the space. A faux bearskin rug lies on the hardwood floor, between the foot of the bed and the doorway. On the nightstand next to the bed were body oils and lit candles. The room was definitely equipped for pleasure as Trey Songz crooned softly in the background. Stacy Wilson laid on the silk sheet covered queen size bed in great anticipation. She was ready to get down to business. Her center was dripping wet and she was drunk with desire. Scanning the room, she smiled, pleased with the results. It had taken her over an hour to get everything ready.

"Damn I forgot the fruit," she mumbled rising from the bed. She was passing the dresser when she noticed the fruit on top of it. "Thank God," she mumbled returning to the bed.

Her baby should be home any minute and Stacy wanted to see her face when she walked in the room. With her luck, her boo would've walked in while she was in the kitchen.

"Stacy," her boo called.

Stacy was so deep in her thoughts that she didn't even hear the door unlock. She yelled that she was in the bedroom. She was in agony as she waited, hearing the echo from the shoes striking the hardwood floor.

"Oh my god," Janelle said with her hands over her mouth. "I can't believe you did all this for me."

Stacy smiled and told her she deserved it. She would do anything to keep Janelle happy.

"I thought you had to work," Janelle said with a raised eyebrow.

Stacy told her she did as she looked around the room.

"So I take it you are pleased."

Janelle nodded in the affirmative, still taking in the room. "Well come show me how much," Stacy said.

Janelle seductively laughed and began removing her clothes to the beat of the music. She slowly raised her red t-shirt over her flat stomach and red short hair while Stacy's eyes stayed glued to hers. Janelle could tell her girl was naked under the covers. Stacy's hands caressed her own nipples while she watched the show. After Janelle's bra hit the floor, she turned around giving Stacy full view of her ample ass. She dipped low and unbuttoned her pants. She pulled them down as she threw her ass in the air, swaying it from side to side. She smiled as she heard

Stacy moan "damn". Her baby loved when she slow wined, so she did. *I'm really about to make her go crazy now*, she thought making her ass clap and jump. "Come here Nelle," Stacy hissed.
"Are you sure," Janelle asked seductively turning to face her lover.
She laughed when Stacy simply nodded her head, unable to speak. The power Janelle had over people because of her looks was intoxicating, and she couldn't get enough of the boost. Janelle made her way to the bed but abruptly stopped. She gave Stacy a naughty smile and laid on the bearskin rug instead.

    Stacy didn't have to be given directions, quickly rising from the bed toward Janelle. She was horny before Janelle got home, but after that performance she felt like a dog in heat. Stacy looked at Janelle in awe, her baby was perfect. The fiery red, short haircut was beautiful against her fair skin. Stacy was hypnotized by Janelle's B-cup breasts and couldn't resist sucking her right nipple. Quickly she had half of her lover's breast in her mouth as she sucked greedily. Stacy had to force herself to stop and continue on her exploration. Her eyes gazed past the small waist and flat stomach, finally landing on the most beautiful, fattest, and wettest vagina she had ever seen.

"Are you going to look at me all day," Janelle asked squirming with desire.
Stacy lowered her head and allowed her tongue to find Janelle's center.
"Shit," Janelle hissed as her fluids mixed with Stacy's saliva. She was bisexual but she would take oral sex from a woman any day. It was as if Stacy had the latitude and longitude of her g-spot.

    The arching of her back alerted Stacy that Janelle was close to her end. She quickly squeezed her lover's clitoris between her two fingers and sucked it.
"Yesssss," Janelle screamed as her orgasm escaped her.
Stacy relaxed her suction, giving just enough pressure to prolong the orgasm.
"Boy I love this," Janelle whispered breathlessly.
Stacy let Janelle enjoy her afterglow and was now beside her, patiently waiting for the favor to be returned.
"Baby," Janelle said sweetly. "I got you after you get Willis."
Janelle knew Stacy hated using Willis. She felt as if she wasn't adequate enough. Janelle tried to explain that she loved being with Stacy, but she was not gay. She was bisexual and she needed a hard dick, plastic or real.

For One Night   Elizabeth LaShaun

Stacy begrudgingly went to the closet. She began strapping on the contraption telling herself that it wasn't a big deal. Yes, Janelle was bisexual but she lived with her. As far as she knew, Janelle had not been with a man since they had been together and never showed any signs of infidelity.

"I am trying baby, I put the thing on wrong," she told Janelle taking the instrument off to begin anew.

"Hurry baby," Janelle whined, her finger deep in her center. Her eyes glued to Stacy's apple bottom. Laughing, Stacy told her she would and allowed her thoughts to float once more. She hated Willis but if she had to wear him to keep the human form named Willis out their relationship so be it.

Janelle's eye lit up when Stacy finally turned around. She was on the verge of gluing the damn thing to her girl. She was well aware of Stacy's disdain for Willis but it was a must for her. She had been good so far, though often tempted. She was faithful, so Stacy had to suck it up. She hissed as Willis entered her slowly. Stacy smiled at the ugly face her lover was making. She started off slow and gradually increased her speed.

"Talk to me baby," Janelle said with her eyes closed.

Stacy rolled her eyes, despising this part. Janelle wanted her to talk dirty to her but in a low tone, like a man. She would have her eyes closed the entire time and never called Stacy by her name. She swore she wasn't thinking about a man, but Stacy wasn't stupid. She hoped it was a celebrity she was fantasizing about, making the request a little less painful.

"Whose pussy is this," she growled in the foreign voice. Janelle smiled as she relished in the feeling, quickly answering with a, "Yours baby". Stacy continued the charade bringing Janelle to her peak twice.

Rolling over Stacy smiled. The serene and peacefully look on Janelle was what she lived for. The smile that touched her lips made the humiliation she felt with Willis not sting as much. She loved Janelle and wanted to be with her forever. She would put on Willis and sound like Barry White to make her happy. *What about your happiness*, her heart threw out. Stacy rolled her eyes and inwardly replied she was happy.

"Happy first anniversary baby," Stacy whispered in Janelle's ear.

Janelle lazily returned the sentiment and drifted off to sleep. She knew she hadn't satisfied Stacy but she would when she woke up. Stacy would understand; she always did.

For One Night   Elizabeth LaShaun
Chapter Two

The diamond necklace sparkled on Janelle's neck. She couldn't stop touching it as she openly admired it in the mirror. Stacy had really outdone herself picking out the lovely piece. *You know you are wrong for forgetting your anniversary*, her conscience scolded her. Janelle felt guilty and made a mental note to buy Stacy something on her lunch break. "She doesn't mind though," she said aloud easing her guilt. "Stacy isn't into the gifts. She's happy when I am happy." Reapplying her lip gloss she left the restroom, returning to work, the shopping trip already dismissed.

Janelle worked at the local gym as a part-time personal trainer. The place was a pit stop in her eyes. She was a model and was waiting on her big break; then she would be living the life of luxury. Janelle hated trying to motivate overweight, unattractive, people she knew wouldn't lose a pound. *Everyone has to pay their dues*, she thought with a shrug of her shoulders, as she approached her next client. Putting on her signature fake smile she greeted Simone.

Simone was five feet and at least seventy-five pounds overweight. She seemed determined to work out showing up everyday, on time if not early. She ate subway for lunch and dinner believing the healthy sandwiches and exercise were the answer. Janelle had given her recipes for meals, shakes, and smoothies, but she couldn't afford the ingredients. That was another thing that drove Janelle up the wall, her clients were broke.
"So Janelle, are we starting with the weights," Simone asked bringing her out of her thoughts.
Janelle told her that was fine and began the mind-numbing task of inspiring the enormous woman.

Glancing in the mirrors that aligned the wall to check her hair, Janelle saw him. Making sure she looked scrumptious she trained her eyes on him as he walked to the treadmill. He had been coming to the gym for two weeks and Janelle wanted him in the worse way. She learned from the towel boy that his name was Chad. She laughed when she recalled how easy it was to get his information. She told Trevor that he was very handsome that day and he was putty in her hands, like most men. Janelle knew she was fine and couldn't understand why Chad hadn't approached her yet. She was starting to believe that he was gay until she caught him checking her out. He was very discreet but she caught him sneak a peek at her ample behind as she grilled Simone. She had been faithful to Stacy thus far but her willpower was wearing thin. She was going to have Chad and that was the end of it.

***

The Morning Perk was buzzing with the early morning rush. The jukebox was playing an Aretha Franklin classic that Stacy found herself singing along too. She was waiting for her best friend, Riley, to show up so they could catch up. She had been so busy with the library and Janelle that she missed just sitting back with her friend. She smiled as her favorite waitress, Jasmine, placed her cappuccino and English muffin on the table.

"It'll get betta girl," Jasmine said with a warm smile causing Stacy to smile as well.

Jasmine nodded her head and told her to call her if she needed her. Stacy told her she would and thanks. She didn't know her melancholy mood was so obvious. She hoped Riley wouldn't notice it because she would never hear the end of it.

"And he would walk in the door now," she mumbled buttering her muffin.

Stacy waved to garner his attention and continued to butter her muffin when their eyes locked. She watched her best friend approach. He was 6'2" and dark chocolate. His shoulder length dreads hung free as he walked with a powerful stride to the table. He smiled at one of the waitresses making her sigh involuntarily. Stacy laughed as she watched Riley's spell capture another woman. Even though she was gay she understood why women were head over heels for Riley. His smile was better than any Colgate model and his eyes made you feel like you were the only person in the room when he looked at you. The nice body he had didn't hurt either. Today a graphic t-shirt and baggy jeans covered it. A smile came across Stacy's lips as she thought about his unusually casual attire. *He is not happy about this early meeting.*

"What it do," Riley said as a greeting kissing her on the cheek.

"It don't do nothing," Stacy laughed as she searched the diner for Jasmine.

"So how are you," Stacy asked after Jasmine waved that she would be right over.

"I'm good, tired as hell," he told her sarcastically.

"Boy you would sleep your life away," she chuckled as she took the last bite of her muffin.

"Refill and a bowl of fruit," Jasmine asked Stacy, who told her of course.

"And what can I get for you," Jasmine asked turning her attention Riley.

Riley ordered a cup of orange juice and an order of pancakes with bacon.

"What happened," Riley asked as soon Jasmine left the table.

"What do you mean," Stacy asked as if she was shocked.

She hated the way Riley was leaning back lazily in the booth giving her his signature knowing look.

"When I talked to you for the five minutes that you could talk yesterday, you were so excited about your anniversary. You even took today off because you were going to be spending the day with Janelle," he grilled her putting emphasis on Janelle's name.

"Damn I said all that in five minutes," she asked sarcastically while searching desperately for Jasmine.

Riley knew Stacy was trying to avoid the conversation, but he wasn't having it. Usually he would stay out of her relationship, but he couldn't today. He was tired of Stacy getting her hopes up just to be disappointed. She never complained or called him in tears but he could tell that she was in pain.

"Stacy," he called her name after Jasmine left the table again.

She had asked the poor waitress every question she could think of to avoid the conversation they were embarking on. He had to say, the waitress was very professional, but she was dying to leave. Her eyes would periodically roam to the table that a man sat at alone eating his food.

Riley didn't mind, he was very entertained himself. He watched as a so called lawyer that sat in the back of the diner talked on his cell phone. Riley seriously doubted that the man was lawyer with the cheap and wrinkled suit he had on. "I'll be damned," Riley laughed when he heard the man tell his caller that he would take the case, but to call him back because he only has free incoming calls.

"You are so nosey," Stacy whispered slightly irritated.

"And you don't like confrontation," Riley returned asking her again what happened.

"Janelle had to work today," she answered tightly.

Riley didn't care for Janelle, but never said anything negative about her. Lately, however, he had begun to make sarcastic remarks or faces. Just like the one he was giving her at the moment.

For One Night   Elizabeth LaShaun

"Say what you are going to say," she asked him eating a piece of watermelon.

"There really is no point, is there," he threw back shaking his head in disgust.

Stacy watched as he cut his pancakes calmly and applied butter. His silence was eating her up. It was as if she was so stupid that he wouldn't waste his words on her. Nothing ever bothered him and if it did you never knew it.

"Let me get out of here," she told him, taking the money out of her jeans pocket and putting it on the table.

Without a word she left the table walking swiftly to the door.

Riley knew Stacy was hurting, but he didn't know what to say to her. To him it was simple, leave the stuck up woman alone. "That's why I'm single," he thought aloud with a shake of his head. Being honest, he understood Stacy. They were a lot alike, reserved and loyal to the few they loved. The difference was Riley was very skeptical of people and always kept his guard up, even if it was only partially. Once Stacy liked a person she would tolerate anything. She became blind. Riley associated their mindset to them both being raised in foster care. They met at one of their numerous foster homes. Stacy was twelve and Riley was fourteen.

Riley was a bad ass to the bone. He had been in the system since he was four. Miss Mary, their current foster mother, was just a pit stop to him. He stayed to himself whenever he was in the house. Stacy was so shy and went out of her way to make friends. Riley frowned as his mind took him back in time. Justin was his age and his foster brother. The boy was trouble from the start, but had everyone fooled except Riley. Not giving a damn, Riley continued doing as he pleased. As long as Justin didn't cross him, he had no problem with him.

Miss Mary was actually a good foster mother, which was rare. Riley considered her an angel from God; most of the children in her home where older children or rejects. She was usually their last hope for forming a normal bond with an adult. She gave her entire heart to each child and for that Riley loved her. Friday was movie night and all the children were in the basement. Riley rarely stayed home for the movies. He was either at the mall or getting into some type of mischief. Miss Mary asked him to stay one Friday and he did, incapable of refusing her.

Everyone was watching the cartoon and eating popcorn.

"Stop," he heard in a whispery crying voice.

"Shut the hell up," came the harsh reply.

For One Night   Elizabeth LaShaun

At first, Riley was going to continue watching the movie, but the cries continued. Slowly he got up and followed the noise. Entering the laundry room he found Stacy on her back, eyes wide with fear and her pants down. Justin had a sinister smile on his face and was pulling out his immature penis. Riley put Justin in a headlock from behind.

"Don't say a fucking word," he hissed in his ear.

Riley wanted nothing more than to kill Justin but he didn't want Miss Mary finding them. She would be devastated and feel personally responsible. Slowly Justin shook his head in agreement and Riley let him go. He reached out to help Stacy up, but she cowered away from him into the space between the washer and dryer.

"I will get him tomorrow I promise," Riley whispered so low that only Stacy could here him. The doubt danced in her eyes causing him to continue. "I can't now because of Miss Mary."

Justin paced in the background nervous. "Stacy get your ass up," he hissed, but was silenced by the evil glare Riley threw at him.

Stacy grabbed Riley's arm bringing his attention back to her. Riley helped her to her feet and turned, facing a pacing Justin, while Stacy gathered herself.

True to his word, Riley and four of his friends beat Justin up the next day. A few years later word reached Riley of rumors Justin was spreading. Justin boasted how he had slept with Stacy on many occasions and she was a washed up slut. Instantly, Riley became livid and regretted not killing the loser years ago. Later that night, Riley found Justin acting a fool and spreading more lies about different people in the neighborhood. Without warning, Riley beat Justin within an inch of his life for spreading horrible lies about Stacy. To this day, he didn't know if Justin died or not that night. He didn't lose any sleep either.

Riley always felt a strong need to protect Stacy but didn't know the cause until years later. Riley's biological family consisted of only his mother. The love the two shared was immeasurable and rare. Lola had Riley at the age of thirteen after being raped. Young, uneducated, and with a feeling of hopelessness, Lola turned to the oldest profession known to man, prostitution. Too young to know exactly what his mother did for a living, Riley did remember her coming home beaten at times. Lola made sure Riley was very bright and told him what to do if she didn't come home. At four years old, the young boy never imagined that he would have to carry out the instructions two weeks after mastering the plan.

For One Night   Elizabeth LaShaun

Lola had been killed by a nameless john. Stacy reminded him of his mother; selling herself short, low self-esteem, a pushover. He believed that was why he took to her and watched over her. For the first time since entering the foster care system, Riley behaved. He was happy at Miss Mary's house and built a close relationship with her and Stacy.

Miss Mary fought hard to keep those two together and used every string she had consumed during her twenty-five years of service in foster care. She saw something special in Riley and Stacy and told them that daily. When Riley reached eighteen he moved out but visited Miss Mary and Stacy often. Reeling his thoughts in, Riley grabbed his money from his wallet when he realized Stacy had left more than enough on the table. She was such a sweet girl and he didn't want her to get hurt. He knew that she needed support and comfort, but he didn't know what to say.

"I'll go check on her," he mumbled as headed towards the door.

He observed Jasmine's crush checking her out. *Jasmine might be getting lucky tonight*, he chuckled as he exited the diner.

For One Night   *Elizabeth LaShaun*
Chapter Three

Pastor Richard Toplin's office was the last place Chad wanted to be. The pastor was his father, but he was a minister first. Chad's eyes fell upon the other attendees of the meeting hanging onto every word that left his father's mouth. It sickened him. The congregation loved Pastor Toplin. The upscale chamber they provided proved it. The desk and chairs cost the moderate sized church a few thousand dollars alone. Chad shook his head as his father's robe caught his attention. *Why it had to be made out of imported silk is beyond me,* he thought, making sure that he periodically nodded his head, as if he were paying attention.

    Chad really didn't need to be present at the meeting; he didn't need to be a member of the Finance committee. On further thought, there was no reason to have the committee; whatever Pastor wanted, he got. Chad surmised that his father's ability to persuade his congregation had to do with his previous career. Pastor Richard Toplin was known as Cream, twenty-five years ago. Cream is an acronym, which means: cash rules everything around me, and Cream made sure he had plenty of it.

    Cream had partaken in almost every illegal path known to man, but settled on pimping. Chad understood his father's decision. The man could give Denzel Washington a run for his money. Standing 6'2", Pastor Toplin's chocolate, toned body garnered women's attention. His handsome face and charisma kept their attention. Chad had often wondered if his father used his charm to get sexual favors from his members. He had never seen anything inappropriate from his father, but the women were vultures, especially Miss Shack, who at the moment was doing everything she could to have Pastor give her breasts some visual attention. She wore a deeply cut gray sweater to help him with the effort.

    Chad turned his eyes to his father. Pastor Toplin spoke to Miss Shack with a smile on his face, but his eyes never left hers. Chad had to give his old man credit for that at least. He was faithful to his wife, Tabitha. Chad loved his mother dearly. It was hard for him to believe that his mother was once his father's bottom whore, but she was.

"Chad what do you think about the new housing development," Pastor Toplin asked him breaking his thoughts.

"I would like to review the entire proposal before I make a decision," Chad answered telling a half-truth.

Personally, he didn't trust the Alderman that was promising most of their underprivileged members the world, but he didn't want to make a decision either. It wasn't that he didn't care, politics just didn't interest him, but again Pastor Toplin didn't seem concerned.

Pastor nodded his head as in deep thought and turned his attention to Trustee Brown, Chad released a subtle sigh, happy to be off the hook, for the moment. He allowed his mind to wander to Janelle. The woman was as beautiful as she was ugly. On the exterior she was breathtaking, shapely, and mesmerizing. It was the interior that turned Chad off. The woman walked around like she was the queen and people should bow down to her. *I wouldn't mind tapping that*, he mused inwardly as her ample behind came to the forefront of his mind. A small smile appeared on his lips as he thought of his father's reaction if he knew his thoughts. *He would kill you*, his mind threw at him. Chad stifled a laugh wholly agreeing.

Pastor, which he made Chad call him, would have a fit if he knew his son was thinking about sex, let alone in church. Pastor would tell him to deny the flesh and handle it himself when it became overbearing. *How an ex-pimp can tell me to masturbate is beyond me*, Chad brooded as the meeting came to an end.

"Chad," Pastor Toplin called just as his son reached the door. He grimaced hearing his name. He was so close to the door, so close to freedom.

"Yes, Pastor," Chad answered facing his father with his best forged smile.

"Son, you need to become serious," Pastor said his smile amiable but his eyes angry and daring.

"Alderman Southby's proposal will affect majority of our congregation," he continued, as Chad looked at him emotionless. "Your stance can make or break your political career," he finished with a deep sigh.

Chad wanted to tell his father for the millionth time that he didn't want to become a politician. His dream was to become a fantasy author. He wanted to tell his father to back off and let him live his life.

"I will research the proposal Pastor after bible class," he said instead knowing it was pointless to speak his mind.

Upset by his son's nonchalant attitude, Pastor Toplin told him fine, dismissing him from his presence. He didn't know what was wrong with his son. He was trying to groom him to become the next President Obama, but he was fighting him at every turn. *If he would just give up this author nonsense*, Pastor Toplin thought. He saw a few of his son's books, mostly by some author named DK Gaston. He had also found some of his notebooks with his own work during one of his regular hunts. He searched Chad's room often; nothing was private in his house. Chad being twenty-two didn't change the fact that it was his house. Age was just a number and Chad's obscene desire to be an author further proved that his son did not know what was best for him. Wizards, witches, and Lycans would not garner him a comfortable life, Toplin was sure.

He doesn't see the opportunities that he has, Toplin thought angrily. He wondered if Chad's attitude was a punishment from God for his days as Cream. Toplin didn't fully understand the power, respect, and influences politicians possessed until he became a pastor. Of course by that time it was too late. He had a criminal record and reputation that was perfect for a redeemed pastor, but not politics. That was why it was important for Chad to reach his full potential and flourish; bringing the Toplin name the prestige and recognition that it deserved not only in the streets, but in every American household.

"Wonder if this is how Joseph Kennedy felt," Toplin sighed closing his eyes in thought.

"Pray and ask for guidance," he mumbled to himself as he opened the top left drawer of his imported Greek desk and retrieved his bible.

***

"Of all the people," Stacy thought as she looked at the woman sitting at one of the tables at the library. Even though it was her day off, Stacy came to work in hopes of finding some solace in the job she loved. Her hopes appeared grim as she took in the young lady sitting at the table with her face in a book. She didn't care for the lady at all. She always came in with the most precious sons but had a very nasty attitude. She had no patience, especially with her sons.

"I'm surprised she is alone," Stacy thought aloud a frown developing on her face.

She couldn't explain why she felt so worried for the boys whenever she saw them but she did. "Wonder what that's about," she wondered as she noticed the woman's tears.

For One Night   *Elizabeth LaShaun*

Despite her dislike for the woman, Stacy had to check on her and began heading that way when someone grabbed her arm. Turning she discovered Riley standing in front of her.

"Can we talk," he asked her calmly.

At that moment they were rudely interrupted as Nash walked up to them.

"Excuse me," he threw out rather harried.

Stacy turned to him responding rather sharply when he described the woman he sought. She could see her words stung him slightly from the small frown on his face. She tried to mumble a slight apology but his back was already to her as he headed for the woman. Stacy was so engrossed in the interaction between the two that she didn't even try to disguise her interest. They seemed so odd together. The gentleman seemed nice, levelheaded. The woman was so haughty and irritable. Riley took her arm once more, breaking the spell as she once again regarded him and he repeated his request to talk.

Returning her attention to the two, Stacy surmised that they were just talking, and led Riley to a quiet corner of the library.

"What's up," Stacy asked avoiding eye contact with Riley. Instantly, Riley was amused at her attempt to be angry.

"And how did you know I was here," Stacy asked irritated with the smile on Riley's face.

"I came to check on you Stacy and I knew you would be here because you love it here. You are here on your off days," Riley joked causing Stacy to smile slightly.

"I am fine Riley," Stacy told him, her eyes reaching his.

"Are you," he returned his eyes piercing her soul causing her to look away.

"Why are you acting like this Riley?"

"I am tired of you being hurt and disappointed Stacy," Riley returned having a hard time controlling his voice. He'd watched her prepared to intervene in someone else's business but she continued to refuse to stand up for herself.

"Riley, I am not hurt or disappointed," Stacy stated exasperated. "I understand that Janelle has to work. If anyone understands that it should be you."

"Understand how she disregards your feelings? Tells you bullshit excuses? What is it that I should be understanding," Riley gritted unable to control himself.

This was not how he wanted the conversation to go. He wanted to have a civilized conversation and how his best friend was looking at him with hurt filled eyes, fighting to keep the tears from falling.

"Janelle is there for me Ril-,"

"Why are you lying Stacy? How many times have you called me disappointed because Janelle forgot a date? How many times have you made up an excuse for Janelle when you are broke and have to bail her out?"

"Are you jealous Riley," Stacy spat the lame comeback

"Jealous of what Stacy? A woman that is using you for the check you get and the pus-".

The slap across his face immediately silenced Riley.

"You slapped me because I talked about a bitch that hasn't done a thing for you?"

"No, I slapped you because you were about to disrespect me and put a major strain on our friendship."

The laugh that came from Riley was throaty and hurt filled. "You let a woman that you have been with for a year disrespect you on a daily basis, but you slap me for telling you the cold hard truth?"

"You know what maybe," Stacy began but grew silent.

"Maybe what," Riley questioned.

Being faced with silence for a few minutes he asked again with more force.

"Maybe Janelle is right. You are jealous because you don't have anyone that loves you so you want to cause trouble in my relationship," Stacy yelled the anger, hurt, and confusion boiling over.

Immediately she regretted her words as she watched the hurt on Riley's face. Quickly it turned into blazing anger and then indifference. She didn't mean to say what she had but each truthful word cut like a knife to heart as they left his lips leaving her exposed.

"Nobody loves me," Riley whispered at first as if it were a question then as a statement.

Shaking his head with a sad chuckle Riley strolled away from her without another word. His head held high, shoulders back.

"Riley," Stacy called after him over and over again falling on deaf ears.

For One Night   *Elizabeth LaShaun*

Chapter Four

Janelle could not ask for a better day. Summer was in full bloom and the sun was kissing her bare back as she made her way to the photo shoot. She changed from her workout gear and was now clad in a peach halter summer dress. It was funny how her attitude and perspective changed when she left the gym.

"Not in your lifetime," she mumbled under breath to the average man in Swan Park checking her out.

Looks and money were important to her and the joker in the Dockers had neither. Thinking about her preference in a partner, her mind went to Stacy. She really loved her and believed she showed that by staying with her. Librarians didn't make much money, but Stacy always went out of her way to make sure Janelle was happy.

Continuing on her journey she came to the Morning Perk and slowed her pace. She wanted to see if she spotted Stacy in the dump.

"Nope," she said after reaching the diner from the huge windows. Taking account of the patrons inside, a slight frown appeared on her face. The people were so mediocre and trifling.

"Look at these fews," she thought taking in two men with scary smiles on their face awkwardly standing in the restaurant. Stacy called the establishment retro, she called it tacky.

"Oh well," she shrugged deciding to talk to Stacy when she arrived home.

You need to be really nice to her tonight, her mind threw at her. Janelle shook her head in the affirmative allowing her mind to wander again, but this time to Mr. Chad. She was going to bed the man, there was no doubt, but she didn't want to hurt Stacy. This afternoon the perfect idea came to her, but she had to be very careful to pull it off.

"Well look at who's on time," her best friend Tamya joked. Janelle looked at Tamya in shock. She was so engulfed in her scheme that she didn't even realize she was at her photo shoot.

"Shut up trick," she joked, kissing Tamya on both cheeks. Janelle took in her best friend and summed her up in one word, decent. Tamya's butterscotch skin covered her 5'10" frame. Her body was very lean and had no curves at all. Her short, edgy haircut complimented her pretty face making her typical model material.

For One Night   Elizabeth LaShaun

In short, she was no competition for Janelle's striking looks, making her the perfect best friend.

    The two entered the shoot and greeted the photographer before heading to make up. The shoot was the usual low budget catalog shoot, but not to Janelle. Every shoot was her potential big break and she quickly told the make up artist what he could and could not do.

"Relax girl," Tamya chuckled sitting next to Janelle. "Let the man do his job."

Janelle rolled her eyes but didn't comment. If Tamya was content with being a catalog model that was fine with Janelle, but she had Paris and Tokyo to conquer.

"How was your anniversary," Tamya asked while the make up artist applied her eyelashes.

Silently, she listened as Janelle recounted every detail of the night and the gift Stacy gave her.

"Sounds steamy, what did you give her," she asked.

Janelle mumbled a nothing while her artist applied her foundation. Tamya gave her best friend a look, of course unseen by her. Stacy was a nice person and she hated to see her mistreated.

    "Who is doing wardrobe," Janelle asked looking in the mirror, somewhat pleased with what she saw.

"Riley," Tamya managed to get out before Janelle began demanding that the artist fix her lip liner.

"This day seems to be going from bad to worse," she spat as she hastily stood and rolled her eyes at the frustrated make up artist.

Riley was a fashion consultant and rarely crossed paths with Janelle. He normally worked with couture designers and the music industry. He had been to fashion week in Paris and New York for the past three years. Janelle loathed the man. No matter how nice she was he would never help her in the advancement of her career. She had told Stacy on numerous occasions that her best friend was gay. He had to be; he had seen her naked at a fashion show they both worked and he didn't even glance her way.

    Tamya was trying not to burst in laughter as she watched Janelle. Her face was so contorted it looked like she had sucked on ten lemons. Her friend hated Riley with a passion, but always went out of her way to suck up to him, learning that her diva persona was getting her nowhere.

Janelle was a bitch with a capital B and seemed to be proud of the fact. At the first runway show Janelle did with Riley she threw a tantrum when he showed her the outfits she was suppose to wear.

For One Night   Elizabeth LaShaun

Riley stood silently as she called him an idiot and incompetent. When the show began, Janelle didn't have anything hanging in her dressing room. Livid, she marched up to Riley and asked what his problem was.

"I was an idiot to think you would look decent in anything that didn't have a name written across the front," he said calmly, really pissing Janelle off. "As soon as I find something of a higher caliber I will make sure you have it."

Nevertheless, she didn't walk the runway and had a hard time finding work for some time.

      Janelle would never admit it, not even to herself, but Stacy was responsible for her career. It was common knowledge that Riley had black balled her from the industry. It wasn't until she began seriously dating Stacy that she began receiving gigs again. Tamya noticed Janelle's attention go to the door and turned to find Riley standing there with a rack of clothes.

"Hey Riley," Janelle squealed with delight, making her way to him.

"What's up," he returned dryly, removing clothes from the rack.

Tamya had to admit the brother had it going on in every way imaginable; the simple red thermal and baggy, not sagging, dark denim and red jeans looking damn good on Riley's chiseled body. The brother definitely had some serious swag. Grabbing her clothes from Riley, Tamya went to the dressing room before she vomited from the performance Janelle was giving.

"You talk to Stacy," Janelle asked making small talk.

"Yeah, for a minute," he returned taking his eyes from the clothing rack and looking into her eyes.

"She seemed a little sad. You know she took the day off, but when duty calls we must answer, huh," he threw out looking at the dreary fitting room before his eyes came back to Janelle's. Before she could open her mouth, he had given her three hideous dresses and told her he would see her around.

***

      "Are you coming or not man," Brandon impatiently asked Chad. Tonight the most popular fraternity was having a party and Chad swore he was going.

"Where is it again," Chad asked stalling.

"Man your ass is not going, stop playing," Brandon threw out turning off his Pontiac. "You always say you are going, but never come," he continued as Chad felt like a punk as he listened in the passenger seat.

96

For One Night   Elizabeth LaShaun

He wanted desperately to go to the party, but he had to visit the sick and shut in early tomorrow morning and his father said he wanted to talk to him tonight. *I think his ass has a fucking radar*, Chad fumed inwardly. It seemed like his father always wanted to talk when he wanted to go out.

"Look man, I have to get ready. Fine ass Raven is going to be there and I am hitting that so I'll holla," Brandon said in one breath and unlocked the door.

Knowing there was nothing else to say, Chad exited the car and made his way to the prison he had called home for the past twenty-two years.

For One Night   *Elizabeth LaShaun*
Chapter Five

"What's up," Chad greeted as he approached Janelle, sounding far more confident than he actually felt.

"How are you," Janelle returned amiably, excited that the chocolate Adonis had finally made a move.

Chad smiled and the two conversed for a few minutes. The conversation was basic and only gave him to time to build up the courage he needed to state his purpose. Sex was what he wanted and nothing else. Chad was tired of living the good holy life to please his father. Overhearing his father promise to take care of an activist by the name of Jaheem chilled him to the bone. Pastor Toplin never went into detail, but his tone foretold his malicious intentions.

"So you wanna fuck," Janelle whispered into his ear, allowing her sweaty breast to touch him.

Chad's mouth slightly dropped and his throat was as dry as the Sahara but he managed a yes.

"I will be in touch," Janelle purred, noticing her next client entering the gym.

Chad watched her hips switch in the tight electric blue biking shorts. Janelle was perfect for his first lay. She was beautiful, shapely, and above all not his type. Watching her bend over as she helped her client stretch, he smiled as his manhood came to life, the thoughts of her spread eagle overtaking him.

***

Stacy was looking out of her bedroom window at the children outside jumping double-dutch. She couldn't help but smile as the girls had a small argument about who was going to jump first. Soon an older boy, she assumed their brother, approached the girls and played mediator. Seeing the handsome and calm young man brought her thoughts to Riley. She hadn't spoken to him since he came to the library to talk to her on her anniversary. He accused Janelle of using her, which Stacy quickly denied. She wanted to leave the conversation alone, but he kept provoking her. Before she knew it, she told him he was jealous because nobody loved him. The look on his face made her shudder as his painful eyes burned into her. She opened her mouth to speak but he quickly left the aisle they were in heading to the exit.

"Dinner is ready," Janelle said sweetly interrupting her thoughts.

For One Night   Elizabeth LaShaun

Stacy smiled and told her she was on the way. She hated that she was at odds with her best friend, but he was wrong. Janelle was not using her and was very remorseful about forgetting their anniversary. Her woman had gone out of her way to make her feel special. She cooked her dinner every night and had a bath drawn for her as soon as she was done eating.

    Janelle watched Stacy closely as she ate. *She betta say yeah*, she brooded, recalling the hard work she put in to make Stacy happy.

"That was great baby," Stacy said pulling Janelle by her arms and leading her to the beige, cloth sofa.

"I am happy that you enjoyed it," Janelle told her before kissing her deeply. "Stacy do you love me," Janelle asked, with just the right hint of doubt.

"Of course, I do," Stacy quickly reassured stroking her face. "Why you ask that," she asked hating that Janelle could doubt her love.

Sighing and pausing for effect, Janelle told her that she didn't think she loved the real her. Seeing the confusion written on her lover's face she hedged forward. She explained that like it or not she was bisexual and was still very attracted to men.

"So you're breaking up with me," Stacy asked with an incredulous look, working overtime to keep her tears at bay.

"No baby," Janelle said. "Never, I want," she trailed off again for effect, causing Stacy to quickly ask her what she wanted. "I want to have a threesome."

    Stacy quickly removed her hands from Janelle with widened eyes.

"See I knew you would react this way," Janelle returned forging hurt.

"I'll do it," Stacy told her as the first tear escaped from her right eye.

The smile instantly came over Janelle's face and she kissed her lover with immense passion. *I knew she would go for it*, she thought cockily. *Okay its time to go in for the kill*, she continued to brood as she began to tug at Stacy's sweats. Giving head was not something that she enjoyed. She only performed the act after she had at least two orgasms herself.

    Stacy moaned deeply as Janelle satisfied her. She was so gentle and attentive, which was rare. Most times Janelle seemed to be in a rush. Pushing the thoughts out of her mind she returned to her boo, who was pleasing her. Janelle brought her to her end twice and never asked for any pleasure or Willis. Instead she simply kissed Stacy on the cheek and went to retrieve a soapy washcloth. Reality set in quickly for Stacy. She had agreed to participate in a threesome. She had never been with a man and vowed to never be with one. *If you don't do it she will leave you*, her heart threw at her. Immediately she resolved to see the threesome through. Janelle had sacrificed a year of her sexuality, she could at least compromise.

"Riley would go off if I told him this," she mumbled as her mind once again went to her best friend.

As much as she tried to block out his words they were ringing loud and clear. The gnawing feeling in the pit of her stomach told her he was right.

***

Janelle stood in the doorway watching Stacy. She heard her comment about Riley and dug her fingernails into her left palm to keep from screaming. She was tired of Riley's ass, but soon he wouldn't be a problem. A sinister smirk appeared on her face just as Stacy turned her attention to her. Thankfully the lights were off, so all she could see was her silhouette.

"Are you just going to stand there," Stacy joked trying to lighten the mood, avoiding her feelings being much easier. Janelle told her she was just admiring her and headed to the bed. Pulling her love close to her warm body, Janelle whispered in her ear, "It's only for one night."

Unable to talk with the lump in her throat, Stacy nodded her head in agreement. Deep down inside she had a feeling that one night would change a lot of things.

For One Night   Elizabeth LaShaun
Chapter Six

Chantrese's thong was soaked and her skin was on fire as her eyes slowly scaled Riley's burly body. The god was perusing samples for a show and had no knowledge that she was watching him. His freshly and neatly twisted dreads concealed his face making him appear untamed. Chantrese felt her nipples begin to her harden and her nerve dwindling. There was no way Riley would be her date for the after party. Chantrese was twenty-two and new to the couture modeling scene. She had witnessed Riley turned down beautiful women and some even said he was gay. Chantrese knew better though, Riley was anything but gay. In the blink of an eye Riley looked up, his eyes connecting with hers.

"Hi," Chantrese managed feeling like a complete fool after they both stared awkwardly for several seconds.

Riley returned the greeting and was heading to the closet when Chantrese blurted, "Who are you taking to the after party?"

Riley stopped in tracks and turned to face Chantrese. It wasn't until that moment that he realized she was interested in him, the slight blush and diverted eyes giving her away. Riley lips quickly prepared to turn her down, but the cold words Stacy threw at him came to him. He would never admit it, but her words had hurt him deeply. Chantrese fidgeting brought his thoughts back to her. He took in the beauty before him. Her creamy peanut butter skin was flawless. He had never noticed her hazel eyes that peaked through her overgrown bone straight bangs. For a model, she was curvy. Her hips were subtle. In her profession, the plump ass she possessed would be a curse but he was loving it. A smile grazed his face as he thought about the sisters that actually wrapped their asses with ace bandages to flatten it.

"I wouldn't mind going with you," he told her as she smiled pulling him into her essence.

***

Stacy was a nervous wreck as she sat in the living room waiting for Janelle's fantasy to walk through the door. She couldn't believe that she was doing this. Her stomach did a summersault as she watched her supposed lover prance around the house in a silver teddy, drink in hand as if she was on top of the world. She couldn't remember when she had last seen Janelle this happy. *You are acting dumb as hell*, her mind threw at her at the same time that

101

her heart told her to be understanding. Before she could get her thoughts together the doorbell rang.

The deep breath she had quickly taken left her when her eyes connected with the sexiest eyes she had ever seen. Before she knew it, damn, had left her lips. Chad expected Janelle's lover to be fine but never as beautiful and erotic as the woman before him looked. Her dark doe eyes penetrated his being and her wild naturally curly black hair was extremely sexy. Allowing his eyes to lazily scan her toned body he had to stifle a moan he wanted her so bad. Her breasts were perky and begging to be released from the satin cloth detaining them. His breathing grew ragged as he looked at her shapely legs. He could tell from her peach nightie that she was reserved and shy. For the life of him he couldn't figure out why, she was breathtaking.

"Well," Janelle said with an edge to her voice. "Chad this is Stacy, Stacy this is Chad," she introduced them through tight lips.
Neither took their eyes off the other as they shook hands. Janelle knew Stacy was beautiful, but she usually downplayed it by wearing oversized clothes, hats, and shades.
"Well don't just stand there let's go to the bedroom," Janelle laughed grabbing his arm and pulling him towards the bedroom.
She had no doubt that once she got him in bed his attention would be back where it belonged, on her. Wasting no time she pushed him hard onto the black satin sheet covered bed. Before he could react she straddled him allowing their lips to connect.

Stacy stood in the doorway frozen. She couldn't believe that she was attracted to Chad, let alone aroused. She couldn't help but yearn for him to caress her the way he was caressing Janelle. Seeing his manhood come to life she clinched her legs as her juices began to pool. *What in the world*, she thought unable to take her thoughts off of him. "Come here," he told her in a commanding and husky tone. Stacy would never be able to explain how she went from the standing in the doorway thinking about sex to riding a dick that she would swear was made just for her. She couldn't explain why she was screaming his name and begging for him to go deeper and never stop, but she was. His hands on her hips were driving her wild and she was at his mercy.

Janelle sat on the bed beet red. Chad and Stacy were in their own utopia miles away from her. She was almost on her way to jail when she reached out to him and he looked at her with a mixture of lust and annoyance.

"No she didn't," she mumbled aloud as she watched Stacy allow Chad to hit it from the back.

It had taken months of dating for Janelle to be able to see Stacy's back. It was grotesquely scarred from the third degree burns she suffered as a child. Her father was in one of his infamous drunken stupors when an electrical fire caused the house to go up in a blaze. Stacy called out her father's name and screamed as the fire danced on her back. Her father looked her in the eyes for a few seconds, which felt like hours and ran out of the house to safety leaving Stacy behind.

Chad kissed Stacy's disfigured back as hot tears rolled from her eyes. Feeling his ending looming he slowed down until he felt her center contract.

"Aargh," Stacy screamed in ecstasy as her head began to spin and her body forsook her.

"OK Chad, its time for you to go," Janelle hissed before he could catch his breath. "Don't call me," she continued throwing his clothes at him. "Or my woman," she said with a threatening stare.

In his weakened state Chad didn't argue with Janelle. He knew he would be seeing Stacy again whether Janelle liked it or not.

For One Night   *Elizabeth LaShaun*
Chapter Seven

Pastor Toplin stared at his son with intense eyes. He couldn't believe he had the nerve to stand in front of him and tell him a lie. He had been lied to by the best and told the best bullshit ever uttered. He knew his son was having sex and it was damn good sex at that. Inwardly he was pleased, at least he knew he wasn't gay, but sex complicated things. Finally Job's ignorant ass was gone and here was another problem.

"I want you to invite this non-existent person to the church banquet next month," he instructed as Chad sighed deeply and stood.

Knowing there was nothing he could say his son gave him a simple head nod before heading to the door.

"Chad," Toplin called after him. "You know I am doing this for your own good and one day you will thank me."

Chad once again nodded and left his presence. Toplin only said the words because it was the first thing to say. He didn't give a damn if Chad thanked him or not. He would be the mayor of the city one day and that was not up for discussion.

***

Stacy sat in a corner booth waiting for Chad. She hated that she couldn't sit by the window like she normally did, but she couldn't risk Janelle seeing her. It was funny that her girlfriend passed the diner everyday but wouldn't step foot in it. Stirring her tea, Stacy reflected on her and Janelle's relationship. She would be lying if she said that she didn't love her, but the love was not the same. Her life once revolved around Janelle. She was finally the center of attention for a change.

"Hey baby," Chad greeted kissing her softly, producing butterflies in Stacy stomach.

"What's up," he asked picking up on her melancholy mood. Stacy told him nothing and asked if he was hungry.

"Stacy you need to leave her," he threw out irritated.

"It's not easy Chad, she was there when no one else was and what did I do in return? I have been cheating on her for a month."

Chad couldn't understand the hold Janelle had over Stacy. If anything, Janelle broke her further. Whenever he told her she was beautiful she looked at him with surprise in her eyes as if no one had ever told her.

"She deserves what she gets if you ask me," Chad began anew.

For One Night   Elizabeth LaShaun

"Chad, you don't understand," she screamed louder than either one of them expected.

"Why don't you help me understand," Chad countered curious about the hold Janelle had on Stacy.

Seeing that Chad would not let the conversation go, Stacy released a heavy sigh and began.

"I have known Janelle for a few years. She is a model and I told you my best friend Riley is a fashion consultant."

"The same Riley that doesn't like her either and you are not talking to because of an argument about her right," Chad asked sarcastically.

Are you going to let me finish," Stacy answered and continued when Chad gave her a lazy shrug of his shoulders. "Well I knew her but we weren't close or even talked. I always thought she was attractive but wouldn't approach her," Stacy paused uncomfortable with talking about her lover with her boyfriend.

Picking up on her apprehension Chad encouraged her to continue.

"Well I was staying with my foster mother if she had an available room and working at McDonalds. Janelle approached me telling me how pretty I was and we started dating. I moved into her place three months later and she encouraged me to apply for the job at the library since I was always there." Releasing another sigh Stacy asked, "Now do you see why I have a hard time leaving her? She was there for me when I had nothing."

Chad didn't see how Stacy could feel indebted to Janelle. He was sure that Janelle had an ulterior motive for her sudden attraction to Stacy. He didn't know how right he was. Janelle knew Riley and Stacy were best friends. She observed the love the two shared for each other. Starting a relationship with Stacy revitalized the small modeling career she had, with Riley's reluctant aid.

"Look," she continued lowering her voice and grabbing his hands. "Let's just go to the hotel and concentrate on us."

A look of disgust came over Chad's face. He had been lying to his mother and Pastor for a month. He was actually falling for her and she was too afraid to leave her trifling ass chick. "I feel sick all of a sudden," he said nastily. "I guess I'll talk to ya later."

Stacy reached out for him, but Chad pulled away. He was risking everything to be with Stacy and she could care less it seemed.

Stacy could not believe Chad was being so inconsiderate and didn't protest when he walked away. She was risking a lot by having an affair with him. If Janelle put her out she couldn't stay with him. He still stayed at home with his parents. She really did care for him and even felt she was falling in love, but she felt obligated to Janelle. She was fully aware of Janelle's eccentric attitude but there was a loving and protective side of Janelle. Just this morning they argued because Janelle said her jeans were too tight and her shirt was too revealing. They had been arguing a lot since their threesome. It seemed as if Janelle's jealously had increased tenfold. She would pop up at her job unexpectedly and had begun checking her phone. With Chad being upset with her too, she felt overwhelmed.

"I need to talk to Riley," she said to herself as she grabbed her purse.

***

The Bears and Green Bay game was tied in the third quarter. Riley had no true interest in the outcome since neither team was his home team, but decided to root for the Bears being that they were the underdog.

"Who is that," he mumbled as he heard the doorbell ring. He wasn't expecting anyone. Chantrese was on location at a photo shoot. Walking down the stairs he saw his front door open and knew only two people had the key to his house. He doubted it was Ms. Mary, but he hadn't seen Stacy in a month. His mouth dropped as she came into full view. She was gorgeous; chic, breezy, happy. Her form fitting cropped pants and pale pink baby doll top were so different from her normal attire. He wasn't aware that she was so curvy. *Does she have on makeup*, he wondered as he examined her beautiful face. *She doesn't have on a baseball cap*, he continued to brood completely taken aback.

"I hope you don't mind me using the key," Stacy stated awkwardly. "I rang the bell a few times and wanted to make sure you were okay," she stammered.

Finally recuperating from his shock, Riley told her to come in and have a seat on the couch.

"Dang I forgot this game came on," Stacy stated excitedly with her eyes glued to the television.

Riley smiled unseen by his best friend. He had missed her a lot. He could see a change in her instantly, but he could see she was still his Stacy.

"Can you get me a beer," Stacy asked absently, still engulfed in the game.

Riley chuckled and headed to the kitchen for the beverages.

For One Night   Elizabeth LaShaun

The last month had felt awkward. Before a day hadn't passed without them talking but he had made it, with Chantrese's help. He was feeling Chantrese but something was missing. The sex was great and she was fun to be around, but he couldn't see himself falling for her. He had thought about breaking it off. It was obvious that Chantrese was falling for him, but he continued seeing her. Since he had never been in love he assumed that he was expecting too much.

"It's about time," Stacy joked when Riley handed her the beer.
"Shut up big head," he chuckled while plopping down on the couch.
The bond the two friends shared was strong and soon they found themselves back in their rhythm. Stacy was rooting for the Packers, just to irritate Riley. They laughed and talked smack for the next twenty minutes. Riley couldn't help but take in her shapely body in her conservative, but sexy outfit. He was curious to know what caused her change, since she always dressed tomboyish.
"So, why haven't you called me," Stacy asked after the game ended.
Riley laughed before giving her a look.
"I guess it's the same reason you didn't call me. I have a girlfriend," he replied snidely.
"What," Stacy asked with wide eyes.
Riley had slept with more than his fair share of women but he never gave any of them titles let alone the coveted title of girlfriend.
"And when did this happen," Stacy asked, sucking her teeth. *Is she jealous*, Riley wondered bewildered.
"We have been talking for about a month," he replied with a smirk.
"You thought you were the only person who could get a woman."
     An unexplainable anger came over Stacy. She didn't know why she was so upset but she wanted to rip Riley's head off right now.
"I haven't been spending much time with my girlfriend lately," she began putting emphasis on girlfriend. "Most of my time has been spent with my new boyfriend."
Riley's jaw clenched and his eyes quickly scanned her body. That was why she had changed so drastically. *She has a man? Naw, not Stacy, she would never be with a man*, he inwardly concluded calming a bit.
"So where did you meet this so called man," he asked deciding to play along with Stacy.
A frown came across his face when she diverted her eyes.

That was the one question she didn't want to answer. She could never lie to Riley, and she knew with the guilt she felt about the threesome attempting to lie would be pointless. "Where you meet him at," Riley asked again forcefully, assuming Janelle had pulled her into some more bullshit. Stacy jumped at the sound of his voice and mumbled, "We had a threesome".

"Why the fuck would you let Janelle convince you to do such a thing," he boomed disappointed.

Stacy quickly explained that she was trying to compromise and be understanding. Riley gave her a look, making her feel a deeper need to explain. "I didn't expect to be so attracted to him Riley," she continued with a lustful look in her eyes as her mind went back in time. "It was like we were the only two there." Stacy was so wrapped in her memory that she shared the details of their loving making with a look of total bliss covering her face.

Riley was fuming as he listened to Stacy talk about this Chad character. Quickly the question of: *why wasn't I good enough,* popped into his head. She didn't even sound like this when she first met Janelle.

"So just because you had great sex he is your boyfriend?"

Stacy quickly rolled her eyes. What she had with Chad was so much more. She told him how he loved reading and wanted to work in the literary industry. Her eyes lit up as she talked about his dream of being an author and the great quality of his work. Joy was in her voice as she talked about the way they could talk for hours about jazz, movies, and current events. *She is in love,* he concluded as she continued to talk and the envy screamed on the inside.

"Well as long as he makes you happy," he said weakly.

"He does," she quickly answered but became sullen when she said, "and Janelle is making me miserable."

Chapter Eight

"Ugh," Janelle screamed as she once again got Stacy's voicemail. "Where the hell is she!" Stacy was changing and it was definitely for the worse. The skimpy clothes and missed calls were driving Janelle up the wall. She wanted the Stacy that doted over her every need back. This new bitch had to go. Janelle found herself checking on Stacy and Chad the best she could. She could never catch them together but deep down she knew they were together.
"Talk about fucking irony," she chuckled as she turned to the mirror to apply her makeup.
She was the one to bring Chad into the relationship and now she was plotting to kick him out.
"Fuck," she hissed as she looked at the pimples that were on her face.
All the stress was causing her to have terrible outbreaks, which was making her lose money. The chirping of her cell notified her that she had a text. If she could break everything in the dressing room, she would. Stacy was sending her a message that she was going to check out a jazz club since she was working late and would see her when she got home. For a second the thought of leaving the shoot and heading to the club crossed her mind but she needed the money badly. She had been cancelled from three previous gigs because of her acne.

***

"Looks like you could use some Proactive," Riley joked as he placed the clothes on the rack and left the room.
Laugh now bitch, she thought as she snatched the lipstick off the vanity. She knew soon she would be getting the last laugh as far as Riley went.
"You are a bad bitch," she repeated to the mirror until she believed it.
Taking a deep breath she went to the clothes rack and grabbed the hideous dress. She would take care of Riley, get Stacy back in line and live the life she was accustomed too. For the first time in weeks Janelle had a genuine smile on her face as she headed to the set.

***

The day was perfect for a picnic. The sun was shining and it was a perfect eighty degrees. Chad had been checking out Swan Park for a few days and determined that it was safe. He had instructed Stacy to meet him in the park for a walk. He wanted to surprise her with the turkey sandwiches, chocolate covered strawberries and champagne. Seeing her crossing the street he hid behind the wall of the parks entrance.

"Boo," instantly Stacy jumped and grabbed her chest. "Aww sorry baby I was just practicing," he whispered in her ear. "That wasn't funny," she pouted walking ahead of him.

Chad laughed and ran to her. He told her that he just wanted to make sure she was prepared for the stalkers that would come since she was dressed so sexy. No matter how hard she tried Stacy could never stay mad at Chad.

"I thought we were going for a walk," she said noticing he was leading her off the walk trail.

Chad didn't answer her, instead he continued to lead her deeper into the park.

Chad smiled as he felt Stacy squeeze his hand. "Aww baby," she squealed before kissing him so deeply that he fell on the ground, Stacy on top of him.

"I get all this for a turkey sandwich," Chad laughed.

"Its so much more than turkey sandwiches," she began as her eyes became misty. "It the fact that you took the time to make the sandwiches or buy them, put them in the basket, and set this up for me."

Chad wiped the two tears that had fallen from Stacy's eyes. That's why he loved her, she made it easy. While other girls expected the moon and the stars, Stacy just wanted him; making him want to give her the moon and the stars. The banquet was in two weeks and he was nervous to ask her until now.

"Baby, I want to ask you something," he began nervously. Stacy quickly kissed his lips reassuringly. "My parents want to meet you at our church banquet in two weeks," he blurted out as a smile came over his lover's face. She knew how much Chad tried to live up to his father's expectation and was floored that he wanted her to meet them. Quickly she agreed kissing him passionately once again. The fire inside of them raged so high that they left without touching their food.

***

"Bitch, I wish you would back out," Janelle hissed through clenched teeth. "Your career will be over before the measly son-of-a-bitch begins," she added for good measure. She heard the other party try to speak but hung up. There was nothing left to say. The job would be done because of self-preservation.

For One Night   Elizabeth LaShaun

Smelling smoke Janelle ran to the kitchen to check her roast. She couldn't believe that she was cooking to make Stacy happy. She had been with a few men and women since the threesome to get back at Stacy but only found herself more miserable. None of them cared about her. They didn't smile because she smiled. It was just sex. She heard the front door open and quickly went to the front door to greet Stacy.

"Hey ba-," was all she managed before Stacy ran to the bathroom with her hand over her mouth.

She heard Stacy's violent hurls and went to the kitchen to prepare some soup. She never heard of someone having the stomach flu in the summer, but assumed it was a fluke.

"At least it's not the nine month flu," she giggled to herself before reality hit her and the can hit the floor.

She couldn't remember Stacy coming on her cycle since the threesome. Blinded with rage she stormed into the bedroom with her eyes blazing. Stacy was wiping her mouth and looking at her with scared, knowing eyes. Her eyes didn't have to give her away because her glow and clear skin did a great job.

    "I can't believe you Stacy," Janelle screamed.

Stacy tried to open her mouth to explain but Janelle continued calling her every foul name she could think of. A couple Stacy believed she made up. Coming to the conclusion that trying to talk was pointless, Stacy simply endured.

"You don't even fucking care," Janelle screamed after ten minutes of rage.

"I do care," Stacy protested before Janelle quickly called her a liar.

The room began to spin Janelle was so furious. She couldn't believe Stacy would cheat on her, let alone get pregnant.

    After several moments Stacy resigned from the awkward stare down.

"Where the hell do you think you're going," Janelle spat grabbing her arm.

Stacy looked at her arm then into her lover's eyes and stated tiredly, "Janelle its over."

Not caring if Janelle had a reply she walked to the bedroom and began to pack.

"No this bitch didn't," Janelle mumbled in total disbelief. Stomping to the bedroom she laughed once she reached the doorway. "So you think Chad is going to want you and your confused ass baby? You were a fuck Stacy, nothing more and nothing less," she continued gaining momentum, while a hurt Stacy continued to pack.

"A dumb fuck I might add since you got pregnant," she laughed in a mean and throaty tone. "Give a bi...," was all Janelle got off before she saw stars.

Stacy had hit her with a mean uppercut right on her chin.

"I will not be another bitch," Stacy hissed with hot tears rolling out of her eyes. Grabbing her suitcase she walked out of the house and into the scary world.

For One Night   *Elizabeth LaShaun*
Chapter Nine

Times like this made Stacy happy that she had a car. She knew she should have been paying attention while she drove but she was thinking. No radio, no regards of the outside world, just her and the open road. Pregnant? A baby? Her? It was impossible. She was not mother material. She never met her own mother. She made the ultimate sacrifice when she had her.

"Naw, I'm not pregnant," she concluded aloud.

Yeah her period had been late and she had been a little moody but she was stressing a lot and was in a relationship with a man for the first time. Hearing the song Closer bellow from her phone she rolled her eyes. She knew it was Janelle and at this moment she wanted to be anything but close to Janelle.

"I can't deal with her now," she hissed as she pressed the ignore button.

She didn't plan on getting pregnant on but she was. The question was if she was going to keep it. She said she would never have an abortion. Ms. Mary always said never say never, and now she understood why.

It was so easy for her to judge others and say they were stupid, but now she was considering calling the clinic. The knock on her window made her jump. Turning her head she couldn't help the tears falling from her eyes.

"You wanna get out the car waterhead," Riley asked with a lazy smile on his face.

Stacy shook her head no. *You always do this shit,* she scolded herself. Whenever there was a problem she wound up on Riley's doorstep, well driveway, but same thing.

"Don't make me call the police and tell them I have a stalker on my property."

Stacy cracked up and gave her best friend the finger before she unlocked the door.

"Is everything alright baby," Chantrese asked standing in the doorway.

Who is this trick, Stacy thought taking in the woman. If her good looks didn't irritate her enough, seeing that she only had on an oversized shirt did the job. Riley nodded his head that they were, his eyes on Stacy's backseat.

"Open the backdoor," he told her.

For One Night   Elizabeth LaShaun

Chantrese knew who Stacy was because of the many pictures Riley had of her. She had also seen her once or twice at one of her gigs, but she didn't remember her like this. The Stacy she knew always had on black oversized clothes and wore hats. Her attire reminded her of Justice in the movie Poetic Justice. The electric blue, fitted dress was a shock. With her hair being up in a trendy hair do revealed how beautiful she was. Instantly Chantrese was not feeling the new Stacy. Riley wasn't doing a damn thing to help either. She never felt threatened by Stacy. Riley had always described her as a little sister and she knew the girl was head over heels in love with Janelle. But the look in Riley's eyes was anything but brotherly. Deep wrinkles were in his forehead as he listened to Stacy talk. His eyes smiled when she made the slightest smile or smirk. At that moment he was breaking his back carrying three bags but put on a smile when Stacy turned to ask him something. Chantrese learned a long time ago that it's what a man does that proves his love not his words. Yes, there was no doubt about it, Riley loved Stacy and not like a sister. Just to be sure, Chantrese leaned in to kiss Riley and he turned his head, giving her his cheek. It was subtle and she was sure Riley didn't even know what he did, but she did. Closing and locking the door she turned and noticed Stacy giving her the once over. *Oh it's on honey, trust.*

Stacy allowed her mind to wander while she unpacked in Riley's guest bedroom. She loved Chad but she wondered if he loved her, and if he did, was it enough to have a child.
"You okay in here," Riley asked as he entered the room. Turning to talk to him, Stacy's words ceased. *Damn he's looking good*, she thought as her nipples hardened. Riley allowed his locks to fall freely and the wifebeater he was clad in showed every muscle on his beautiful torso. Stacy snapped out of her lust filled trance when Riley snapped his fingers in front of her. "Oh, I'm sorry Riley. I'm fine," she answered discreetly increasing the distance between them.

Riley watched as Stacy bent over and the form fitting dress hugged her ass so tightly he thought he heard the seam give way. "God...I hope the room is to your liking," he said, happy he was able to clean up his previous statement. Inwardly he cursed as she stood to her full height. He had never seen anything more beautiful than her bent over.
"You need to stop it boy," Stacy chided as she folded a pair of short   shorts.

For One Night   Elizabeth LaShaun

"You know I love this room, I decorated it," she finished and took in the room.

The walls were a butter crème color, which was beautiful against the rich purple ceiling. The queen size mahogany sleigh bed sat in the middle of the room covered by a shiny, silk plum quilt. Riley was fully aware that she was pleased with the room he just needed to catch his slip-up. He hadn't asked her why she at his house with bags. She would tell him soon enough. The thing plaguing him was the joy he felt removing her bags and bringing them into his house. *She is your fucking sister man*, his head screamed at him. Riley heard the logic but his body and heart were calling it a damned lie. Stacy was a beautiful, giving, compassionate woman that deserved the world. She deserved to be loved and cherished. "She deserves me," he mumbled absently.

"What did you say?"

Riley quickly told her nothing and asked if she was hungry. "A little. Did your girlfriend cook," she asked taking great effort not to roll her eyes when she said girlfriend. Riley laughed and told her Chantrese had left. Unseen by him, a huge smile appeared on Stacy's face.

"I'll order a pizza," she offered and he readily accepted.

***

The apartment was dark and eerie, just the way Janelle wanted it. She wanted to wallow in her self pity and plot. She couldn't believe Stacy was pregnant. It was the ultimate betrayal. *Be careful what you wish for*, her minute conscious told her. "She was never gay," she hissed.

For the past three days Janelle had only left her room to urinate or eat. Her body was screaming for some personal hygiene care. Today was a different story. She was going to the gym so she could get Mr. Chad's address. She knew Stacy was shacking with him, but not for long. Janelle was going to get her woman and take her to the clinic. During the second day of her isolation, Janelle came to the conclusion that everyone was entitled to one mistake and this was Stacy's.

Janelle rolled her eyes and loudly sucked her teeth when she heard her phone go off. She knew from the ringtone it was her mother. She thought about not answering, but knew she would only call back. Taking a deep breath to calm her nerves she answered the phone.

"Child, what took you so long to answer the phone," her mother asked in her nasally voice.

For One Night   Elizabeth LaShaun

Janelle quickly lied and said she was in the shower. She didn't know why she bothered because her mother would find a problem with any answer she gave her.

"At this time of day," she came back with, proving Janelle's point.

"What can I help you with Mother," Janelle managed through tight lips.

"You really need to stop being a bitch Janelle. It gives you premature winkles and you know you need all the help you can get," she continued casually. "But I was calling to remind you of your sister, Jessica's, engagement party. You and Samantha can come but please don't act all funny around my friends," she lowered her voice; the word gay being unspeakable.

"Try to look pretty and if someone asks what you do say you are in law school. It makes no sense to say you are a model when no one has seen you," Janelle continued to listen mutely and keep her tears at bay.

She was waiting for the turn of the knife and her mother did not keep her in suspense long.

"Jessica is going to be doing fashion week in Paris so get the book, 'Law for Dummies' or something and read it. That is all," and with that Melody Parisher hung up. There was no how are you? I love you, just one insult after another.

Janelle's desperation to get Stacy back had just increased tenfold. If she weren't at the party with her, she definitely wouldn't hear the end of it. The sound of the ringing phone caused her to grimace. It wasn't her mother but it wasn't her lover either. The way her day was going she couldn't fathom the phone call bringing good news. Seeing Chantrese's name on the caller ID, she answered, her curiosity piqued.

***

"Have you talked to Stacy," the woman asked after the typical greeting. Janelle was thrown by the question, but answered as vaguely as possible. "Well she has been at Riley's for the past three days," Chantrese returned bursting Janelle's lie wide open.

Instantly the migraine began to settle down in her head. *No wonder she hasn't called me. She is with that homosexual*, she thought bitterly. Her mind quickly went to the look she had seen in Chantrese's eyes when she talked about Riley. *Would she? Naw not my Stacy. The same Stacy that is pregnant by another man*, her mind reminded her. Red appeared before her eyes and she gripped the phone so tightly her knuckles were white.

"Have you seen Riley," she baited her caller. She wasn't surprised when Chantrese told her no. When one of them needed the other they blocked out the world to help, another reason she hated Riley. Chantrese didn't know about the threesome and Janelle decided to use it to her advantage.

"The reason I haven't seen her is because we broke up," she began with a shaky voice.

"She is pregnant. I didn't want to believe it was Riley's," she broke down in fake sobs as Chantrese told her it would be okay.

She could hear the wheels turning in her callers head and decided to go in for the kill.

"I know you love Riley and he has hurt you too. I for one am not going to sit back and let them play me for a fool."

"What do you have in mind?"

The devious smile on Janelle's face stayed in place as she unraveled her plan to Chantrese. After thirty minutes and heavy persuasion they agreed on the plan. Janelle's faith that Chantrese would carry out the plan? There was no greater motivator than pain and humiliation.

Chapter Ten

"Ahhh," came the deep moan followed by a sharp hiss. Pastor Toplin felt his end nearing, but wanted to prolong the ride. He moved back half an inch in the chair to relax himself. "Lawd," he mumbled as Sister Thompson pulled his manhood back into her mouth weakening his legs. Toplin grabbed the back of her head and played in the curly hair at the nape of her neck. The slurping sounds she was making driving him crazy. When the good sister softly gripped his balls, Toplin lost his battle, finishing in her mouth. A lazy grin appeared on his face when she swallowed and zipped his pants up. Sister Thompson left without being asked already knowing the routine.

Some drank when they were stressed while others exercised or cleaned. Oral sex was Pastor Toplin's stress reliever. He took his vows with his wife serious and had not put his penis in another woman's vagina since they exchanged vows. Pastor Toplin didn't consider oral as sex because the mouth was not made for sex. There was no connection with Sister Thompson. She was only twenty-five. She was a beautiful young lady. Her family was Creole. Sister Thompson had the fair skin and long curly hair, but he didn't know she was Creole, until their first sexual encounter. Marie was a very docile young lady with beautiful green eyes. She walked into Toplin's office a year ago after bible class and told him he was tense. Toplin told her he was and asked that she pray for him. Assuming she was leaving, he turned his swivel chair and began going through the mail. To his surprise when he turned back to the desk, Marie was on her knees with a fire in her eyes. The rest was history.

Toplin shook his head as he thought about Marie. She would have made someone a great wife. She was educated, classy, and beautiful. "But she's a hoe," he mumbled once again shaking his head. Toplin had no respect for a female that gave a man oral sex. He wasn't trying to hear that lady in the street but a freak in the bed. She had to be a lady at all times. His logic stemmed from his days as a pimp. There was no greater form of submission than for a woman to have a man's dick in her mouth. Unless a woman was a bonafide freak, most did it to show their love and need to please her partner. If a woman wouldn't suck his dick she couldn't be in his stable.

For One Night — Elizabeth LaShaun

With a sigh, Pastor Toplin brought his attention back to the cause of his stress. Tithes and offering had dropped by a quarter percent and he couldn't have that. He didn't want to do it, but he would. It was time for him to pimp his predominantly female congregation again. He would give them his puppy dog eyes and throw a few scriptures damning them to hell their way.

"This recession is killing us," he mumbled content with his plan for the moment. "Now to take care of my other problem," he said aloud as he picked up the phone then quickly returned it to its cradle. "I don't wanna call him just yet." A laugh escaped his lips as he thought about the drastic measure he was about to take.

Chad had been tight lipped about his lady friend, but he knew better than to bring a less than worthy woman to the banquet.

"Lord pimping aint easy," he huffed as he checked his Rolex and realized it was time for the trustee meeting.

***

It had been a week and both Riley and Stacy were high strung. If the sexual tension wasn't enough, their personal problems being added to the mix was more than enough. Riley couldn't figure out what was so bad that Stacy wouldn't talk to him. The last time she had been this secretive she was coming out the closet; which wasn't a big shock because even though she was standing in the closet, the door was wide open. Hundreds of scenarios had crossed his mind but the one that stuck out was that she was getting married. He was preparing her favorite meal, tacos. He hoped if they sat back ate and caught another preseason game she would open up.

***

What is she doing leaving Pastor's office, Chad thought to himself. Chad had never caught his father cheating but he had his assumptions. Turning on his heels he headed back up the church stairs and out the door. He could always tell his father he knocked but nobody answered. If Pastor didn't have an attitude he was definitely fucking around. Starting his black Volvo he dismissed his father's antics and focused on his own dilemma. His ex-girlfriend Jiya had came to pay him a visit few days ago. He wasn't surprise to see her there. His mother and Jiya remained very close. She was his father's head nurse at the church and took the job very serious.

Jiya and Chad had been separated for almost six months now. They began dating because of Pastor Toplin and it dissolved because of him. Jiya was everything Pastor wanted; beautiful,

For One Night — Elizabeth LaShaun

classy, and a devout Christian. The problem was she was dating Chad and not Pastor Toplin. Everything they did his father knew. When they shared their first kiss his father was notified the next day. The last strike was when she suggested they called his father when he expressed his desire to have sex. He couldn't help but laugh in her face when she said they needed to pray for the thoughts he was having.

The breakup was relatively smooth. Jiya was going away to complete her junior and senior year of college to study theology. His father suggested they try to maintain a long distance relationship, since sex wasn't involved. To please his father he agreed but quickly deleted her number.

Three days ago she stopped by but nobody was home except him. Chad invited her in and told her she could wait a few minutes if she liked. Quickly agreeing and asking for some juice, Jiya made herself at home. Heading to the kitchen, Chad grabbed his cell to call his mother. He was supposed to be meeting Stacy in an hour and didn't want to be late.

"Are you serious," he said into the phone as he poured the juice into the glass. His forehead knotted as his mother told him it would be at least two hours before she got home.

Frustrated he turned to find Jiya standing before him naked as the day she was born. *That explains the trench coat*, he thought as he took in her toned body. Her father told him she had decided on a university in California and he had to admit the sun was doing her body damned good. The bronze tan was striking against her hazel eyes and golden streaked hair. Chad would have sworn he told Jiya to put her coat back on. He would also swear that he told her to stop when she began to walk toward him with sexy fire engine red stilettos on. In front of God himself Chad would have insisted that Jiya had some magical power that put her on top of the island and his dick inside her. That would have been the end of his testimony because every stroke and moan was his doing. He couldn't help himself. Jiya was so tight and had learned a few tricks in bedroom 101 while she was studying about the Lord up high.

That's why he found himself in front of the Holiday Inn prepared to meet her for the third time. It was also the reason that Stacy was furious with him. He had missed their dinner date and didn't call her until the next morning. He felt like a complete jackass as he listened to his woman cry about her fears of him being hurt. She claimed she wanted to talk to him about something very important and he wouldn't answer the phone. Chad heard it ring but there was no way he was going to stop what he was doing to answer it. He was receiving oral sex for the first time and to say it was phenomenal was an understatement. His dick jumped while he was on the phone with Stacy from the memory. Stacy told him she had to clear her head and she would talk to him later. "You're still coming to the banquet right," Chad asked softly. After an awkward pause and heavy sigh Stacy agreed. That was three days ago and besides four very brief conversations Chad hadn't spoken to Stacy. He was too busy spending most of his free time inside Jiya. Did he know he was wrong? Yeah, but he blamed it on him having a late start. It was simply him sowing his oats. He would give Stacy her space and after the banquet he would be faithful.

***

The hot shower was pouring over Stacy's body but her tears were cleansing her face. Moments ago Stacy looked in the mirror and didn't know who she was. Two months ago she would have been a woman in love with the woman that gave her purpose. A month ago she was in love with a man that showed her love that was indescribable. Today she was a pregnant woman that wanted nothing more than for her best friend to hold her in his beautiful arms. *How can you have a baby,* her reflection asked her. *You don't know who the hell you are.* Stacy climbed in the tub defeated. And now she was choking on her own sobs. She could sense the impatience increasing with Riley. The smell of tacos invaded her nostrils, instantly causing her stomach to flip. Quickly she jumped out the tub, sliding across the marble floor trying desperately not to fall, and dry heaved into the toilet. Pushing her hair back, she stood on weakened legs.

"Pull yourself together girl," she told herself before pulling on one of Riley's oversized shirts.

For One Night   *Elizabeth LaShaun*
Chapter Eleven

"So you want to tell me what the hell is going on," Riley asked through clinched teeth as soon as Stacy returned to the living room. They were having a great time watching the football game and all of a sudden she started crying because he didn't buy her favorite flavor of soda. Riley tried apologizing but Stacy still had a slight attitude. Just when he thought they were over that bizarre hurdle she rushed to the bathroom vomit shooting through her closed lips.

"Can you come sit down so we can talk," Stacy asked as Riley put the mop away.

Riley complied and sat next to her on the white sofa. Taking a deep breath Stacy explained that she was pregnant by Chad. She went on to say she conceived the night of the threesome. Seeing the disapproval and shock in her best friend's eyes she decided to focus on the cable remote sitting on the glass coffee table. Continuing she told him about Janelle finding out pretty much the same way he did and her reaction. Stacy eyes went to him as he began to laugh.

"What? I would have loved to have been there for that ass whipping," he laughed causing her to join.

"Anyway," she said playfully rolling her eyes. "That's my story."

Riley nodded his head in a steady rhythm while processing the information she had just told him.

"Does he know," he asked looking into space still gathering his thoughts.

A slight frown appeared on his face when she told him no. "I was afraid to tell him," Stacy quickly added defensively. "We were supposed to go out a few days ago but he stood me up." The frown deepened on Riley's face, unseen by Stacy. "I was actually happy he did," she added in a whispered voice. "I didn't want to tell him about the baby."

For the first time Riley looked at her and asked, "Why the hell not?"

Stacy didn't know how to explain it. Even if she did find the words she doubted Riley would understand.

"Stacy," Riley called with more bass in his voice. He was prepared to go and kick Chad's ass.

"He says he loves me but I don't know. I don't know me so how can he," she returned more to herself as she grabbed one of the brown throw pillows placing it on her lap.

For One Night   Elizabeth LaShaun

"Follow your heart and mind," Riley told her as he placed his hand on her shoulder. He saw the tears in her eyes and he felt helpless.

    Stacy laughed a mocking laugh and told him they were totally at odds. Her heart had too much on it and her mind said fuck it all.

"What's on your heart," Riley whispered in her ear becoming lost in her essence.

Stacy was still focused on the remote and slowly began to speak from the heart. She spoke to herself more than to Riley when she said, "If I want to keep the baby, the pain from me and Janelle's relationship ending, the new love and doubts I have about Chad, the love and desire I have to have you." Stacy quickly covered her mouth regretting the last sentence and turned hesitantly to Riley. She didn't know if he was going to call her a slut and tell her to get out or what.

"Look Riley," she began looking to his unreadable eyes. "I am so..." was all she managed before his lips were on hers. The kiss they shared shooting electricity through both their bodies.

"You. Can. Stay. With. Me. Stacy," Riley managed in between kisses.

Stacy couldn't say a word as his hands caressed her hardened right nipple. Gently, Riley laid her down on the couch and began slowly kissing and licking her toes. He was intoxicated off her aura and wanted to discover every part of her. The moans coming from her mouth almost made him climax. He had seen first hand *some* of the trial and tribulations Stacy had been though. He had seen the effects *all* of her trials and tribulations had on her. At this moment, his goal was to allow her to escape it all. For her to experience nothing but bliss for as long as he could. Working his way up to her navel Stacy forced him to look at her.

"Take me there Riley," she pleaded.

Without hesitation Riley unbuckled his pants and prepared to enter her.

    The banging on the door caused both of them to pause. Giving each other looks they prepared to continue since they both looked confused by the visitor.

"Riley, I know you are there. I see your truck outside," Chantrese screamed.

In the blink of an eye the lust had escaped Stacy's eyes and was replaced with doubt, sadness, and regret. He tried to reach out to her but she moved away and pulled her t-shirt down. Opening his mouth to speak he heard.

"You know I am your girlfriend Riley. Did you forget that? We have a commitment."
There was nothing more he could say. Chantrese had just destroyed any chance he had to talk to Stacy.

***

"I miss you too baby," Stacy said into the phone while shaking her head. She couldn't believe she was on the phone telling her supposed boyfriend and baby's father a bold face lie. Not just ten minutes she was on the couch with Riley. Looking out the window she could see her reflection and quickly closed the purple curtains. Some girlfriend she was. She didn't even tell him she had left Janelle. *Because you don't want to tell him where you are staying*, her conscience chastised her.
"Baby did you hear what I just said," Chad asked breaking her thoughts.
"Uh, I'm sorry baby I didn't hear you," she returned feeling like a dork.
Chad told her it was fine and that he wanted to know what she had to tell him.
"Its nothing honey, I will tell you at the banquet," she said, immediately kicking herself in the butt.
Chad told her that was fine and that he was going to a men's retreat and wouldn't be back until next week. He explained that he wasn't allowed to have his phone on so he would call when he got back in town. Looking at the ceiling Stacy mouthed 'thank you God'. Disconnected she stayed in the room until she heard the front door close. Luckily her window faced the front of the house. Getting out the bed she looked out the window and saw Chantrese and Riley getting in his truck. For a brief moment Riley paused and looked up at her window.

***

Jiya loved to see a plan come together. Chad was lying next to her in a coma like sleep. He had rented a room for the week in a quaint suburb forty minutes away from the city. She didn't like to toot her own horn, but she must admit she was damned good. Jiya knew people, especially the hypocrites at her church would think she was wrong if they knew what she was doing, but they were delusional. She believed in God and could quote the bible with the best of them; she also knew God helped those that helped themselves. And that was exactly what she was doing. Her going away to college was one of the biggest mistakes of her life. During her one and a half semesters she learned that she wanted to be a housewife, Chad's housewife. At the time she didn't know why she stayed in touch with First Lady Toplin, but boy was she happy that she did. She was able to keep close tabs on Chad and more importantly his future. First Lady bragged about him going into politics and rubbing elbows with the likes of Alderman Southby. The dollar signs danced in front of her eyes as she continued to talk to First Lady.

Day in and day out Jiya prayed that the Lord gave her another chance with Chad and it came a month ago. She was leaving her young adult ministry class when she received a call from Pastor Toplin. Jiya was surprised that he was calling her, but the surprise was pleasant. She admired her Pastor. He had come from the pits of hell and turned his life around. Chad thought his father was controlling but Jiya saw him as protective. Listening to Pastor Toplin speak she could see how he was a pimp. The man definitely had a way with words. Never did he tell her what to do but he told her that Chad was distracted by a young woman and he believed they were sexually active. He told her that he didn't want his son going to hell with some trap. He said that he knew premarital sex was a sin but sometimes we have to walk the walk and talk the talk of sinners to save them. Bottom line, he wanted her to fuck his son silly and take him from the chick he was with. The small doubts she had were erased when Pastor told her how she would make a fine wife and mother someday.

"I wish you were my daughter-in-law to tell you the truth," he added causing her to salivate at the mouth. Everyone knew that Pastor was in control of Chad's life. So for Jiya the conversation translated to this: Fuck my son silly and I will make sure he marries you.

That day Jiya learned everything she could about sex which was not hard. The saying that preacher's kids were the worse was the absolute truth. After mastering her skills, Jiya packed her bags and returned home. Checking to see her future was still asleep, she smiled admiring his nude chocolate body. *That ass, that ass*, she thought to herself almost squeezing it. Realizing she had business to take care of she sighed and sent the text to Pastor Toplin. Moments later his reply came and she smiled.

"Now I can play," she said licking her lips then placing her tongue on the top of his Chad's butt. *God do I love my job*, she thought before Chad roughly laid her down.

For One Night   Elizabeth LaShaun
Chapter Twelve

The hustle and bustle of the day revitalized Stacy. It was just afternoon and the Morning Perk was quickly filling with blue and white collar workers looking for a great meal. A few years ago, mostly blue collar workers patronized the diner. With the recession affecting everyone, CEOs, and Vice Presidents began to be seen sprinkled in the establishment.

"Here you go," Jasmine said placing her turkey club and fries down in front of her.

"You OK girl," Stacy asked picking up on the sadness in Jasmine's eyes.

Chuckling, Jasmine told her she was great now that she was back. Stacy decided not to push and told her favorite waitress that she was definitely back.

"Now if I can keep this food down," She thought aloud after Jasmine walked away.

Applying salt and pepper to her fries Stacy looked out of the window and saw a group of children walking past. She assumed they were heading to the park. It was a precious sight, twelve kids not older than six holding hands and smiling. Her smile widened as she observed a little girl wipe her partner's tears away.

"Aren't they adorable," Jasmine said returning with a refill of her iced peach tea.

"They sure are," Stacy said then thanked her.

***

Jasmine was placing one of her customer's food into a to-go container when he walked into the diner.

"Thank God," she mumbled to herself and gave him a genuine smile when their eyes locked.

She knew something was wrong with her second favorite customer and didn't like it. She did love her new attire; today she had on a strapless black top and white skinny jeans. Jasmine knew the woman was cute but she had no idea she was so beautiful. *Wonder if he is the reason for the change*, she thought to herself. Usually she would tell her if she was meeting someone but she didn't. *She looks like she needs to clear her head*, she thought to herself. *And you do too*, her mind threw at her. Jasmine sighed agreeing with her thoughts. She couldn't believe her mood was so noticeable. Looking at the clock behind the counter she moaned.

"Please don't let him be out here again." Removing her apron and placing it neatly into her locker, she turned to Gladys the waitress taking over her tables. "Make sure you take care of my girl," she said and smiled as she saw the man approach. They really made a cute couple. They were even matching. She chuckled as she took in his black button up and white khakis. The woman wasn't smiling but she had a feeling things would work out.

***

"Would you say something all ready," Stacy told Riley her eyes meeting his. "And sit down for heaven's sake," she added looking around the diner.

Riley had been standing at her table for the last minute or so staring at her. At first, she tried to act indifferent, but his stare was too much for her to handle.

Riley didn't know what to do, his emotions a melting pot. On one hand, he was happy to see her. The other hand, he was furious that she left his house leaving behind a letter filled with bullshit almost a week ago. All he wanted to know was why and he asked.

"Riley, you already know why," she answered rolling her eyes. "No the fuck I don't," he answered his voice thick with venom. Seeing the fear in her eyes he softened his voice. "Stacy do you know how I felt coming home and not finding you there? I thought something had happened to you."

"I left you a note," Stacy cut in defensively, hating the pain that was in his eyes.

She never meant to hurt him. She was trying to avoid both of them a lot of misery. Riley laughed a mocking laugh as he reached into his right khaki pocket and pulled out the letter. "You thought that bullshit was cool," he asked throwing the paper on the table. "All it says is that you were leaving. I figured that shit out when I got home," he continued his anger increasing as he thought of the worrying and panicking he had been enduring for the last week.

"Look Riley, we are best friends and I love you," Riley's heart skipped a beat as she proclaimed his love for him. They had told each other 'I love you' countless times but this time was different. "But the reality is I am with Chad and about to have his baby a…," she managed before Riley cut her off asking, "So you are going to have the baby?"

"Yes I am, and you are with Chantrese, remember," Stacy spoke with more confidence than she possessed.

"You're right," Riley threw back with a bone chilling glare. "I am with Chantrese. You enjoy your life with baby daddy that hasn't called your ass one time that I can recall."
Stacy opened her mouth to speak, but Riley but up his hand and continued.
"I wish you nothing but the best," and just like that he got up from the table and headed toward the door.

Steady tears streamed down Stacy's face as she watched him exit the restaurant and walk past the window near her table. Riley never looked at her as he passed. Stacy was utterly distraught and confused. She had fantasized about living with Riley and cooking for him, making love until the wee hours of the morning. She dreamt of greeting him at the door with a kiss and listening to him tell her about the crazy ass models he worked with, but that was all make believe. Reality set in and one detail was missing from every daydream, her child. Numerous times over the past week she had picked up the phone to call the abortion clinic, but couldn't. She felt that Chad had a right to know about the baby.

Looking around the diner she noticed that it wasn't so cheery and pleasant. Even the kids returning from the park didn't bring her joy. Across the street near the bank, she noticed a couple holding hands and laughing. The sight brought a mix of emotions. Loneliness filled her along with fear. The couple reminded her of Chad, which in turn brought the banquet tomorrow to the front of her memory. Paying her tab, Stacy left the diner and headed to the mall. She needed a new dress.

***

"Didn't I tell your simple ass," Janelle told Chantrese. They were sitting inside Chantrese's Buick across the street next to the bank. "You're lucky we didn't get caught when she looked this way," she continued while Chantrese sat in the driver's seat shocked. "Now do you see that he doesn't want your ass," Janelle drilled sucking her teeth, with no regard for Chantrese's feelings. *What the fuck does she have*, Chantrese wondered while she watched Riley walk away livid. He was never that upset at her. She had done a few things to test him, but he didn't react like a man in love would.
Janelle played on her dumb comrade's pain. She repeatedly told her how Riley was playing her. Pointed out the gigs she had missed to spend time with him. By the time they pulled off Chantrese felt nothing but pure hatred for Riley.

For One Night   Elizabeth LaShaun

Jiya's bronzed face was twisted with fury as she listened to Chad. He was definitely his father's child, giving long speeches instead of spitting it out. At the end Jiya came to the translation of: The fuck was good while it last, but I am going back to my girl. *This motherfucker has lost his mind*, she thought as shook her right leg vigorously while sitting on the bed.

"Listen, Jiya don't go off on me, I never told you we were a couple," Chad readily told her.

He could see the steam coming from her head. He planned to break the news to her this morning, but she caught him in the shower and he was preoccupied. They had to check out in ten minutes and he wanted her to leave understanding where they stood.

"Oh I understand Chad," Jiya began, her voice calm but her eyes blazing. "I understand that you must think I am a damned fool to agree to this bullshit," Chad shook his head at her ghetto antics. "Where was your girlfriend when I was sucking your dick," she asked him.

Chad knew he had messed up and didn't have answer for her. Sighing he lamely told her, "I love her". Jiya recoiled from the sincerity in his words and stomped out of the room. She really needed to text Pastor now.

For One Night   Elizabeth LaShaun
Chapter Thirteen

Riley worked on autopilot. He didn't remember pairing the outfits or switching garments that didn't compliment the models body types but he did it.
"Great job Riley," Pierre, the photographer told him.
Riley threw him a thank you and continued getting the next shoots wardrobe prepped. He was supposed to be online researching trends but he couldn't focus. He hated being on the computer. He could perform his real job, dressing with his eyes clothes. He loved the space he was given to work with. It reminded him of his humble beginnings in his first apartment.

Riley always had an eye for fashion, but was too afraid to pursue it. What straight man from the projects would be a stylist? When he first got his own apartment he dabbled in selling weed and a little bit of cocaine, but Ms. Mary put a stop to that. She came over to his house, of course unannounced, and told him to stop bullshitting himself. Riley laughed now thinking of Ms. Mary's straightforward attitude. He would never forget the words she told him, 'boy I know the game and I know that everybody won't have a nine to five. If I thought you didn't have nothing to offer but being on the corner I would keep my mouth shut, but you do. Stop being afraid of what others think, because nobody is taking care of you'.

The next day Riley enrolled in school. He had created his best work in a room similar to the one he was in now, small, with peeling yellowed wallpaper. The room was the size of a small living room and had over forty clothes racks crammed in the space allowing only enough room for a narrow walkway. "This would look perfect on Stacy," he thought regarding a gold, sequin mini dress, immediately having a sour taste in his mouth.

He hated that he always thought about her. *Face the fact that she doesn't want your ass,* his mind threw at him. Sighing, Riley resolved he would leave Stacy alone. If she wanted to be with a nothing like Chad, that was fine with him. He couldn't stop that or be mad at her; it was her decision to make. What hurt was the way she talked about the baby. She made it sound like he wouldn't take care of the baby like it was his own child. He loved every part of her and that included the baby.

For One Night   Elizabeth LaShaun

The models had begun to spill into the tight room hoping to get the best outfits. Riley again did his job his mind, still on Stacy.

"Riley, you didn't notice me," Chantrese asked him after he pushed an outfit in her hands. Riley looked up and immediately apologized. "It's been a long day baby," he said with a sigh and absently giving her a quick peck. *I just bet it has*, she thought but asked if they could go out later.

Declining was Riley's first thought but he knew he needed to move on. He would always be there for Stacy but he had to live his life. "I would love too".

***

Chad felt like a complete jackass as he drove his Volvo to the banquet. He had a beautiful woman that wanted nothing more than to love him and he was busy fucking his ex. Glancing at Stacy, she smiled lighting up his world. A smile appeared on his face when he thought about her reaction to seeing him after almost two weeks. She rushed to him planting hungry kisses on his lips. After several minutes he pulled away and was able to take her in. She was absolutely stunning in the lavender silk halter dress. Her pearl accessories went great with the dress. On her feet were deep purple stilettos. Due to it being a church banquet, Chad understood the shawl but he wanted her to take it off now. Nothing was going to hinder his view of her in the gown.

"So how was the retreat," Stacy asked bringing him back to the present.

Chad groaned as he thought of the lies he would have to tell her. "It was really nice," he told her hoping she would let it go, but she didn't.

For the next twenty minutes Chad told her the lie he had concocted.

***

Stacy had never been to a church banquet before but she never expected such grandeur. A massive and exquisite chandelier illuminated the foyer of the pavilion. The doormen at the door were dressed in black tuxedo's directing them to the corridor that led to the grand ballroom. Stacy oohed and aahed at the expressive artwork that lined the ways, causing Chad to chuckle. He had never met anyone as appreciative as Stacy. She never expected anything and was grateful for everything. Unable to help himself, he kissed her lips with great passion.

For One Night   *Elizabeth LaShaun*

"Boy we are at a church banquet," she scolded putting emphasis on church. "That is beautiful," Stacy said as she stared at the colossal hand crafted wooden door that held the festivities.

Chad squeezed her hand and turned slightly hearing the steps of running children. Hearing Stacy gasp he returned his attention to the forefront.

Chad had to admit his father had really outdone himself this time. The silver, silk and suede blend drapes hung beautifully on the walls, giving the room a majestic atmosphere. Turning to his right he noticed the purple lighting against the walls.

"This is beautiful," Stacy whispered in utter shock. "Look at the tulip centerpieces against the silver and purple place settings." Chad squeezed her hand once more and continued to survey the room. *I shoulda known*, he thought seeing Alderman Southby and his wife.

                               ***

Of all the fucking people, Pastor Toplin thought, noticing his son, and more importantly his date as soon as they entered the ballroom. Pastor diverted his eyes to his black Armani tuxedo sleeve for five seconds, not wanting to stare too long. He was sure he knew the young lady, but it had been years since he had seen her. Returning his eyes to the couple, his jaw clenched as he saw the evidence proving it was indeed her. The young lady had a shawl draped around her shoulders but a small portion of her back was exposed, revealing the grotesque burn. *This boy is constantly fucking up*, he inwardly fuming taking a sip of his water, wishing like hell it were brandy.

                               ***

Stacy indulged herself and ate her lemon tart as well as Chad's. She always ate when she was stressed and today was no exception. She could feel the storm brewing and no matter how many reassuring hand squeezes Chad gave it seemed to be moving fast. A couple of warnings went off in her head. The first one being that they had been at the banquet for a little over an hour and Chad's parents had not made their way to the table to greet them. She told Chad they should go over but he said later. Noting the longing in Chad's mother's eyes, she could tell his father was the one that refused to interact with them. Pastor Toplin was vaguely familiar, but Stacy couldn't put her finger on how she knew him.

"Hello there Chad," Alderman Southby said walking to the table, his wife in tow.

"Hello Alderman," Chad greeted putting on his phoniest smile ever.

Stacy knew that Chad didn't like the man from their previous conversations, but greeted them both amiably when he introduced her as his girlfriend. The two had never put a title on their relationship and a genuine smile was on Stacy's face as she shook Mrs. Southby's hand. The woman's eyes were filled with misery and her handshake was weak. *Is that a bruise*, she wondered seeing where makeup had worn from the woman's wrist. The look in Mrs. Southby's eyes confirmed her suspicious as she quickly covered her hand with her purse.

I can not believe this is happening, Chad thought as he noticed Jiya sweep into the ballroom. The Alderman was still talking about God knows what as his focus remained on Jiya. He couldn't believe how angelic she looked in her long crème gown. She looked so innocent and sweet. Deep lines creased his forehead as he watched his father hug her and rather loudly say, "She was almost my daughter-in-law, I hope she will be," locking eyes with Chad.

From the start Chad knew his father didn't approve of Stacy, his dismissive behavior speaking volumes. Taking a sideways glance to gauge Stacy's expression, he couldn't, her tresses concealing the profile of her face.

Finally the Alderman got a clue and excused himself. Pastor Toplin was laughing with one of the Trustees close to the door, away from his wife. "Let's go speak to my mother baby," Chad told Stacy, who readily agreed. Stacy's stomach began to flip as she walked the dreaded twenty feet to his mother. She was stunning in her black silk gown and matching jacket. Her hair was in a tight bun at the nape of her neck, giving her beautiful pecan skin its just attention.

"Mama this is…"

"Boy, hush," First Lady Toplin shooed Chad. "This is a beautiful young lady," she finished his sentence with a radiant smile. "My name is Tabitha and yours is," First Lady asked shocking Chad. His mother never told anyone her first name it was always First Lady Toplin. With shaky hands Stacy shook her hand and introduced herself.

"Nice to meet you ma'am and I'm sorry I didn't introduce myself earlier," she told her giving Chad a sideways glance.

"Well why don't you introduce yourself now," Pastor Toplin said sneaking up on Chad and Stacy from behind.

For One Night   *Elizabeth LaShaun*

"I heard your name is Stacy, but you are who to my son," he asked amiably. Stacy saw the smile but she could feel and see the coldness coming off the good Pastor. Stacy thought Chad would say something but when he didn't she spoke up, "I am dating your son."

"Really," Pastor said looking at his son before returning his eyes to Stacy. "You don't remember me do you," he asked with a smirk.

Stacy shook her head no, but added that he did look familiar. "I use to counsel you at Ms. Mary's," Pastor Toplin said as recollection hit Stacy full on. "How is your father? Is he still drinking," he asked the smile never leaving his face.

"Excuse me," Stacy quickly said her face full of shame as she retreated to the restroom.

Pastor Toplin saw the look his wife gave him but disregarded it as he turned his attention to his son. In a low growl he spoke, "How dare you bring that trash in here," his eyes blazing. "You will never have a political career if you marry her." Chad was sick he actually felt the bile begin to rise.

"I love her so fuck you and politics," he hissed his eyes meeting his father's.

"You're fucking with the right one," Pastor Toplin said in his ear, right before Mother Patterson asked the two to take a picture.

***

"Why him," Stacy whimpered as the tears cleansed her face. She had locked the bathroom door after she had thrown up her dinner and prized tarts. Looking in the mirror she shook her head as she thought about the things she shared with Pastor Toplin, her father's alcoholism, the fire, her pain, her fear. *The rape*, her mind threw at her causing her to shudder from the recollection. She had never told a soul until Pastor Toplin came along.

Ms. Mary told her that the pastor was a newly changed man and he was here to talk to her. Stacy didn't trust him, but Ms. Mary explained that God was there for her and she should talk. At first, they played board games and cards during his visits. Slowly gaining her trust, Stacy told him about her father and his drinking. She recalled the night of the fire and the fear she had of sleeping.

"Stacy, you are not telling me everything," Pastor Toplin told her one day. "You don't trust me," he asked.

A then twelve-year-old Stacy felt the pastor was her friend and she didn't want to upset him. She explained that Riley had gotten in trouble for beating up Justin.

For One Night   *Elizabeth LaShaun*

"Why did he beat him up," he asked.

Stacy said he was taking up for her providing nothing else. Pastor Toplin knew there was more to the story and forced Stacy to tell him what Justin had done, which she reluctantly did.

"Well you should be happy right," the pastor asked confused. "But he wasn't there to protect me the other times he did it," Stacy said before breaking down in heavy sobs.

Banging on the door brought Stacy back to the present. Fixing her face and preparing to leave the washroom, Stacy realized the relationship was over. She saw first hand that Chad couldn't stand up to his father. Without thinking she dialed Riley's number, but hung up on the second ring, remembering he had a relationship. Exiting the door she saw Chad and his father posing for a picture. Shaking her head she headed for the exit.

"Excuse me," Jiya said running to Stacy before she left the ballroom.

"Yes," Stacy returned warily.

"You're Chad's girlfriend right," Jiya baited not waiting for a response. "Well Chad left this and if you could be a doll please return them," she finished handing Stacy the bag. Looking inside Stacy saw the red polo and jeans she'd brought him as a gift inside. She also saw a few of his underwear. Hearing her name being called she looked up with teary eyes to see Chad running towards her. Outdone, Stacy dropped the bag and took off running, Chad hot on her tail. She made it outside and was about to go down the first step when Chad grabbed her arm. Furious and with all her might, Stacy yanked away loosing her balance and tumbling down nine marble-tiled stairs. Her head and back hit the pavement with a loud thump, blood oozing from her head and between her legs.

"Stacy," Chad screamed yearning to be at her side but being pulled away by his father and three deacons as someone rushed and called 911.

Chapter Fourteen

Riley took hurried and fearful steps toward the hospital. He had received a call while he was at dinner with Chantrese. The nurse was vague only saying that someone he knew was in the intensive care unit. Finally making it through the long white corridor, Riley rounded the corner looking for the nurses' station. Tons of people were huddled inside the small emergency room waiting area. Mustering the small amount of self control he had, Riley waited behind the Spanish man as he tried to check in.

"Boy relax," Ms. Mary scolded him, while he sighed heavily. Riley had picked her up as soon as he received the phone call. Though they never said her name, Riley knew in his heart of hearts that it was Stacy.

Ms. Mary decided to take control the situation and asked the nurse if Stacy was a patient. She steeled her self as the Middle Eastern nurse typed in the information in the system. "She is in ICU room twenty three," the nurse replied without emotion, her eyes still on the screen. Instantly, Ms. Mary began to pray as Riley all but dragged her to the elevator. Glancing at Riley she could see the deep concern and fear in his eyes. He was walking so fast that she was actually trotting to keep up.

"Naw, Stacy," Riley mumbled astonished as he entered the room.

He had tried to prepare himself as they made their way to Stacy's room. ICU was no joke and he had resolved himself to be strong for Ms. Mary. Quickly his resolve left as soon as he saw Stacy. She was not swollen, there weren't various tubes covering her body. She appeared, she looked, dead. Riley was rocked to his core, approaching the bed. *She is still warm,* he thought expecting her to be cold. Touching her face, he brushed her cheeked softly and whispered that he was there.

"Hold on Stacy, please," he pleaded, praying that she heard him. With his hand still in hers, Riley studied the monitor that registered her vital signs. He had watched enough medical series to know that her blood pressure and pulse were weak. Rage filled him as the thought of losing her began to creep into his mind.

She was supposed to be at fucking banquet, he thought behind closed eyes. Opening them, he saw Ms. Mary standing in the shadows with her eyes closed, praying he was sure. On closer observation he could see the tears steadily roll down her tired and wrinkled face. Ms. Mary was a plain lady, wearing a flowered dress and casual walking shoes. Kissing Stacy on the cheek, Riley swiftly passed Ms. Mary and was out the door; the pain of possibly losing the love of his life, and the woman who raised him broken, too much for him to bear.

***

"Is she going to make it doctor," a distraught Chad asked the doctor. The nurse told him who the doctor was and he was lucky enough to stop him as he left another patient's room. "Right now it is too early to tell. Ms. Wilson has lost a substantial amount of blood. She also has some edema on her brain," he frowned from the look Chad gave. "She has swelling. Where you with her during the accident," he asked Chad.
"Yes I…"
"We were all present," Pastor Toplin cut in while the other deacons present nodded in the affirmative. "It was a horrible accident," he added refusing to go into details. He didn't want to incriminate them in anyway. A scandal of this magnitude could be detrimental to Chad's career. Doctor Blackman immediately had a bad feeling about the pastor and returned his attention to Chad.
"I understand that she fell down the stairs, but with the injuries she sustained there had to be great momentum," the doctor said looking into the Chad's eyes. "As if she was pushed," he added regarding the young man closely. 'Can you tell me what happened?"
"That's what the fuck I would like to know," Riley finally spoke up. He had been listening unseen by anyone for quite some time. Chad immediately knew who Riley was.
"Have you seen her? How is she doing," Chad asked wearily. Riley looked at him like he was scum and said nothing.
"I'm sorry, let me introduce myself, I'm Chad," he said reaching out his hand, again clueless to what was going on. Pastor Toplin was not and immediately sensed the rage in Riley.
"I'm Pastor Toplin from Fellowship Baptist. We are just as concerned as you are," Pastor Toplin said with a smile sickening Riley.

He could smell a fake a mile away and the good pastor's stench was strong. "What happened," Riley said again his blazing eyes on Chad. "I don't know," Chad sighed. "She was running to leave and I chased after her…"
"You don't know owe this man anything," Pastor Toplin spoke up, giving Riley a condescending look.

Turning his attention to Chad he never saw Riley coming. Riley punched him in the jaw and kicked him as the deacons pulled him off of him.

"I will kick your fake ass," Riley yelled. "Fuck playing with me and your punk ass," he said turning his fury onto Chad. "You know what the fuck happened, but you too scared of your bitch ass daddy," his anger was so high that he was trying with all his might to escape the men's grasp. "I am going to see your stupid ass, soon. The question I have is, how could you let her fall when she's pregnant with your child?"

"What," Chad and Pastor Toplin said simultaneously as the shocked deacons released Riley and threw questioning glances at Chad. "Is everything alright," the security guard asked Doctor Blackman. Feeling a genuine sense of concern from both men the doctor excused the guards.

"Did she," Chad asked unable to finish the question as the guilt crushed his heart. "Unfortunately, the fetus did not survive," the doctor answered sorrowfully crushing Chad. Pastor Toplin did not allow the smile to come to his lips but his eyes gleamed which was enough for Riley. Before the pastor could react Riley was raining punch after punch on him. Security was still close and quickly came breaking up the fight. Dr. Blackman intervened when the guards put the handcuffs on Riley. He had seen the total disrespect Pastor Toplin had displayed as well.

"I think it is best that you leave," the doctor said to Chad.

Chad was about to protest until he was able to get a good look at his father's face. Blood was coming from his nose and his eye was swollen. Shaking in his head in defeat, Chad slowly walked away, repulsed at his father and more so at himself.

***

Pastor Toplin was furious when he saw the damage to his face. His nose wasn't broken but it was close. He had thought about pressing charges against the petty thug but didn't want the headache.

"Especially with the bitch still being unconscious," he mumbled to himself while he looked for his phone in the desk drawer. "He betta answer the fucking phone," Toplin thought as the phone began to ring. He had been calling the man unsuccessfully for three days now.

"How can I help you," the caller answered his annoyance evident.

"It's like that Lock," he asked the man looking at the phone.

He couldn't believe the man was talking to him like that. "I know you are doing big things now, making it easy to forget our humble beginnings."

Ray Lockhart immediately picked up on the underlying meaning and sighed. "I have a lot going on now," Ray told him the half truth as he scanned the court documents.

Ray wished Cream would just get to the point of his call. The man had saved his life when they were teens and never let him forget his debt. Slowly, he tuned back into the conversation when Cream finally got to the point. *He is such a cocky bastard*, Ray thought.

"You have nothing to worry about. It was a mere accident and you have more than enough witness. She pulled away," he answered, pinching his nose in irritation. *That boy can't run his own life, so what makes him think he can run for office*, Ray brooded as Cream continued to talk.

"Cream I really have to go, but let the young man be. You said you didn't want Chad with the lady," he reasoned and prepared to disconnect.

Ray felt that he had paid his debt and more to Cream. He had to take care of the situation, but with things in such an uproar on the home front, he might have to outsource. Scrolling through his rolodex, he smiled as he came to the contact.

***

"Uggh," Riley groaned as he repositioned himself in the hard chair he had been sitting and sleeping in the past three days. Many nights he wanted to get in the bed with Stacy and hold her, but he didn't, afraid of the damage he could cause. Turning to look at her, he was surprised to see her eyes looking back at him.

"Hey," she whispered, the tears rolling down her cheeks.

"Hey to you," he smiled rushing to her side. "When did you wake up girl,' he asked stroking her cheek.

Stacy explained she had been up for a while and managed to press for the nurse.

"Are you in pain," Riley asked and was relieved when she said she wasn't.

Without asking, Riley climbed in the bed and lay next to Stacy, holding her tight. Looking deeply into Stacy's eyes Riley became lost. No doubt, he had many questions that he wanted to ask her, but he didn't. Riley just wanted this moment of peace to never end.

"Riley," Stacy attempted before Riley kissed her lips softly. Stacy shook her head no. She had to say what she had to say. She couldn't be with him, Janelle, or Chad.

"Damn it Stacy, stop fighting this because it is going to happen," Riley said with an edge to his voice startling her. "I am going to be here and you can't stop me. I am going to love you with everything in me," he said while wiping her tears.

"Riley, you don't want me," Stacy proclaimed. "You are confused."

"No, you were confused," he chuckled "Real confused, but you finally got it right."

Stacy laughed despite herself as her resolve began to crack.

"You lied to me about that pain too," Riley said noticing the slight grimace.

Riley waited until Stacy dozed off to leave. He had to meet Chantrese and tell her it was over. He knew she would be hurt, but he had to honest. Calling the florist and ordering Stacy a get well arrangement he pulled out of the parking lot.

For One Night   *Elizabeth LaShaun*
Chapter Fifteen

"Slow down," Janelle scolded Chantrese. They were both sprawled across Janelle's bed naked. Chantrese was busy snorting cocaine off a small compact mirror. Janelle sucked her teeth in total disgust as she observed the woman. Chantrese's drug habit was her leverage at first to get her to take Riley down. Since they followed Riley at the diner the woman's habit had worsened.

"You care about me baby," Chantrese asked with glassy eyes and hardened nipples.

Thankfully, Chantrese's phone rang sparing Janelle from hurting her feelings. Seeing Riley's name on the caller ID, Chantrese sucked her teeth and answered the phone.

Janelle was disgusted at Chantrese. Her eyes were glassy and jumpy as she frantically looked in her purse for more drugs. It was amazing how she should sit and have a perfectly normal conversation while cocaine covered her nose like old cake batter. Janelle began to wonder if Chantrese's habit had worsened or did she just show her true self to Janelle because she was comfortable.

The frown stayed at bay until Chantrese muted the phone and began brushing the drugs off her nose in her hand and licking it. She was so engrossed in getting high that she was snorting like a vacuum attempting to get every morsel of the powder. Janelle listened to Chantrese talk and wanted to ring her neck. From what she could decipher Stacy was in the hospital and had woken up this morning.

Junky bitch, Janelle inwardly fumed with a calm face. Chantrese never told her Stacy was in the hospital. *Maybe because you keep telling her you love her,* her mind threw at her. Janelle decided to play it cool. Once Riley was out the way she would dump Chantrese and fix her and Stacy's relationship.

"Simple bastard," Chantrese huffed after hanging up the phone. "We have to do it tonight," she threw out nonchalantly searching her purse for more drugs.

"Why?"

"He's going to break up with me tonight," Chantrese answered dumping the contents of her purse on the bed. "I could hear it in his voice."

Why am I stuck with the dumb ass, Janelle wondered as she grabbed Chantrese by her arms and forced her eyes to look into her own.

141

For One Night   *Elizabeth LaShaun*

"You need to get yourself together Chantrese! We can't pull this off if you are high out of your mind," she continued, shaking Chantrese at this point.

Chantrese wiped her running nose and resumed searching her purse.

"Stop looking for that shit and listen to me."

"Okay, okay I won't do anymore, but I need some kind of high," she giggled opening her legs and exposing her hairless pussy.

***

Stacy woke up and discovered she was alone, relief washing over her. It was time that she was honest with herself and move forward. Absently she began to rub her stomach and stopped. Before she could stop them, heavy sobs ransacked her body. Stacy secretly felt the miscarriage was a blessing. She wasn't prepared to take care of a baby, especially after the hideous experience at the banquet.

"Lord please give me a sign," she prayed with a heavy heart. After an hour of prayer she glanced out the window and saw a Whole Foods truck in the hospital parking lot. *That's odd*, she thought. There was no Whole Foods store anywhere in the vicinity and it surely wouldn't be delivering to the hospital. Before Stacy could give it further thought her phone began chirping. It was a text from Riley. It read 'I love you for you.'

"OK God, I got the message," she mumbled as contentment fell over her and she replied. Before long she drifted into a contented sleep.

***

Was she always like this, Riley thought as he opened the car door for Chantrese. They were at her place after a very interesting dinner. Riley shook his head as he recalled how obnoxious Chantrese was acting. She had been extremely rude to the waitress and hostess at the restaurant. Dismissing her actions as irritation that they hadn't spent any time together Riley endured. He surmised it was the least he could do since he was ending the relationship. His patience was worn thin; however, when she became very raunchy and overly sexual at the table. Honestly, Riley was taken aback by her behavior.

Walking to her door Riley's thoughts increased his anger and embarrassment to the point that he had to speak. "Listen Chantrese," Riley began when they made it to her door. "I have been trying to tell you this all night and…"

"Riley, I don't want my business in the streets," Chantrese chuckled unlocking the door and walking inside.

Sighing deeply Riley followed wanting to state his piece and leave. He missed Stacy something terrible and wanted to get back to her.

"Look Chantrese," Riley said the edge to his voice taking Chantrese by surprise.

"Riley let me get us a drink and we can talk," she threw out heading to the kitchen before he was able to reply.

Just be patient, Riley thought as he sent Stacy a text message. Smiling at the almost instant response, he saw Chantrese return.

"To happiness," Chantrese said as they clinked glasses and drank their cocktails. "Now talk," Chantrese said with a warm smile.

"Chantrese, you are a nice lady and will make any man happy," he began. "But unfortunately my heart is with someone else," he said as sense of warmth washed over him. The smile on Chantrese face was one of malice, but Riley didn't notice, his eyes focused on Chantrese perky breasts teasing him in the silk halter she had on.

"Didn't I make you happy Riley," she asked with artificial pain lacing her voice.

Riley mumbled that she did. His vision was becoming blurry and he was seeing double. Instead of being alarmed, he felt an uncontrollable since of pleasure as he now had four breasts to peruse. Slowly Chantrese untied her top exposing her breasts.

"Don't you want to for old times sake," she asked as Riley nodded that he did.

Something is wrong, Riley inwardly panicked. His eyes were half cast, he was drowsy and horny. His entire body felt tingly and aroused. Standing Chantrese grabbed his hand and led him to her bedroom, winking at Janelle, who was in the closet. Janelle told her to only put one X pill in his drink, but she put two, knowing how freaky the pills made people. She wanted their last fuck to be the best.

***

They sure don't keep you long, Stacy thought with a chuckle as she began to pack her toiletries. The hospital was discharging her in an hour and she was ecstatic. Her first thought was to call Riley, but decided against it and opted for surprising him. "Let me know when you are ready Ms. Wilson and I will call the cab," Paula, the nurse's assistant told her peeking in the door. Stacy told her she would and went to the bathroom to see if she left anything

For One Night   *Elizabeth LaShaun*

behind. Satisfied that everything was packed, she returned to her room and was taken aback by the unwanted visitor.

"What do you want," she asked tightly as Chad looked at the floor.

"I thought I had the wrong room," he began uncomfortably. "I thought you would be in bed. I know you aren't being discharged this fast."

      Stacy started to explain that she was put in a medically induced coma and had been awake for almost two days. She wanted to tell him that she needed a blood transfusion and it was his entire fault.

"What do you want," she asked again instead.

"I'm sorry Stacy," Chad solemnly replied as she began to fold the other clothes Riley had brought her.

You sure are sorry, she thought while throwing her jacket into the overnight bag.

"Can I explain," Chad asked softly, her silence killing him.

"I really don't see what there is to explain. You played me and your father disrespected me," she spat her blazing eyes on him as he cowered, the words cutting deep.

"Just what I thought," she added, completely outdone.

"Where you ever going to tell me," he asked taking most of the wind out of Stacy's sail.

"Would it have changed things Chad? Could it take back who I am," she asked quietly.

"I never meant to hurt you Stacy," he threw out sincerely. Stacy chuckled at the statement and turned to face him, bag on her shoulder.

"I know you didn't, but you did and I must thank you and your father. You opened my eyes to the man I should have been with from the beginning."

The anger consuming Stacy began to shrink as she looked into Chad's eyes. He was a hurt and lost young man. Part of her longed to hold him, help him, but she couldn't. She needed to help herself and so did he.

"Goodbye, Chad," she softly said kissing his cheek.

      "What the hell," Riley shouted jumping out the freezing shower. Instantly, he grabbed his head the migraine weakening him. "What happened," he mumbled as he clumsily made his way to the living room.

He didn't see Chantrese, but he saw his clothes sprawled on the floor. Nearing the couch, he saw the crimson stains on the beige carpet. "I know that's not blood," he mumbled still holding his head. Making his way to the light switch, he moved it up only to return it to its prior position. The light was killing his eyes. Hearing noise, he followed the noise to Chantrese's bedroom.

The room was also dark, with no lighting, the curtains being closed. Riley made his way to the window and pulled back the curtain enough to give the room some light. "Chantrese, Chantrese," he called yanking on her arm. "What you doing up boy," she slurred leaning forward and face coming into the light. Riley gasped. She resembled a scary sadistic clown. Blood tinged cocaine covered Chantrese's once beautiful face, like a mask; her cheeks having a mixture of cocaine and mascara appearing as dirty clay. Her right eye was swollen and her lip was split in several places.
"Who did this to you," Riley asked forgetting all about his headache.
"You did," Chantrese giggled. "After you raped me."

Riley quickly let her go, causing her to fall hard on the bed. "I didn't rape you," he told her as his mind raced trying to remember the night before.
"That's what Janelle said," Chantrese giggled again quite amused with contradicting tears coming from her eyes.
"Janelle," Riley hissed as his head really began to spin.
"Don't tell me you want Janelle," Chantrese pouted. "Didn't I make you feel good Riley," she asked fondling her nipple. "The boys told me what to do to make you feel good."

Riley watched as Chantrese mumbled about one guy after another. Sickened he went to the living room in search of his phone. Finding the device under the coffee table he noticed he had ten missed calls from Stacy and just as many messages. Riley was happy to see that she was out of the hospital and wanted to ring Chantrese and Janelle's neck for putting him in this mess. With his phone, Riley returned to Chantrese's room and prepared for a long night.

***

Stacy was beyond worried as she sat in the window sill with her knees to her chest. It was eight o'clock at night and she had not heard from Riley, which wasn't like him. She sent him an instant message that she used her key to get in his place, but he hadn't replied.
"If he is not hurt I am going to kill him," she said pushing his cat, Roady off her leg. As soon as she stood the doorbell rang.

For One Night   Elizabeth LaShaun

"It's about time," she thought as headed towards the door. Stacy had ordered a pizza and assumed it was the deliveryman. Opening the door with major attitude, her frown quickly turned to astonishment.

"Aren't you happy to see me baby," Janelle asked with a wicked grin on her face.

Brushing past Stacy she was happy to see that the house was empty, with the exception of Roady.

Stacy watched, still in awe as Janelle sat on the couch and crossed her legs. She opened her mouth to speak, but the doorbell rang once more. "Now he wants to come," she mumbled as she headed to the door. Janelle was quite amused as she listened to Stacy tell the deliver not to even think about a tip.

"A little dick has given her some spunk," she said absently. Janelle had no worries; she would quickly retrain Stacy and have the love of her life back. *She has gotten a little thick*, she thought lustfully as she watched Stacy walk to the kitchen with the pizza.

"What the hell is going," Stacy thought aloud as she sat the pizza on the island. "First Chad, now Janelle."

Well you did run from your problems, her conscience piped in. "I guess I did," she mumbled as she steeled herself to face Janelle.

"Your poker face is cute," Janelle smiled as Stacy sat in the chair opposite of the couch. *She's damned thick*, Janelle thought once more as she took in Stacy's outfit. The long turquoise form fitting summer dress was beautiful against her chocolate skin. She loved the soft touch of makeup Stacy had on and the new updo hairstyle.

Stacy had begun to feel uncomfortable under Janelle's gaze and fidgeted slightly in her seat. Janelle had always had that effect on her and she despised it.

"What do you want Janelle," she finally asked with a roll of her eyes.

"I want you to come home," Janelle answered matter-of-fact. "I know that you made a mistake with Chad, but since you came to your senses," she continued and focused on Stacy's stomach. "You can come home."

Stacy burst into laughter at Janelle. "Thank you for the invitation Janelle, but I am happy."

Now it was Janelle's turn to laugh.

"You think Riley wants you Stacy," she said and lit a cigarette. "Yeah a bad habit I picked up," she added after taking a long drag from the cigarette. "Riley is on some macho male bullshit. He found out you were with a man and now he has to be the next one to tap that girl," Janelle could see signs of Stacy's armor cracking. It came from being with her for over a year and knowing when she was being swayed. "When was the last time you heard from him anyway," she threw out.

Stacy did have some questions for Riley, but she would never disclose that to Janelle. The smooth ballad playing let her know she had a text. Retrieving the device from the end table, she opened the text from Riley. 'Baby I know that you are upset but I can explain,' it read. 'I will be in front of the house in 10 minutes and I need for you to come outside.'

Stacy quickly replied that she would try but Janelle was at the house. Almost instantly she got a reply that had her puzzled.

"Are you done being rude," Janelle snapped.

"Sorry about that Janelle," Stacy answered humbly, deciding to play along to get Janelle out of the house. "I have to go and handle something, but I will definitely come by your place tonight to talk. I just need answers to a few questions."

Janelle worked hard to keep the smile from her face as she stroked Stacy's cheek.

"I'll be waiting love," she whispered before kissing Stacy passionately and walking out the door.

For One Night *Elizabeth LaShaun*
Chapter Sixteen

Riley was making sure that he followed all the traffic laws as he headed to his house. He had murder on his brain and needed to talk to Stacy before he did something he would regret. He didn't know which pissed him off more, the women underestimating him or what they had planned. Stacy had just texted him that Janelle was gone, but he didn't want to put anything past the woman.

Pulling in front of the diner, he saw Stacy chatting with the waitress and blew the horn. Not wanting to be rude, he waved at Jasmine as Stacy hopped in the car. The ride was quiet and Riley knew that meant Stacy was pissed and she had every right to be.
"Baby, I need for you to let me explain and have my back on this."
"Riley, has there ever been a time that I didn't have your back," she asked.
Riley answered her no but this time it was different and the consequences were a lot higher. Stacy was about to ask him for more details when he parked. Looking around, Stacy surmised that it was a decent, newly developed area. There were newly developed townhouses lining the streets and a small recreation center across the street.
"Who's place is this," Stacy asked as Riley opened the door with a key.
"Chantrese's," he answered without looking back. Hearing her smack her lips and mumble Riley turned around and said, "I really need for you to trust me on this one."

Stacy nodded her head in agreement and was rewarded with a passionate kiss that had her ready to give him her all at she possessed at that very moment. With great effort, Riley pulled away. "We have to stop because you have to heal first," he whispered in her ear. Stacy licked out her tongue at him, chuckling. In her mind the scenario made no sense, but Riley had never put her in harm's way before. *More than you can say for most people*, her heart threw at her as they climbed the stairs inside the dwelling.
"Brace yourself," Riley told her standing before Chantrese's bedroom door.
"Oh my god," Stacy proclaimed with her hands over her mouth.
Chantrese was still lying in the bed, naked with drugs covering her face.

"What happened to her Riley," she asked as the tears began to well in her eyes.

"Janelle," he answered bitterly.

"Janelle was with me Riley," she answered naively.

"Baby, I heard rumors that Janelle was getting close to the girls that she felt were her competition and getting them strung out on coke. She would tell them she was doing it but she would actually be snorting flour," he explained as Stacy listened flabbergasted.

"I didn't know she had turned Chantrese out too," he continued his eyes on Stacy; this was where he needed her to understand and trust him. Taking a deep breath he continued. "I left the hospital so I could break it off with Chantrese. We went to dinner and she wouldn't let me get a word in honestly. We came back here and she made me a drink. She must have put something in it because I blacked out."

Stacy's facial expression told him that she wasn't buying his story.

"I woke in the shower with a killer headache and found Chantrese in here. I know I wouldn't beat her like that. She was so high she told me everything."

Pulling his cell phone out of his pocket he pressed play on the recorder.

Stacy's head began to spin as she listened to Chantrese tell him how they were going to set him up for rape. She told him that it was Janelle's idea and she was tired of him causing problems in her career. At first they were going to just set up him for a robbery at one of the shoots but when she discovered his feelings for Stacy it all changed. Stacy could tell Chantrese was crying when she asked him why she wasn't good enough and why Stacy was so special. A smile glowed on her face as she listened to his answer.

"I have always loved Stacy and always will. She is my everything."

Chantrese explained that they drugged him with E so they could have sex. Janelle was there and beat Chantrese to a pulp.

"You started getting real hot," Chantrese's slurred. "I thought you were going to have a seizure or something and asked Janelle to help get you in the shower," the recording continued. "You know what the bitch said," Chantrese chuckled. "Let his ass die."

The tears began anew when Chantrese explained that she began to get high because she was so nervous after she managed to get him into the tub.

"The bitch thought she had me though, but I got the last laugh," she stated icily, sending a chill down Stacy's spine.

"I am sorry I keep dragging you into my problems," Stacy said once she managed to find her voice.

Riley knew she was also referring to Justin as well.

"This is not your fault Stacy," he told her as he brought her into his arms.

"I just feel like I bring you nothing but drama," she told him as she laid her head on his chest.

"Are you done yet," he asked her.

"With what?"

"This pity party, I know what I want and I want you. Janelle, Chantrese, Chad, nor anyone else will stop me," he told her with a kiss.

"What are we going to do about her," Stacy asked looking at Chantrese with great pity.

"Don't worry about her, I'll take care of her," Riley answered. Stacy broke their embrace and looked deeply into Riley's eyes. She heard the tone in his voice and knew what Riley was capable of.

"Please don't hurt her Riley," she asked him.

Riley looked away unable to make that promise and told Stacy to make sure that she didn't leave anything behind.

"Baby, please," she begged. "I know you are upset, but she is a victim too. Janelle tricked her. That could have been me."

"No, it wouldn't Stacy because you wouldn't have taken the drugs and you wouldn't set anyone up for rape," he combated.

"No I wouldn't, but I don't think Chantrese would have either if she was sober. Janelle is a user. You know Chantrese has a good heart. She saved you," Stacy reasoned. She knew that ultimately it was Riley's decision and she would stand beside her man regardless, but she felt a connection to Chantrese. Stacy wasn't high off of cocaine, but at one point she was high off Janelle.

For One Night   Elizabeth LaShaun
Modern Technology

The lights were low as they swiped across the runway. It was the fall premiere and the designer had decided on an African motif, since most of his patterns had animal prints. The runway had the audience buzzing. The designer was known as much for his eccentric runway as he was his clothing. He did not disappoint this year. The models would walk on two ten feet runways that would then intertwine into the shape of Africa. The runway was one and a half feet in depth and filled with water, which the models would tread barefoot. At periodic intervals, sand and glitter would be blown onto the runway. At the end of the walkway were fifteen feet ivory elephant tusks.

Sean created his walkway to entertain his audience, but also to demand the best in his models. Sean was a top designer and sometimes had to do casting calls for his Paris show because models were afraid. Janelle was not afraid and was happy that she had finally made it to the crest of fashion, where she belonged. Standing behind the black imported silk curtains, Janelle smiled as her mind wandered.

It had taken her a year to get here, and she didn't regret anything along the journey. She had not seen Chantrese since the night she beat her in her apartment. She had left her and Riley for dead, but she guessed they both had another life left. A month after the ordeal, Riley had returned to work, but by that time Janelle had made a name for herself and was busy working. She still thought about Stacy periodically, but she was happy in her personal life. She was seeing a bisexual woman named Kai and a heterosexual male named Jonas. "Life is definitely good," she mumbled as the coordinator shoved her towards the runway.

***

This is beautiful, Stacy thought as she settled into her seat. She had been to a few runaway shows but none as breathtaking as this one. Stacy watched as the show began with high anxiety waiting for Janelle to walk onto the runway. Scanning the audience she confirmed that Riley's featured guests were in attendance and from the look on Janelle's face and extra bounce in her stride, so did she.

***

What are they doing here, Janelle thought, seeing her mother and sisters in the second row at the premier. It was the first time she could remember them looking at her with pride in their eyes.

Janelle gave a subtle wink and put more attitude into her walk. *What is that*, she thought, as they were being handed portable televisions.

***

Riley was happy that he listened to Stacy. After Chantrese was sober, she shared with them that she had recorded the night of the botched rape. She explained that she didn't trust Janelle completely and wanted some insurance. Seeing the fear and regret in her eyes, Riley promised that he would not implicate her if she went to rehab.

"Riley, Sean is furious," Dave, his assistant said in passing. Riley couldn't help the smile on his face as he stood backstage and watched Janelle take the stage once again.

***

Janelle was on top of the world as she hit the runway again. The zebra hooded coat and leather mini skirt were made for her. Once again when she made it to her family, she gave them a subtle wink, but saw the tears and anger in their eyes. *Now what is wrong with them*, she thought trying to analyze the daggers. Coming off the stage, she saw Sean glaring at her. He almost made her fall; he grabbed her arm so hard.

"What the hell is this," Sean asked his French accent gone.

"What," Janelle asked trying hard to bite her tongue.

Instead of answering the designer simply pressed play on the recorder.

Janelle watched in horror as the video showed her place pills in a drink. It then shows her drag a person into the bathroom. Her stomach turned as the camera zoned in on her snorting the flour.

"But...Se," She attempted before Sean told her to keep watching. Hesitantly she returned her eyes to the screen and witnessed herself beating Chantrese without mercy. The recorder had volume and she could hear the smacks and moans coming from Chantrese. She grimaced when she heard Chantrese ask, "What about him?" She knew her reply and grabbed the recorder.

"This is bullshit, I was framed," she bellowed.

Sean grabbed her into one of the vacant dressing rooms and closed the door.

"Janelle are you going to sit here and tell me that's not you," he asked sickened.

"It's me, but the video was edited. Chantrese was the woman and Riley was the man I..."

For One Night   *Elizabeth LaShaun*

"Janelle please stop while you are ahead. You are lucky that it doesn't show the people's face you were drugging and attacking."

"Sir," One of Riley's assistants said while he knocked on the door. Sean quickly told him to go away. "But sir, there is an emergency. The other designers are frantic about some video."

"Janelle, I swear if this is what I think it is, your career is so fucking over you won't be able to model socks in the local pharmacy," Sean gritted before leaving the room.

Janelle knew it was the tape and was sure that was what her family was looking at as well.

Janelle looked at the table and sighed. "My life is over."

***

    Tabitha looked over the congregation and saw that the sanctuary was filled to its capacity before sitting next to her husband. Cream had his most radiant smile on his face and talked to worshippers as they passed. To the outside world he was his normal, friendly self. Tabitha knew better however, she could see the guard her husband had up. She noticed the way he looked into the worshippers eyes when he greeted them. Tabitha eyes went to the person who's attendance she had mandated, her son. *It's time*, her spirit spoke to her. Looking at her husband again, she shook her head slightly in total agreement with her soul.

"We are going to begin the meeting," Deacon Richardson stated. Tabitha stood and made her way to the pulpit. She almost laughed as she saw the look her husband gave her.

"Good evening church," she began and paused so they could return the greeting. "I called this meeting because I feel that as First Lady I have a responsibility," she continued with her eyes on her husband. "And it's not just to visit the sick or shut in or organize the church anniversary. My first obligation is always to God," she continued with her eyes blazing on her husband.

A small smile came to her lips as he shifted in his seat.

"Then my responsibility is to my family," this time her eyes landing on Chad.

She left them on him until he looked up at her. The tears welled in her eyes as they silently spoke volumes to each other. Blinking away the tears she continued, "And lastly my obligation is to you my church. I have called this meeting so I can put everything in order."

The "amen," and "preach," that came from the audience were abundant. "Church I want you all to remember a few things tonight. One is this, brother will betray brother to death and a

For One Night   Elizabeth LaShaun

father to his child," she quoted the scripture. For the first time Pastor Toplin's fear showed. "This is life and so I have no hard feelings or hatred at this," she continued and pressed play on a remote control. The congregation gasped as the projector showed Pastor Toplin receiving oral sex from countless members.

Tabitha kept her eyes on her husband as the church became alive with chatter.

"Let her finish church," Deacon Richardson stood up and spoke.

"Thank you," she directed towards the deacon before continuing. "Like I said I am not upset because I can see why women were attracted to my husband, which brings me to my second lesson. Judge not lest thou be judged, I was a prostitute as you all know," she continued her eyes scanning the congregation. "I have slept with plenty of married men in my time. My husband is very charming and was able to convince me to give him money I earned. I do not blame my husband for any of my actions however, because I was a grown woman. The bible tells us of the sins of the father with the story of David and that is one of the reason's I stand before you."

Chad watched his mother with great pride and respect as tears rolled down his face and she continued to speak.

"I have lived my life and so has Pastor Toplin," Tabitha continued. "The sins we made and will continue to make are our own. I have sat back and watched him try to make my son what he feels is the perfect man. Son you are perfect in every sense of the word. You lost a love, but not the love of your life. Your name is Chad Toplin, it is not Pastor Toplin."

Tabitha saw her husband reach his boiling point and prepare to stand.

"You will sit Cream," she stated firmly.

Slowly she watched him return to his seat.

"My lesson is that there is a season for everything and my season with Pastor Toplin and as First Lady of this church has passed. I have been seeing Trustee Johnson for some time now," once again she paused as the congregation gasped and began to chatter.

"I know that it is a sin and it is surely one I will pay for. I don't owe anyone an explanation, but I will say that I was lonely and seeking happiness, which I found. So church we've come full circle as I tell you pray for me."

Tabitha smiled as Trustee Johnson helped her down from the pulpit. They passed the first pew when her husband grabbed her

For One Night   Elizabeth LaShaun

arm. Trustee Johnson went into attack mode when she grabbed his hand, stopping him.

"Let it go, Cream," she told him with weary eyes and walked away. Making it to her son, she embraced him with all her might, cleansing both of them.

For One Night   Elizabeth LaShaun
Epilogue

Ms. Mary smiled as she stirred the greens on the stove. She had known since days after Riley and Stacy met that they would be together. She never doubted it when they went their separate ways. "God's will shall be done," she said as she checked the turkey in the oven. "Mama, what are you in here cooking," Riley asked when he entered the kitchen.

"None ya," she chuckled and hit his hand when he tried to peep into the pot.

"You know you're being selfish right," Riley laughed.

"Mr. Fashion Designer can you please go pick up Mrs. Literary Agent so she can get ready."

"Yes ma'am," Riley laughed before quickly looking into the pot.

On the way to the airport, Riley was in awe as he thought about the past year. He had started his own clothing line at the insistence of Stacy. The line was doing great. He couldn't wait to see Stacy and increased the speed of the Altima. She was a literary agent now and was flying in from a tour she had done with one of her authors. He missed her immensely and couldn't wait to get her back home.

***

The airplane was waiting for a gate for almost ten minutes. Stacy decided to read a magazine to pass time. *Oh my god, she looks just like Janelle* she thought, becoming melancholy. Janelle had committed suicide the night of the disastrous premier. Stacy shook her head sadly as she thought about her actually putting the blow dryer in the shower. Grabbing her blackberry she prepared to text Riley, but noticed she had an email. It was from Chad; he was one of her clients and was now on tour with another suspense author DK Gaston. Riley didn't have a problem with Chad being her client. He knew she loved him, but he would never let her go on tour with him, she was sure. She would never want to go either. After responding to Chad's email, she read Ms. Mary's email and was laughing so hard there were tears in her eyes. The email simply read, 'Get your butt home.'

***

"Can you please hand me that bottle," Chantrese asked the little girl in her class. She now worked at a daycare for children born addicted to drugs. Chantrese had begun working there after having her drug addicted son.

For One Night   Elizabeth LaShaun

"Trese Ray looks like he wants to crawl," Tiffany a fellow teacher joked as she entered the classroom.

Chantrese laughed and told her she thought so as well. She enjoyed spending time with the children was excited to be able to talk with an adult.

"Girl I love her hair do," Tiffany began anew showing her the magazine. Frozen with fear, Chantrese's mind began to swirl. *It can't possibly be her*, Chantrese thought looking at the model who appeared to be Janelle.

Chantrese was at the show the night Janelle committed suicide. Her therapist and counselors had told her not too but she wanted and needed closure, and had planned on talking to Janelle. Tiffany keyed on Chantrese's mood and grabbed the baby her co-worker was holding. Frantically flipping through the magazine Chantrese read the article about the model. The woman was in fact Janelle's paternal sister. The article went on to say that Chloe didn't learn about her sister until her death. Chantrese became physically sick as Chloe went on to say how great of a person Janelle was and how her sister was too good for this world. *Humph, she destroyed lives and had no regard for the effects her actions and scheming would have on people,* Chantrese thought angrily.

And you do, her mind asked her. *You have made decisions without regarding other people's feelings.* A heavy sigh escaped Chantrese's lip. She wished she had never seen the magazine, so she shouldn't have to think about her dark past. Yes, she made some decisions that she wasn't sure of, but she just wanted the drama to end. *It might not be his child*, she screamed at her irritating heart. *Yeah right. He looks just like him and you know it. Ray, boy wonder where you got that name from,* her mind laughed at her.

Before Chantrese could give her situation any more thought she was literally saved by the bell, the school bell. Yes Ray looked like Riley but she was not one hundred percent sure it was his son and there was no reason for her to get him involved in her life again.

***

Chad did not understand everything his mother was saying when she left Fellowship Baptist, but at this moment he did. They were burying his father, who was murdered from a single gunshot to the head. Chad had love for his father, but he did not love his father. During the service the words, only for a season repeatedly ran across his mind. His felt his mother squeeze his hand and looked over to see her smiling at him. Kissing her on the cheek, he continued to scan the congregation and noticed Stacy and Riley.

For One Night   Elizabeth LaShaun

He always knew he and Stacy would have a connection, but he never thought it would be a professional one. She was happy, which made him happy. A small part of him wanted to rekindle a relationship with her but the small bump in her belly and the love that shone in her eyes when she mentioned Riley let him know it would never be. Yes this was definitely the season for Chad Toplin to be happy being Chad Toplin. Looking at the mahogany coffin he had to admit that he had his mother, Stacy, but most of all his father to thank for making him the man he was today; a strong man, a wiser man.

***

Riley sat in the church feeling nothing. He was here only in support of his fiancé. Many of his friends and even Miss Mary couldn't believe that he didn't have a problem with Chad being her client. Riley couldn't lie, at first he did feel insecure about Stacy working with Chad. She had loved the man deeply at one time and he was her first. Stacy had asked him to read Chad's book and if he still felt uncomfortable she wouldn't be his agent. Riley had to admit it was a great book and understood why Stacy wanted to work with him.

Never willing to admit this to anyone, Riley had so much to thank Chad for. His mistake gave him his soon to be wife and unborn daughter. The book was a bestseller and put Stacy on the map in the literary game. Did he still have ridiculous thoughts at times, yes, he was human. But he worked with beautiful, at times naked, women all the time and his fiancé trusted him so he could do the same. *I am still watching him though*, Riley thought locking eyes with Chad. He had full trust in Stacy. Chad was a different story. He had made it through a lot, but Riley was still a young man from the ghetto that could return to his roots if need be.

THE PREREQUISITES OF PERDITION

Keith K. Williams

I dedicate the Prerequisites of Perdition to the Readers in Motion Book Club, the first book club to show me real love and support. It was through your website that I met my amazing co-authors who have become family in every sense of the word. Without YOU, there would be no Crossroads. My heart has been broken for a while. On the days when the pain of its wounds have bothered me more that usual, you all have taken turns being the ones to ease it.... I'll always love you, members old and new. Thank you.

The Prerequisites of Perdition   Keith K. Williams

PART 1
Welcome to the Morning Perk

The patrons of the Morning Perk Diner were absolutely ravenous. Some scarfed down food like savages as they kept their eyes on the time pieces on their wrists. Others gulped down piping hot coffee to burn the last remnants of sleep from over-worked, fatigued bodies. A few stuffed their mouths with sweet pastries to get the sugar rush they needed to keep them going. This was the early morning rush.

Everyone seemed to be running late except for Nash. He ate his breakfast slowly and was in no hurry to be anywhere else. He'd already called in to his office to let them know that he was running late. His mind was so preoccupied that he didn't even notice Jasmine, his waitress, as she refilled his coffee cup for the third time. Normally, such a juicy, shapely woman would have warranted a lust-filled look from him; especially the way her uniform hugged her hips. Even she was surprised that today, he paid her no mind. She almost overfilled his cup as she studied his face. His expression was anxious and his eyes never left the front door of the diner. Nash was one of her regular customers, usually friendly and flirtatious, so his behavior struck her as odd. She figured that he must have been having some sort of personal problems. She shrugged and moved on to take the breakfast order of the man in the booth behind him that seemed to have turned it into his own personal office.

While everyone else was buzzing around him, Nash felt like he was trapped in a bubble where time stubbornly stood still. The more anxious he became, the more he felt like a creep. He sat there, eating his breakfast as slow as a snail, late for work, waiting for someone to come into the diner who probably wasn't even thinking about him at all. As this realization dawned on him, he didn't know if he should be angry with himself or just feel stupid. He pushed away his plate of unfinished food and signaled for Jasmine to bring his bill. Just as he was about to stand to leave, disgruntled and frustrated, Brenda Swan walked into the diner and ordered a cup of hot chocolate with whipped cream. Finally, his wait was over.

The Prerequisites of Perdition   Keith K. Williams

"Where're the kids today?" Fats, the owner of the diner asked Brenda. He found it strange that she was alone because every morning, without fail, she always walked in to have breakfast with her two little boys as well as her pet Shih-Tzu tucked away safely in its designer bag. Fats hated her bringing the miniature mongrel into his establishment but, even though he owned the business, Brenda's husband owned the building. Nash sat back down. He went back to babysitting his cold breakfast and wondering the same thing that Fats had asked.

"They're fine," Brenda answered without really answering the question.

Fats recognized how hastily she dodged the question so he immediately dropped the subject. He was three months late on the rent so he wasn't exactly keen on angering his landlord's wife.

Nash tipped back his cup and gulped down his coffee. Even from afar he could tell that something had her on edge. Jasmine tried to pour him more coffee but he waived her off and paid his bill instead. He pretended to be interested in his food but continued to keep a keen eye on Brenda. Something was definitely wrong. Her thick, jet black hair was usually neat and perfectly styled. Now, it hung wildly and uncombed over her shoulders. This morning she hadn't bothered to straighten it. A good portion of it was draped in her face, not unlike the dark curtains of a theater. She made no effort to brush it away either, almost as if she didn't want anyone to see her face. Usually, her clothes were as neat and stylish as her hair. Her smooth, honey-colored skin was always covered in classy designer fashion and no one could mistake her for not being a woman of wealth. Today, dressed in her tight jeans and plain white T-shirt, she resembled one of the kids from the nearby college campus.

Brenda paid for her hot chocolate and slowly sipped it until it was done. Even her posture suggested that something was amiss. She sat hunched over the front counter of the diner. After the last sip, she wiped the excess cream from her mouth with her hand and wrist, no regard for her watch. From the way the diamonds reflected the early morning sunlight, it must have been worth a small fortune. It probably cost at least two year's salary for most of the other patrons of the Morning Perk. She waved goodbye to Fats and without another word to anyone else, Brenda

The Prerequisites of Perdition   Keith K. Williams

walked out. Nash immediately got up out of his seat and followed her, trying his best to remain inconspicuous.

PART 2: Pursuit

As Brenda walked ahead of him, Nash was very careful not to let her know that he was following her. Again, he found himself feeling like a creep and a stalker. He failed to fully understand why he had always been so obsessed with this woman and he was equally unsuccessful subduing the shame he felt because of it.

Brenda wouldn't have noticed if the ground collapsed behind her as she strolled along aimlessly. She was lost so deep within herself that she didn't even feel alive. Now she understood how ghosts felt as they lingered, lonely and intangible. As everyone went about their morning routine, no one even seemed to take notice of her as she wandered into Swan Park. That is, no one except for the man that followed her.

With every step Nash took behind Brenda, he felt worse and worse. He knew that following her around like a stalker was wrong on many different levels but he couldn't stop himself. He was drawn to her even though he knew that his obsession was unhealthy. Fear of discovery kept his heart racing until he followed her into the park. He relaxed once he passed through its gates and found himself under the protection of the shade provided by the towering trees. With so many people in the park enjoying the sunny, spring weather, it was unlikely that she would take notice of him. As he kept moving forward with his eyes on her, he blindly walked into a flock of geese pecking at scattered bread crumbs. The birds avoided being trampled by his feet but he nearly bumped into the man who had been feeding them. In life, there are people that you make eye contact with and realize that they are not to be trifled with. The man that Nash had almost carelessly crashed into was definitely one of those people. This man coldly stared back and made no effort to step aside. Nash decided it was best if he just went around.

As their shoulders touched, an abnormal, eerie chill swirled in the air. Nash didn't look back as he continued on his way although he felt the enigmatic stranger's eyes on his back.

The Prerequisites of Perdition   Keith K. Williams

Nash continued on his obsessive, creepy quest and as Brenda reached the opposite end of the park, a strange thing happened. Out of nowhere, without a cloud in the sky, it started to rain. Brenda covered her head with her hands and dodged a few cars as she ran across the street to the library. He watched her jog up the stairs and walk inside. He followed but then, another odd thing happened. As soon as he got to the steps, the spring sun shower suddenly stopped.

The overwhelming noise of the streets outside seemed instantly muted as he quietly let the library door shut behind him. At first, he nearly panicked because he had no idea where Brenda had gone. He decided to inquire at the main desk where one of the librarians appeared to be engaged in an intense conversation with a tall, well-dressed dread. Nash politely interrupted and explained that he was supposed to be meeting someone. He gave the librarian whose name tag read *STACY*, Brenda's description and she quickly pointed him in the right direction. She seemed incredibly annoyed and in a hurry to get back to her conversation which came across as very *un-librarian-like* on her part. They were usually polite, mild-mannered and most of all, patient. Whatever she was discussing with the man at the desk had to be something serious.

Nash walked down one of the aisles and ended up at a quiet, deserted corner of the library. He spotted Brenda as she pulled a book off of the shelves and sat down at a table to open the huge hardcover she'd selected. He walked closer as she turned to some random chapter, somewhere in the middle and literally buried her face in the pages as if the book was a pillow. With her eyes closed he felt brave enough to get closer to her. He stood behind the table where she sat and pretended to search the shelves.

This close to Brenda, what caught Nash's attention was the fragrance she wore. It added spice and flavor to the musty air that circulated feebly in the library whose windows were rarely opened. It stood out from the scent of rotting paper and old wood. He couldn't help but grin as it pleasantly reminded him of how his own mother used to smell. It caused the most pleasant memories to float to the surface of his psyche. Finally, he relaxed enough and made a very serious decision to sit down where she was. Nash didn't want to startle her so he slipped stealthily into the chair opposite her at the table.

The Prerequisites of Perdition   Keith K. Williams

Brenda appeared to be caught in the embrace of deep sleep with her face buried in the book. Her messy black hair spread across and contrasted with the off-white pages. It spread everywhere like ebony liquid that flowed freely from a dark fountain on her head. She was so still that she might have been dead or at least unconscious. In fact, as Nash pretended to read while watching her, she remained so still for so long that he became worried. Then, just as his anxiety built up to the point where he was about to tap her on the shoulder, she popped up and looked around nervously. Her dreadfully dark and bloodshot eyes still managed to burn brightly, even from behind the tears that flowed ceaselessly from them. He imagined that she must have washed away all of the ink on the pages she had been using for a pillow. Her honey brown skin seemed to glow a little less than he remembered and her nose was red from crying. She wiped the tears from her eyes and then stared at Nash with a blank expression. His heart stopped.
"Why'd you follow me here Nash?" Brenda asked. He fumbled for the right words before he spoke.
"I was worried about you. You didn't look right so I wanted to make sure you were alright," Nash explained. Brenda laughed and then spoke with a voice laced with venomous sarcasm. "You were worried about me? Really? Since when?" she asked.
"Since the first day we met," he told her, hoping that she would sense how sincere he was being.
She rolled her eyes in disgust but kept them fixed on him.
"Is that so?" she answered.
Nash recognized that nothing he could say would lessen her hostility. Today, her attitude could not, and would not be tamed so he asked the question that he had wanted to ask her since she walked into the Morning Perk Diner earlier.
"Where are the boys?" he asked her. The question seemed to hit her like a sobering slap to the face. Brenda looked away from him and bit her bottom lip to keep herself from bursting into tears again. She covered her mouth with a hand that quivered uncontrollably. Now, the concern he'd felt before multiplied tenfold. As he studied her face and the distant look in her eyes, he could tell that even though she sat right in front of him, she was lost. Nash reached out and touched her arm from across the table. This startled her and ripped her back to reality.

The Prerequisites of Perdition   Keith K. Williams

"Don't touch me!" she yelled, her voice shattering the hush of the library. Nash took his hand off of her arm.

"Where are the boys?" he asked again, this time with authority.

"What does it matter to you?" she asked in a much softer voice this time.

Again, she dodged the question she'd been avoiding since the diner. Now, Nash completely lost his patience. To avoid his eyes, she bowed her head and once again, her wild hair covered her face. Nash grabbed her by the arm again.

"I asked you a question Brenda. I suggest you answer me right now! No more games," he said. His kept a steel grip on her forearm. She raised her head slowly so she could look at him.

"A game is all this has been Nash. Go away and stay out of my life. Don't worry about what's going on with me," she told him.

"I didn't ask you anything about your life. I don't ever interfere with your life," he answered.

"Oh, so now you don't interfere in my life? Really? So what would you call the last three years of my life?" she demanded.

"Don't go there. We made a mistake three years ago. We've both been paying for it since then," he answered.

"Both of us? How have we both been paying for it Nash? I've been the one that's had to keep the secret. I've had to face it and deal with it every day," she said.

"And what do you think my life has been like?" he asked in a harsh whisper through gritted teeth.

"Don't you dare! Don't you dare compare the two! I regret that day every morning that I wake up. I lie to my husband with every breath and in every moment that I spend with him. On top of that, I do what you asked me to do every single morning. I even have to lie to my boys to keep our dirty little secret. I feel cursed," Brenda told him, pulling her arm away from him.

"You're so selfish. All I ever asked for is to be able to see my son. Do you think it's easy for me to only see him from a distance? I've watched him grow for three years and he has no idea that I'm his real father," Nash complained.

"Selfish? I'm hurting myself to please everybody! How the hell am I selfish?" she asked. She didn't take care to whisper nor was she concerned with whoever became annoyed by her raised voice.

The Prerequisites of Perdition   Keith K. Williams

"I'm not saying it's been easy for you but," Nash started to say, trying to calm her down but she cut him off mid-sentence.

"Let me tell you how easy it's been for me. Three years ago, we met in the diner on one of the worst days of my life. I'd just had the biggest fight with my husband, all because I'd taken Demetrius to see my husband's mother whom he hated. I left my son home with his father because I couldn't stand being in the house another minute. That's how you met me Nash. I was upset and vulnerable. I should have been stronger. I should have stayed home with my family," she reminded him.

"I understand. I just saw you upset and you looked like a nice person. You were so sad that it hurt to look at you. At first, all I wanted to do was ask if you were alright," he answered.

"I looked like a nice person? Are your serious? No, Nash, you liked the way I looked so you decided to be nice to me because of that," she corrected him.

"I never meant to take advantage of you, or your situation," he explained.

"All the same, look what happened? Because of that one day, that one mistake with you, I got pregnant with Douglas. Ever since then, my life has been a living nightmare," she said.

"I never meant for things to be the way they are," he told her.

"Yeah, if you say so. I explained that I was married. I regret even telling you I was pregnant after we did what we did. I don't know what I was thinking. Then you insisted on the impossible. You didn't care that the truth about you being the baby's real father could ruin my life." she said.

"I understand that but what kind of man do you think I am? Do you think I could live with myself knowing that I had a child in the world that I never saw at all? I don't think that under the circumstances I'm asking for too much," he answered.

"And so, just to keep you happy, I bring my children to that diner, every morning, just so you can look at your son. I've been doing that for you for three years," she reminded him.

"And I'm grateful for that but do you know what kind of torture that is for me? I can't talk to him, hug him or let him know that I love him. It fuckin' kills me," he said, trying his best to show her things from his perspective.

The Prerequisites of Perdition   Keith K. Williams

"It kills you? How do you think I live with the lie? I wake up every day with it. I live it. I gave up my career to have my first child because my husband is totally against abortion. I had to have your child because I couldn't have hidden an abortion from him. I didn't even have to tell you that I got pregnant. You better remember that!" she asked Nash.

"Yes, I know," Nash answered.

"Good, so don't talk to me about being selfish. I've given up too much and risked everything for everybody else. I'm the one who has to keep secrets and I'm the one who gets tortured every day by the truth. I'm the one who's sad all the time. I'm the one who doesn't remember what it's like to not be depressed," she told Nash.

At that moment, there was something in her voice that frightened him. Somewhere, hidden in her angry, hushed whisper, there was a terrible thing clawing to escape. Nash was terrified to hear what it was but he had to know exactly what she was avoiding telling him.

"Brenda, where are the boys?" he asked and waited for her to answer.

Somehow, the look on her face when he asked this time let him know that he was about to get his answer. She paused and then took a deep breath before she spoke. Her confession had finally fought its way from the recesses of her mind until it found her lips.

"This morning wasn't any different from any other morning. My husband had his coffee way before I woke up, kissed me goodbye and left for work, long before the sun came up. I told him to have a good day, went back to sleep and waited for the alarm clock to wake me again. Once I was up, I got my boys out of bed and started to get them ready for daycare and school. I put them in the tub together to take a bath. I usually stayed with them, made sure they got clean and played safe. I don't know why I left them alone. I knew it wasn't safe," she began her story. Nash's heart was racing and fear gripped him mercilessly.

"What did you do Brenda?" he asked, disturbed by the direction her story had taken. Her mannerisms were disturbing as she retold that morning's events. He watched horror creep across her face until her features contorted as if she was in pain.

"I don't know what was wrong with me. I just felt so tired. I knew that I shouldn't have left them alone in the bathroom. There was more than enough water in the tub so I don't know why I left the

The Prerequisites of Perdition   Keith K. Williams

tap running. I sat down on the couch in my living room. I couldn't see them but the house was quiet and I could hear them splashing and laughing," she continued.

Her voice was barely a whisper and all of the blood seemed to have drained from her caramel face. Her eyes were wide open but she didn't seem awake. Nash sat on the edge of the uncomfortable wooden chair and when she stopped talking, fear gripped him again.

"Brenda, what happened to the boys?" Nash asked, frightened of what her answer would be.

He gripped her arm firmly to get her talking again. She continued with her story although she still appeared to be mentally missing, lost in the memories that replayed in her mind.

"I don't know what was wrong with me. The sunlight from the window was warm on my face but the room felt dark. I sat on my couch and felt like I didn't want to move, ever again. I felt like I was too heavy to move. I wanted to just sit there forever. I was chained to my life by secrets and lies and I didn't want to be. Then, I realized that I didn't hear them," she said.

"What do you mean you didn't hear them?" Nash asked.

"I didn't hear them splashing. I didn't hear them laughing. I just sat there with my eyes closed and acted like nothing was wrong. I should have panicked when I didn't hear them. Any good mother would have panicked but I didn't. I didn't move. For a split second I wondered if they'd drowned. For a split second, I wondered if my little boys were dead. And may God forgive me, I felt free," she said.

Horrified, Nash reached across the table and grabbed Brenda by both of her shoulders.

"What have you done?" he asked.

"And then, it was like I stopped dreaming. I ran to the bathroom and I found them both standing outside of the tub, watching the water overflow, terrified that they were going to be in trouble. I turned the water off and hurried them out of the bathroom. The wet floor soaked my socks and I wanted to throw up. I almost wanted to drown myself because I knew that for a split second, I had wished my children dead. I'm a monster," she finished. She hung her head and stared at the grain of old wooden

168

The Prerequisites of Perdition   Keith K. Williams

table. She didn't want him looking into her face. Nash let go of her shoulders and slumped back in his seat.

"Where are the children?" he asked.

"I left them with my husband's mother," she answered.

"I want my son," he told her.

"What?" she asked. His request snapped her out of her trance and back to reality.

"You heard me. I can't let him stay with you if you're going to hurt him. I won't let him get hurt just because you're tired of your life," he said firmly.

"Are you out of your mind? Do you hear yourself? Do you know what you're asking?" she asked.

"I know exactly what I'm asking. And before you even ask, no, I don't care about what happens to your marriage. I only care about my son," he explained, making his position clear.

"Oh, you don't care about my marriage? Well, you should Nash," she said.

"And why should I choose to protect your miserable little marriage and risk losing my own flesh and blood?" he asked.

"Because, to threaten my marriage is the same as threatening your flesh and blood," she told him.

"No, you're worried about what your husband will do to YOU if he finds out the truth! I'm worried about my child's safety if he stays in your custody," he answered.

"You should be just as worried about my husband as I am," she warned him.

"And why is that?" he asked.

"Do you have any idea who my husband is?" she asked.

"Actually, I don't. You never wanted to tell me," Nash reminded Brenda before he locked eyes fiercely with her.

She took a deep breath before she answered.

"Nash, I'm married to Dirk Swan, as in *Swan Park* that we just walked through. My last name is Swan as in, *my husband owns this city* in one way or another," she explained to Nash.

His eyes opened wide in disbelief. That bit of information that Brenda had withheld certainly changed the dynamics of the mess he'd gotten himself into. Immediately he became angry with himself. He was also far from foolish so he understood that there was a very good reason to be alarmed. He hoped Brenda didn't notice the change in his facial expression. He quickly composed himself.

"I don't give a fuck. That doesn't change shit!" he told her.

"Nash, stop it. My husband is one of the wealthiest men in the country. He is not rich. He's wealthy. You have no idea what he's capable of. Whoever you may know, or whatever street trash may owe you loyalty because you grew up with them, cannot compare to how strong, or how far my husband's reach is," she warned Nash again.

"So what am I supposed to do, just sit back and wait until something happens to my son?" he asked.

"If my husband were to find out the truth, he'd have all three of us killed. Don't doubt me on this. I know his heart. He has the resources to have it done, the right way and by the right people. People like my husband are above the law. He would just as easily have us killed to wipe away his shame as another man might swat a fly. Do not try him. I'm trying to save us all, **our** son included," she said, bursting into tears again.

"So, what am I supposed to do?" he asked.

"Nothing, unless you want us all dead. Tomorrow, I'll make sure everything is back to normal," she said, wiping her face. Her words gave him no comfort.

"Normal? Is that what you call this?" Nash asked, getting up out of his seat. Without another word, he walked out of the library.

The Prerequisites of Perdition   Keith K. Williams

Part 3: The Ex Mrs. Swan's Song

Outside the library, Brenda hailed a taxi-cab. She got in and gave the driver her mother-in-law's address so that she could pick up her sons. The driver started the meter and she closed her eyes, hoping to get a little sleep before she got to her destination. Even though their meeting today had been filled with subtle unpleasantness, Brenda was glad that she had spoken to Nash, even if their dialogue only served to weigh his soul down with even a small portion of her burden. She definitely felt lighter. She also hoped he took heed to her warnings of how ruthless her husband was. She knew better than anyone that Dirk Swan was not to be trifled with.

Brenda's husband was the sole heir to a massive fortune left to him by his father. Dirk owned real estate in almost every part of the city. This well-known fact would make any stranger wonder why the mother of this ridiculously wealthy man would be living in one of the most decrepit parts of the city, District 19. How things had come to be the way they were was an interesting story.

***

When Dirk was five years old, his mother walked out on his father. She chose to leave him behind because her son *just didn't fit in* with her plans for living a new life. While she was gone, it was as if she fell off the face of the earth. There were no phone calls, letters or any other sign that she was even still alive. For a time, because his young mind couldn't comprehend how his mother could just abandon him completely without even a word, he actually believed that his father might have had her killed. Dirk was ten by the time his mother's *new life* collapsed on her, leaving her in the world with absolutely nothing. She had no choice but to crawl back to Dirk's father who opened his doors to her as if she had not been the one to walk out of them in the first place. Mr. Swan convinced himself that he took her back for the sake of his son. The real truth was that he still loved her. On the other hand, after she'd left, she hadn't looked back. Before she left, she called her husband weak and less than a man. Perhaps he also took her back to prove that he was more than what she thought of him. Dirk's

The Prerequisites of Perdition   Keith K. Williams

father showed infinite benevolence the day she showed up at their estate with the same suitcases she had packed and walked away with all those years before. Unfortunately, his wife wasn't home long before he realized that he had made a terrible mistake that couldn't easily be corrected. Dirk himself made no secret the contempt he held for his mother and it pained his father to see his son so miserable. His last attempt to rectify the situation was his last will and testament where he'd left everything to Dirk, along with a letter of apology.

In that letter, Mr. Swan apologized to his son for taking the boy's mother back. He admitted that a small part of his reasons for doing so was the love that he himself still had for her. Even after all that she'd done, he confessed that his heart would never have totally been rid of his weakness for her. He warned his son that real love always leaves deep scars. He also wrote that his main intention had been to give Dirk back the mother who had abandoned them both. His father explained how painful it had been to watch his only son grow up without a real mother. He admitted that he never anticipated how much more pain he had caused by allowing her back in their lives. Finally, Mr. Swan wrote that he had often wondered if it would not have been a better choice to have just re-married. In his will, he named Dirk as the sole heir to everything that had been his.

Dirk's first course of action after putting on his father's crown of wealth had been to evict his mother. At the time, he hadn't grown ruthless enough to let her starve so he bought her a cheap home in one of the low-income communities in the city. Because she had no other means to support herself, she reluctantly and painfully accepted his charity, if that's what it could be called. She found herself banished to live out the rest of her days in a slum. Brenda often accused him of being a sadist. She believed he maintained the distant, cruel relationship simply to pour salt in his mother's wounds as she was constantly reminded of being *cast out of heaven*. He found pleasure in dangling the life she could have had in front of her face.

Brenda was immediately reminded of her husband's cruelty as the taxi sped through the decaying neighborhood. Everything seemed dead or impatiently waiting for death. The main signs of life came in the form of the abundance of young children in the streets. The poor always seemed to produce more offspring than

The Prerequisites of Perdition   Keith K. Williams

the wealthy. Brenda couldn't imagine raising her sons in such a neighborhood. The criminals were grim reapers and the addicts were like dead limbs on a dying body. There was the overwhelming feeling that anything that even managed to grow there wouldn't survive for long.

***

Brenda told the taxi-driver to wait while she went to pick up her children. His expression made it clear that he wanted desperately to get out of there as soon as he could. He reluctantly agreed to wait only after she promised him a big tip. She secretly hoped that he used some of it to buy deodorant. She hadn't realized just how bad he smelled until she stepped out of the taxi. She didn't know how she hadn't noticed it before but it was refreshing to inhale even the polluted air instead of the cabby's overwhelming body odor.

Brenda pushed open the rusty gate in front of the dirty brown house. She carefully walked up the crumbling brick stairs until she got to the front door. The doorbell dangled from its base and was only supported by its exposed wires. She was sure it didn't work so she banged on the heavy, metal front door instead. Before long, her mother-in-law appeared at the front window and peeked through the curtains.

"Hello Brenda," her mother-in-law greeted her as she opened up the front door.

Somehow, even with her years showing in the age lines and crow's feet that marred her appearance, her beauty wasn't diminished. In her youth, when life had been more kind to her, it was undeniable that she must have been comparable to a goddess among women. Even now, if you stared into her deep blue eyes, you'd feel as if you could drown in the depths of the deepest ocean. Only a single, majestic streak of gray stood out against the golden, blonde hair that fell past her shoulders and almost to her waist. Brenda always thought that the woman resembled what a fairy-tale princess would look like, long after the *happily ever after* ending of the story. It seemed absolutely surreal for this white woman to be living in this part of town, a place where Blacks and Hispanics were usually condemned to live their entire lives as prisoners of poverty.

"Hi Mrs. Swan," Brenda answered.

The Prerequisites of Perdition   Keith K. Williams

"I keep telling you to call me Emily sweetie. My married name still makes me cringe when I hear it. Besides, you're more than welcome to the title," Emily told her.

"Of course. I'm sorry Emily. Anyway, I'm here to get the boys. Are they ready?" Brenda asked.

"Well, there was a problem. Something happened today," Emily explained, nervously rubbing her hands together.

"What's wrong? What happened?" Brenda asked. She noticed that the children's grandmother rubbed her hands together until her knuckles were white.

"Demetrius is fine but little Douglas got hurt today," Emily answered.

"Oh my God, what happened to little Dougie?" Brenda asked, frantically.

"Well, I only left them alone for a second. I left them in the backyard playing while I came inside to answer my phone. I heard Demetrius shouting so I ran out to see what happened. When I got outside, Demetrius was holding little Douglas in his arms and there was blood everywhere," Emily explained.

"Blood? Oh my God! What happened to my baby?" Brenda asked, grabbing Emily's hands in her own as tears started streaming down the boys' grandmother's face.

"They were playing and little Douglas sliced his thigh open on a jagged piece of sheet metal. I'm so sorry. I was only gone for a second," Emily sobbed.

"Where is he?" Brenda asked.

"I called an ambulance. I couldn't get you on the phone so I called Dirk to meet us at the hospital," she answered.

"Is Dougie alright?" Brenda asked, letting go of Emily's hands. Now, Emily was sobbing so hard that Brenda could barely understand her.

"I don't know. I don't know. As soon as Dirk got to the hospital he sent me away. He was furious. He wouldn't even look at me," Emily answered. Brenda turned away and ran back down the crumbling stairs.

"I have to find my boys," Brenda shouted as she flew through the rusty gate.

"I'm sorry!" Emily called out to her as Brenda jumped back in the taxi.

PART 4:
Observations, Speculations & Revelations

"I'm just glad that he's okay. I hope there isn't any permanent damage," Brenda said as she flopped down on the couch, exhausted. She found it unnerving that she sat in the same place where earlier, she'd almost let the son that she was now so worried about die in the bathtub. After racing frantically to the hospital, only to discover that her boys were not there, she was relieved to find them safe at home.

"Dr. Griffin said it looked much worse than it really was. By the way, why were the boys at my *wonderful* mother's house in the first place, if you don't mind me asking?" Dirk asked from behind the bar in the enormous living room. "I mean, I'm in the middle of an important meeting when I get a frantic phone call from this woman I don't even speak to."

Brenda leaned her head back to look behind her. From an upside-down viewpoint, she watched him put ice in two shot glasses as he prepared to make two drinks.

"I needed a break," Brenda answered, trying her best not to appear nervous. More than anyone else in the world, she knew how shrewd and cunning her husband was. The hairs on the back of her neck stood up.

"If you needed a break, why didn't you just leave them with Helga? That's what I pay her for," Dirk questioned his wife. He grimaced as he drank both of the drinks he'd poured and immediately started to mix two more.

"Because your mother hadn't seen the boys in a while and I figured she would be happy to see them," Brenda answered, secretly praying that he wouldn't pry further.

"Yeah, that makes sense since my mother has such *awesome* maternal instincts. Of course," he said.

His voice was laced with sly malice and Brenda imagined that she could feel the poison of it coursing through her veins.

"Dirk, I don't think that's fair," she replied.

His strained relationship with his mother was one of the things they always argued about. Brenda never understood why he wouldn't just let the past go. She thought it was cruel for him to

The Prerequisites of Perdition   Keith K. Williams

torture and torment the woman until the end of her days. Often, she'd found herself wondering what kind of man she'd married.

"Oh my love, I'm pretty sure I know what I'm talking about," Dirk answered.

"Don't you think you've done enough to that woman?" Brenda asked.

"Actually, no. In fact, I've done *to her* almost exactly what she's done *for me*, absolutely nothing!" he said.

"All I'm saying is that maybe it's time you had a conversation about what happened and why she might have left. We don't always understand the things our parents did in their past until they explain themselves," she said, trying to reason with him.

Secretly, Brenda also hoped that the spotlight would be taken off of her and her strange behavior that day. It was better for her if her husband's thoughts were turned to his feelings towards his mother.

"Why? Nothing she could say would change my feelings about the whole nasty business of what she did or how she did it," he answered. He tossed back both of the drinks he'd poured. Brenda heard the ice clang in the glasses and knew that she was about to be in for an *interesting* night.

"You men will never understand what it's like being a mother. You assume that we're just supposed to be naturally good at it. Motherhood is harder than you think. Parenthood is complicated for us too," she sighed.

"Speaking of parenthood, have you ever noticed anything different about our little Douglas?" Dirk asked.

"Different? How? What do you mean, *different?*" Brenda asked. Dirk came from behind the bar with two fresh drinks in his hand. He didn't sit down next to his wife even though he handed her one of the shot glasses of liquor as he passed her. Instead, he sat in the plush recliner directly in front of her, on the opposite side of the coffee table. He put his glass down and fumbled in his sport coat pocket for a cigar. He reached forward and pulled the ashtray close to him before he lit the cigar and answered her. He inhaled deeply, causing the end of it to glow bright orange.

"Well, for one thing, he's much darker than Demetrius," Dirk began. Smoke from the cigar escaped his lips, mixed with his words and created the illusion that his insides were on fire. It was unnerving to look at.

The Prerequisites of Perdition   Keith K. Williams

"And? You're a white man and I'm a black woman. That does happen you know?" she answered, annoyed and terrified of where Dirk was probably going with this. He smiled before he took his second pull from the expensive cigar he'd just lit.

"Hmm," was Dirk's response as he sent a cloud of cigar smoke tumbling towards his wife.

At first he fixed his eyes on the vaporous nicotine as it filled the air between them. It gave the appearance that a storm was brewing in the room. Then, he fixed his cold gaze on Brenda.

"What the hell is that supposed to mean? My mother was a light-skinned black woman. She was even lighter than I am. My father was as black as coal. So, it stands to reason that our *mixed-race* children could have totally different complexions. Doesn't it?" Brenda asked matter-of-factly.

"I guess it does. But, I still find it strange," Dirk said, leaning forward to pick his shot glass up off of the coffee table. Now, he studied Brenda's body language while the liquor burned his throat and the intensity of his gaze burned her skin.

"Where is all of this coming from anyway? Is it because you saw your mother today?" Brenda asked. She took a sip of the drink he had given her. She fidgeted nervously on the couch while her husband watched her every move. Unlike his mother, Dirk's hair was as dark as black ink, something he definitely inherited from his father. Brenda had even found the resemblance between the two men uncanny. An enormous picture of a young Mr. Swan hung in Dirk's study and the only thing that distinguished father from son was that Dirk opted not to wear the thick moustache as his father had. Otherwise, they could have almost been twins. Brenda thought that her husband's father closely resembled George Orwell's *Big Brother* from his classic novel, "1984." At that moment, the one trait that the two men did not share helped to make Brenda incredibly uncomfortable. Her husband had the same deep, blue, powerful eyes as his mother. She knew that as he smoked his cigar, those eyes attempted to peel back the layers of her soul. Her skin crawled while her guilty conscience wrestled with her tongue to keep certain details hidden. To slip now would lead to disastrous results.

"Well, I guess I would say that it's the strangeness of today. Everything seemed, well, I guess, just out-of-place," he answered.

The Prerequisites of Perdition   Keith K. Williams

"Out-of-place? How so?" Brenda asked, trying to avoid his eyes as she stared at the ice cubes in her glass. They floated smoothly in the brown cognac like icebergs in a polluted ocean.

"Well, first you took the kids and left them with my mother instead of taking them to school. Then, I get a phone call from my mother saying that she's at the hospital and that one of my children has lost a lot of blood. Then, in total confusion I rush to the hospital while wondering why my wife isn't answering her phone. I get to the hospital and something even stranger happens when I try to give blood to my own son," Dirk continued before he took another pull from his cigar. It was so quiet in the room that Brenda heard it crackle as he inhaled.

"I still don't see where you're going with this," she lied. She knew exactly where he was going and the panic was written all over her as plainly as if it had been a tattoo. Dirk smiled, pleased with himself. Again, he sent a cloud of cigar smoke floating in his wife's direction.

"Do you know how I've managed to hold onto my fortune when most rich kids would have frivolously pissed away everything they'd been given?" Dirk asked, tapping his cigar on the edge of the ashtray, causing grey ash to crumble from the end of it.

"No, but I'm sure you're about to tell me," Brenda answered. She pouted and prepared for the psychological assault that she knew was coming. Her husband never asked a straight question and rarely gave a straight answer. It disgusted her how much he enjoyed toying with people. She finished her drink and banged her glass on the coffee table out of anger and frustration. She was trapped and there was no escape.

"I've actually expanded and quadrupled what my father left me. Know why?" Dirk asked.

"Because you're sooooo smart," she answered sarcastically, folding her arms and looking away from him.

"Actually, I'm a little bit more than just *smart*. From where I'm standing, I'm actually not much different than Superman," he began to explain, extinguishing his cigar in his glass of liquor instead of using the ashtray. The hissing sound unnerved her. Brenda felt like a cobra waiting to strike, and not a man, sat on the other side of the coffee table.

"Oh really? Now it all makes sense to me," she answered and slapped herself on the forehead as if she'd just stumbled upon

The Prerequisites of Perdition   Keith K. Williams

an obvious truth. She shook her head and chuckled nervously. They both knew that her laugh was hollow. She was afraid and well aware that there was no humor in her current predicament.

"Don't laugh. I'm very serious. Let me explain," he told her, getting up from the recliner. Dirk walked to the window, closed the blinds, and the curtains. Brenda's heart began to pound in her chest. He walked over to the lamp in the corner and turned it off. A sliver of moonlight still forced its way into the room through the thin gap in the curtains but it was not enough to conquer the sudden absence of light. Brenda began to wonder exactly how much her husband knew and more importantly, what he was going to do in the next few moments.

"By all means, please explain it to me. I can't wait to hear this," she said. He loosened up his necktie and walked towards her. Even in the gloom, she could see the wide sinister grin on his face as he walked over to her.

"Aww, c'mon honey. With all this power, how am I NOT Superman?" Dirk asked, throwing both of his arms up in the air like a referee signaling a touchdown in the NFL. He flopped down on the couch and tried to put his arm around her *affectionately*. His hug was anything but gentle.

"Do you hear yourself? How many drinks have you had exactly? Now I can see why your father hated that damn comic book collection of yours," she said, sliding further down the couch in order to escape his *loving* embrace.

"Of course I have powers. In fact, I have the same ones as Superman," he told her.

"How so?" she asked nervously. Her face was still turned away from his so he grabbed her chin firmly and forced her to look at him before he spoke again. He pulled her face close enough to his that she could smell the liquor on his breath.

"For example, right now, I'm using my x-ray vision to see right...through...you. You might as well be invisible. Without even asking you the questions I really want to ask, your body language is telling me everything. I can see it all, from the hairs standing up on the back of your neck to the goose bumps that rose up on your beautiful, honey-brown skin," he said as he ran his finger delicately across her cheek. "I saw how you tensed up when I asked about Douglas. I noticed how you panicked inside when I mentioned *his* blood and mine in the same sentence."

The Prerequisites of Perdition   Keith K. Williams

"So, what am I supposed to be so afraid of Dirk? What have you said to make me panic?" Brenda asked, roughly pulling his hand from her chin.
"Oh, my love, it's not anything I've said, yet. What has you on edge is the chill of my voice. You know exactly where this is going. And, you and I both know that right now, I should be spitting flames in your direction. Instead, my coolness petrifies you," he told her before blowing her a kiss. Brenda couldn't take it anymore. She got up off the couch, walked to the window and pulled the curtains open. The moon was still high in the sky but now it was hidden behind dark clouds.
"Why don't you just say what's on your mind? Why do we ALWAYS have to do this?" she asked, folding her arms in a desperate attempt feel some small sense of safety. She knew that her husband certainly wasn't going to comfort her.
"Because, if I did things any other way, I'd die from boredom," he answered flippantly. That described exactly who Dirk was. He was the guy that ripped the wings off of flies and watched them die. That was the part of him that frightened her and killed her love for him slowly over time. The kindness he faked was a mask. This grim, malevolent spirit was who he really was. It was who he had always been. That was the truth that had tormented her no matter how hard she tried to ignore it. That was why she had slept with Nash that day, three years before. Brenda had wanted to tarnish the false reflection of her marriage so that she could never be fooled by the lie it had become, ever again.
"No, you do things the way you do because you're cruel," she responded.
"Maybe, but realistically speaking, don't you think Superman would have been cruel as well with all of that power? How could he NOT be? In fact, I believe he was a very cruel being. For example, don't you think it was sadistic for him to even put on the guise of Clark Kent? I mean, I know most people would say that he only wanted to feel a little less alone by pretending to be normal but I don't buy that theory. If he really was as much the hero that everyone believes, wouldn't he have wanted to spend ALL of his time helping humanity instead of treating the fate of the world like a part-time job? I have a completely different theory. I believe that inside the hero that we all know and love, there was a darker side in plain sight that everyone chose to overlook. I think he was

The Prerequisites of Perdition   Keith K. Williams

intoxicated from the sense of satisfaction he got from hiding himself among normal people, watching them suffer, knowing that they needed him to save them. I believe Superman was a sadistic voyeur with a hero complex," Dirk explained to Brenda in a creepy, lifeless, monotone voice.

"That's just sick and demented. That's like saying Santa Claus was a burglar who liked to break into people's houses on Christmas Eve," she answered, continuing to look out of the window to avoid looking at him.

"Maybe, but that's how I see it. Now, I'll move on to the part of my Superman comparison/analysis as it relates to our little life. Now, I know I'm the resident comic book expert here but, do you remember what the Man of Steel's one weakness was? That was an easy question by the way. It's fairly common knowledge," he said and waited for her response.

"Kryptonite?" Brenda asked, even though she was sure of the answer. She didn't want to play along with him any more but at the moment, she was absolutely sure that it was dangerous not to.

"Yes, Kryptonite. But, I see it differently too. I think he had two weaknesses," he said.

"Really? Pray tell, what was the other?" Brenda asked.

"Lois Lane!" Dirk answered, raising his pointer finger high in the air. "Aside from his sadistic voyeurism, she was part of the reason why he chose to pretend to be Clark Kent. She made him want to be weak like normal people. I remember that in one of the movies, he even gave up being Superman to be with her," he said.

"That's what love will do," she sighed, remembering a time when she believed Dirk was her own, real-life superhero.

"True, but do you remember that at first, Lois Lane wasn't even interested in Clark Kent at all? However, she immediately fell in love with Superman from the very first time she saw him. Know why? It was because she was attracted to all that power! She only lusted for Clark Kent AFTER she figured out that he was really Superman. And you know what? For a long time, I though you were my Lois Lane," he told his wife. Now, Brenda turned around to face him.

"And here I was thinking that I was just your black girl fantasy all these years," she answered. Dirk laughed out loud at her *assumption.*

The Prerequisites of Perdition   Keith K. Williams

"Did it ever occur to you that, because of my mother's past, detestable indiscretions, I chose a woman as different from her as I could find? But, sadly it seems my father and I were both cursed to love the wrong women because here I am, standing in his shoes, like he left them for me as part of my inheritance," he said.

"Don't you dare compare me to your mother! I'm still here and I haven't left you!" Brenda yelled.

"No, you haven't but you have deceived me in the worst possible way. You've wounded me as deeply as if you had," he told her.

"Dirk," she said. Brenda started to walk towards him but he put his hand up and stopped her. She might as well have been rooted in place as she dared not move a step closer.

"I don't have to wait for the results of the paternity test I took to get the truth I'm looking for. I already have my answer," he solemnly declared.

"Dirk, let me explain," Brenda pleaded but again, he put his hand up and silenced her.

"Surprisingly, I'm not as angry as I should be. Of course, I'm sure that our little Douglas's real father is nowhere close to being a man of any significant power or influence. Basically, he's probably very normal. Otherwise, you would have probably left me for him already," he said, putting his hand to his forehead as if he was in pain.

"Is that what you think of me?" Brenda asked.

"I must say, I'm actually intrigued and excited that Clark Kent, and NOT Superman won Lois Lane's heart in our little slice of reality. Still, I'm a little conflicted and confused. I was sure that you were my Lois Lane. Now, I'm thinking that you might just be my Kryptonite," Dirk said before he got up and left the room without another word. Brenda was left standing alone in the moonlight with her secrets stripped away, feeling as naked as a newborn child.

PART 5: He Knows

Half a pack's worth of stepped-on cigarette butts lay at Nash's feet as he chain-smoked in front of the Morning Perk Diner's entrance. This morning, he didn't bother with the charade of pretending to eat breakfast inside. He was so anxious that there was no way that he would have been able to sit still. The bags under his eyes and the liquor that lingered on his breath were evidence of the drunken night he'd had. His crushed jeans and wrinkled short-sleeve shirt told the story of a man who had slept in his clothes. The night before, he'd been haunted by thoughts of Brenda and the son they secretly shared. As he stood there in the blinding sun, he was tormented by random thoughts and worries as he waited for them. He had no way to contact her discreetly without putting their secret out in the open. For now, his hands were tied. Nash coughed heavily as he lit another cigarette. Despite nearly drowning himself in alcohol, he'd decided on his next course of action with a surprisingly sober mind. He was concrete in his resolve. On that day, no matter what, his son was going to know who his real father was.

Everyone on the street noticed the black Bentley with the limousine tint as it pulled up and double-parked outside of the diner. It wasn't common for a vehicle of that caliber or class to just cruise through a blue-collar, working class neighborhood. Out of everyone, Nash paid it the most attention as he remembered who Brenda said her husband was. His heart stopped beating and the cigarette fell out of his mouth when the passenger side window began to roll down slowly. After expecting to be showered with a hail of gunfire, he relaxed slightly when he saw that the driver was Brenda. She waved frantically and beckoned for him to come over to the car. He looked up and down the street tentatively before he dared to walk over.

"Get in," she told him as he leaned down to look inside the car.

"Where are the kids?" Nash asked, noticing that the back seat was empty.

"We don't have much time. Get in. We have to talk, NOW!" she ordered him, nervously checking the side-view mirror first and then

The Prerequisites of Perdition   Keith K. Williams

the rear-view mirror after. Without questioning her, Nash got in the car. Somehow, he knew that he should do as she said. As soon as he was in the passenger seat, Brenda pulled off and sped down the street before his door was even shut properly. Nash quickly buckled his seat belt as she exceeded the speed limit recklessly and changed lanes erratically as if she was in a high-speed chase, constantly checking her mirrors. It was obvious that she was terrified or paranoid about being followed.

Aside from the insane way she was driving, Brenda seemed more like herself today. She had abandoned the grunge look and was back to displaying her high-class fashion sense. She definitely looked like she belonged behind the wheel of the four hundred thousand dollar car. The sunlight bounced brilliantly off of her diamond jewelry as it poured in through the windshield. However, hidden behind her designer sunglasses, Nash couldn't see that her eyes were red from crying. He kept quiet at first with his stomach in knots as she took risk after risk to weave in-between cars and traffic. Only after she stopped at a red light that would have been too dangerous to run through did he dare break the awkward silence.

"Where are the boys?" he asked again.

"They're in school," she answered.

"Why didn't you bring them with you today? I wanted to see them," he inquired. Because of the story she'd told him the previous day, Nash was worried for their safety.

"I couldn't," she answered as the traffic light turned green and she floored the gas pedal again.

"Why not?" he asked, grabbing her by the arm.

A frightening possibility dawned on him. He wondered if Brenda was running from the police and if that was the case, he shuddered to think what heinous act she might have committed. Only a day before, she had been willing to let her children drown in the bathtub.

"Because he knows," she answered, quickly pulling away from him.

"Who knows what?" he asked.

"Who else? My husband. He knows that Douglas is not his" she answered.

"How?" Nash asked. He was relieved that the news was not as evil as he'd expected but, he had a feeling that this new twist in the plot wasn't going to play out much better.

The Prerequisites of Perdition   Keith K. Williams

"It doesn't matter. He just does," she told him.

"So what now?" he asked, looking away from her.

He didn't dare look at the streets in front of them for fear of throwing up. Instead, he stared up at the few clouds that graced the clear blue sky. Even elevated up to incredible heights in the lofty breeze, they didn't seem to move, almost as if the heavens themselves paused to witness the unfortunate events that were certain to follow.

"What now? What now is that I'm sure I won't be able to go anywhere without being followed," she explained.

"Followed? Followed by who?" he asked, turning to look out of the rear window of the car again.

"Followed by whoever my husband chooses to pay to follow me. After what he knows, you think he'll ever trust me again? No, not likely. The only reason he even let me come to the diner at all this morning was for me to give you a message," she said.

"And what message is that?" Nash asked.

"My husband wants me to tell you to go away. He said that you took something important from him and so he's going to take something important from you. This is the last time you're going to see me and you'll never see Douglas again," she told him, relaying her husband's message.

"So, if he's the one who sent you to see me and he already knows where you were going this morning, why are you speeding through the streets like a maniac to get away from whoever you think is following us?" he asked, checking the side-view-mirror.

"Because, fuck him! I don't appreciate being followed by his flunkies," she exclaimed.

"What about the rest of it?" he asked.

"What of it?" she asked in a tone that expressed how ridiculous she thought his question was.

"You really mean to never let me see my son again?" he asked in disbelief.

"You really think my husband was joking?" she asked.

"I don't give a fuck what he said!" Nash yelled.

"Well you should, because if we do anything other than what he said, he'll kill us all," she warned. "And that includes our son."

"He can't do that," he started to say.

"And why not? You act like I didn't explain to you who my husband is. With his money, he can do whatever he wants, and get away with it. You know why? Because he can afford the people who will do the job right. He can afford to pay off whoever he needs to pay off. Make no mistake Nash. This is his city and we are trapped in the middle of it," she told him.

"He can't keep my son from me. I'll kill him," he raged. Brenda laughed so hard that he wanted to slap her face.

"You can try but you won't be able to," she said.

"I know people too. I can get him touched," Nash threatened. Again, Brenda laughed out loud at how naive he sounded.

"Are you serious? Do you really think that my husband can be dealt with like any common street thug? You may not know, but I know enough for both of us. I've heard things. I've seen things. I know the types of monsters my husband has at his disposal for the unpleasant things he does from time to time," she said.

"Are you trying to tell me that *Dirk Swan* is some kind of criminal kingpin?" Nash asked, clearly feeling that she was blowing things way out of proportion.

"Not at all. He's worse. What I've been trying to explain to you is that my husband IS money. And that goes hand-in-hand with the fact that he IS power. All of his businesses are legitimate and legal. That doesn't stop him from keeping ties to unsavory individuals. Of course, he doesn't have to. I think he does it for the thrills and just because he can. Even the criminals respect and fear him. A man with money is a dangerous thing," she said.

Nash leaned back in the passenger seat and held his head in his hands as it pounded painfully. He wasn't sure if it his hangover was to blame or the things that Brenda had just told him. His migraine made him feel as if his brain was going to swell and crack his skull open.

"I can't believe this is happening," he said.

"Well, believe it," Brenda told him as she pulled into the Lakeshore Movie Theatre parking lot. She drove into an empty parking space and turned off the car's engine. She took off her sunglasses to see him clearly as tears streamed from beneath the hands he used to cover his face. She knew that he loved the son they shared.

For so long she had been so angry with her own circumstances that she'd never considered how difficult the situation must have been for him. Only being able to see his child from a distance, as a stranger, had taken its toll on him. Now that he faced the possibility of never seeing his son ever again, it was

The Prerequisites of Perdition   Keith K. Williams

too much for him to bear. Every time thoughts of Nash had ever floated into her mind, Brenda had always classified him as just another mistake in her life. Now, for the first time, she viewed him as a decent man. If things had been different, she was sure that he would have been a good father.

"There has to be another way," he said to her, finally lowering his hands. The look on his face nearly broke her heart. She hadn't realized how much her second son looked like his real father until that moment. His pain immediately became her pain. It almost felt as if she stared at her own child as a grown man through a looking glass that showed the future. Still, she gave Nash the only answer that made sense.

"There is no other way. This is how it is and how it has to be," she told him. She looked away from him and there was a long silence between them.

"I wish we'd never met that day," he said. His words seemed harsh but they were heartfelt and true. Brenda's silence after he spoke them suggested that she completely felt the same way. There was nothing they could do about it now and there really wasn't anything more that she could tell him. They were cursed and damned it seemed. Brenda sighed and started the car's engine.

"I'll take you back to the diner now," she offered.

"No thanks, I'm good. I'll find my own way back," he answered and then paused. "You know, I never met my father. I swore that I would never do that to my kids and here I am," Nash said, opening the car door and getting out.

Brenda watched him walk away. He looked like a man who'd just had everything taken from him. The man himself was the product of an entire generation of fatherless boys and it tortured him to know that he would have to abandon his own. It saddened her but she knew that this was the best thing for everyone involved. She remembered the look in Dirk's eyes when he had given her his deadly ultimatum. His speech had been completely cold, ruthless and most importantly, sincere.

Still, as she started to drive away, a tiny spirit of rebellion began to build in her heart. Her mind began to work on overdrive as a dangerous idea dawned on her. She pulled the Bentley up to Nash and beckoned for him to come over to her window. As he walked over, she reached into the backseat for her designer clutch. She fumbled in it until she eventually found a pen to write with.

The Prerequisites of Perdition   Keith K. Williams

The only paper she found was a faded receipt for some expensive trinket she'd bought and long since forgotten.

"What is it? Nash asked, annoyed and disgruntled. The pain in his head had spread to his neck now. He felt like he was being compressed by the weight of the insane situation he now found himself in.

"I have an idea. There may be a way for you to still see our son. There might be one person in the world who won't be afraid to help us," she explained quickly. On the back of the thin paper of the receipt, she scribbled an address and a time.

"What's this?" Nash asked as she handed it to him.

"Be at this address in two days, at that time. Don't drive your car because they probably know it by now. Take a cab instead. I'll figure out something by then," she told him.

"Thank you," Nash said. Brenda didn't answer. She rolled her window up and sped away.

The Prerequisites of Perdition   Keith K. Williams

PART 6: Fork in the Road

As Brenda drove away, she thought about the morning that had changed her life forever, just a little over three years ago. She wondered how different things might have been if she had stayed home with her husband instead of storming out of their home in anger. She thought about all the grief she could have saved herself if she'd just gone for a long drive to clear her mind instead. She might have avoided so much pain if she had just ordered breakfast from a fast food drive-thru.

Brenda had gone to the Morning Perk that day because she longed for somewhere familiar. It had been the place she'd had breakfast almost every morning when she'd been in college. She was drawn there that day because it was the closest thing to a second home in the city where her husband seemed to be a god. The argument that had prompted her to storm out of her home was about much more than just her decision to take their son to see his paternal grandmother against her husband's wishes. It had simply been the catalyst for the confrontation and although it was also the focal point of the shouting match, the real *issues* ran much deeper than that. For a long time, Brenda had been second-guessing the life she'd found herself swept up in. At times, she felt like a leaf in a hurricane, only kept aloft until the wind stopped blowing. Every day that passed, she felt more and more lost in the world. She blamed it all on her marriage to a man that she'd slowly begun to realize she didn't know. Although she held her tongue, she had seen and heard things that troubled her. He always treated her with the tenderness but, some of the things he'd been rumored to do were borderline monstrous.

***

Not long after she'd graduated from college, she met Dirk Swan. He'd held the door for her as she entered an office building where she was scheduled to have her first job interview. She remembered him as dashing, polite and handsome which helped to slightly remove some of the butterflies from her tummy. She blushed when he smiled at her, thanked him and tried to remain calm as she signed in at the security desk. Dirk was still smiling at her when the guard directed her to the elevators. Her day did not improve

The Prerequisites of Perdition   Keith K. Williams

unfortunately. After much stuttering, sweating and fumbling for answers, she knew that the interview had not gone well. A horrible feeling twisted in her stomach as she got off the elevator and walked into the building's main lobby. She was in a hurry to get back to her tiny apartment before her roommates got home so she could cry alone.

To her surprise, she found Dirk patiently waiting to hold the door for her again as she left. (Eventually, she would find out that he owned the entire building and had instructed security to let him know when she was on her way back down.) She thanked him again as she stepped outside, fighting tears while trying to hail a taxi-cab. That's when he put his hand on her shoulder and offered her a ride instead. Although hesitant at first, she eventually agreed. She was in shock when Dirk's driver pulled his car up front as soon as he raised his hand. As Dirk opened the door for her to get inside, she got the feeling that he had been completely certain that she would accept his offer. Brenda found that level of confidence overwhelmingly sexy. It also helped that he was *movie-star* handsome as well.

Within a month, Dirk and Brenda had fallen in love and found themselves married in what seemed like the blink of an eye. No other man in her life had ever made her feel more like a princess in a fairy tale. Because Dirk was white, she hadn't told her parents about their relationship until after the wedding, a decision she would come to regret dearly. It had been her secrecy and not Dirk's race that had wounded her family most deeply. In the end, it caused them to shun her and she hadn't been in contact with them since.

As is the case with all fairytales, there eventually comes the time beyond the climax and the last page is read. Usually, after the *"and they lived happily ever after"* line, nothing else is said, leaving the details of the ever after a mystery. That was the confusing place that Brenda found herself. It was in those uncharted waters that she discovered the storm of doubt that was causing her inner turmoil. A portion of the fascination, the fiery lust and the element of pleasant surprises were gone. She was married. She had a child. It was a horrible time to discover that she really didn't know who her husband was.

The argument had started because Brenda had taken their newborn son, Demetrius, to see her husband's mother for the first

The Prerequisites of Perdition   Keith K. Williams

time. It was also the first time she'd met her mother-in-law. Dirk hadn't had contact with his mother for years and he remained tight-lipped about the cause. In fact, Brenda had to do a great deal of detective work on her own to even find the woman. Eventually, it was Helga, the Swan's long-time housekeeper who had aided in the search. She always had a special relationship with Dirk's mother and had secretly stayed in contact with her over the years. Although her mother-in-law was overjoyed to meet her new grandchild and daughter-in-law, she refused to shed any light on the non-existent relationship with her Dirk.

When she arrived at the woman's home, she couldn't understand why her husband's mother lived in a slum, apparently abandoned and forgotten. Frustrated, Brenda finally pressed her husband for answers instead. To her shock and dismay, the man she'd barely heard raise his voice the entire time they'd been together suddenly flew into a rage. He'd even gone as far as to raise his hand to slap her; something she thought she'd escaped by not dating any more men from where she was from. No matter how she yelled, begged or tried to reason with him, he told her nothing. That part of his life remained a mystery and reality began to heavily outweigh the fantasy that had seized her heart, once upon a time. It only added to her suspicions that he was keeping more dark secrets that she was doubtful she could stomach. It hurt that she had willingly, deeply wounded her own family for the sake of the dream she had been living. She loved her husband because he was nothing like any other man she had ever met but she wondered if that was enough to justify their hasty marriage. On top of everything else, she'd brought a child into the world and unfairly doomed him to be caught in the middle of it all. It wasn't a situation that she could easily walk away from. She had become a caged songbird.

***

That's exactly where Brenda's head was as she slowly sipped the last of the hot chocolate in her mug at the Morning Perk. Before she knew it, tears wet her lush eyelashes and streamed down her soft cheeks. She covered her face and became lost behind the darkness of her own hands. By the time she'd composed herself, Nash was sitting at her table with a friendly offering of a fresh cup of hot chocolate.

"I like my hot chocolate with whipped cream," she sniffled and tried to smile.

The Prerequisites of Perdition   Keith K. Williams

"Sorry," he answered, playfully apologetic.

"I'm just kidding. Thanks," she answered. He winked at her to let her know that she was welcome.

To Brenda, Nash wasn't particularly handsome. In fact, she found him quite plain except for the light in his eyes and the warmth in his smile. It complemented his dark brown skin which seemed so strange to her because she'd grown accustomed to only paying attention to the pale, distinguished charm of her husband's face.

"I know it's none of my business but, you wanna talk about whatever's got you all upset?" he asked.

"No," she answered dryly. Mentally, she reminded herself that she was a married woman and no longer an adventurous college student.

"Ok, since you don't want to talk, how about I talk until I make you smile?" he asked.

"Fine, suit yourself," she answered. "But, you look like the sort of man who has things to do. Shouldn't you be on your way to work or something?"

"Not today. It's my day off. I'm just here out of habit. Well, habit plus the fact that I would probably burn my kitchen down if I tried to make my own breakfast," he told her.

For almost three hours they sat in the diner and spoke about nothing and everything. Brenda was pleasantly surprised by how charming Nash was. He never seemed to flirt. If he did, it was very subtle and easily interpreted as him just being friendly. She found his mellow vibe hypnotic. As he spoke to her, the world around them fell away and she felt as if they were alone, even in the middle of the hustle and bustle of the busy diner. She found herself glued in place because without being forceful or aggressive, his presence was just that strong. Subconsciously, she covered her wedding band with her right hand. That's when a dangerous thought crept into her mind. Somehow, without the flash or the money, Nash was beginning to have just as strong an impact on her as Dirk had when she first met him, on the morning of her first job interview. She began to wonder if she really had been blinded by the glamour and the glitz. Brenda contemplated what would have happened if she'd met Nash first and gotten lost in the honesty of his dark brown eyes, instead of being dazzled by the brilliance of Dirk's bright blue gaze. In her mind, her family as well as society

The Prerequisites of Perdition   Keith K. Williams

would certainly have been more accepting of a union with a man that looked more like her. All of these notions plagued her as they continued their conversation and Nash continued to make her feel like the only girl in the world.

"Are you going to be alright?" Nash asked kindly. It appeared as if their conversation was finally coming to its end. He seemed content to know that her tears had stopped flowing. He had even gotten her to laugh heartily a few times during their chat. There was one problem. Brenda wasn't ready for things to end just yet.

"I guess so," she answered at first. "No," she answered right after. An idle mind is just as dangerous as a confused one and at that moment, Brenda couldn't have been more confused. A reckless spirit replaced all caution and every single warning in her heart.

Nash remained silent at first. He had managed to calm the storm inside him as he counseled and consoled her, innocently enough. He admitted to himself that her obvious vulnerability had drawn him to her but in her moment of weakness it felt unfair to try to seduce her. However, he recognized that something else began to burn underneath her skin and there was nothing vulnerable about it. He couldn't lie to himself or pretend that he hadn't desired her. She was an absolutely gorgeous woman. Even as charming and smooth as he was, it wasn't often that a woman like Brenda paid him much attention.

"What do you…?" he started to say before she cut him off.

"Let's leave," she answered quickly. She called for the bill and paid it, even after he tried again and again to take care of it.

"You can pay for the room," she told him which finally shut him up.

Nash swallowed hard at her bold suggestion. Without further protest or even another word, he walked out of the Morning Perk, right behind her.

The Prerequisites of Perdition   Keith K. Williams

PART 6 ½ : The Room

Brenda and Nash's awkward shame lessened the further they walked down the fancy hotel's lobby, away from the desk clerk's judgmental eyes. Even though it wasn't nearly a tawdry, *motel of ill repute*, their intentions were the same and the clerk knew it. The way he sneered at them as he exchanged the room keycard for the cash made them both feel filthy. Brenda had almost changed her mind while Nash was filling out the paperwork.

When the elevator opened in the lobby, Brenda and Nash stepped inside like strangers. They both behaved suspiciously, as if the whole world was the audience for the sin they were about to commit. She still couldn't believe what she was doing and Nash couldn't believe that she was about to do it. He had been with his share of good-looking women but none of them were quite like Brenda. None of them had been as refined. None of them had ever felt this much like forbidden fruit. Just being near her was intoxicating and Nash was still taken by the realization that she was about to let him drink his fill of her. He knew that what they were about to do was wrong on every level. He just couldn't stop himself because it wasn't every day that a man had the opportunity to touch what he wanted instead of what he had been forced to settle for. She was exactly *his type*, which was a very dangerous thing. A man could easily lose his soul in such an entanglement and Nash was very aware of the risk to his own sanity. He decided to enjoy everything they were about to do while keeping his own desires under control. He refused to poison himself with the notion that she would ever be his and his alone.

While Nash hardened his heart and focused on cold sexuality, Brenda's heart beat frantically, supercharged with trepidation. She was about to do the wildest, most reckless thing she'd ever done. Brenda hoped that by doing this thing that she had set her mind to, she might re-establish a sense of reality in her life. She would open her legs and by doing so, have the fairytale destroyed. After holding back the waves for so long, she wanted to let the sea reclaim the castle made of sand that she'd been living in. She believed that she was doing what was necessary to wake up from the dream.

The Prerequisites of Perdition Keith K. Williams

By the time Nash hung the do-not-disturb sign on the knob and locked the door behind them, Brenda was already partially nude. Her full breasts swayed beautifully as she bent over and slipped out of her jeans. Not even once did she look up at him as she slid her panties off, first past her round hips and then finally past her ankles. She didn't have to. She could feel his eyes on her soft flesh. She climbed on the bed and slowly spread her legs, seductively. Her clean-shaven lips glistened with anticipation. Again, Nash was awestruck by how beautiful she was. He half-expected to wake up.

Nash got to his knees in front of Brenda but she closed her thighs and picked his head up. She wasn't in the mood for any of that. She wasn't interested in romance, affection or any of the pleasantries that of foreplay. What she wanted was raw, animalistic and very basic. She was determined not to turn their encounter into anything more than what it was supposed to be.

The way the soft flesh of Brenda's thighs rubbed against Nash's sides was blissful to him as he moved powerfully between them. She raised her legs up off of the mattress and wrapped them around his waist. The initial sensation of penetration was amazingly overwhelming for him. She moaned deeply which let him know that it had been for her too. He quickly found himself drenched, and sliding into her smoothly with every push; at first with just a part of him until he was able to work in everything. Still, the sexual excitement he felt was limited to just that and that alone. Although her body was warm, wet and tight, there was an unseen barrier between them. Her body moved as if she welcomed him but, he could feel that she purposely held back and refused to give him everything. As much as he liked her, he was disappointed. She'd allowed him to walk into her garden but he knew that she had not allowed him to pick any flowers.

Every time Brenda felt Nash deep inside her, she knew that she was wrong but things had gone too far to turn back. The entire time she never let him move her into any other position besides the missionary they had started off in. They never kissed and she didn't let him know what it was like to have her soft, delicate hands lovingly caress his rigid, tensing and flexing flesh. Oddly enough, she did keep her eyes fixed on his face the entire time. She feared that if she ever closed them then it would make everything seem less real. As her body rocked on the hotel mattress

The Prerequisites of Perdition Keith K. Williams

from the force of his movement, she accomplished what she wanted. Her fairytale was definitely over. Her life was on a different road now and she knew it as soon as they had finished.

PART 7: Unlikely Accomplice

Just as Brenda had instructed, Nash showed up at the address she had given him, at exactly the time she had told him to be there. He paid the cabbie his fare and stepped out onto the cracked, weathered concrete. He wondered why she had wanted to meet him in such a grimy part of the city as he stared at the shabby brown house. It was hard to imagine that the decaying dwelling had ever been brand new. The rusty black gate screeched horribly as he pushed it open. He walked up the crumbling brick stairs and banged as politely as he could on the heavy, metal front door. Judging by the condition of the doorbell, he was certain that it didn't work. To his surprise, a middle-aged Caucasian woman with the most beautiful blue eyes he had ever seen answered the door.

"Good afternoon. I'm Emily. You must be Nash," she greeted him, reaching out and touching him on the shoulder.
"Hello, I'm supposed to meet Brenda here," he stuttered nervously. He was totally confused and had no idea what to expect.
"Yes, my daughter-in-law is inside waiting for you," Emily told him.
If she hadn't kept her hand firmly on his shoulder, he would have taken a step back. Instead he found himself being led politely inside the run-down brown house. He wondered why Brenda would have him meet her at her husband's mother's house and how long it would be before the goons threw a black hood over his head. Now he knew how a rat felt right before the metal bar on the trap smashed its neck. When Emily closed the front door behind them, he knew it was too late to turn back. All Nash could do was take a deep breath and let whatever was going to be, just be.

"Relax. I can see the worry on your face. Brenda has already told me the whole sordid story," Emily explained, taking him by the hand. She walked him down a narrow, cramped hallway with old, wooden doors on either side of it. Nash assumed that they must have been closets and the entrances to other rooms.
"But you're her husband's mother," Nash started to say.
"I know what you're going to say. This is true but Brenda has always been kinder to me than my own child. He and I have not

The Prerequisites of Perdition   Keith K. Williams

been on good terms for a very long time," she told him. There was something about her voice that made Nash believe her. There was something overwhelmingly convincing about those deep blue eyes, almost as if they were incapable of lying.

The long, narrow hallway came to its end at the beginning of a dimly lit living room. The only light came from a lamp in the far corner of the room but even in the gloom, Nash recognized Brenda as she sat on Emily's sofa with her legs crossed. Behind her, the heavy curtains on the large windows were drawn tight, blocking out the bright afternoon sun.

"I'll leave you two to speak while I go get something for everyone to drink from the kitchen," Emily said as she left them alone. She patted Nash reassuringly on his back before she walked out.

"Hello Nash," Brenda greeted him.

"Well, this is the last place I'd expect you to have me meet you," Nash answered.

"That's good. I'm hoping that my husband is thinking the same way," she answered.

"How can you be sure that you can trust your husband's mother?" he asked although he assumed that she must have had her reasons. He just wanted to know what they were to put his own mind at ease.

"Trust me, I'm sure," she answered.

"Are the boys here? Can I see Douglas?" he asked.

"Yes, he's in the backyard playing with Demetrius," she answered and pointed to the windows behind the couch she was sitting on.

Nash hurried to the window and opened the curtains, just enough to see outside. His heart soared as he watched his child, laughing and playing. As always, Nash's happiness was also accompanied by a crippling sadness. He could only watch his own flesh and blood from the shadows like a ghost. All the same, given the circumstances, he supposed that he should be grateful for even this.

"Thank you," he told Brenda.

"You're welcome," she answered. "It's too risky to do this too often, especially the way things are now but, I'll arrange it for you as often as I can."

Nash watched Douglas and was afraid to blink, almost as if he'd miss something important if he did. He tried his hardest to commit every precious moment to memory because there was no

The Prerequisites of Perdition   Keith K. Williams

telling when he would be afforded this opportunity again. He understood the stakes of the game he and Brenda were playing. He also felt selfish and guilty because if what Brenda had told him about Dirk's threat was true, he was also putting the child he cherished in grave danger.

"Why are you doing this, even after your husband's warning?" Nash asked.

"Because fuck him! He's cruel and it's not his right to say I can't. I was wrong for doing what I did and then keeping the truth from him but I'm not about to be punished for the rest of my life for it," she answered with such conviction that Nash had heard all the explanation he needed from her.

At that moment, Emily appeared with a pitcher of homemade lemonade on a tray with three glasses with ice in them. She set the tray on the coffee table and poured Nash a glass of lemonade first. She walked over to the window and handed it to him with a smile. She was sure that he had no desire to move from that window until the time for him to leave had come.

"Thank you," Nash told her. Emily winked.

"You're welcome," she answered before she went back to the couch and sat down beside Brenda. She poured a glass of lemonade for herself and then one for her daughter-in-law.

"Thanks," said Brenda. Emily nodded to let her know that it was fine. After a few healthy gulps, Emily reached into her glass for an ice-cube and crunched it to pieces in her mouth. Then, she took a neon-pink lighter from her jeans pocket as she took a cigarette from the red pack that sat on the coffee table. She offered Nash a smoke but he politely declined. She didn't bother to ask Brenda because she already knew that her daughter-in-law had conquered her nicotine addiction years before, while she had been pregnant with her oldest, Demetrius. When Emily had finished her cigarette, she addressed both of her guests.

"I hope the two of you know that I'm not exactly an eager participant in your little web of espionage. To be honest, I feel terrible about having anything to do with this. No matter how badly my son treats me, he's still my son. As much as he ignores and mistreats me, Dirk is still my child. Somewhere, deep in my foolish heart, I've always held onto the hope that some day, things could be right between us. If he ever found out about my part in

The Prerequisites of Perdition   Keith K. Williams

this, all hopes of ever fixing things with him would be gone," she told them and put her hand to her chest, covering her aching heart.

"I understand what you're doing for us," Brenda said, reaching out and putting her hand on Emily's.

"I doubt you really do sweetie. Hopefully, you'll never have to find out. Children never understand the choices or decisions their parents make. They certainly never forgive us for the mistakes either," Emily warned.

"I'm so afraid of that. I try not to think about the day coming when I'll have to tell my boys the truth. I don't know if I can. This lie is eating me alive and the older they get is the worse it gets for me," Brenda said.

"Sooner or later, they're going to have to know," Nash said dryly. It was no secret what his position was on the whole situation.

"I wish it was that easy and that simple," Brenda snapped.

"Maybe not for you. I've never wanted to lie about this," Nash answered.

"And what do you suppose would have come from that? What would have that accomplished?" Brenda asked. She shifted on the couch so she could look behind her and stare into his face.

"My son would have known his real father. He could have known I loved him and he could have had the chance to see his father's face," Nash answered. The conviction in his voice enraged Brenda. She didn't understand how he couldn't see the absurdity of the course of action he was proposing.

"You wish he could see your face? You mean visit your grave! And that's only if he wasn't buried in his own by then. Haven't you been listening to anything I've been telling you? Don't you understand that Dirk would kill us all?" Brenda yelled.

"I think that might be a little extreme. He may be cold-hearted but I don't think he'd do anything that monstrous," Emily interrupted.

"Then you don't know your son," Brenda answered. "I'm starting to feel like I'm the only one in this room who knows what he'll really do."

"Well, like I told you before, I'm not afraid of him," Nash told her.

"Good for you. I KNOW why I am! As a matter of fact, why don't you just kill yourself before you get us all murdered?" Brenda roared. Unmoved by her outburst, Nash coldly turned his attention back to his son playing in the backyard. Emily sighed and ran her fingers through her long, mostly blonde hair. She gently patted Brenda on the knee and encouraged her to calm down.

"His father was such a kind, gentle man. For so long, my heart hurt thinking about where he got this mean and spiteful spirit from. The only thing I can think is that he got it from me because my late husband was nothing like that," Emily sadly stated.

"That's not fair. Don't say that. Dirk is the way he is because he chooses to be that way," Brenda consoled her.

"That's sweet of you to say honey but it's also very far from the truth. I'm an aging, fading woman who's too old to tell lies about herself anymore. My dear daughter-in-law, when I was your age, there was a selfish fire that burned inside me that could not be put out. Dirk and his father felt the pain of it when I left them. I'm sure that my son carries that same fire in his soul now. My husband was a good man. There was a time when I didn't understand him though. I didn't appreciate who he was. I even went as far as to call him weak and blame him for why I left. I was wrong for that. He only hand a soft hand when it came to me. He deserved for me to love him more. In my heart, I know that's why my son is the way he is. You see how he treats me? I guess he's showing me that he's not weak like I thought his father was," Emily explained. Her bottom lip quivered and she seemed on the brink of tears. Brenda moved closer and wrapped her arms around the trembling woman. Emily eagerly put her head on Brenda's shoulder. The two women shared the hollow hope that Dirk was a good person at his core but his true nature is what bound them in the same sadness.

"Quiet! You hear that?" Nash asked suddenly. They all kept quiet and listened for what he might have heard. Before long, they all heard it again.

"Bang! Bang! Bang!" was the sound on Emily's heavy, metal front door.

"You expecting anyone?" Brenda asked Emily.

"No, no one," Emily answered.

"Stay here," Brenda told Nash as she took Emily's hand and got up off of the couch. "We'll go and see who it is," she said as she took her unfinished glass of lemonade with her.

***

The two women were still holding hands when they got to the front room. Both of their hearts were beating furiously.

The Prerequisites of Perdition   Keith K. Williams

"BANG! BANG! BANG!" the knocking came again, even louder than before. Emily had never heard anyone pound so hard on her door. It almost sounded like it was about to buckle and shake off of its hinges.

"Check the window and see who it is," Brenda told her. Emily nodded and walked over to the curtains to carefully peek at who was banging on the door. After a quick glance, she immediately backed away from the window.

"Well?" Brenda asked.

"I don't know them but," Emily started to say but then stopped mid-sentence.

"What is it? Why do you look like that? But what?" Brenda asked while moving her frozen mother-in-law aside so that she could see for herself. After one look, Brenda's eyes opened wide and her glass of lemonade fell out of her hand. The sound of it crashing and breaking against the old wooden floorboards made Emily nearly jump out of her skin.

Brenda had seen the stout man in the dark red business suit that was presently banging on Emily's door before. She remembered his dark, thinning hair, slicked back with tons of grease. He saw her as she peeked through the curtains and smiled with unusually full lips, surrounded by a dark goatee. She could almost swear that he had red pupils and quickly looked away from them. Parked at the curb in front of the house was a vintage, candy red, '69 Chevy Impala with a white, leather interior. Leaning on the car with a cell-phone to her ear was the man's lover and counterpart. She was considerably taller than him and her short, cropped hair was bleach-white, matching the color of her tight, short dress.

She was stunningly gorgeous and in another life, she might have been a super-model. Brenda watched in horror as the woman's black lipstick-covered lips moved as she spoke into the phone. She also spotted Brenda in the front window. She winked at Brenda with her green eye. Her other eye was completely cloudy as if it had no pupil at all. The woman ended her call and bent over to reach into the back seat of the Impala. As she did, her short skirt rode up and exposed the bottom half of the luscious cheeks it barely covered. Once she got what she had reached for, she turned around and pulled her dress down, trying to cover the pale, shapely legs that seemed to go on forever. Then, as if she was a limousine

The Prerequisites of Perdition   Keith K. Williams

driver at the airport, she held up a cardboard sign with *BRENDA SWAN* written in black lipstick.

"Oh my God!" Brenda exclaimed before she turned and ran back down the narrow hallway. "Don't open the door!" she yelled back at Emily who was still rooted in place.

***

Dirk had sent Grendel and Gretchen to claim his wife.

The Prerequisites of Perdition   Keith K. Williams

PART 8: His Due

A few of the customers seemed slightly curious but Fats was the only one that swallowed hard as the white limousine appeared in front of the Morning Perk. He was the only one who knew exactly who had come to visit. Only moments before, Fats had been deep in thought about how he was going to replace his establishment's outdated television set with a fancy, new flat screen. He now knew that in a few moments, he was about to have much bigger problems on his hands.

***

The two towering men that walked in the diner's doors behind Dirk were obviously bodyguards but Dirk preferred to call them *personal assistants*. Immediately, anyone who laid eyes on them would find something unusual about them. Usually, men of their profession practiced and perfected their poker faces or scowls. It added to their grim persona and solidified their intimidation factor. This was not the case with Sam and Simian. They both wore subtle, permanent grins. It was slightly disturbing at a quick glance but after being in their presence for a few minutes, their creepiness multiplied exponentially. Dirk would say that he paid them to enjoy their work and that he expected them to smile.

Fats half-heartedly raised his hand to greet his landlord. Dirk didn't smile or return the gesture. Instead, he tilted his head to signal Fats to join him at one of the empty tables at the rear of the diner. There weren't many customers back there and Dirk wanted privacy for the conversation they were about to have. Fats complied with unwilling feet. All of the cheer had vanished from the jolly owner of the Morning Perk. Sam and Simian remained standing but Dirk sat down and continued reading a comic book as Fats sat down.

While serving one of her customers their plate of eggs and grits, Jasmine noticed her boss walk by her as if he was on his way to his own execution. She loved Fats like a father and it frightened her to see him so terrified. Also, to her, the three men whose company he now shared had an ill look about them. The two goons in black suits who stood on either side of the table grinned continuously like lunatics. There was also something sinister about

The Prerequisites of Perdition   Keith K. Williams

the strikingly handsome man who was obviously their boss, seated directly in front of Fats. She started to walk to the back to take their orders but her real purpose was to eavesdrop. Her plans were quickly thwarted when Simian put his hand up and stopped her before she could get anywhere near their impromptu *pow-wow*. His unnatural smile and the way he winked at her before she turned away sickened her stomach. She hoped Fats was going to be alright. Just in case, she set an extra pot of coffee to boil. She didn't know how much she could do against those two grinning gorillas but, she would do what she could if she had to. No one liked hot coffee thrown in their face.

***

"Good morning Fats," Dirk said without looking up from the comic book he appeared to be engrossed in. He hadn't looked up from its pages since he sat down.

"G'mornin' Mr. Swan," Fats answered. He didn't know which was worse; Dirk's icy indifference or the shadows that Sam and Simian cast over him.

"Relax Fats. A grown man's voice shouldn't tremble, even in the face of trouble. And, it's just Dirk today. I'm here on personal business," said Dirk.

"D-D-D-Dirk," Fats stuttered.

"Know why I'm here?" Dirk asked, slowly turning a page in his comic.

He still had not looked up at Fats who now perspired profusely and had to wipe his forehead with his sleeve.

"Well, about that. I'm sorry. Things have been kinda slow and," Fats started explaining. Dirk shut him up by simply looking up at him with the most serious face Fats had ever seen on any man in his entire fifty-seven years on this earth.

"Obviously you don't, so stop talking. I'm here about some troubling business with my wife. Now, you know her don't you?" Dirk asked.

"Yeah, kind of. She eats here with her boys almost every morning but I haven't seen her here today. I make small talk but I don't really know her," Fats answered.

"I know you haven't, and I'm sure you don't, and stop rubbing your hands together like that. It's annoying," Dirk told him.

"Ok," Fats answered, putting his hands flat on the table. He felt like a five-year-old in public school all over again.

The Prerequisites of Perdition   Keith K. Williams

"Good. Now, I have some questions. If you tell the truth, we won't have any problems here this morning. Now, I know that there are all kinds of reasons that people tell little white lies to cover up huge, black, ugly truths. I get that. However, let me please stress to you that this morning is not a good morning for little white lies. I will not suffer them to be uttered in my presence today. I'm here sitting with you for a reason chubby guy. I'm on a mission to uncover some ugly black truths. Understand?" Dirk asked.

"Yes," Fats answered.

"Good. Now, why do you think my wife comes here for breakfast when we have a chef at the house?" Dirk asked, his blue eyes seeming to grow cold and frost over like a placid lake in the winter.

"I asked her the same thing once. She told me that she likes my hot chocolate and that the boys think my cook makes the best pancakes," Fats answered.

"And that's the only reason? Are you sure there isn't anything more to it? You've never noticed anything strange going on? Never noticed her speaking to any of the customers?" Dirk asked.

"Not that I noticed. To tell you the truth, the time your wife usually comes in is the morning rush for us. I'm so busy I don't usually get a chance to pay attention to anyone in particular. But, I've never seen her talk to anyone in here aside from myself of course and maybe the waitresses sometimes. She pretty much keeps to herself," Fats answered.

"You're sure about that?" Dirk asked.

"Positive," Fats answered, looking Dirk directly in his cold blue eyes.

Somehow, Fats knew it was a bad idea to look away. He was far from a scholar but he was certain that Dirk was studying his body language. He definitely didn't want to be mistaken for a liar when he was telling the truth.

"So, you *see no evil?*" Dirk questioned him, putting his hands up to cover his own eyes. He slowly put them down and then stared intensely at Fats.

"I, I'm not sure what you mean but I ain't seen anything strange," Fats answered, disturbed by Dirk's behavior.

He wanted him to finish with his damn questions and be gone. Dirk was about to speak again when his cell-phone rang.

"Excuse me," he said before answering it.

The Prerequisites of Perdition   Keith K. Williams

"Of course," Fats answered and got up in his seat, assuming that Dirk wanted privacy.

Sam's grip forcing him to sit back down assured Fats that his presence was still required. After what he was about to hear, Fats wished that they had let him leave.

"You saw her at the house?" he paused. "Bring them to me and kill her," Dirk spoke into the phone.

As he ended the call and put it back into his pocket, Fats struggled not to throw up as his stomach churned at the thought of the order Dirk has just given so nonchalantly in front of him.

"You probably shouldn't have heard that," Dirk said.

"I didn't," Fats answered.

"I didn't think you did," Dirk said with a smile. Then he covered his ears with his own hands in the same manner that he had covered his eyes before. "I see you *hear no evil* as well?"

"Never," Fats answered. He was no fool.

"That's good," Dirk said as he got up out of chair. "I'm glad I can trust you to speak no evil as well," he continued. This time, he reached across the table and covered Fats' mouth with his hand. Fats flinched in surprise but dared not move.

"My old pappy always told me that a man must know how to mind his own business in this life," Fats answered after Dirk moved his hand away.

"Well, your old pappy was a wise man. It's the safest way for him to hold onto that life. And speaking of business, start paying your rent. This ain't a charity you know. Give the comic to your son. It's a rare copy. It'll be worth something one day," Dirk said, leaving the mint condition, vintage comic on the table.

He flashed a grin that gave no hint that he was the ruthless person that, only moments before, almost caused Fats to pee in his pants.

PART 9 – The Fallen

"They're not going to open the door," Grendel called out to Gretchen as he walked back down the stairs. His voice was deep and seemed to come from somewhere else besides his body. Two teenage boys who were passing by, bouncing a basketball on their way to the park were spooked when they heard it. They picked up their dribble and hurried along.

"I just spoke to him. He says to kill her and bring them to him," Gretchen answered.
The sound of her voice was soft and feminine but slipped from her lips with a sinister hiss. Grendel gripped her by the back of her neck and kissed her passionately. His hand found its way up her skirt and the smooth lips covered by her lace thong. She gripped him by the crotch and felt him grow from her touch.
"A little bit of kidnapping and a little bit of wet work it is then," said Grendel. His voice always made her shiver deep inside.
"Yes," Gretchen answered, eager and excited. "This kind of work always makes me wet."
"I can tell," he said as he removed his hand from under her skirt. "Let's get to work."

The lovers walked to the rear of the Impala and popped the trunk. They both picked out their weapons of choice from the arsenal inside. Grendel armed himself with two desert eagle handguns, equipped with silencers but Gretchen lifted an assault rifle that looked like it could take down a helicopter. Grendel smiled as he lit a cigarette and watched as she loaded ammunition in the fearsome weapon.
"I think a little discretion is called for with this one," he told her.
"Fine," she sighed and put the monstrosity back in the trunk.

"You know I love your enthusiasm though," he told her, trying to ease her disappointment. She rolled her eyes as she wielded a grisly, razor-sharp machete instead. There was still gore on it from the last time it had been used.
"Yes, yes but I'm going to ruin my dress now and it's my favorite," she said, running her hand smoothly across her hip, caressing the thin material.

The Prerequisites of Perdition   Keith K. Williams

"You have a closet full of white dresses," Grendel laughed. "Come on, time to clock in."

***

"What's wrong?" Nash asked as Brenda came bursting frantically into the living room.

"We have to leave, NOW!" Brenda yelled.

"Why? What's going on?" Nash asked. The way Brenda was acting, he expected the whole house to blow up any second.

"Go through the back door and get the boys inside quickly," she ordered him.

Nash didn't hesitate. As he turned his back to go over to the door that led to the backyard, Brenda smashed Emily's lamp over his head. The entire room started swimming until blackness took him.

"Why'd you do that?" a shocked and horrified Emily asked. She covered her mouth in horror as she watched blood leak from the gash in the back of Nash's head.

"I had to. If they find him here, they'll kill all of us for sure. If we hide him in the closet, all they'll do is take me and the boys back to Dirk," she explained to Emily.

"But, what about what you said he'd do to you? He threatened to hurt all of you," said Emily.

"I know. I don't think he's that much of a monster. Now hurry up and help me hide him in the closet before they find a way in," Brenda pleaded.

Emily quickly helped her drag Nash across the living room floor and over to the nearest closet.

After they'd secured Nash's unconscious body in the closet, Emily was the first to turn around. Her mouth hung open in shock and all the color drained from her face.

"What's wrong?" Brenda asked, afraid to know what was behind her.

Emily didn't answer so she turned around slowly, her body trembling without even knowing what was wrong. She gasped when her own eyes saw what had spooked the soul right out of her mother-in-law.

Somehow, Grendel had got in through the backdoor of the house without them hearing. Somehow, he had managed to bring Brenda's sons inside quietly as well. He stood in the living room, holding Demetrius and Douglas' hands. Both boys were visibly confused but sensible enough to remain silent.

The Prerequisites of Perdition   Keith K. Williams

"Go to Mommy," he told them as he let go of their little hands.

His voice was absolutely terrifying. Demetrius and Douglas ran to their mother and hugged her tightly. She wanted to cry but held back her tears with all of the strength she could manage. She knew that the children were frightened and with good reason. She had to make sure that they felt safe, even though they weren't. Grendel took his guns from their holsters and held them casually at his sides. Brenda was certain that they were all going to die when she saw the silencers attached to barrels of his gun. Her knees almost buckled.

"Tell the boys to close their eyes now," Grendel said. His voice seemed to make every vein in her body vibrate like the strings on a cello. Brenda knelt down and kissed both of her babies on their cheeks. She closed their eyes with her own hands as she touched their precious faces for what she believed was the last time.

"Now, don't open your eyes until I tell you," she told her sons. Brenda silently made her peace with God and waited for Grendel to raise his guns to take her life. Then, she heard the most sickening sound she had ever heard in her life. There were no words that she could find to describe it but as she looked beside her, she saw what it was.

Tears flowed freely from Emily's eyes while a feminine hand covered her mouth to muffle her screams. Her beautiful blue eyes were opened wide and bulging in their sockets. They seemed to fade as Gretchen forced the machete brutally though her body. Amplified a thousand times, Emily heard her insides being maimed. Brenda watched in horror, then screamed as the tip of the machete emerged from the front of Emily's body.

"He said to tell you that he knows that you're the one who's been helping her keep secrets," Gretchen whispered in Emily's ear as she began remove the blade, slowly, and sadistically. Right before the last light left her beautiful blue eyes, Emily's tears became blood. It was the most horrible thing Brenda had ever witnessed. All she could do was keep her hand over her children's eyes.

"Why are you doing this?" Brenda sobbed.

"*WHY* is a silly question to ask us. I'm sure you could answer your own question better than we could. We make it a point to never ask. We don't know and we don't care. We don't have consciences

The Prerequisites of Perdition   Keith K. Williams

because we're just the weapons and the tools of the people who send us to do unpleasant things," Grendel explained indifferently.

"All over my dress, just like I said," Gretchen complained as she let Emily's body fall to the ground in a mangled heap.

Her white dress was stained with crimson. Brenda felt trapped in a horror movie. Gretchen stared at her with her *green eye* but it was the cloudy, white one that nearly stopped Brenda's heart from pumping. Blood from the machete trickled down the blade and dripped onto the floor as Gretchen held it at her side. Brenda didn't want to die but if she was about to, she hoped that Grendel would just shoot her as opposed to getting hacked to pieces by the woman in the bloody white dress.

"There was supposed to be a man here too. Where is he?" Grendel asked.

"He was supposed to meet me here but he never showed up," she lied.

Even if she was about to be killed, she had no desire to see anyone else slaughtered in front of her. She felt responsible for bringing this calamity into Emily's life. She hoped that maybe saving Nash might wash some of the sin off of her soul.

"Cowardly that he didn't show up but, smart I guess," said Gretchen.

"Take them to the car while I finish up in here," Grendel told her.

"Ok, but hurry up. I want to get out of these clothes," she answered, winking at him with her healthy green eye.

"I'll help you with that," he said, licking his lips.

Gretchen took Brenda by the arm and began to lead her out of the house with the children in tow. Her skin crawled when she saw that Gretchen's filthy hands had smeared poor Emily's blood all over her arm. She was sickened by what she had just witnessed but also relieved to still be alive. Gretchen dragged them outside to the car. She didn't know what was going to happen next but she knew that she would do whatever it took for her sons to survive this ordeal. As they were forced into the car, Brenda began to pray and hope that someone, anyone, was listening.

***

Grendel looked down at Emily's body and sighed. A pool of blood had formed underneath it. He'd always felt that Gretchen was too messy. As he began to drag the body over to the couch, he told himself that he would have given the woman a much cleaner

The Prerequisites of Perdition   Keith K. Williams

death. After he'd propped her up on the couch as if she had been sitting there all along, he took one of the cigarettes from the coffee table. He put it between his lips and lit it with a wooden match from his pocket.

"Horrible brand," he said to Emily's dead body before he spit the lit cigarette onto the floor. A black flask of alcohol from his pocket provided the fuel to assist the tiny flame grow into a mighty blaze. He watched solemnly as it grew and spread across the floor until it became an inferno.

"I'm sure we'll meet again," he said to Emily's lifeless body as if he expected her to answer.

He kissed her cold lips as the inferno that he had started engulfed the entire room. Her beautiful blue eyes were still open, staring off into nothingness. He lowered her eyelids for the last time with his fingers.

***

As the house burst into flames, Grendel walked out through the front door calmly, his clothes still smoking. He didn't look back as he walked down the crumbling brick stairs and passed through the little black gate.

"Let's leave this place," he told Gretchen as he climbed into the passenger seat of the '69 Chevy Impala.

He shook his head in disbelief when he saw that Gretchen had inadvertently smeared blood all over the white steering wheel.

The Prerequisites of Perdition   Keith K. Williams

PART 10 – Inferno

Nash lay flat on his stomach on the grass in the backyard. He nearly hacked up his lungs which were scorched from the black smoke he had just escaped by way of a miracle or more likely, divine intervention. His head was still reeling and he wanted to vomit. He couldn't block out the image of Emily's body burning on her couch. Brenda and the children weren't outside and he could only pray that they had escaped the flames. Tears streamed down his soot-covered face as he realized that they might be burning to death inside. In the distance, he could hear the wailing of the fire engine's sirens. With every bit of strength he had left, he forced himself to crawl to the fence that led to the neighbor's yard and climbed over. There would be too many questions that he couldn't even begin to answer if he stayed.

***

Dirk sat on the steps of his home with his two personal assistants standing watch like pillars on either side of him. His tie was loose around his collar and he looked disheveled, as if he had just got home from a hard day's work at the office. Even in the failing light of the setting sun, you could see that his bright blue pupils were surrounded by redness. He had been estranged from his mother longer than he remembered but, once he had given the order that would ultimately end her life; he felt a doom casting a shadow on his life. He had wept just as he had when he had lost his beloved father, all those years ago. He hadn't imagined that he would have felt anything at all but he mourned her. For years he told himself that he hated her. He felt cheated by the huge white lie he had held onto for years which had now been made reality by his own hand. It was a crippling, painful truth. To finally prove to her that he did not inherit his father's weakness, he had damned himself.

Dirk lost track of time as he sat on the stairs with his head in his hands and a half-empty bottle of liquor at his feet. Most of its contents now coursed through his system. The rest of it would soon follow. Beside his other foot sat a black briefcase full of money. It was Grendel and Gretchen's payment. Their services were not cheap. Dirk reached for the bottle and guzzled down its

The Prerequisites of Perdition   Keith K. Williams

contents, ignoring the burning sensation in his throat. To his drunken eyes, the world seemed to sag and wane as if it was made of wax. He was certain that he'd lost his mind when he thought he saw his father's ghost coming up from the main gate below towards him. He slurred apologies as his father's apparition continued to cruise up the driveway until he realized that it was only the headlights of a candy red, vintage car. Grendel and Gretchen had arrived to make their delivery and collect their money. Sam and Simian walked down the stairs to meet the car once it came to a full stop.

***

The boys both cried for their mother as Sam walked them inside the house, past their own father who dared not look into his children's eyes for fear that they might see him for what he was. Brenda kicked, screamed and cursed as Simian dragged her out of the car. She only stopped fighting momentarily when she got to the steps where Dirk was sitting. She looked down at her husband in disgust and he looked up at her like a lost soul. Their eyes locked and she spat directly in his face. His expression remained the same and he made no effort to wipe away her spit. It ran slowly down his cheek and dripped from his chin. He waved his hand and Simian continued to drag her, kicking and screaming, into the house.

Gretchen shook Grendel, who was slumped all the way back in the passenger seat, sound asleep. If his snoring wasn't louder than the car's engine, she would have thought he was dead. She muttered about *having to do everything herself after driving all the way there* and got out of the car, slamming the door as she did. He still didn't stir from his deep slumber.

Dirk was not prepared for what he was about to see. He quickly shut his eyes after seeing Gretchen walking towards him with her blood-stained hands and dress. To him, she looked like a demon and as she got closer, he covered his eyes with his hands. Gretchen found his behavior odd but, she had grown accustomed to all manner of eccentricities from the clients in her line of work. She shrugged it off and picked up the briefcase.

"Did she suffer?" Dirk asked as Gretchen walked back to the car.

He opened his eyes to watch her leave, almost to make sure he knew that this was all real.

"What do you think?" she answered, showing him the gore on her hands and clothes as she walked backwards to her car.

The Prerequisites of Perdition   Keith K. Williams

Without another word, she got behind the bloody steering wheel and drove away, leaving Dirk alone on the steps of his mansion, fighting for breath in a sea of regrets.

***

"Did you count it?" Grendel asked, rubbing sleep from his eyes. He was surprised by how dark it was. When he had closed his eyes, it had been bright out.

"Oh, so now you're awake," Gretchen answered.

"Oh hush woman. Did you check it or not?" he asked again, this time slipping his hand between her thighs.

"Do you really think he would play with our money?" Gretchen asked.

"Of course not, you're right," he answered. He slipped his fingers into her panties and parted her second set of juicy lips.

"You're going to make me crash," she moaned.

"So pull over," he told her.

PART 11 – Purgatory

Nash paced up and down his condo with a troubled mind. He was certain that he had barely escaped the scene of a crime. He strongly doubted that Emily's house fire was an accident. His scorched lungs had him coughing violently and served as a constant reminder of Emily's burning body on her own couch. He just thanked God for waking him before he was burned alive in some stranger's closet. The gash at the back of his head was also a reminder that someone had tried to bash his skull in. Worse than anything else, he didn't know if somewhere in that inferno lay the slain bodies of Brenda and the boys. He had barely escaped the flames himself. Then, the evening news came on the television and the story at the top of the hour was about a mysterious home fire. Nash grabbed the remote control and turned the volume all the way up.

The news reported that Mrs. Emily Swan died when her house caught fire and burned to the ground as she slept. The authorities were still investigating the cause of the fire. When the news report was over, Nash clicked off the television and sat in the darkness. He was relieved and deeply troubled at the same time. The news didn't report that anyone else had died in the fire which gave him hope. However, he still didn't know what had become of Brenda and the children. He hacked and coughed in the dark. He knew that he should have gone to the hospital. Still, the physical pain that lingered was nothing compared to the anguish of simply *not knowing*. Sleep was something he knew would soon wickedly elude him until he found out exactly what had happened to them. The storm and turmoil inside him was too much to bear.

All in one day, he had become a shade, trapped in-between life and death. Everything seemed to have less meaning than it used to but he wanted to go on, driven by his desire to see his son again. If Douglas was gone, there would be nothing left for him on this earth. That is how deeply Nash Tate had learned to love his son while being forced to watch him grow up from a distance. Now, he was trapped in a purgatory he had taken all of the proper steps to design himself.

The Prerequisites of Perdition   Keith K. Williams

PART 12 – Dearly Departed

Brenda hugged her babies tightly as she cowered in the dark of the closet in the boys' bedroom while Sam and Simian stood watch outside. Both of her boys were tired, afraid and hungry. She continued to whisper quiet prayers as she listened to their tummies growl. She begged for mercy from the heavens because, at this point, she knew she would receive none from her husband. After all that she had seen, she had never been more terrified in her life. With every second that passed, she expected to see the platinum blonde with the one, green eye walk into the room and hack them all to pieces. When it happened, she would beg for mercy for her boys. Every minute that crawled by felt like a century. Not knowing how this was going to end was torture. Just as the anxiety of it all threatened to strip away her sanity, the closet doors opened and she knew that in the moments to follow, she was about to have her answer.

***

At first, Dirk towered over them silently. The light that suddenly poured into the darkness of the closet caused her to squint. Mercifully, the children had fallen asleep. Her husband reached for her arm to help her up but she recoiled from his touch. She never wanted him to touch her ever again. He remained silent but answered instead with a sad smile as he stepped back to give her room to get up. One at a time, she put her precious sleeping boys into their beds and tucked them in. she kissed both of their foreheads and then turned to face her husband. For a few moments, there was an intense stare-down as they eyed each other like strangers. Dirk was the first to break the silence.

"I suppose that's it between us," he said. He closed his eyes and sighed as if he was relieved.
"After the things you've done? Yes, this is it between us," she answered.
"It couldn't be avoided. This is who I am. I did warn you," he reminded her.
"I never thought you'd go this far. You're a fucking animal!" she snarled.

The Prerequisites of Perdition   Keith K. Williams

"But you knew that. Somewhere inside, you had to know that but you still pushed me. I didn't want any of this. I practically begged you to not make me have to do this," he said.

"No, you fucking threatened," she said.

"Same thing, at least to me anyway. Now I have to do things that I never wanted to do," he continued.

"What do you mean? Your own mother is dead. You had her house burned to the ground with her in it! What more do you want? Isn't that enough? You still want more blood?" she asked.

"Not much more," he answered.

"So, you're going to have us killed too?" she asked. She wanted nothing more than to break down in tears but defiantly refused to. She wouldn't give him the satisfaction. If this was how it was going to be, she wasn't even going to beg. There was a long silence between them before he spoke again.

"Take Douglas and leave my house," he ordered her. "I don't care where you go as long as you're not here."

"But what about Demetrius?" she asked in disbelief.

"My son stays with me," he answered.

"Oh God no!" she bawled. "He's my child too. You can't do this!"

"Don't bother to beg. My mind is made up," he told her.

"You're casting us out like you did your mother?" she asked, barely able to find breath to speak.

"No, this is nothing like that at all. I had always hoped that that woman would have found a way to redeem herself in my eyes. She never did. Instead, she betrayed me by helping you to keep secrets. Now, I want you and your son out of my sight so that I can pretend both of you are dead too. One day, this will all just seem like a bad dream to me," he said, in a voice so pleasant that it took cold, calculating cruelty to new heights. Brenda was beside herself with grief.

"And what if I won't leave my other baby? What if I won't let you separate us?" she asked even though, judging from the expression on Dirk's face, she already knew the answer.

"Then I'll kill you and Douglas. He's not my son, and you're not my wife, just like Emily showed me that she was never any kind of mother to me. One way or another, I'll be rid of all of you," he told Brenda with such conviction that she had no choice but to despair.

The Prerequisites of Perdition   Keith K. Williams

PART 13 – Perdition

The sun still rose the next day despite the dark events that had transpired the day before. The world would not stop turning, no matter what horrors its inhabitants faced on a daily basis. In Swan Park, the geese still congregated to be fed by their mysterious benefactor.

Elijah was enjoying another warm morning in the park. Feeding these beautiful creatures gave him a calming sense of balance. He was able to maintain this amazing relationship with these animals that were as free as the wind that blew through the leaves of the trees above his head. Of course, they would never hold conversations with him in the traditional sense but, they shared a magical, unspoken understanding.

With only about two handfuls of breadcrumbs left in his small brown paper bag, he knew that reality was just around the corner. Once he had emptied it, Elijah felt the small slip of paper at the bottom of the bag. He removed it and tossed the empty bag into the trash bin next to the bench he was sitting on. The dollar amount written on the slip of paper was impressive. As usual, a single name was inked on it as well.

The slip of paper read: <u>NASH TATE</u>

The Prerequisites of Perdition   Keith K. Williams

PART 14 – Welcome to the Afterlife

Nash had never been more relieved in his life than when he received that first phone call from Brenda. Through fits of hysterics, she'd told him everything that had happened since she'd smashed the lamp over his head and locked him in the closet. He heard the grief in her voice when she explained how she had to abandon one child to save the other. He could tell that she mourned her first-born as if he had died. The circumstances she found herself in as a mother were horrible. Nash pitied her but at the same time, considering the alternative, things could have been much worse. Terrified and having nowhere else to turn, the first thing she'd done was call him. He's told her to come over to his condo but she preferred to meet in a public place, just in case Dirk was still having her followed.

***

Nash waited for Brenda under the warm spring sun on a bench in Swan Park. There were no clouds in the sky, birds chirped as they returned home and he believed that it was the most beautiful day he had ever seen. Even the buzz in his ear from the occasional flying insect couldn't dampen his spirits. He was aware of the danger but remained too excited to waste thoughts on the possibility of retribution from Dirk for past transgressions, even in the ill shadow of the things he'd witnessed. Nash was going to meet his son for the very first time.

The sunlight glistened on the lake in front of him as the geese swam gracefully on its surface. It seemed like an eternity passed as he waited. Every second that went by felt like an hour and every minute a day. Then, just as eager anticipation nearly turned to frustration, from the corner of his eye he spotted them, Brenda and his son. For a moment, everything else in the world slowed down as they walked down the paved, tree-lined path. Nothing had ever felt more like a dream and he was afraid he would suddenly wake. He stood up to greet them.

Little Douglas looked nothing like how a boy should, in a park with his mother on a sunny spring day. He clung tightly to the hem of his mother's white summer dress as if it was the first time he had ever been outside. Brenda looked into Nash's eyes for a

The Prerequisites of Perdition   Keith K. Williams

brief moment before she turned her gaze downwards at the one child she had left. The pain in her face broke Nash's heart. Without a word, he stepped closer to them and hugged Brenda tightly. He felt her body shake as she cried in his arms. He hushed, soothed and squeezed her until she calmed down enough to speak. When he let her go, he took a step back to give her room to breathe.

Brenda held her head down and looked away from him as a mild breeze blew through her hair as well as the thin material of her dress. Fear, hurt, horrors and unmistakable tragedy also draped themselves around her. Even with the weight of all of those things, somehow her spirit wasn't completely dead. In Nash's eyes, there was still a small piece of something inside her that had the potential to burn brighter than the sun. At the moment, he just didn't know how to keep her from drowning in despair. He reached out and took her hand in his own.

"Thank you," she said.

"You don't have to thank me. I'm just glad that you're alright," he answered.

"I guess we're as alright as we can be," she said.

"Can I?" Nash asked.

"Of course you can," she answered.

With her permission, Nash waved hello to his son for the very first time. Douglas didn't wave back as he still clung to his mother. Nash felt a lump in his throat as the million things he wanted to say all came to him at once. Every word, from every missed moment tied his tongue. He had never believed this day would ever be possible. Brenda sensed the uneasiness and bent over to speak softly to her child.

"I know this is all confusing baby and I'm very sorry. Remember what we spoke about? This nice man is your real father," she told Douglas.

She knew that this wasn't the best way or the best time to tell her child the truth. At his age, she doubted he even understood the magnitude of the situation. She was grateful to Nash for being willing to help them and it was for his sake that she parted her lips to finally speak the truth. An eruption of emotion overwhelmed him and Nash's eyes filled with tears.

***

At the last moment, Elijah decided to grant Nash a final mercy by not blowing his head off. Some semblance of humanity

The Prerequisites of Perdition   Keith K. Williams

deterred this professional executioner from horrifically ending his life in front of this woman and child with a head shot. Dirk had allowed Brenda to go free with her son for a much more sinister purpose than she could have ever imagined. He knew that she would seek out the boy's father and she had unwittingly played her part as bait to perfection. Nash never saw the scope attached to the sniper-rifle that would guide a bullet directly to his heart. A single slug ripped through his chest and he fell to his knees. As he clutched at the wound, his hands became soaked in his own blood. The geese on the lake took flight at the sound of the gunshot as it echoed throughout the peaceful air of the park. Brenda's white dress was splattered with crimson as she screamed frantically for help. Douglas watched silently as the man his mother had just told him was his real father died in front of him.

"I love you," were the words that Nash gasped with his final breath. He touched his son's face for the first and last time as he inadvertently smeared the boy's cheek with blood. Through watery eyes and fading vision, it was the last image Nash would see in this life. It was a beautiful death.

IN DESPERATION

DK Gaston

I like to thank my writing conspirators. I've learned a lot from them while working on the anthology and hope that a little of me rubbed off on them. And I especially like to thank all the booklovers that enjoy reading what strange thoughts come out of my head.

In Desperation
Part 1 Anthony

DK Gaston

She slapped me? She actually slapped me! I stood there stunned, cheek burning, rubbing the right side of my face to work the sting away. I quickly scanned the neighborhood hoping no one had seen. The Connolly's were pulling into their driveways, a man with his dog walked casually down the sidewalks away from us, kids played in the street. All were too busy to see what happened. Before I could react, Yolanda was stomping off in an angry huff, carrying an overstuffed gym bag. She hadn't even told me what I'd done.

Bounding from the front porch in a Michael Jordan leap, over the three cement steps, I ran after her. She was making her way around to the driver's side of her BMW before I was even halfway down the cracked sidewalk.

I yelled for her, "Yolanda, can we talk about this, baby?"

With her hand on the car handle, she shot back a stare that gave me pause. There was hatred in her eyes; pure, unadulterated hate.

What had I done? I moved beside her as she opened the car door. "Wait! Can you just wait a minute? Can you at least tell me when you're coming back?"

I'd known Yolanda's answer as soon as I saw her clothes and toiletries in the backseat of the car.

She didn't look at me when she said, "I won't be coming back, Tony." Her voice was as cold as ice.

My eyes began blinking. She might as well have kicked me between my legs. Air left me in deep, violent waves. I felt dizzy and my legs began to buckle. Desperately, I grabbed her arm. I spun Yolanda around, probably a bit too rough, trying to make her look at me. Her teeth clenched, but made no sounds of protest or pain.

"Baby, what's this all about? What have I done?"

Slowly her gaze came to mine.

Her expression changed from icy rage to uncertainty. I loosened my hold. "You hurt me, Tony. I thought you were the one person I could trust…"

Her eyes filled with tears.

I don't recall ever seeing her cry before.

Her lower lip began to quiver.

223

In Desperation   DK Gaston

I wanted to comfort her. To hold her in my arms until whatever this was could be forgotten.

She pulled away from my grasp. "...I don't ever want to see you again," she said with newfound resolve before tossing the bag inside and getting in the car. Yolanda drove off leaving me alone in the middle of the street without a clue.

      Just last night, we had a romantic dinner together at the club Deluge where we first met. I presented her a beautiful diamond engagement ring, asking her to marry me over candlelight. I made arrangements with the band to play Janet Jackson's *When I Think of You*, her favorite song. She said yes quickly, as though I might take it all back. Everyone's attention turned to us. Our joy gave off an electric vibe that must have sent out a jubilant shockwave that affected the club's patrons. Later, at my place, we made passionate love, awoke in each others arms and had a relaxing breakfast. Everything was perfect.

What had happen from the time I went to work to the time I came home?

What had she meant about me hurting her? I hadn't hurt her or betrayed her trust. I would never do that. My mind raced, but there was nothing.

I yanked my cell phone from its holder on my belt and pressed the speed dial. I had to know why. It rang three times before going to voicemail.

"Baby, I would never—"

Never what?

I let out a long exaggerated breath before I spoke again more slowly, "Call me, okay? We can work through this, whatever it is. Just call me back, please." I hoped she would call back.

In my heart, I knew she could carry that temper of hers into the next century. There was a better chance of Ike and Tina hooking back up than Yolanda returning my call.

My arm dropped to my side as though it held a heavy weight instead of a cell phone. The only way I was going to find out what happened was to search for the answers myself. Once I had that, maybe, and that's a very iffy maybe, I could calm her down long enough so that we could work this out. Yolanda meant the world to me. I don't know what I would do without her in my life.

      Defeated, my head slumped between my shoulders. The sun glinted on a small reflective object on the street. I didn't recognize it at first. My lips pressed together in a tight pinch. I fought back tears trying to burst their way out. *Men don't cry*, I heard my father's exacting voice.

When I was a boy, my dog Toby, jumped the backyard fence, running off forever. I cried all night praying for him to return. The next morning, Daddy came to my room, sat on my bed, gave me a stern look that resembled steel and said, "Men don't cry." He hadn't meant it in an unkind way. Daddy wasn't much of a talker when it came to emotional situations. It was meant to tell me that bad things happened in life, crying wouldn't solve my missing dog problem. Thinking that was enough for a nine year old to understand, he smiled, patted my leg, and then brushed that same hand through my hair as though I were Toby. Strangely enough, it made me feel better.

I bent over reaching for the shiny object on the asphalt at my feet. It was the engagement ring. I hadn't caught the sound of it dropping to the pavement when she got into the car. She had discarded the symbol of my devotion without the slightest hesitation. Was this how we were going to end our two years? I had the sudden impulse to fling it in the air. Instead, I calmly stuffed it inside my pants pocket and stood up.

My thumb stroked the cell phone in my hand. I wondered what I should do or if I should do anything at all. This could all blow over in a few hours. She could come to her senses. I remembered all her things in the back of her car. Waiting for this to resolve itself wasn't going to do it.

I pressed the speed dial number for Pam, Yolanda's best friend. She answered on the second ring, when she spoke, she sounded almost in tears, "Oh Tony... It's horrible... I don't know what happened."

My first thought was something happened to Yolanda but that was crazy of course, she just left me. "What is it? What's wrong?" I asked trying not to sound as frantic as Pam.

"She called me a slut! Said that we were no longer friends! She said she hated me!"

Pam was one of the strongest sistahs I'd known and to hear the distress in her voice, it took all my strength to continue speaking. "Who?"

"Yolanda..." she gasped before a long pause. I think she muffled her side of the phone with a hand because the feedback sounded like listening to a seashell. When she spoke again, her voice carried more strength. "Yolanda said those things to me. She wouldn't explain. I thought she was going to hit me. What's going on Tony?"

"I. Don't. Know."

I wanted to believe this was a terrible nightmare but the diamond in the ring bit into my leg letting me know I wasn't dreaming. I dug it from my pocket. It lay in the center of my palm, weightless, cold, unmoving, ugly. It'd lost the beauty it held a short time before. My fingers closed around it. My hand became a fist. I raised it up high, at first wanting to blame God for this day, but then I lowered it. This wasn't God's fault.

Not wanting to say it, I said, "She told me she didn't want to see me either. I had hoped you could give me some answers."

Pam's silence spoke volumes. She wouldn't have any answers. She was as lost and confused as I was.

When a car horn blared behind me for me to move, I realized I was still standing in the middle of the street. The driver, Miss Johansen perhaps the oldest person I'd known, who was rumored to be nearing one hundred, waved to me with her wrinkled hand as I stared at her. She said something I couldn't make out as she passed. Without even thinking about it, I nodded politely to her and headed back toward the house. The phone stayed frozen to my ear.

When Pam finally broke her nervous quiet, what strength she'd found had abated. Her words sounded choked, "I don't know what to do. She won't take my calls. What are we going to do, Tony?"

We? In a strange way, knowing I wasn't alone in this made me feel--to some extent--better. What's the old saying: 'Misery loves company'?

Raising my fist to God told me something. I needed answers that I wasn't going to get by doing nothing. Yolanda was the most pigheaded person I'd known. If she was angry at us for something we'd done, Pam and I would have to pry it from her, because otherwise answers would not be coming.

I asked, "Are you absolutely sure she hadn't said or done anything that could tell us something about what's going on?"

"No. She came to my desk shouting at me this morning..."

I cut her off. "What time?"

In Desperation — DK Gaston

This morning Yolanda left the house all smiles, ready to shout to the world that we were getting married.

"Around eleven, I think. She came charging into my cubicle after she finished talking with someone at hers." Pam and Yolanda worked together at the University's Human Resource Department.

"Did you see this person...? The one who she was talking to?" I asked, grasping for straws. It was Yolanda's job to speak with the University's employees and family members.

"No, I wasn't paying attention; I had someone in my cubicle at the time." She was quiet for a long moment. "Wait a minute. When Yolanda started shouting at me, I jumped up from my chair in surprise. I caught a glimpse of the back of a woman's head leaving her cubicle. She had short raven black hair and she was dark skinned, darker than Yolanda."

Yolanda's deep brown color reminded me of a rich chocolate.

"Do you think someone else in your office would recall seeing her?"

"I don't know, I supposed it's possible. Why? Do you think this is important?"

Barely noticing the three short steps I took up the stairs I was back on the porch standing motionless in the very spot Yolanda had lashed out at me. I was locked in place, unable to move, the memory of the slap looping over and over in my mind. The diamond chewed into the flesh of my palm, snapping me from my frozen state. My legs regained mobility.

I forced myself to head inside where Yolanda's sweet perfumed smell would probably still linger. A vision of her standing naked and arms opened, waiting for my warm embrace, appeared. I quickly brushed the mental picture aside, returning my focus to the conversation.

"I... I don't know, Pam. Is there anything else you can remember?"

"After she finished biting my head off, she up and left, without so much as another word." Another pause, "I heard she then marched into the manager's office and quit."

Yolanda loved her job and the people there. I wondered just how far she would go not to see Pam and me. Would she move out of her apartment? Would she move out of the city, perhaps state? Panic overwhelmed me. If she did leave, without a single clue as to where she was going, there would be no way I could ever find her. Yolanda's parents were dead; she hadn't spoken to her brother DeShaun in years. The only remnant of his existence in her life was some old instant Polaroid of him hugging her. I found it lodged between pages of a book I pulled from a bookshelf in her apartment.

"Pam, tomorrow morning, I want to meet with you, there at your work." I would have preferred tonight but I want to try to track Yolanda down before she'd disappeared.

Concern filled her voice. "Tomorrow's Saturday. No one will be there to question."

"I don't want to question anyone. I want to take a look inside her cubicle."

"Okay. I know the guard who works there on weekends. He won't give us any trouble."

"Perfect. We'll meet at around eight in the morning, have something to eat to get our heads straight and then we'll make a beeline for your office."

For the first time since she answered the phone, I heard some of Pam's old zeal. "Sounds like a plan."

After the phone call I searched the house for God knows what. She might have left a note or some type of clue inside. She must have come directly from work, to have removed all her stuff before I got home. Pam said, their fight was around eleven, it takes about twenty minutes to drive from the University to my place.

She had nearly five hours to take whatever she wanted. I hadn't even made it inside when she stormed out of the house onto the porch. She had a gym bag. When I tried to kiss her, she shoved me aside, ran down the stairs to her car. On the sidewalk, she whirled around so quickly she appeared as a blur. I stood there dumbstruck until she'd marched back on the porch, thinking she would explain. What I got was a savage slap to the face and no answers.

I moved about the house in a state of bewilderment, scarcely aware that I was in the living room when I stepped on something that crunched. There were more crunches from shattered glass with the shifting of my foot. A picture torn in two lay with its back facing up. I don't know why I was compelled to pick up the torn picture. Perhaps it was the same unknown force that wouldn't let me put the engagement ring back into my pocket. Or maybe I was just a gluten for punishment.

In Desperation   DK Gaston

I flipped the torn photograph around. It was the one taken on our first vacation together. We were outside the CN Tower in Toronto. A sidewalk photographer took it while we were sharing cotton candy. She and I had sticky apple red and sky blue candy garlanded on our faces. We looked like a pair of circus clowns. I hadn't wanted to keep it because we looked silly but Yolanda loved it for that very reason insisting we buy it. She had it framed.

She kept it here at my place I think just to taunt me. The photo never meant much to me before, but with the glass from the picture frame in a hundred pieces, holding the ruined halves in my hands, it started to mean something.

I opened a drawer in the display cabinet that held decorated plates; she had talked me into buying the monstrous cupboard to add a little life to the bland living room. It always struck me as strange that she'd placed more of her attention in beautifying my house than in her own apartment. In the drawer, under a pile of paid receipts, I got the invisible tape, determined to bring the halves together. Shutting the drawer harder than intended, one of the cabinet's doors slowly creaked open. I rarely unlatched it except for dusting. The catch had been pried open. That's when I noticed all the plates inside were broken. They looked like a hammer was taken to them.

I fell back into a chair, my strength completely drained. She bought those for me. They'd cost her a months pay. Knowing that she would do that, sacrifice so much money for me, was when I first realized she was in love with me. Like the plates, my heart lay shattered, and broken in small pieces.

***

I parked outside of Yolanda's apartment building just after seven. The evening sun remained bright and high showing little signs that the night would shortly be forcing it into retreat. I gazed up toward the fifth floor. Had I expected her to be waiting at her window, ready to throw down her hair for me to climb to her rescue? This was no fairytale. She would not be waiting for her knight to come, although I prayed for the happier-ever-after ending. Looking away from the building, I'd called her number, both cell and phone, collectively more than ten times. I stopped leaving messages after the fifth.

In Desperation — DK Gaston

I approached the front entrance. I almost pressed her apartment number. If she was there, how would she react? Would she run and hide? I had a key. I could simply show up and surprise her. Without thinking, the key was in my right hand, perched between my thumb and index finger, opening the downstairs front door.

Exiting the elevator on the fifth floor, I hesitated. I knew no more now than I had earlier. What would I say to her? How do I prove my innocence, when I don't know what I have done wrong?

Innocence.

The word echoed in my mind as though it was shouted across the Grand Canyon.

Innocence.

I was headed down the empty hallway getting angrier with every step.

Innocence.

She's the one who went into a rage, not only with me but her best friend! It was Yolanda who smashed things we'd cherished, not me! I couldn't understand why I was the one ready to apologize for something I most likely hadn't done.

I was going to make her explain what was going on, one way or another. Stopping in front of apartment 517, my tightly wound fist was ready to pound the door down. But was that the right thing to do? I took several deep breaths getting my temper under control. I realized I'd let my anger blind me to the fact that the key to her apartment was in my pocket. I used it and stepped inside.

The door swung opened and, still carrying some of my anger, I shouted, "Yolanda!"

A part of me expected the place to be completely empty; no furniture, no pictures, and no cat--just an empty apartment with the lingering scents of her perfume. The sparse decorations still hung on the walls and cluttered her shelves. I closed the door behind me and stepped further inside.

"Are you here, it's Tony," I asked softly.

The perfumed aroma I expected was not there but a faint unpleasant smell hung in the air. It seemed to be everywhere. It wasn't overpowering but it was enough for me to scrunch my nose in mild disgust. Yolanda wasn't the most responsible person when it came to the upkeep of her place. She would leave clothing on the floor for hours, leave dishes in the sink for days, and not take out the garbage. I, being the complete opposite, would sometimes remind her, in a nice way, to clean up after herself. The odor could be rotting meat she had put out and forgotten about. I ignored the smell for the moment.

I searched the small apartment for her. She was not home, not even the cat, Wanabe (pronounced, Wan Na Be). I bought the gold and tan Tortie Smoke Persian cat six months ago on a whim. Yolanda gave her that stupid name as a joke. She kidded that I *wanted to be* this or I *wanted to be* that, just because I spoke of wild dreams for our future or what I wanted to do with my career. Most of those dreams I let go for the security of a steady paycheck. Others stayed in the back of my mind.

Those months ago, when she was mad at me; and when I gave her the cat as a peace offering, she said, I *wanted to be* forgiven; that led to the cat's name. Despite my mixed emotions of anger and fear, a small smile fought at the edges of my lip. It was something I did every time I thought about Wanabe's name. Though I now found little humor or even comfort in it.

The edges of my mouth cracked with sudden dryness. I licked at my lips. They too were dry, as was my throat. Worry was robbing me of needed fluids. My throat ached for some type of relief.

In the kitchen, I opened the refrigerator looking for something sweeter than water. It was stocked. She hadn't cleared the fridge out which meant she might return. Whether that would happen tonight, I had no idea. Still, I decided I would wait for her. I quickly downed a can of Mountain Dew with a single swig. The soft drink was there for me; Yolanda never touched the stuff. Caffeine kept her up. When I lifted the trash lid to drop the green aluminum can in, I dropped it to the tiled floor instead.

I'd discover the nauseating odor.

Inside was Wanabe. Her head twisted backwards. Blood dripped from her still opened eyes and mouth.

In Desperation   DK Gaston
Pam

Speaking with Tony made me feel a little better but not much. Placing the cell phone back in my purse, I looked out from my patio to feel the warm sun on my face. I wondered what he expected to find in Yolanda's cubicle.
And what was going on in that girl's head anyway? Why did she call me a slut?

Had Tony said something to her about *us*? But there was no *us* to talk about. He and I were friends and that's all. Besides, he wouldn't hurt Yolanda for the world. I'd never seen a man so devoted to a sistah in my life. I wished I could find someone like him. Oh, let me honest with myself for once. I wish I found *him*. Just listen to me; Yolanda goes off the grid for one minute and I already have thoughts of taking her man.

I looked up at the sky staring directly into the sun, hoping to burn the thought from my brain. Yolanda's a good friend—the best in fact. She doesn't need me daydreaming about Tony—not now—not ever. I needed to focus on finding her and finding out what was happening.

Quickly spinning around, I stepped back inside the apartment. I heard the loud voices of Mo'Nique and Countess Vaughn throwing one-liners back and forth at one another, a rerun of The Parkers. On cue, a dubbed laugh track followed their wisecracks. The invasive sounds were irritating, giving me a headache. Throbs at my temples came rapid and continuous as though Sheila E were playing a drum solo on my brain. I quickly found the remote and put the TV on mute.

Though there was no sound, I could still see the Parkers were arguing. Whatever problems they were having would be resolved at the end of the show. I wished life was like that. Have major crises, break-ups, arguments, dragged out cat fights, or mental breakdowns that would be solved in less than thirty minutes. But life wasn't like that, was it? Life was unpredictable and complicated.

The phone rang and disrupted my thoughts. "Yolanda," I said even before picking up the handset, but the caller-ID displayed my mother's number. Putting the handset to my ear, I collected myself, and said, "Hi, Mama."

In Desperation   DK Gaston

"Hey, Coco," she said.

I hated when she called me that. I hated it when I was a kid, and I hate it even more as an adult. But she's my mother, so what could I do?

"What time will you be stopping by the house tonight?" she asked. The question threw me. We hadn't scheduled anything, so whenever she hit me with the dropping-by-the-house question, I knew she was fishing for information. "What do you mean?"

"What do you mean, what do I mean? Yolanda said you would..."

My heart pounded in my chest. I gripped the handset tighter. "Yolanda? Did she call?"

Concern rose in Mama's voice as she asked, "What's wrong, Coco?"

I took a deep breath before continuing. "Nothing's wrong. I just want to know if she called you today, that's all."

"No, Yolanda didn't call me today." Disappointment brought my heartbeat back down to a normal pace. That was until Mama added, "She came by. Left about thirty minutes ago and dropped off some boxes."

Boxes? Why would she leave boxes? "Can I assume you've already went through them?" I asked, knowing she had already inspected every item inside.

    Mama was the type of person who sat on the couch all day in the living room, staring out the front window to watch her neighbor's going-ons. She'd known everyone's business and never minded sharing it with anyone who'd listen. Her nosiness extended beyond the neighbors and intruded into my life. In all my years living under my parent's roof, it was like being under guard by Homeland Security. There wasn't an entry she hadn't read from my diaries, a number she hadn't called back after I talked with friends on the phone, or a boyfriend she hadn't scared off after giving them the third degree. Even after years in my own place, she made frequent stops to my apartment and called me incessantly to keep tabs on my life.

    Anything left at the house straight away fell under her prying scrutiny, especially if Daddy wasn't around to stop her. He wouldn't be home--a senior police homicide detective--he'd be on duty.

Mama said innocently, "Now Coco, you know I wouldn't—"

In Desperation   *DK Gaston*

I was on a short fuse and not in the mood for her blameless act. "Oh, come on Mama. What did Yolanda drop off?"

Unexpected silence fell on the other end of the line. She debated whether to reveal what was in the boxes and confessing the truth about her perusing. Finally, she said, "It's filled with things you've given her, birthday gifts, clothing, pictures, and… and…" Mama's tone softened, underlined with snooping concern. "Is there something going on between you two? Yolanda seemed… Well, hot and bothered. Did you two have a fight?"

    My hand again tightened around the handset. I couldn't find the words to respond. But I had to say something, the last thing I needed was to have Mama involved in my personal life, again. If anyone could make a situation worse, it would be her. With that last thought, I said, "It's nothing, don't concern yourself."

Mama waited for more.

Instead of responding to her curiosity, I asked, "What did she say, Mama?"

"Not much at all. Yolanda seemed distant, angry even. She told me to tell you, not to look for her. When I'd questioned her about it, Yolanda went into a huff, dropped the boxes to the floor and stormed out of the house."

"Really?" I asked, more to myself than to Mama.

She repeated. "Is there something going on, Coco?"

    For Mama, Yolanda might as well have thrown fuel on top of a proverbial fire. She wouldn't let the matter go, no more than I would. I'd have to give her some type of explanation before she involved Daddy. "We had an argument okay, that's all. She and I will work it out."

"I hope this isn't anything to do with Anthony, I know how you feel about—"

"Mama, please don't! This isn't about Tony." I hoped. "Anyway, there's nothing going on between him and me. Get that straight in that head of yours, okay?"

    I lied and she knew it. Due to her prying into my life and going through my personal journals, Mama knew I'd always had feelings for Tony. That woman was a better detective than Daddy.

She went on ignoring me. "You don't ever want to be that other woman. Yolanda and Anthony are good together. If your father ever cheated on…"

In Desperation   DK Gaston

I stopped listening and moved the handset from my ear, dropping my arm to my side. She was ranting. It could go on for hours. I grabbed the remote and turned the television sound back on to drown out her chattering.

I wished I had a remote control that could put Mama on mute like in that Adam Sandler movie. I would rewind back to the morning and play everything that happened at the office to figure out what made Yolanda so upset. She'd always been a little flaky, but never as much as that morning. We had our arguments but at the end of the day, we always made up. Maybe not as conclusive and clean as a sitcom, but enough that we stayed best friends over the past two years.

Two and a half years before

I just finished with a client when Jan, my department manager, appeared outside my cubicle. Beside her was this dark skin sistah who, in heels, was an inch shorter than me, putting her around five seven. The stranger wore a bright blue dress with yellow flowery trimmings around the breasts and on the skirt's lip, which offset her deep chocolate complexion. She didn't have on any jewelry or makeup. I thought that was unusual in this day and age of pretentiousness.

Her wide, friendly grin was as vivid as her clothes. It was infectious and I couldn't help but return her smile. Without her saying a word, I found myself liking this stranger.

Jan said, "Pam, this is Yolanda. She'll be starting today. She's replacing Debbie."

Debbie used to work in the cubicle right across from me. She wasn't what you would call a people person and hadn't gotten along with anybody in the HR department. I doubted she even had a friend outside of work and probably lived in a house filled with stray cats. She quit more than a month ago after finding another job, leaving a vacancy in the department Jan desperately tried to fill.

Yolanda stretched out her hand in greeting. "It's nice to meet you, Pam."

Her grip was tight. I felt calluses on her palm. It was like shaking hands with a man. I doubted whatever she'd done for a living before was in an office environment.

I said, "Nice to meet you too. Welcome." She let go of my hand which was a relief. I gave her a double-take, reevaluating my first impression. Jan didn't move after the introduction. "Is there anything else?"

Jan winked. "As a matter of fact, there is. Would you mind getting Yolanda acquainted with everyone and explain how things operate around here? I have a meeting in a few minutes and simply don't have time."

I frowned, curling a corner of my lip and arching an eyebrow. Jan was always dumping her work on me. "Sure. Why not?" I asked, exaggerating like an overzealous dingbat.

It was quiet now.

Yolanda looked embarrassed and Jan maintained her perky disposition, unaffected by my clear reaction to her request. Standing, the squeaky wheels from my chair slowly rolling backwards broke the edgy silence.

Jan said, "I'll leave you two to it then." She whirled around on her high heels, humming a tune and quickly disappeared down the hall.

"Does girlfriend always trip like that?" Yolanda asked, in a low voice.

"Girl, you haven't seen nothing yet," I retorted playfully. "I don't know where you worked before, but this will probably be a whole new world to you."

I left it out in the open for her to say something about her last job. All she did was giggle. When she finally spoke, it was about work at the university, not what she'd done previously. It was like that for a several weeks. She knew about everyone in the office, but no one really knew anything about her. I even went so far as to access the personnel records on Yolanda just to find out where she had been employed. All I could find was a name, the *Erikson Group*. Digging deeper, I tried to find information about the Erikson Group by calling the company directly and going on the Internet, only discovered they did contract jobs. It wasn't until months later at a company party that Yolanda finally started talking about herself. After a few sips of *Sex on the Beach*, I couldn't shut girlfriend up.

Yolanda told me she worked for a contract company for five years. She didn't go into detail about what she did there or the name of the business. Not that I needed the latter, my inherited nosey nature already dug up that bit of info. I kept that part to myself, though.

She also told me that she had just gotten out of a bad relationship and wasn't trying to begin a new start with her life-- new job, new friends, new environment, new everything. I'd recently broken up with my man as well. That common bond had us going on for hours. Still, she hadn't said much more regarding herself. I never heard so much talk about nothing in my life. Regardless, she was an interesting person and surprisingly we had a lot in common.

We declared our friendship that night.

Present day

I placed the TV back on mute and returned the phone to my ear. "Mama, Mama… Can you stop talking for a second? Thank you. I'm coming over, okay? Yes, right now. I'll be there in twenty minutes."

Mama talked for another ten minutes before I convinced her that I was really coming over. I swore that when I eventually had children, I would never be like my mother. Admittedly, she provided a momentary break from what was happening with all her badgering.

I needed to refocus my energy and find out what was going on in Yolanda's head rather than figuring out where she was. Yolanda might have left more in the box with my returned gifts, maybe a note or something that she couldn't say to me in person.

I grabbed my purse and ran out of the apartment determined to find the truth, one way or another.

In Desperation　　　　　　　　　　　DK Gaston
The Bald Man

Hidden behind the dark tinted windows of his car the bald man watched Pamela Reeb with great interest as she left her apartment building. Her clothing was simple, geared more for comfort than fashion. She was dressed in skintight white denim jeans, a loosely fitted yellow tee-shirt, and white tennis shoes with yellow Nike symbols. Even her hair was practical, dark waves were pulled to the back of her head into a large tight bun.

The camcorder zoomed in on her so that he could get a clear shot of her face.

"She's pretty," he said aloud, stretching the words out sounding like a hiss. The bald man's breathing became heavy and his heart raced in his chest. "So very pretty."

A voice, not his own, boomed in his earpiece. "You need to keep your focus."

The camcorder slowly pivoted on the woman's body from head to toe, lingering here and there as beads of sweat ran down the bald man's forehead.

She moved with the fluid grace of a dancer.

He could hear his own breath much clearer now. It drowned out the dogged voice in his ear. He wanted to get out and meet this Pamela Reeb personally, not peer at her in secret. He yanked his right hand away from the camcorder and dropped it to the passenger seat where the knife waited. His index finger gently, slowly, caressed the sharp edges of the blade. His fingertips were flawless against the steel, sliding back and forth along its six-inch length. The mere act should have been enough to draw blood, but he was careful with the blade.

"No, it won't be my blood it spills," the bald man said in a low self-gratifying groan.

"What's that?" It was the voice in his ear.

The bald man returned from his reverie and wondered if he had been talking aloud again. "It was nothing." He wiped the sweat from his brow. "The woman has exited her apartment building. She's headed for her vehicle."

The voice said, "Excellent. Once she's gone you know what to do."

He smiled. "I do."

The bald man turned off the camera. Act I, of his masterpiece was done. Later, Act II in her apartment, where she thought she would be alone, safe and secure. He tried hard not to think beyond that. Things always got kind of crazy into the third Act.

Not crazy in a bad way, at least, not for him.

The pretty woman was in her black and gold Mountaineer, making a U-turn on the street. As she drove by, he blew her a kiss through the dark tinted windows. She saw nothing. Still, he knew Pamela Reeb desired him, wanted him so bad.

He wanted her too.

"Later," he thought. "There'll be time enough, later."

***

Inside Pamela Reeb's apartment the bald man began his work. He had much more equipment than his assignment required. It wouldn't delay him. He'd be out of the place on schedule. The bald man had done this many times and it had become an art. He was only supposed to install the audio listening devices, but to film his second Act he needed to install video cameras as well.

Placing the silver case on a tabletop in the front room and opening it, he whistled, *Pop Goes the Weasel*. The sound made was a sick reverberation inside the apartment.

"You enjoy your work too much," the voice said over the earpiece. The bald man stopped his eerie whistle. "What's life, if you can't enjoy yourself?"

He looked around taking in the entire place, searching for the best placement of his paraphernalia. The apartment was picturesque, uncluttered, without unnecessary embellishments.

Adorning the living room was a medium length auburn couch, a matching glass coffee table, a stylist metal display case and in two flanking corners long slender lamps. Curved at the apex, with the yellow covers, looking like drooped over tulip petals yet to blossom. Large African vases stood to each side of the sofa. The polished wood floors gleamed with sunlight penetrating through long clothed blinds on the patio doors. The fragrance of fresh apple spice potpourri filled the room.

From the display case, he picked up a picture frame with a photograph of pretty Pamela Reeb and two other people, Anthony Holman and Yolanda Blakely. The bald man stared at the trio for a long time, studying their every detail. He placed his gloved thumb

In Desperation   DK Gaston

atop Yolanda's image. He wanted to press his finger through the glass and frame, poking her out.

An ache in his right leg throbbed; a recurring throb from a wound that never fully healed.

    He spun the frame around to its backside and examined its black vinyl spine. Laying it back on the display case, he retrieved a small circular device from his equipment bag, pressing it on the spine. The bug matched the dark texture perfectly, it was seamless. Careful to place the picture back in its original position, he again looked at the images and once more his pain returned.

He'd thought Yolanda was pretty once. Not anymore.

He didn't know how long he stood there staring, hating.

The voice said, "What's your progress? Have you gotten to the phones yet?"

    The bald man blinked, and then looked at his watch. His face twisted into a distorted angry mask. He'd lost ten minutes.

He growled. "Keep your shirt on, I haven't been in the apartment that long. I'll be done, when I'm done."

He hated being under anyone's leash. He liked to work alone.

Had Rembrandt been overseen as he painted? Had someone been watching over Shakespeare's shoulder as he wrote? Had Luther Vandross been towered over as he sang?

No. Artists should be allowed to do what they do best alone, in their own time and in their own way.

The bald man was an artist too.

His canvas was human flesh, his paint, blood. His pen was his knife. His voice was the soulful wails of his guns.

Yes. He was an artist; an artist of pain and death.

Part Two: Anthony

"Oh God, Wanabe!"
I looked away repulsed by the sight of Wanabe's mangled carcass in the kitchen garbage can and the strange foul odor I smelled as I entered her apartment, but now it was much stronger, putrid. Cuffing my nose and mouth with a hand, I choked back the vomit that tried to work its way up my throat. With my other hand I held the garbage can lid in the air chest high like a shield as though I could fend off what had happened.

Suddenly it struck me that Yolanda might be in the apartment, somewhere hurt or worse. I slammed the lid back on the can and rushed from the kitchen. "Yolanda!" My shout echoed in the small apartment. I began another search, this time more thoroughly, checking behind furniture and looking inside closets.
After fifteen minutes, I stood outside of her bedroom closet, propping my forehead against the door frame. There was no sign of her. I had discovered that a lot of her clothing was missing, along with several suitcases. I hoped she made it out before whoever killed the cat had entered. Wanabe's death changed everything. This wasn't just about my fiancé running away.

My mind raced with unanswerable questions because someone dangerous might be after her: To do what, hurt her? Kill her? Did she have a craze stalker? Was she out there, alone, unaware that someone may be threatening her? I slammed the side of my fist against the drywall. It gave under the impact, leaving a fist sized hole. My thumb throbbed with pain. I stared at the injury. Luckily, I didn't break the skin.
The sting gave me the opportunity to think straight. Lifting my head from the door frame, I pulled out my cell phone and dialed Yolanda once more. My heart skipped a beat when I heard a familiar sound come from the front of the apartment.
It was Yolanda's phone.

My fear morphed to hope as I raced out of the bedroom running toward the sound. She must have come in moments ago. In the hallway I had a clear view of the front room.
It was empty.

But I could still hear the ring-tone playing John Legend's *Heaven*. She bought me his CD for my birthday. I hadn't cared for his music at first. It'd grown on me sometime later after she had played his music and played it again and again in her car. My birthday present became her present.

Eventually, I found her cell phone under the couch. Had she ditched it there rushing out of the apartment? I flipped it open and looked at her messages inbox. Pam and my name filled the display. All were unanswered.

I continued to scroll down the listing and saw something odd. There was a PRIVATE number. Yolanda was vigilant about who she gave her number to. Someone with a PRIVATE line never would have been added to her short list. A severe violation like that would have definitely been ignored by Yolanda. This particular caller had tried to reach her several times since nine this morning. Counting, I came up with seven times. Whoever it was seemed to really want to talk with her but left no messages. That was a serious mistake. Perhaps if this person said something, the message would at least have been heard.

Yolanda had a single landline with a private number that she'd only given to Pam and me. She had no computer for Internet access. It took Pam and me months convincing her to buy the cell phone. Even then, it was under my name on the contract, not hers.

I sat on the couch drained of all my energy. If she didn't have her phone on her, there was no way to contact Yolanda unless she decided to call. The stench in the air reminded me that she may be in danger. I dialed the police and prayed that I hadn't waited too long.

***

Initially, a uniformed officer arrived at the apartment to verify my story. She questioned me for about ten minutes before being convinced there might be a real threat to Yolanda. She made the call to her department. Because Wanabe had not died of natural causes and because there was the possibility that Yolanda was in mortal danger or dead, the Police Department sent two Missing Persons detectives to investigate, Sergeants Larry Madden and Paula Dixon.

Knowing the detectives came from Missing Persons made me feel even more jumpy than I had been before I called the police. I sat on the living room couch as Madden questioned me. His partner, Dixon, was searching around the apartment being careful not to touch anything.

Madden asked, "You entered the apartment an hour ago correct?"

I nodded. "Yes, that sounds right." The words came out sheepish as I tried to hide my nervousness.

He looked at his wristwatch. "So, that would mean you came in at around seven o'clock."

"Yes." There was irritation in my words. "Why don't you have a forensics team here or something? We're wasting valuable time."

He paused and looked me over. "I'm sorry, Mr. Holman, do you have a background in police procedure?" His voice was even but I sensed I might have hit a nerve.

I shook my head, no.

He continued, "Have you personally been involved in a police investigation?"

Again, I indicated, no.

His blue eyes narrowed to thin slits and he spoke through gritted teeth. "Then don't assume you know how we should conduct our investigation, Mr. Holman. If we determine that crime scene investigators are needed, then we'll send for them pronto. For now, I need you to answer my questions."

Madden, stood over me in his dark grey two-piece suit that looked cheap, like it came off a JCPenny's rack. His tan skin gave him an olive coloring. He was shorter than me by two or three inches, which put him around five ten or so. Still, as I sat, he towered over me giving him the appearance that he was much taller and intimidating. He looked a lot like Ray Liotta from that gangster movie, Good Fellas, which added to his tough guy persona.

I heard myself say, "I'm sorry." But I wasn't. I wanted these two to get off their butts and find Yolanda before it was too late. "I'll answer your questions."

"Thank you, Mr. Holman."

I noticed he kept repeating my name. I wondered if he did this to commit it to memory. I couldn't imagine how many suspects, victims and lawyers he spoke to on a day-to-day basis as he investigated various crimes.

Before he said another word, I said, "Tony."

"Excuse me?"

"Not Mr. Holman. It's Tony."

He nodded politely, understanding. "Tony it is then. You said you arrived here at seven. Was Ms. Blakely expecting you?"

"No." I decided not to elaborate. The less I said the less chance of me saying something stupid, especially out of anger.

"Hmm. So do you often drop by without letting her know ahead of time?"

"Sometimes, but not often."

"Why this time?"

"Why this time, what?"

"Why did you come over without calling?"

"I had called her. Several times in fact."

His left eyebrow shot up. "Did you now?" He folded his arms together. "Care to explain what you mean by that?"

I let out a frustrated breath. "We sort of had…" I tried to think of the right word but nothing came to mind. We hadn't exactly had an argument. She slapped me and walked away. Finally, I said the only thing that came to me. "We had a disagreement."

"A fight?"

"No. A fight takes two people."

He gave me a wry smile. "One would think that a disagreement was much the same, Mr. Holman." He snapped his fingers realizing his mistake. "Sorry, I mean, Tony. You said something about calling her several times. Was it because she wouldn't pick up?"

"That's right," I answered guardedly. I was starting to feel like a suspect.

"So, after you two had your… Disagreement, was it?"

I just looked at him.

The detective continued, "Anyway, after your disagreement, you came here to what? Make amends?"

"Something like that. Yes."

"How did you get inside the apartment?"

"I have a key."

"Did she give you the key?"

"Of course she gave me the key!" That upset me and I felt the anger well up. "We were going to get married."

His partner, Dixon, chimed in. "I looked around. I didn't find any wedding invitations or bridal magazines."

244

In Desperation   DK Gaston

Surprised by her voice, I twisted my head around and looked up at her stunned.

She made her way back into the living room and stood behind the couch where I sat. She had a hard edge to her demeanor that wasn't there before and gave her partner a stare that I couldn't interpret. He, on the other hand nodded his understanding.

Madden in the front of me, Dixon at my back. The room suddenly felt smaller, claustrophobic.

My head darted from her to him and back to her.

Fighting the urge to shout, I asked, "What are you trying to say?"

She shrugged her shoulders in an 'I don't know' fashion. "I'm just saying I didn't see any proof of an impending marriage, that's all. I mean, if I were engaged, I would have something to show for it. Wouldn't any woman?"

My teeth were gritted now. "I asked her last night. She hadn't had time for any of that."

Madden asked, "Last night, huh?" I craned my head toward him. "Yesterday, you two were love birds and today, you two had a disagreement. Don't you find that kind of strange?"

Dixon directed her attention to her partner, ignoring me all together, and said, "I do. Maybe, the husband to be chickened out and tried to back out of the marriage. Maybe that's what started their argument."

"Disagreement." Madden corrected her. "It takes two to have an argument, remember?"

Dixon said mockingly, "Oh that's right. How stupid of me."

I bolted to my feet.

Madden put his palm against my chest. "Sit down, Tony!"

I had the feeling that if I refused, he would have put me down by force. I sat voluntarily. "I called the police remember? Why are you treating me like I'm guilty of something?"

"Are you guilty of something?" Dixon asked. "Maybe you killed the cat out a fit of anger."

"What?"

"Perhaps, you broke off the marriage, because you discovered that your fiancé wasn't as faithful to you as you might have hoped."

What was happening? Why was I suddenly being treated like a criminal? The lingering smell of death from Wanabe was making me sick. I was about to vomit. This time I knew, I wouldn't be able to hold it back. I threw a hand over my mouth and lurched from the couch almost knocking Sergeant Madden off his feet, heading directly to the bathroom; neither detective tried to stop me and I barely made it to the toilet before the tide came.

I emptied my stomach and I felt like I was there for an hour even though it had not been more than a minute or two. My heavy breathing echoed inside the bowl, drowning out the footsteps that entered the bathroom behind me.

Lifting my head, a towel appeared beside me.

I looked up to see Madden offering it to me.

He said, "Clean yourself up, Tony. You're getting your wish. I'm calling for a forensics team to check out the apartment. In the meantime, you need to come with us. We have a few more questions for you."

The tidal wave began again.

In Desperation   DK Gaston
PAM

After carrying the five boxes Yolanda left to my old bedroom at my mother's, I spent the past few hours going through them. At first, Mama pretended to help as she tried to pry more information from me and to continue her tangent about my fooling around with my best friend's man. She left me alone twenty minutes later, having said her piece and not gaining any further explanation from me.

With everything piled on top of the bed, the items sketched out the two and half year history between Yolanda and me. Pictures of us doing our *thang* at the clubs, playing volleyball at company picnics, and double dates we shared. She gave back everything we treasured as friends. It was as though she was trying to erase her past. I sat on the edge of the bed, holding a photograph I took of her and Tony. It was the night Yolanda and I met him.

Twenty-eight Months Ago

Hanging at Deluge after work, it was a girl's night out on the town. It was hopping and filled to capacity. Yolanda and I sat at a table in the corner away from the long bar with two other women from our department, Georgia and Kara. The music was live that night, jazzy and sexy. All of us may have had too many drinks but the dawgs were on the prowl and they kept buying us whatever we wanted. Between the four of us, we must have had over twenty drinks starting with a simple Long Island Ice Tea and ending the night with Bahama Mamas.

For twenty minutes this tall, skinny brother who wore too much cologne gave me his best pickup lines. He actually bounced back and forth between Yolanda and me, hoping one us would bite, probably envisioned having a little ménage à trios with us.

Had to admire his audacity; not many men would attempt this maneuver, but this brother did it with finesse. He was wasting his time, but we let him stay since he kept paying for more drinks. Besides, he wasn't bad on the eyes, um, man-candy, and some of what he was saying was kinda cool. A few more Long Islands and who knows? Maybe he would have gotten both our digits that night. Of course, neither she nor I let him know this.

247

In Desperation   DK Gaston

Finally, he picked up on the fact that he wasn't making any headway with us, before moving on to another table filled with women that looked tipsier than us. From their scantily appearances, they would probably be more open to the suggestion of ménage à trios than we were. The tall, skinny brother with too much cologne told us exactly what we were missing. But I'll keep those naughty comments to myself. Anyway, everyone had a good laugh at the table and joked about giving him another shot.

Yolanda and I got up to go the ladies room. I didn't realized just how drunk I was until I started to walk, if you want to call it that. It was more of a sway or maybe a full blown stagger. Yolanda on the other hand had total control of her faculties and was graceful. Though I knew she had more drinks than me. She could always drink me under the table. The only thing she didn't seemed to be able to handle was wine, believe it or not. The only time I'd ever seen her drinking wine was during that first office party when she opened up to me.

I bumped against everyone in bumping distance trying to make it to the ladies room. Halfway there the room began spinning. I felt myself going down. Yolanda whirled around to catch me and as fast as she was, I knew it was too late, and I was going to hit the floor hard. Sinking backward in my downward spiral, all I could see was the intense glow of the ceiling's spot lights. I closed my eyes and braced myself for the crash landing.
It never came.
A pair of strong hands caught me from behind, held me in place, keeping me from dropping any further.
I heard a man ask, "Are you all right?"

I tilted my head in the voice's direction. I'm pretty sure there was only one person there holding me up but I was seeing double. Both images were handsome with these amazing brown eyes staring down at me filled with genuine concern. His body gave off a blend of Perry Ellis 360 cologne and subtle perspiration. I could see he was sweating even though it was cool in the bar. He probably had been on the dance floor. His caramel brown skin was cast in shadows and the bar's dim glow as patrons navigated by us disrupting the overhead spotlight.
I was breathless.

He brought me upright and waited until my feet found its footing before he let me go. Again, he asked, "Are you okay?"

248

In Desperation   DK Gaston

"Y..yes... I'm okay and so embarrassed," I finally said. Now that I was on my feet, his twin image disappeared and I was staring at one of the finest brothers I have ever laid my eyes on. Six feet something, short hair with a bald fade, well dressed in his blue pants and shirt, clean shaven face and those eyes. He reminded me of Boris Kodjoe from that Undercover TV series.

Oh God, I think I might have been staring at him too long. He noticed.

Smiling, he said, "Don't be. I doubt that anyone even noticed."

"You did and I'm thankful for that." I tried to sound sexy but I think the alcohol might have caused my words to slur a bit. I wasn't sure.

I was about to say more when Yolanda chimed in, saying, "You have a name, Mr. Knight in Shining Armor?"

He looked from me to her. In comparison, I must have looked a mess. My hair was thrown, I couldn't stand straight and on top of that I was drunk. Yolanda looked like she just stepped off that show Models, not a single strand was out of place and she was dressed to kill that night.

"My name is Anthony but you can call me Tony," he said forgetting all about me.

In retrospect, I couldn't really blame the brother for not showing me any interest.

Present day

       For a split second a rush of anger filled my thoughts as I remembered that night. If I had been sober. If I had not let her interrupt. If I went to the ladies room alone. It all could have gone differently.

       When I felt the photograph beginning to crumple under the weight of my fingers, I realized that I was being stupid and loosened my hold. I believe in God and in destiny. If Tony and I were meant to be, then we would have gotten together that night. In the last two years we built a friendship that was as close as Yolanda's and mine. That's something I would never regret having. I wasn't about to let what could have been interfere with me finding my friend. Instead of putting the picture back in the pile, I placed it inside my purse. Where I can have it close to remind me of the friendship the three of us share in those times that I once again start to have my doubts.

In Desperation   DK Gaston

      I was about to close the purse when my cell phone rang. I took it out and saw a number I did not recognize on the display. I was hesitant to answer it at first. Lately, I've been getting random cold calls from sales people trying to sell me something. I'm constantly trying to remind myself to put my cell on the Do Not Call watch list but keep forgetting. I was in no mood to deal with a salesperson but something, maybe because of the strangeness of the day, caused me to answer.

I said, "Hello."

I waited for the caller to say something like, *Hello is this Pamela Reeb. I would like to offer you, blah, blah blah…* But instead I got something I didn't expect.

It was Tony.

He was being questioned by the police.

In Desperation DK Gaston
The Bald Man

Once the bald man had installed the bugs and cameras into pretty Pamela Reeb's apartment he headed over to Anthony Holman's house. Being there, inside this man's dwelling, made the bald man sick in the pit of his stomach. It was his ulcer acting up again. He started getting them when he learned of Yolanda's latest love interest.

He hated Holman because Yolanda loved him; or at least as close to love as she could get. Looking around, he bit down hard on his bottom lip until blood trickled out. His tongue slithered from his mouth like a venomous reptile and he slurped the blood away. Peering down over the living room couch, his thoughts wandered off his work. She and her latest love had watched movies here, talked about their future together here, and made passionate love right here on this overstuffed couch.

The urge to burn it all to the ground was overpowering. He shouted, "Burn it down and kill the boyfriend!" A devilish grin spread across his broad face.

"You need to control your anger," the voice ordered. "You are not there to burn anything. Holman isn't your assignment just a means to our true objective. Do you understand?"

"Yes," the bald man said with a momentary grimace. "I haven't forgotten my mission." His frown turned back into a smile as he imagined the house in an inferno with Holman caught helpless in its wake screaming for his life.

"Good. Proceed with your placement of the listening devices."

On the floor, ripped pictures, shattered plates, and other keepsakes lay scattered as though a storm had swept across the room. He knew that it was Yolanda's doing. He'd experienced that temper of hers himself.

She was a hellcat when it overcame her. The rage rivaled his. Hit the right button and Yolanda could be the most dangerous person on Earth. Holman only experienced a tamed variation of it so far. But that was going to change soon. The bald man knew Yolanda better than anyone alive. Her anger would fester. She'd need to direct it at something or someone. That someone of course would be Anthony Holman. He'd made sure of that.

In Desperation   DK Gaston

Pam

I was furious and stormed passed my father's executive assistant, Vicky, without asking her if he was busy. One thing I'd definitely inherited from Daddy was his temper, and I was ready to blow. Vicky saw the fire in my eyes and knew better than try to stop me. The white stenciled Chief Reeb on his door caused most that approached to pause. Most of the time, the visitor was either about to be reprimanded or was delivering bad news. All it had done for me was made me even angrier. How could Daddy let his officers interrogate Tony? He'd known him for years and knew Tony wouldn't harm anything, not even a cat.

Pushing open the door, I stomped in, my finger wagging and my mouth primed to let him have an earful. But he held up his hand, stopping me before I uttered a single syllable. Sitting behind his large black desk, Daddy was on the phone giving whoever was on the other end, the treatment I'd intended to give him. He was shouting at the top of his lungs, bulbous veins ran across his shining shaved head. Momma always said some day one of them would burst if he didn't take it easy.

I wanted to scream. I wanted to throw something. But instead I kicked the door close with the toe of my shoe, crossed the office and sat in the chair opposite Daddy. Folding my arms, I crouched in my seat like I'd always done when I was upset with him. A quick twinkle flickered in his eyes as he stared toward me, but was gone in a flash. I imagined that for a moment, he saw me as his spoiled little girl. Uncoiling my arms, I sat up straight. I needed him to see me as a grown woman.

After five long minutes, Daddy finished his tirade and hung up. I opened my mouth, only to be halted by his hand again. Daddy pressed the intercom button. When his assistant answered, he said, "Vicky, please hold all my calls."
"For how long, sir?" Vicky questioned.
Daddy looked thoughtfully at me and then said, "Until I say otherwise." He released the button before Vicky could respond.
"Can I talk now?" I asked.
"No."
"Excuse   me?"

His face became stern, his body rigid as he sat stoically upright. I'd seen it many times before, when he was about to give me a life's lesson. "I said no, young lady. Before you say anything, I need you to understand there are certain protocols and procedures that have to be adhered to. Just because I know someone personally doesn't automatically negate my officers from performing their duty."

I leaned in closer, holding my expression was as hard as his. "But it's Tony. He wouldn't hurt a fly, let alone do anything to harm Yolanda."

"I know no such thing. One thing I've learned over the years is anyone, under the right conditions, can be pushed beyond his breaking point and do things, friends and family never thought possible."

My eyebrows shot up. "Come on, Daddy, you can't seriously believe that."

"I've seen it more than once, young lady."

"But we're talking about Tony," I repeated, unable to come up with anything else.

He let his shoulders relax and his face softened. "I know. And because of that fact, I've already stretched my authority further than I should have when I had him brought here to headquarters instead of one of the precincts."

Daddy thought that flexing his muscles a little around the precinct would appease me, but it didn't change the fact he was treating Tony like a common criminal. "If you truly believe he's capable of doing Yolanda harm, because they had an argument, you might as well question me too."

He leaned in, placing his arms across the top of his desk. "What's that supposed to mean?"

"Yolanda yelled at me this morning, accusing me of hurting her and then stormed off before I could find out what she was talking about."

Daddy looked ready to ask me a question, hesitated, looked down at his hands, shaped them into a pyramid, and then stared up at me again. "Are you and Tony sleeping together?"

I came out of my seat, almost knocking the chair over. "What?"

For a brief moment he looked embarrassed, before then his calm demeanor returned. "I've seen how you looked at him when you thought no one was watching. How you talk about him, especially when Yolanda is not in earshot. It's obvious you like Tony. I suspect he likes you too."

"No, we're not sleeping together. He's dating my best friend." I couldn't believe what I was hearing, Daddy accusing me of betraying Yolanda.

Daddy let out a sigh and cocked his head, looking relieved and let his hands lay flat again on the desk. "I thought as much, but I had to ask."

I took a step closer, my eyes narrowed in disgust. "What do you mean, you had to ask? Are you interrogating me now, Daddy?"

Daddy's voice brimmed with good spirits. "No, baby, of course not. This was just a father-daughter conversation." He evaded my first questions.

I gave him my best *you-don't-really-expect-me-to-believe-that* stare. "What aren't you telling me?"

He wiped a hand slowly across his bald head. His dark brown eyes, that had always provided me with reassurance, now made me very nervous. "Until we get things sorted out with Tony, maybe you should stay away from him for a little while. I wouldn't want you to be inadvertently pulled into his troubles."

Shaking my head, I said, "Um, um, Daddy. That's not going to fly. Tony is one of my closest friends. I trust him," I said wagging a finger at him. "Look, I don't know what's going on, but I'm sure as hell going to find out."

He stood raised his open hand and softly said, "I'm trying to protect you here, sweetheart. I'm not your enemy."

"It sure doesn't look like that from this side of the desk, Daddy."

His eyes glared as he stood up tall. In an instance, I felt like a little girl again about to be scolded. "How dare you talk to me that way, young lady! I'm putting my foot down, stay away from Tony. That's an order!"

"I'm a grown woman, Daddy. I don't take orders." I couldn't believe what I was saying. Yes, we had heated disagreements in the past, but never to the point where he was giving me orders. Whatever the police had on Tony, it must be bad.

"Fine," he huffed. "If you want to know what's going on, I'll tell you. My detectives found photographs in Yolanda's apartment of her sleeping with another man. We're thinking that Tony might have discovered them, confronted her and went into a rage."

I reeled in astonishment. "I can't believe that, Daddy. Tony would never—"

He sliced his hand through the air cutting me off. "We obtained a warrant and are searching his house even as we speak." Lowering his hand, he let out a heavy sigh. "I'm sorry sweetheart, but I have a job to do. My detectives feel there's enough on Tony to suspect he may have harmed… Yolanda."

I suspected Daddy stopped short of saying, *or killed.*

"I want to talk to him, Daddy."

"I don't think that's a good idea. Especially after telling me you and Yolanda had an altercation this morning."

I shook my head and asked, "So it's okay to shield me from your detectives, but not Tony?"

He wagged a finger at me. "Now see here—"

It was my turn to cut him off. "Does Mama know that you let Tony be arrested?" Mama thought of Tony as the son she never had. I thought Daddy felt the same way, but I saw that I was wrong.

His eyes danced around in his sockets. "Your mother doesn't need to know this," he said, knowing Mama would nag him about it from dusk till dawn if she found out. "Besides, Tony isn't under arrest. He's only being questioned."

I folded my arms. "So he can leave whenever he likes?"

Daddy nodded resignedly. "Assuming he hasn't implicated himself, of course."

"I can't believe you're saying any of this, Daddy. I thought you liked Tony."

"I do," he admitted. "I love him like a son, but evidence so far is saying he might be guilty."

"Of what? For all you know, Yolanda simply packed up and left. Your detectives are most likely making something out of nothing."

"I hope you're right. I really do."

"I'm seeing him, Daddy and you can't stop me," I said more forcibly than I meant to.

He sat back down, shaking his head, looking defeated. "Fine, honey, go see him. But understand this, if the District Attorney decides there's enough evidence against Tony, I won't have any choice but to have him arrested. It's nothing personal."

Though I felt like hitting something, I couldn't take my anger out on Daddy. In the end, he was right. He was only allowing his detectives to follow the chain of evidence. It wasn't Daddy's fault that Tony was a suspect. I let my arms go slack. "You don't have to protect me Daddy, I'm a big girl now."

He gave me a slight grin. "I see that. You're a firebrand, just like your Mama."

"No need to insult me, Daddy."

We shared a laugh, though it sounded forced from the both of us.

I was opening the door to leave when Daddy shouted, "Don't tell your Mama about Tony. I'll never hear the end of it, baby."

Glancing over my shoulder, I said, "I'll think about it."

Part Three: Anthony

I was in the interview room at police headquarters. Because of my connection to the police chief's daughter, I rated a bit more importance than most people of interest, so Sergeants Madden and Dixon brought me downtown. I was looking down at the table, fiddling with an empty paper cup. For the past half hour the detectives had hammered me about my relationship with Yolanda as though I had something to do with her disappearance. I had a hard time believing just finding Wanabe in the trash would spark so much trouble for myself. As much as I loved that cat, he was just that, a cat. It wasn't as though Yolanda was lying on the floor dead.

That thought sent my eyes back up toward the detectives, who had moved away from the table to converse quietly near the door. They seemed to be arguing about something. Perhaps one of them realized they were wasting valuable time investigating me, when they should be out searching for Yolanda. Letting go of the empty glass, I rubbed my bruised hand. Dixon narrowed her eyes on me.

Unable to take her suspicious gaze or the silence, I asked, "Do you have information about Yolanda you haven't told me about?"

"What makes you say that?" Dixon asked, shoving past her partner. I nervously rubbed my hand faster. "Maybe because you're treating me like crap, as if I had something to do with my girlfriend's disappearance."

"Did you?" It was Dixon again. "'Cause right now, nothing really explains why she would simply pack up and leave, unless you provide us something that makes sense."

I pushed the chair back and got to my feet, pointing an accusing finger at her. "I don't like what your insinuating, Sergeant!" It was time I called an attorney; things were getting out of hand.

Dixon calmly approached the table and sat in a chair staring at me intently. "What happened to your hand?"

"What?"

She pointed at my wagging hand. "It's bruised. How'd that happen?"

"I hit it against a wall," I answered without thinking, already regretting it.

Madden folded his arms and looked thoughtful. "Do you like hitting things, Tony? Is that something you do when you're angry? You hit things, maybe people too?"

Surprised by the question, I staggered back as if a blow struck me in the face. "No, of course not! It was... I was just—" *Shut up. Shut up. Shut up.* I had said enough and was digging a deeper hole for myself. "I'd like an attorney."

Dixon glanced over her shoulder toward her partner. "Typical."

My hand turned into tight balls. "You know I'm getting tired of your attitude, Dixon!"

She turned back and grinned. "I'll betcha anything you want to hit me? Guys like you enjoy hitting women."

Guys like me? I instinctively opened my hands. "Look, I think you two got the wrong idea in your heads. I love Yolanda and I would cut off my own limb before I'd hurt her."

"You know that's what my Pop used to tell the social workers that came by the house, after a teacher reported my injuries to them," Dixon said, her mouth tightening into a stubborn line. "Same damn thing my boyfriend said after nearly beating me to death. It's always the same with you type. The same damn thing!"

Dixon seemed to realize that she'd said too much and then frowned, while Madden maintained his thoughtful expression. After a long, awkward silence, Dixon got up and moved to her partner's side. "Since you opted to lawyer up, we're not allowed to ask you anymore questions," she huffed and stormed out.

Madden gestured with a nod to follow him. "I'm taking you to a phone so you can call your attorney. Though I have to say I'm disappointed that you decided to go that route. We could have worked this out, nice and neat, without involving a third party."

Nice and neat, for the police, maybe. But I had the distinct feeling that Madden and Dixon were out to bury me. With his partner out of earshot, I decided to once again ask, "Did you find something in Yolanda's apartment that makes you think I had something to do with her disappearance."

"Yes," Madden said poker faced, offering nothing else.

In Desperation   DK Gaston

"Come on, man, throw me some kind of bone. Dixon is on a witch hunt. I don't know if you're playing the good cop here or what, but I get the feeling you don't share her opinion."

He narrowed his eyes at me. "I like to think I can read folks fairly well. You don't have that scumbag vibe Dixon and I often have to deal with," he admitted freely. "But that doesn't necessarily mean I don't agree with my partner. Sometimes my readings are way off the meter. But I will tell you this much. Yes, she's on a witch hunt. You heard her story, Dixon came from a home where her father beat her most of the time. Later, Dixon ended up with the wrong men in her life, men that tended to be like her father."

I was beginning to understand. Dixon hated men that hurt women. "I never laid a hand on Yolanda. I would never do that," I said with a sincere conviction.

Still poker faced, he said, "You can't talk to me about this, son. You're lawyering up, remember?" He gently took me by the arm and guided me to a row of phones lined up on a wall. "Use your own dime to call your attorney." He sauntered away out of earshot. Left alone, I wondered what Dixon had found in the Yolanda's apartment that had made her go from calm to enraged. When I searched her place, I didn't find anything out of the ordinary. Well, that wasn't exactly true, I found Wanabe's twisted corpse in the trash. I was kind of frantic when I was there and could have missed something. Still, what would make Dixon think I would hurt Yolanda?

I picked up the handset and was about to dial, but paused. Why had I been directed to a payphone? The police had my cell phone. All they had to do was give it back to make my call. They might be checking my calls. But wouldn't the police need a warrant for that? And if they had a warrant for my phone, what else might they have one for? Searching for change in my pocket, I realized one other thing; I didn't actually have an attorney to call. I only said I would call one, because I was nervous and wanted to get the hell out of there.

I thought about picking up the beat up copy of the Yellow Pages lying on the floor, but it was after office hours. Lawyers would be hanging out at some bar enjoying the beginning of the weekend. I banged the handset against my forehead, trying to recall if I knew any attorneys. One name eventually came to mind, my cousin Eddie. He was a glorified ambulance chaser. I wasn't sure he ever had a case that went to court. Letting out an exhausted breath, I'd had no one else to call. It was either him or a complete stranger who might not be any better than Eddie. Digging in my pocket, I pulled out some change.

The call was picked up on the third ring. I said, "Hello."

No answer, though there was the faint sound of breathing on the other end.

"Eddie, it's me, your cousin Tony."

"Whaddup Tony," Eddie's boisterous voice said. "I didn't recognize the number on my caller-ID, I thought you might be a bill collector."

Eddie was always behind on his bills. He lost his house, his car, and dog, to debt collectors. He was the only person I'd known whose dog was repossessed. Eddie lived in his car and his so-call office was in a booth in the back corner of a coffee shop. Though most of the time he appeared to have lost everything, somehow he managed to always land back on his feet. There was always someone who needed a lawyer, some more desperately than others. Never thought that someone would be me.

"I need your help, Eddie. I think I'm in trouble," I choked out, hardly believing that I was forced to seek help from the man who could be the poster boy for ill fortune.

"Um huh," he said cautiously. "Are we talkin' 'bout a payin' gig or are you askin' to help you move furniture for free?"

"You'll be paid. I need your..." I couldn't believe I was about to say this. "Your skills as an attorney."

He yelled, "Yes!" His end went silent.

I imagined he was pumping one arm and leg, up and down in the air, gesturing as if he just won the lottery, viewing me as his next meal ticket.

After a while, he said in a calm, professional voice, "Tell me about your problem Tony."

In Desperation DK Gaston
Pam

I entered the interview room expecting to see Tony being given the third degree, instead I find him sitting, leaning his elbows against the table, face in his hands. His fingers were spread wide apart and I could see his eyes behind them, staring back at me. Occupying the empty chair opposite him, I reached out and gently touch his arm.
"You okay, Tony?"
"No, I'm not Pam." He lowered his hands to the table. Tony had bags beneath his bloodshot eyes and peered about wild-eyed. "They think I did something with Yolanda. Can you believe that?" His voice sounded strained as if it hurt him to speak.
"No," I said reassuringly. "Have the detectives finished questioning you?"
He shook his head. "I told them I wanted an attorney. All conversation ended after that."
"Is he on his way?"
He wiped sweat from his forehead. "Who?"
"Your lawyer. When will he be here?"
"Your guess is as good as mine," he said, looking as if he was ready to burst into a forced laugh.
I squeezed his arm to get Tony to focus. "Either he's coming or he's not. Which is it?"
"My attorney's car is having engine problems. He doesn't have enough cash to take a cab, so he's catching a bus downtown to meet me here."
I thought he was joking, but his stoic expression said differently. "Please tell me you're pulling my leg."
"I wish. I was foolish enough to call my cousin."
Shocked, I pulled my hand away. "Eddie?"
"Eddie," he replied with defeat in his voice. "Eddie."
The interview room door opened and a woman stuck her head in. Her eyes went directly to Tony's and then swiveled toward me.
"You the chief's daughter?" she asked.
"Yes. And you are?"
"Sergeant Paula Dixon." She stepped fully into the room, letting the door shut and approached us with an indifferent expression.

261

"Mind if I ask you a few questions while we wait for Mr. Holman's lawyer?"

I had the sensation of a spider crawling up my back. As Daddy had feared, I may have placed myself into the investigation just for trying to be a good friend. Trying not to show my concern, I calmly said, "I don't think so, sergeant. I'm here to take my friend home."

Dixon gawked at me in disbelief. "Excuse me?"

"Is Tony under arrest?" I asked.

"No, but—"

I held up a hand stopping her mid-sentence. "Is he currently being charged with anything?"

Dixon let out a heavy breath. "No."

I stood and gestured for Tony to do the same. "Is there anything stopping him from getting out of that seat and walking out of here?"

Dixon went to the door, grabbed the knob and pulled it open. "No ma'am, there's absolutely nothing stopping him from leaving," she said sarcastically. She leveled her stare toward Tony. "I'm sure we'll be seeing each other again real soon, hotshot."

"What about my cell phone?" Tony asked.

Dixon reached into her pocket, pulled out the phone and tossed it underhand across the room. Tony caught it and examined the device like he was looking for damage. After a few moments, he looked satisfied and put it away.

"Anything else I can do for you, hotshot?" Dixon's face contorted like saying the words was painful.

Tony shook his head.

As I was walking by the detective, she stopped me by touching my arm and whispered, "You better watch out for this one. You can't trust him. You can't trust any of them." After saying her piece, she let me pass.

In the corridor, I asked Tony, "What's her beef?"

"Her partner said she had it rough when it comes to men." He glanced around as if to make sure no one was listening. "As far as she's concerned, Dixon thinks I killed Yolanda and buried her somewhere."

"What about her partner?"

"Sergeant Madden? I'm not sure about him. He's as expressionless as a Vulcan. But I suspect he doesn't share Dixon's conviction."

We stayed quiet until we were outside. I said, "The police are searching your house."

Tony didn't look surprise and only nodded. He padded the pocket where he placed his cell phone. "I think my phone logs were checked too."

We started down the long row of stairs leading to the sidewalk. "Daddy won't help you."

That got a surprised reaction, but he said nothing, only nodding his understanding.

I took his hand. "We're going to figure this out, Tony. We're a team, you and I."

"I'm not sure if that's a good idea. I don't want you dragged into this, Pam."

"Yolanda is my friend too, remember. You're not alone in this."

Tony smiled. "You're a good friend, Pam." He squeezed my hand.

A rush of heat swept into my belly and I wondered if he felt that same sensation. We held hands all the way down to the bottom step. A bus pulled up to the curb. The silhouette of a man stood behind the door. When the door swung open, Tony's cousin Eddie, wearing a frumpy two-piece suit stepped out, smelling of coffee. In one hand he carried a tote bag with Boy Scouts of America stenciled on its side; his poor man's version of a briefcase. Startled by his sudden appearance, our hands fell apart.

Eddie stared at us wide eyed. "You're out?" He sounded disappointed.

"Turns out, they couldn't hold me," Tony replied.

Eddie's frown deepened. "I was all set to go in there like Matlock and fight for your freedom. On the bus, I wrote an entire speech I intended for the arrestin' officers." He dug into the breast pocket of his wrinkled coat and presented evidence of his work.

Tony looked down at the wad of crumpled paper in his cousin's hand and then at me, grimacing. "Gee Eddie, I'm sorry, I had to miss seeing that."

Eddie turned to me. "Hey beautiful, long time, no see." He never could remember my name and called me beautiful, gorgeous, or princess to cover his lack of memory.

I grinned, acknowledging him, but said nothing.

Eddie's attention went back to his hand, obviously disappointment in his expression. Finally, he stuffed the wad back into his pocket. "Do you still need me or did I waste bus fare comin' here?"

Tony gave Eddie the abbreviated version of what happened during the day. I chimed in, giving my portion of the story and leaving out the part about the pictures Daddy told me about. I didn't want Tony finding out about them, not like that. It would require a little finesse and much more privacy. His cousin listened wordlessly. When we were finished, Eddie placed a consoling hand on Tony's shoulder. "I see you do need me, cuz. Don't worry, I got your back."

"That's comforting," Tony said with a cautious smile. "But what advice can you offer me in the meantime?"

He looked up to the night sky as if in deep thought, and then lowered his gaze to Tony. "Do nothing, cuz. Let me handle things from this point on." When Tony opened his mouth to argue, Eddie stopped him by giving his shoulder a squeeze. "Look, cuz. I know you want to be proactive about this, but you can't. Anythin' you do would only make you look more guilty to the cops."

"Yolanda might be in trouble. I can't sit back and wait," Tony yelled.

Eddie gestured for him to lower his voice. "Or she might be chillin' in Hawaii for all you know, sipping a fruit drink with an umbrella. Besides, you don't have any experience with findin' missin' folks. Let the professionals do their job. You'll just be in the way."

I wrapped my arms around Tony's to reassure him. "Maybe he's right."

Tony looked at me as if I struck him. "Not you too, Pam. I thought you understood more than anyone."

"I do, but Eddie made some good points."

"At least, sleep on it. Don't go looking for her tonight. Okay?" Eddie asked.

Tony reluctantly nodded his agreement.

"Great," Eddie said triumphantly. "Now that that's settled, I'll just go inside police headquarters, hunt down the investigators and bust a few balls to find out what's really goin' on with the case." He swung his gym bag over his shoulder. "Don't worry, cuz. You're in good hands." Eddie, happy to be working, literally skipped up the row of stone stairs, whistling.

"I can't believe I'm putting my life in his hands," Tony said nervously.

In Desperation   *DK Gaston*

"You're not," I said. "We're going to stick with our original plan and check out Yolanda's cubicle in the morning."

He regarded me quizzically. "I thought you said we should listen to Eddie?"

I grinned. "I only said that so he wouldn't keep pressing you to stop. Tonight, we need to go over everything that has happened in the last 24 hours and figure things out."

Tony's eyes glinted under the moonlight. He offered his hand to me. "Partners," he said.

I shook his hand. "Partners."

In Desperation DK Gaston
The Bald Man

He backed off, leaving more space between him and the black and gold Mountaineer than he should have, but he wasn't worried about losing them. The bald man knew exactly where Pretty Pamela Reeb was driving. The pair were predictable and predictability was a weakness he could exploit. Humming, *Pop Goes the Weasel*, he drummed his fingers on the steering wheel keeping cadence. Things were shaping up exactly as he had orchestrated. The police suspected Yolanda's boy-toy of foul play. At the same time Holman and pretty Pamela Reeb were pursuing their own investigation of Yolanda's disappearance.

"What your status," the voice buzzed in his ear, interrupting his thoughts.

He stopped his drumming and twisted his hands around the steering wheel imagining it was his controller's neck. "Reeb is driving Holman to her apartment. I'm trailing them at a safe distance," the bald man explained.

"Excellent. Will you need backup to assist in overnight surveillance?"

Why is he always questioning my abilities? Doubting my skill as an artist?

"Negative. I suspect the pair will stay in place for the night. I'll have time to doze a couple of hours before the sun rises."

"If the target shows up, you may regret that decision."

"If the target emerges from hiding, it won't be me who'll have the regrets. That I promise you."

"Very well. Keep me advised."

"Sure, whatever you say."

Up until that point the bald man had been having a decent day, as he watched all his work successfully unfolding before him, but now he was angry. He needed to desperately hurt someone. Pressing his foot on the accelerator his car jettisoned through traffic, closing in on the Mountaineer. He no longer cared if he was spotted, after all it wasn't like either Reeb or Holman could see his face through the dark tinted glass.

He drove up along the driver side of the sports utility vehicle and matched its speed. Pretty Pamela Reeb gawked at his car as if he were insane. The bald man gunned the engine several times. Smiling, he pressed his foot all the way down on the gas pedal and rocketed passed the SUV, swerving into the lane in front of the Mountaineer. Slowing to nearly a crawl, he forced Pretty Pamela Reeb to veer into the next lane. When she honked her horn, the bald man laughed.

He gunned the engine again and shot away down the street. Taunting them was a distraction, but it wasn't enough to ebb his anger. Driving into the worse crime infected section of the city, the bald man drove up and down the neighborhood until he found exactly what he needed. On a corner, leaning nonchalantly against a streetlamp, two young men barely out of their teens, looked to be simply hanging out. But the bald man knew differently. Folks didn't hangout on street corners unless they had something to sell.
The bald man approached the street corner, casually stopping in front of the young men. He lowered the passenger side window down and turned the interior lights off, making it difficult to see inside. One of the men, wearing pants that hung down past the top of his underwear and a red sleeveless shirt, pushed off the lamp post. A gun bulged under his shirt. He cautiously approached. An open window was an invitation. The man held his hand underneath his shirt, gripping the gun.
"Yo, you want somethin' dawg?" the man said, squinting to see into the darkness.
The bald man laughed. "As a matter of fact, I do."

He lifted his silenced pistol, firing once into the young man's face. As soon as the body toppled out of the way to the pavement, he saw that the second man was reaching for his gun. Firing three times, two to the chest, one to the throat, the bald man watched his victim crumble to the ground. Laying the pistol down in the passenger seat, he let out a satisfied sigh. He rolled up the passenger window and pulled away from the curb. With his anger finally abated, he began humming again, drumming his fingers against the steering wheel.

In Desperation   DK Gaston
Anthony

Opening my eyes, I realized immediately it was morning. I was so exhausted I must have blacked out on her couch seconds after we sat down to talk about the previous days events. Looking down, Pam was leaning against my chest like it was a pillow. My arm was slung over her shoulder and wrapped around her chest like it belonged there. She held adoringly to my arm. She looked so beautiful and peaceful, I hated to wake her, but nature called.

    I was about to give her a gentle shake when I caught movement in the blacken television screen. It was the slender reflected silhouette of a woman. I blinked several times, trying to focus, to make sure it wasn't my imagination. Swallowing dryly, trying hard not to get my hopes up, I jerked my head around. I thought a faint shadow passed by my peripheral vision, but I couldn't be sure. No one was behind us. I snapped my head back to the television. The silhouette was gone. Had it been my imagination?

Pam stirred against my chest. "Um, what's going on?" she asked.

"Sorry, I didn't mean to wake you. I thought I saw someone."

Her eyes came alive with alertness and she shot up, staring around. "You saw someone in my apartment? Are you sure?"

"I might have been dreaming. It looked like Yolanda."

Pam shot up to her feet. Staring down at my wrinkled shirt where her head had laid moments ago, she looked embarrassed. "I'm sorry, Tony. I didn't mean to—"

I held up a hand. "It's all right, we were both tired last night. It wasn't like we slept together." I didn't know exactly why I added that last part. I felt as embarrassed as Pam looked. What made matters worse was the bulge in my pants. I jumped to my feet and turned away from her. "Ah, maybe I better check out your place. Make sure no one else is here." Before she could say anything, I circled the couch and headed down the hallway.

    I took the time to take a quick scan inside the two bedrooms and the linen closet before hiding myself inside the bathroom. I leaned against the door and took a deep breath. I couldn't deny that I had some feelings for Pam that extended beyond friendship, but I had been able to suppress those emotions because of Yolanda. With her running out of our lives, I was having a hard time smothering my fondness for Pam. I felt like a jerk. It wasn't long ago I asked Yolanda to marry me, and now my thoughts were on Pam.

Turning on the cold water in the sink I splashed my face once, twice, three times. I stared into the mirror, blowing out a hard breath. "You're in love with Yolanda, remember," I whispered. Maybe that was the reason I saw her in the blackened television screen. It was a sign for me to get my act together. The priority was to find her, to make sure she was safe. After that, I'm going to have to deal with the feelings I have for Pam. Straightening, I looked down. The bulge was still there. I was going to need a very long and cold shower.

A soft rap on the door, snapped me out of my thoughts. "Tony," Pam called out.

"Yeah?"

"You okay in there?"

I was far from all right, but I answered, "Things are good." Things are good? What kind of response was that. "I mean, I'm okay."

There was a moment of awkward silence. "I think you were right," she said.

Cocking an eyebrow, I stared at the door. "About what?"

"I think someone has been inside the apartment."

The bulge in my pants deflated like a tire with a huge hole. I yanked open the door. Pam was standing there with a gun in her hand. She looked surprisingly calm for a person whose place might have just been broken into. Maybe it was spotting the gun that projected the confidence I noticed in her.

"What do you mean?" I asked, not knowing really what else to say.

"The backdoor in the kitchen was unlocked. I never leave it unlocked," she whispered. "Did you check the rooms?"

"I stuck my head inside each of the bedrooms, but I didn't do a full search," I answered with a stronger voice than I'd expected. Like Pam, nervousness seemed to be vacant from me. I was actually angry; feeling violated knowing that someone had invaded her home. "I'll check again."

Pam inclined her head gesturing for me to follow. "We'll do it together."

"You wouldn't happen to have another one of those," I asked pointing at her gun.

In Desperation   DK Gaston

She shook her head no.

I shrugged my shoulders. "Didn't think so."

Together we checked out her bedroom and then the spare bedroom. Both were clear. So were the linen closet, living room, and kitchen. Whoever broke in had slipped out silently. I wondered again if it could have been Yolanda's reflection I'd seen in the television screen? But if it was, why would she sneak in and then leave without saying anything?

"Should we call the police?" I asked.

She frowned at the idea. "And tell them what? Nothing was stolen, no one was hurt. All they'd think was that I forgot to lock up. Besides, if my parent found out, Mama would have me packed and moved back inside the old house before nightfall."

"No argument there," I said. Both her parents were a force to reckon with, but her Mama was the definition of control freak. I rubbed the back of my head, thinking of the best way of phrasing my next question. "Do you think we should cancel going to your job this morning? I mean I understand if you don't want to go, seeing what happened."

Pam stared at me with a commanding resolve that reminded me of her father. "I have the strange sense that the break-in is connected to Yolanda's disappearance. Don't ask me why. So no, I don't want to cancel. I want to go more than ever now."

I grinned. "Okay then."

She touched my arm. "There's something I should tell you before we go. Something my Daddy told me yesterday at the police station."

I stiffened, already not liking what I was going to hear. "What's that?"

"The reason Dixon is so fired up about your guilt is because she found pictures of Yolanda sleeping with another man in her apartment. Dixon thinks you might have found the photos and then snapped."

I took a step back, stunned as if I took a blow to the face. "Yolanda wouldn't sleep—" Staggering weak kneed into the living room, I plopped down onto the couch, hardly able to breath. Pam trailed behind me saying nothing. "No, I can't believe that," I finally said.

270

Pam sat beside me and threw her arm over my shoulder. "I don't believe it either, but if it's true, Eddie should be able to verify this. Maybe the photos are shots of an old boyfriend. It doesn't necessarily mean she was cheating on you."

I looked at Pam, regarding her critically. "Why didn't you mention this last night with Eddie?"

"I didn't think it was the right time. Maybe there's no right time to tell you something like this. I'm sorry."

"Don't be," I said sinking my face into my hands. I tried to picture times when Yolanda could have cheated. It wasn't like she traveled much and when she wasn't spending time with me, she was with Pam. I didn't think it was possible for her to have an affair. Pulling my hands away, I looked at the darkened television screen waiting for another omen to appear. "Even if she slept with someone else—"

Pam rubbed my shoulder. "It's okay, Tony."

"Even if she slept with another man, I would never hurt her. You believe that don't you?"

"If I didn't, I wouldn't be helping you." Her head leaned on of my shoulder to comfort me.

"Did I tell you that Wanabe is dead?"

"Yolanda's cat?"

It was time I made a confession of my own to Pam. "It's why I'm so worried about her. Why I'm so desperate to find her. I think someone is out to harm Yolanda. If the break-in here is related. You might be in danger too."

"I can take care of myself," she said. "Yolanda is tough too. You know that."

"Yeah, I do," I said recalling the slap across my face. That's one thing Pam and Yolanda shared, toughness. That was probably why they got along so well.

Pam stood up. "Let's get something to eat and then head straight to the university."

My legs no longer felt wobbly when I got to my feet. I was being hit with so much, so fast, it was hard to think straight. Despite Pam's reassurance, I had to accept the fact that something bad might have already happened to Yolanda. But there was one thing I knew for sure, I wasn't about to let that same thing happen to Pam. Whatever dangers were out there, we were going to face them together.

Pam

Breakfast was the perfect distraction I needed. Though I hid my true alarm from Tony, I had to admit that the break-in at my apartment threw me for a loop. I literally was fighting to keep my hands from shaking. Taking hold of the cup as though my life depended upon it, I let the heat of the coffee warm my numb hands. Across the table, Tony was staring out the window, lost in thought. Refusing to go home to change he was still wearing the previous day's clothes.

I understood his home was the last place he'd seen Yolanda and would only bring him bad memories. All I wanted to do was to reach out to him and make him feel better. He had so much on his mind; her betrayal, the police suspecting him of a crime, and now believing that whoever might be after Yolanda may want to harm me as well. It was a lot to take in for any sane person. The waitress arrived with the food, gently dropping huge platters of pancakes, eggs and sausage in front of us. Tony turned around and stared at the waitress. "Jasmine," he said politely. "Have you seen Eddie this morning?"

Though the food was excellent at Morning Perk, the reason we selected the restaurant was in hopes of running into Eddie with news of the investigation. We tried calling his cell phone but immediately received a disconnection notice. It was just like Eddie not to pay his phone bill. It was a miracle Eddie's phone was still activated when Tony tried him from police headquarters.

Jasmine wiped a lock of curls from the front of her eyes and considered the question. Finally she shook her head, "Can't say I've seen him this morning. But his tab is due, so he might be avoiding the place for a while." Her pleasant face broke out into an addictive smile.

"It figures," Tony said grinning, caught up in Jasmine's natural charm.

She moved on to another table. I looked down at the amount of food on the platter and said, "No way, I'm eating all of this. We should have shared a plate."

He took note of the food for the first time. "Wow. That is a lot. Guess our eyes were bigger than our stomach this morning."

We shared a nervous laugh.

A large part of me wanted to talk about our awkward reactions on the couch. The way he jetted down the hall, claiming he needed to check out the place, seemed to me, to be something more than worries about our safety. For a brief moment, we were connected, like being pulled together by a magnet. But I knew better than to bring it up. Our concern needed to be finding out what happened to Yolanda.

"Do you think you can get more information from your father, regarding the investigation?" Tony asked.

"Not a good idea. He didn't want to tell me anything at all to begin with. Daddy definitely doesn't want me helping you."

"Does he think I'm guilty?"

"No," I snapped out too quickly. "But he doesn't exclude you either. He's a cop first, he's suspicious of everybody. He even questioned me last night."

Tony's eyebrow shot up in surprise. "Really? What did he ask you?"

"I told him about Yolanda yelling at me. He thinks you and I might be sleeping together, which was why Yolanda was mad at us."

"That's silly, right?" he said sheepishly.

There was a long awkward silence.

"More coffee," Jasmine said breaking the quiet, holding a pot ready to pour.

"Sure," I answered.

Jasmine's gaze toggled between Tony and me. "You two haven't touched your food. Is there a problem?"

"No," Tony said. "We seemed to have lost our appetite, that's all."

"Don't let the food go to waste honey, there's a lot of starving folks in the world that would like to have it." Jasmine refilled my cup and disappeared into the milling crowd of patrons.

"We better eat. We need our strength," I said.

When the front entrance opened, a hush suddenly took hold of the shop. Two huge men walked inside Morning Perk. Grins that looked more threatening than friendly adorned both their faces. Behind the pair another man entered who didn't grin. He wasn't as big as the other two, but he seemed just as, if not more, menacing. The owner of the shop smiled nervously and raised his hand in greeting. The only response from the grim-faced patron was a subtle head tilt toward an empty table.

In Desperation   DK Gaston

I looked at Tony and asked, "What do you think that's about?" Tony stared through the window at a limo parked out front. "Trouble we don't want to know anything about," he answered.

***

We'd arrived at the university an hour later with full stomachs. Like I told Tony earlier, we didn't have a problem with security. The Human Resources department was dark except for the daylight that filtered through the blinds. Knowing the layout, there was no need to turn on the lights. Tony trailed close behind me, taking in the office. To the best of my recollection, I think it was the first time he had been there.

"Man, I thought my office was sterile. No one even has a plant in their cubicle here."

"My office manager thinks having plants is a sign of individuality, which may lead to distractions." I waved my hands in the air to showcase the entire department. "Here, we are all of one collective mind, whose primarily focus is to serve the universities staff and student body."

"That probably suited Yolanda just fine," he said sadly.

I nodded. "Actually it did. She was never the plant owner type. For that matter, Yolanda really never expressed herself much at all."

"Tell me about it," Tony agreed. "I had to fight, just to get her to open up about her feelings. I still don't know much about her life before we met."

I looked at him, shaking my head. "You're preaching to the choir."

We maneuvered around a couple of corners before stopping at Yolanda's cubicle. "Here we are."

Tony looked inside, scanning every inch of it. "It's not much." His eyes stopped at a pile of paperwork. "I see she's as cluttered at work as she is at home."

"Yet, she's strangely efficient at what she does. Her work is either done before or on schedule. I think that's the only reason my office manager never got on her about the mess."

Tony stared at the half full plastic trash can. "Did the janitorial staff have the day off or what?"

"Yolanda didn't want them in her cubicle. She was afraid they couldn't distinguish between her garbage and her clutter. Whenever she wanted them to take out the trash, she would place the can outside her cubicle. When she stormed out of here yesterday, I guess she didn't even bother with it."

Tony looked satisfied with the answer and then stared at me, asking, "So where do we start?"

I pointed at one end of the cubicle nearest the computer. "I'll poke around this pile." I said, and then indicated another. "You take that one. Good hunting."

Tony sat in the chair used for clients and didn't hesitate going through the mound of paperwork. Not having a clue of what might be constituted as evidence of her disappearance, we knew we were looking for the proverbial needle in the haystack. We searched for nearly twenty minutes, sorting through everything on the desk, in the drawers and cabinets, before taking a break.

"Have you seen anything out of the ordinary?" he asked.

"No," I said frustration in my voice. "You?"

Tony let out an exhausted breath. "Nothing."

"Maybe there's something on her computer," I suggested, spinning around and switching on the monitor. The computer was already powered. On the screen the user login waited for a password. I stared at the image as if I were reading Latin. "Crap. I wasn't thinking. I don't have her password." I had my fingers hovering over the keyboard about to type anyway.

"No, don't," Tony yelled, placing a gentle hand on my shoulder. "Most IT departments only give you three tries before a user is completely locked out." Tony automatically jumped into tech geek mode. He worked in an Information Technology department. "Let me try."

I scooted my chair to the side giving him plenty of room to roll his beside me. My gaze went from the screen to his face. "So what are you going to do? Use some kind of software to hack the computer."

"No," he said, studying the display. "You and I are going to work together to figure out her password. Remember, we have three tries. And this is all dependent on how fast the university's IT team is. Yolanda's access might already been deactivated."

She wasn't exactly the technical type, so we knew she wouldn't use anything that was too complicated. At the same time, she wouldn't use anything that was easy to break. We discussed possible words and number combination that Yolanda would use, listing the top five. Odds were definitely against us, but we had to

In Desperation   DK Gaston

at least try. Tony typed in the first code. Nothing. He typed in the second. Nothing. He wiped sweat from his head. "We're down to the wire," he said.

      We look at the three remaining choices, unable to decide which to enter. All three were related to the few sentimental things she shared with us. Like Tony said earlier, she kept her feelings bottled up. I couldn't imagine she would use something she felt sentimental about as her password. Then it struck me that Yolanda had a sick sense of humor. I put myself in her place, recalling times we shared a laugh. Only one instance stuck out in my mind.

Tony was about to type the next password, but I said, "Stop."

He looked at me curiously. "What is it?"

"Try, ménage à trios," I said, remembering the night a smooth operator tried to pick Yolanda and me up simultaneously at a club the night we met Tony.

Tony winced. "Excuse me?"

"I'll explain later."

      He typed it and hit enter. The login screen faded. We accessed her computer. Tony scratched his temple. "I can't believe that worked," he said, and then stared at me. "Maybe I don't want to know why Yolanda had that as her password."

We went through her files and emails with a fine toothcomb. After an hour of searching we decided that nothing relevant was there. "What a waste of time," Tony said, his head slumped. Frustrated, he picked up the keyboard as if to throw it.

"What's that?" I asked pointing at a slip of paper hanging limply from the bottom.

Flipping the keyboard over, he scanned it then pulled the sheet free. "Looks like a prescription of some type. But I can't make out the writing." The paper had been underneath the keyboard for so long, much of the lettering had faded. The only thing visible was a name: Milroy. He glanced at me. "I've never seen her take so much as an aspirin. Have you?"

"No. She didn't even like taking vitamins," I said, shaking my head. Tony balled up the paper and threw it into the half empty trash can. "Big waste of time," he repeated. Then we looked at each other. We checked everything in the cubical, except the trash. He said, "I guess it's worth a shot."

      I picked up the can and we began rummaging through. Sitting on the top of the pile was a manila envelope. There was nothing inside. Flipping the envelope over, written on the face: Lightning Strike Courier Service.

"Didn't you say you saw someone leaving Yolanda's cubicle, when she suddenly started yelling at you?"

I nodded, recalling a woman walking away. She was wearing a one piece number, like a jump suit, a uniform of some kind. "It could have been a delivery person. The university doesn't get many female couriers."

Tony snatched the trash can from my hand and dug deeper. He came out with a handful of photos. He brought them so close to his face I couldn't see what they were shots of. Tony scanned each with numbed horror. "Oh my God," he said.

"What?"

His hands dropped to his lap. "God, no."

The pictures were face up. They were of Tony and me from various camera angles. We were naked and making passionate love.

In Desperation
The Bald Man

DK Gaston

"You blew it," the voice yelled in his ear, his irritation palpable.

"How many times are you going to remind me?" the bald man retorted.

Earlier, while he was sleeping, the target had somehow slipped in and out of pretty Pamela Reeb's apartment without detection. If he hadn't overheard the two talking about the break-in, he wouldn't have known anything about it. The bald man had been getting berated ever since, being reminded ceaselessly of his failure.

"The entire operation could be over, if not for your blunder."

"I told you, it won't happen again," the bald man said for the umpteenth time. He wouldn't say it again. "Now get off the air so I can concentrate on Reeb and Holman."

With a heavy sign the voice in his ear warned, "One more failure and I will bring in another team. Your contract will be terminated." He snapped off.

The bald man knew what termination meant, his death at the hands of another assassin like himself to his target. Switching his mind to his mission, he looked up at the HR building where the duo had been searching for clues of their friend's whereabouts. He had followed them first to a coffee shop and then to the university. They'd been inside for nearly two hours. The bald man wondered if maybe the duo became aware of him and left through another exit. He quickly let the notion pass. Reeb and Holman weren't professionals. They wouldn't have been able to detect him.

Still, he was getting impatient. What if the target had snuck inside the university and was with the pair? From his vantage point, it was impossible to see a thing. He needed to observe things first hand. Lowering his gaze, he looked at the front entrance. Through the glass doors, he spotted a single guard sitting in the lobby, looking bored. There were also security cameras throughout the building, but he could easily avoid those.

Making his decision, he made sure a round was chambered in his pistol. Storing the weapon beneath his suit jacket, he got out of the car and proceeded to the front doorway. As he expected, once the guard saw him, he got out of his chair to greet him. The bald man smiled, reached into his jacket, pulled out the pistol and fired through the glass two times.

Small holes appeared in the glass and then through the guard's chest.

The bald man pushed the glass doors open, stepped over the dead body as if it wasn't there and headed directly to the stairway.

Pretty Pamela Reeb was only three floors up.

The bald man hummed, *Pop Goes the Weasel* as he scaled the steps.

In Desperation   DK Gaston
Anthony

"**W**hat the devil is going on, Pam? This never happened between us."

"I'm aware of that," Pam answered, sounding stunned.

I stared at the pictures again and again, unable to comprehend any of it. Who would go through all the trouble to doctor pictures of Pam and me sleeping together and then have them delivered to Yolanda? At least it explained a lot, like why Yolanda slapped me and called Pam a slut.

"The police found pictures. Maybe they're as fake as these," Pam said, thinking the same as me. "Someone is setting you up for a major fall."

"But I don't have any enemies. Why would someone do this?"

"Maybe you're not the prime target," she said almost to herself.

"Yolanda never mentioned enemies to me. You?"

She shook her head. "No, but that doesn't mean anything." Looking directly into my eyes, she asked, "What do we really know about Yolanda, really? I mean beyond the two years we've known her."

I saw where she was going. "You're right. All that I know is that she has a brother somewhere. I found his picture stuffed between pages of a book." Then more slowly, "Like she was trying to hide it."

Pam touched my arm. "Maybe the way to find out who's after Yolanda is by figuring out who she was before we met her."

"And how are we going to do that?"

"We start at where she used to work. If anyone can tell us anything, surely her old employer can."

I stood up, rubbing at the back of my neck. "I don't have a clue where that was. She never talked about it."

Pam gave me a reassuring smiled. "It's on record here at the university. All I have to do is access her personnel file." She spun around, jumped behind the keyboard and began typing.

While I waited, I decided to get something to drink. My throat was dry. "You want a pop or something from the machine. I saw one in the hallway."

"Mountain Dew," she said, never looking away from the screen.

In Desperation   *DK Gaston*

    I hoped I could find my way out of the dark maze. Luckily the layout wasn't as formidable as I thought and it didn't take me long to find the hallway. At the vending machine, I punched in the code. It dispensed the Pepsi with a loud thud. Lifting the bottle, I thought I heard a noise from down the long corridor, something like humming. Listening, all I heard was silence and decided it was just my nerves. The machine made another thud as the Mountain Dew came sliding out.

    To my right, I thought I saw movement. I looked, expecting to see the security guard, but there was no one. "Hello?" I yelled. When no reply came back, I suspected paranoia was kicking into overdrive. I carried the soft drinks back to Yolanda's cubicle.

Pam peered up at me, grinning. "I found it."

"So where's it located? In Timbuktu, I suppose." It wouldn't surprise me if she really had worked in some faraway place. After all, I was finding that I really didn't know Yolanda at all.

Pam stood, handing me sheets of paper she'd printed while I was gone. "Actually, it's only an hour's drive away. The company is called, The Erikson Group."

"Never heard of it." Scanning the printed pages, the company described itself as a consulting service. But it didn't say what exactly it consulted. "This is all you could find on it?"

"The internet is surprisingly vague when it comes to The Erikson Group. It's strange, even its own website only shows a photograph of the exterior of the building. There aren't any pictures of the interior or its staff. All I could pull up was an address and phone number."

I scratched my head, confused. "What kind of consulting firm can do business that way if no one knows exactly what it does?"

"Only one way to find out," she said, moving past me.

"Where are you going?"

"To The Erikson Group building. Where else?"

"Can't you call them?"

"Tried that. All I'm getting is the runaround from the person answering the phone. Though I was told, they were open on Saturdays." She grabbed me by the arm and began pulling me along with her.

"So we're just going to barge our way in through the front door and expect them to tell us everything about a former employee? If they're so secretive that they don't supply basic information about themselves, what makes you think they'll talk to us?"

"We can try at least. Otherwise, there's nothing else for us to do but twiddle our thumbs."

She made a good point. So I stopped resisting and let her lead me out into the hallway. I handed her the Mountain Dew. "Last thing you need is caffeine in your overactive system, but here it is anyway," I said.

"Just what the doctor ordered," she joked.

That reminded me of the prescription we'd found. I couldn't remember what I had done with it and checked all my pockets. Pam seemed to sense what I was searching for, reached inside her purse and pulled out the prescription, showing it to me.

"I dug it out of the garbage in case it was important," she said.

Taking a quick peek inside her bag, I also spotted the doctored photos and her gun.

"Is that really necessary?" I asked.

She snapped her purse closed. "You never know. I feel safer with it than without it."

I wasn't worried that she didn't know how to use it. She'd told me her father had been taking her to firing ranges since her breasts started to show. I was more concerned that we may find ourselves in a situation where she might actually have to use it. Down the corridor, the unmistakable sound of a door creaking closed reverberated. We looked at each other. Maybe the humming sound I thought I heard earlier wasn't my imagination after all.

"Is there someone other than the guard working this weekend?" I asked.

"I checked the schedule, yesterday. No one was on it."

"I thought you might say that." Suddenly I was glad she had the gun.

Pam opened her purse and stuck her hand inside, but she didn't pull out the weapon. Just because there was a creepy creaking door in a completely empty dark floor, didn't necessarily mean that we were in danger. But if I heard the all too familiar ch ch ch, ma ma ma, theme from Friday the 13th start playing, we would be making a break in the opposite direction.

The sound of retreating feet padded down the stairway. Pam turned to me. "Well, whoever it was is gone now." Taking her hand out of the purse, she said, "It was probably the guard just doing his rounds."

Taking the elevator, the doors slid open to the lobby. The front desk was empty. Maybe she was right about the guard walking his rounds. The lobby was well-lit and a lot less scary than the darkened floor upstairs. There was a huge section of the tiled floor covered in water, like the cleaning staff did a half baked job.

"Sloppy work," I said.

Pam shook her head. "What a mess."

As we circled around the puddle, I took note of something being mixed in with the water, floating to the top. It was red and thick. I wondered if someone had spilled some paint and did a quick and sloppy job of cleaning it up. Pam was giving the floor the same interest, although she appeared to be more concerned about it than I was. There was also a strange coppery smell. I was about to ask if she noticed it too, when Pam grabbed my arm just under the elbow.

"That almost looks like—" Her cell phone rang, interrupting her.

We continued outside, the sun immediately assaulted us. I was thankful for the Pepsi and drank some while she listened intently to someone on the other end and then gave short, quick answers. When her bottle shattered on the ground, I almost choked on the drink. After nearly hacking up a lung to clear my throat, I asked, "What's wrong?"

Pam looked catatonic, staring off into space. She slowly pulled the phone away from her ear, her gaze falling on mine. "That was my father. He asked me if I knew where you were. I told him no, because he didn't want me helping you." She paled. "There's a warrant for your arrest."

"What? Why?"

"The police found Yolanda's car. It's being pulled out of the river as we speak."

In Desperation
The Bald Man

DK Gaston

After getting close enough to overhear Reeb's and Holman's conversation, the bald man scarcely had time to make it down the stairway and clean up the mess he created. The bald man dragged the guard's body behind the front desk. When the next guard came in for his shift, he'd be in for a big surprise. The hardest part was filling the mop bucket with water and cleanser before the duo came down. But he'd done it. If he hadn't, his controller would surely have sanctioned the bald man before the day ended.

Coming out of his hiding space, he watched them standing in the parking lot. Pretty Pamela Reeb had dropped her soda and looked dumbstruck. Bad news, he supposed, wondering exactly what she had been told. Holman looked as if he had seen a ghost as she relayed information to him. The bald man had to admit, he was impressed by their ingenuity and dedication to find their friend. He never expected them to go as far as wanting to go to Yolanda's former employer. The bald man considered if he should allow it, or simply take them out before they became a bigger problem.

He raised his hand like a gun, aiming at his two targets. "Bang, bang," he sounded out.

"What was that?" the voice asked.

The bald man grimaced; he'd been talking aloud again. "We have a new hitch," he said.

"And that would be?" the voice was shrilled with impatience.

"Reeb and Holman are headed to The Erikson Group."

A long silence and then the voice said, "That's unfortunate."

"Maybe it's time to terminate them."

"No," the voice ordered. "The target is the priority. Their visiting The Erikson Group is only a hiccup. They will learn nothing."

The bald man bit his bottom lip. He was ready to perform act III with Pretty Pamela Reeb. Act III was the best part of his masterpiece. "Fine, I'll keep watching them for the time being. But I have to be honest. This is getting boring."

"Then you're going to have to find a way to entertain yourself until the target has been dealt with. Understand?"

"Sure, whatever." In the back of the bald man's mind, a nagging memory was fighting to the forefront of his thoughts. But he couldn't exactly place his finger on what that memory was. The one thing he had known was that Reeb's and Holman's going to The Erikson Group was a very bad idea.

In Desperation   DK Gaston
Pam

"My God, did they find Yolanda?" Tony was frantic. He dropped his Pepsi and grabbed both my arms. "What did your father say about Yolanda?"

"Nothing. They only found her car," I explained. "They're not sure how the car ended up in the river, but they can't take a chance that foul play was involved."

"We need to go there now!"

"You're not thinking straight, Tony. The police would arrest you the moment you showed your face. Daddy wants me to talk you into turning yourself in."

Realization sank in. He let go of my arms, his hand dropped to his side. "Why is this happening?"

Taking his hand, I said, "That's what we're trying to figure out. We can't go and see about the car. We need to head to The Erikson Group. Our answers are there. I can feel it."

"Do answers even matter if she's dead?"

"You have to believe she's not."

He looked at the ground. "Two years in a relationship and I'm finding I don't know anything about her."

"Don't give up on me now, Tony. This isn't only about you. She's been my best friend for over two years too. I need answers. Don't you?"

His gaze came up to mine. "It's really that important to you?"

"It is."

My heart pounded in my chest waiting for him to respond. Would he abandon finding Yolanda just like that? I wondered if I would be able to continue without Tony.

"I guess I can't go on without knowing the truth. Besides, knowing you Pam, you will just go on to The Erikson Group without me."

I grinned. "You know I will."

With that settled, we headed to the Mountaineer. I glance over a shoulder back to the lobby. I hadn't noticed it before, but there were cracks in the glass. The guard hadn't returned either. Maybe the university was being vandalized. I pushed anymore thoughts of the school out of my head. I needed to focus on the task ahead of us.

Once I was behind the wheel, Tony gave me a sidelong glance. "You know once your father finds out I was with you all this time, he's going to kill you."

Turning the key in the ignition, I said, "Let's not go there, okay?"

During the hour long drive to The Erikson Group building, Daddy called me four times asking about Tony. Mama called me eight times to talk about nothing. Tony was smart enough to have turned off his phone and pulled out the battery to guarantee police couldn't track him through his cellular signal. Unless Daddy got a subpoena to track mine, which I doubt he'd ever do, because Mama would kill him, I thought we were under everyone's radar. So why was it I felt like we were being watched?

The Erikson Group's site was built like a prison. The complex took up nearly four football fields. Its sterile gray color and blocky configuration seemed out of place in the green scenery that encircled it. Large twenty foot walls surrounding the building sat in the center of the property. At the front gate, a guard built like a linebacker greeted us.

"Ma'am, sir," he said with military curtness.

"Hi," I responded pleasantly. "I'd like to speak to someone in the HR department if that's possible."

The guard stared at a clipboard, frowned and then looked back at me. "Do you have an appointment, ma'am?"

"No. But this is really important. I do need to talk with someone here."

"What's this regarding ma'am?"

"A former employee that used to work here."

The guard's stoic expression was nerve wrecking. "Employee's name, please."

I turned to look at Tony not sure if I should say.

Tony shrugged his shoulders and said, "Can't hurt."

Turning back to the guard, I answered, "Yolanda Blakely."

The guard disappeared into the security booth. Long seconds dragged on. I thought for sure he would be sending us away. Instead, he stepped out and waved us inside. He had me stop when I drove up beside him.

He pointed toward the facility. "There's a parking structure subbasement just down the road. You are to enter Lot B and take the elevator to the main lobby where someone will meet you, ma'am."

Pulling into the visitor's underground parking facility. The Mountaineer was the only vehicle in the entire structure. Our footfalls echoed off the concrete floors. We followed a line of arrows to a bank of elevators taking one up to the lobby.

The interior wasn't what I expected. Modern paintings hung on the walls, the marble floors glistened as if recently polished, contemporary jazz played softly in the background. The room felt more like a lobby for a five star hotel than a place of business. There wasn't a receptionist. The only place to sit was oversized beanbag style chairs that looked to be filled with some kind of weird liquid gel. Tony was braver than me and collapsed backwards into one.

He looked as if swallowed by quicksand, but after a few seconds, the chair seemed to mode into a comfortable shape for his body. "I am in love with this chair," he said, closing his eyes looking totally carefree.

"I'm glad you like it," a man's voice said startling us. Wearing a black two-piece suit that looked to be custom fitted, he seemed to have materialized out of nowhere. "My name is Albert Milroy. And you are?"

I offered my hand. "Pamela Reeb."

He gave me a weak shake. "Charmed."

Tony was struggling to get out of the chair, but he kept slipping back. I helped him out. Looking royally embarrassed, Tony stuck out his hand toward Milroy. "Sorry about that. I'm Anthony Holman."

Milroy laughed. "I can't tell you how many times I needed help out of one of those chairs. They are very comfortable to sit in, but require the limpness of youth to get out." He gestured for us to follow him. "I'm told that you are here to inquire about a former employee. Is that correct?"

"Yes, Yolanda Blakely," I told him.

He nodded and led us into a plush office, with a huge oak desk. He circled the monster of a desk and indicated for us to take a seat opposite of him. "Do you mind telling me what your relationship is to Ms. Blakely?"

"She's my fiancé," Tony answered.

Milroy cocked an eyebrow, intrigued. "Fiancé you say? Interesting." He turned to me. "And your relationship to her?"

"Yolanda is my best friend." On his desk, a name plate sat on the front edge. Albert Milroy. Seeing it in print, brought back the memory of the prescription slip Tony and I found under the keyboard. "Are you some kind of doctor?"

Shock flitted across his face, but quickly subsided. "Yes, I am. Has something about me given that fact away?"

I said nothing.

Thankfully Tony chimed in with his own question. "Your website says you're a consulting company. What type of services do you actually offer?"

Milroy smiled, look thoughtful and then asked, "What exactly can I do for you two?"

"Yolanda is missing," Tony blurted out. "We think she might be in some kind of trouble."

"Oh dear," Milroy said, looking generally concerned. "Did the trouble happen shortly after you asked her to marry you?"

Tony leaned forward in his chair eyes narrowed with suspicion. "The day after as a matter of fact."

Milroy rubbed his chin, lost in thought and then looked as if coming to a decision. Reaching into one of his desk drawers, he pulled out two identical sheets of paper, passing one to me and the other to Tony.

"What's this?" I asked.

Milroy's gaze swiveled between the two of us. "Confidentiality agreement forms. Before we discuss this further, you have to sign that document. Nothing we say goes beyond this room."

After reading through the document, we signed our names at the bottom. Sliding the paperwork back into front of him, I asked, "What is this place, really?"

Milroy grinned. "You are sitting in the most sought after psychiatric hospital in the world."

"A mental hospital?" Tony asked jumping to his feet. "But your website said consulting firm."

Milroy gestured for Tony to sit and waited for him to comply before speaking. "Not only are we the most sought after, but also the most secretive. Our elite clientele require confidentiality. They range from highly placed politicians to spoiled actors. We have a success rate of ninety-eight percent. So yes, we place some false information on our website, in case someone becomes curious about us."

"Did Yolanda work here?"

"No," he said flatly.

I wagged a finger at him. "But when she started working at my company, she listed The Erikson Group as her previous employer."

Letting out an exhausted sigh, Milroy said, "We strongly suggest that some clients, especially those that have been long time patients, rejoin the world by seeking work. You see, some never worked a day in their lives, while others started from nothing and built an empire. Those that want to seek work are encouraged to use The Erikson Group as a reference. We comply when employers are doing background checks or such."

Tony gripped the edges of his chair. "You're saying Yolanda was patient here?"

"I'm saying no such thing. I'm not allowed to talk about our clients. I'm only telling you about some of the services we offer at The Erikson Group," Milroy explained.

"I get the impression that your clientele are very rich," I said.

Milroy shook his head. "That's not necessarily true. Sometimes our less fiscal responsible clients are sponsored by outside benefactors. But as for the rest of them, they're filthily rich if I may be so bold."

"Yolanda is barely scraping by on her salary," Tony said throwing up his hands in disgusted resignation.

Milroy leaned across his desk. "Hypothetically speaking, certain clients are so repulsed by their fortunes that they abandon everything they own just to etch out a life they would deem normal."

Tony pointed a finger toward Milroy. "You're telling me, Yolanda is rich?"

Milroy leaned back in his chair, his face scrunched into a deep frown. He looked to be debating something in his head. Coming to a decision, he said, "Let me be blunt. Again, I must insist that what I say stays in this room. I will deny otherwise, if I am ever question about this."

"Go for it," I said encouragingly.

"The only reason I speaking with you, is because your lives may be in mortal danger." Milroy pointed to Tony. "You most of all, Mr. Holman, because you asked her to marry you."

"Say what?" Tony asked.

"Being as non-technical as possible, Ms. Blakely had suffered from what is most commonly known as multiple personality disorder. Three in fact. One, of course being Yolanda, the second being her factious brother DeShaun. The third and most dangerous being an assassin with no name. Under the latter personality, Ms. Blakely had nearly killed two innocent people. Both former lovers."

"We've known her for more than two years. We never saw any evidence of this," I said.

"I had hoped that I'd cured her. She was placed on a strict medication to assist in controlling her personality disorder."

I pulled out the crumpled paper from my purse and showed it to Milroy.

He recognized it immediately. "It would take weeks of her not taking the medication for her to slip back into her previous condition." He swiveled in his chair to a computer and began typing. After several minutes, he faced us again. "It seems that Ms. Blakely has not refilled her prescription in nearly a month."

"This can't be happening," Tony said his face pensive. "We were supposed to be getting married."

"Has Ms. Blakely been behaving strangely?" Milroy asked.

"She killed Wanabe," Tony said, clasping his chin.

"I beg your pardon?"

"We think she might have killed her cat," I explained. "We thought at first someone else had done it, but after this, well, I just don't know anymore."

"Anything else?" Milroy pressed.

Hesitantly, I said, "She might have had pictures doctored of Tony and me sleeping together."

Milroy shook his head sadly. "That's not good for either of you. It seems she made you two the target of her wrath. Killing the cat would indicate the Assassin personality, though it strikes me as odd that she hasn't outright attacked you. With the previous boyfriends, she came at them with knives, but she now appears to have become more creative. And I haven't known her to involve women before in her fantasies."

"You don't sound very hopeful," Tony said lifting his face out of his hands. "What are you getting at?"

"Without examining her, all I can do is offer a speculation. After containing her multiple personalities for so long, it's possible that she might have created others. This may or may not be a good thing, but count yourselves lucky thus far. If I were you, I would stay away from your home and workplace until Ms. Blakely is returned to medical care."

"It may not matter anyway," Tony said looking sick to his stomach. "Police found her car in the river. Yolanda may be dead."

"Was a body found?" Milroy asked.

"No," I answered.

Standing Milroy leaned forward and rested his knuckles on the desk. "Then I would assume she's very much alive. If she has accessed her vast fortune, she's quite capable of faking a great many things, especially her death."

Milroy escorted us out, reminded us repeatedly about the confidentiality forms we'd signed. At the elevator he added, "The Erikson Group guarantees success for its clients. When they do not succeed, we do not succeed. Rest assured my staff will be working diligently in finding Ms. Blakely before she does any serious harm to herself or anyone else."

After we got back to the car, I asked, "Do you think Milroy was a little too forthright with us? I mean for a business that promises secrecy, he told us a hell of a lot."

"I was thinking the same thing," Tony said. "I also got the impression he was scared. He covered it up well, but it was there."

"And if he's afraid, should we be?" I asked more to myself.

In Desperation   *DK Gaston*
Part Four

The Bald Man

While he'd been waiting, the bald man had been listening to news reports of Yolanda's car being retrieved from the river on the radio. Divers were in the water searching for her body. He knew they wouldn't find Yolanda. It was all a ploy in hopes of throwing off the bald man's search for her. His leg throbbed from the old wound she had given him years before. He considered all the ways he was going to make her pay for injuring him.

    Yolanda's apparent death also gave her some autonomy to move with relative ease through the city without detection. If police were spending their time dredging for her body in the river, less time would be spent looking for her. Even without finding a body, it would no longer be a simple missing person's case. In one brilliantly bold stroke it would become a homicide, casting even more suspicion regarding Holman's guilt; meaning the troubles for Holman would increase ten-fold.

    That was unfortunate. Holman was his primary link to the target. If he was to be arrested, she may not come out of hiding. Her revenge on who she'd believed to be the cheating boyfriend would be satisfied. Still, there was pretty Pamela Reeb. No doubt, Yolanda would have something equally devious planned for her. After all, the bald man went through a lot of trouble to guarantee that Yolanda think Reeb was that *other* woman. That was another unfortunate mess. The bald man had his own plans for pretty Pamela Reeb for his third act and he didn't want anything to interrupt that fun.

    His thoughts were interrupted when the front gate opened at the facility. Watching the pair drive off The Erikson Group complex, the bald man wondered what bologna cover story Milroy had supplied. Milroy was an idiot with his smug, high and mighty way of thinking. His approach was to give information seekers half-truths and insinuations for misdirection.

What kind of false trail has Milroy sent you to follow?.

In Desperation
Anthony
DK Gaston

We rode back to the city in relative silence. I knew that was mostly my fault. Pam had been trying to have a conversation, but I wasn't in the mood. Too much was floating in my mind, most prominent not knowing whether Yolanda was still alive or somewhere beneath the river. I thought back to Pam's apartment when I caught the image on the television screen; then about what Milroy said, *"Then I would assume she's very much alive. If she has accessed her vast fortune, she's quite capable of faking a great many things, especially her death."*

Sitting up straight, I glanced at Pam. "Yolanda is alive. I know it!" Shouting my epiphany after nearly an hour of silence, startled her.

She nearly bumped the car in the next lane, regaining control at the last moment. "Jeez, Tony, you almost gave me a heart attack."

"I'm sorry. I'm just excited. I think she's alive," I said calmly, though internally, my feelings were hopping with uncontrolled excitement.

Pam looked hopeful. "Tell me why."

"In your apartment this morning, I saw her."

"The break-in," she said curiously. Pam considered it. "You believe it was Yolanda's reflection you saw on the television?"

"I'm sure it was her."

"Yolanda does have a spare key to my place, for emergencies. I guess she could have simply walked in through the front door. We were so exhausted, a bomb could have gone off and we wouldn't have noticed."

"When I woke, it must have spooked her and she ran out the rear door. It makes sense."

A shadow of doubt creased her lovely face. "I don't know."

"Why do you say that?"

"You heard Milroy. Yolanda may want to hurt the both of us. If she was really in my apartment, she had the perfect opportunity to get us both. But she didn't. Why?"

"I told you, I spooked her."

"Maybe," Pam said still sounding doubtful. "I just don't know how much of what Milroy's story we can believe. It bothers me that he was so open to us."

I couldn't argue. Milroy seemed nice enough, but there was something about him that didn't appear right to me. "If he lied to us, for the life of me, I can't figure out why. He didn't have to tell us anything. For that matter, he didn't even have to let us through the front gate."

"Exactly," Pam snapped. "Why talk to us at all?"

"Nothing has been making any sense lately," I admitted. "Maybe, we should do what Eddie suggested and let the police do their job. We can give Detectives Dixon and Madden what we have so far."

"Keep in mind we're not supposed to talk about what we've learned from The Erikson Group until you want to compound your troubles with a lawsuit from them."

"Screw them. I'm trying to keep my butt out of jail."

"Milroy said he would deny everything. The police won't have any reason to investigate The Erikson Group. As far as the world is concern, they're a consulting business, remember?"

She was right. I lost some of the vigor I'd acquired and slumped a little in my seat. Then with a little hope, "We can tell them Yolanda was in your apartment."

"No proof, sorry. The police won't take your word for it; you're their number one suspect. All I can say is that my backdoor was unlocked."

I folded my arms together defiantly. "You're just full of good news aren't you?"

"Sorry," she said and then her eyes lit up. "What about the photographs we've found. Police should be able to verify they're fake, right?"

I thought about that. "It's not as easy as you think. It could take time. And keep in mind the moment we give them the pictures, it automatically implicates you in this crazy setup. Dixon and Madden will think you and I are working together. It won't matter that you're the Chief's daughter."

She grimaced. "My parents would love that."

"Your parents would kill me," I countered.

"Yeah... They would."

"The only way to clear our name is for Yolanda to make another appearance and someone see her."

"But if what Milroy said was true—" Pam's voice trailed off.

She didn't need to finish, I knew exactly what she was thinking. The next time Yolanda showed up, we may not be as lucky as the last time. She may hurt, or worse, kill us both. How had Yolanda gone from woman in love to homicidal maniac in such a short period? Had things been spiraling downward sooner than that? I mean the old prescription slip and the fact that Milroy said Yolanda's medication ran out over a month ago.

Pam tore me from my reverie. "Speaking of the photos. Yolanda must have had that done some time ago. I'm having a hard time believing she arranged the doctored pictures in a few hours."

Pam and I seemed to be eerily in the same mindset. "I was just considering that too. I think all of this had to be planned weeks before. Maybe just after she stopped taking her medication, but why?"

Pam gritted her teeth, as if holding back something she didn't want to tell me.

I touched her thigh and felt her trembling. "What is it?"

"I promised Yolanda I would never tell you, but under the circumstances, I don't see a choice." She glanced at me and then back at traffic. "Yolanda knew you were going to ask her to marry you. She found the engagement ring over a month ago and told me about it."

I yanked my hand away. "She knew?"

Pam nodded. "That might have been why she stopped refilling her medication. She didn't want to spend her life with you on some type of dependency."

That sounded like something Yolanda would do. She had this need to be strong all the time. Medicine would have been a weakness. A rush of guilt filled my entire being. Was my proposal the catalyst for her mental relapse? It was all my fault.

"Don't blame yourself," Pam said, again reading my thoughts. "Yolanda was the one responsible for taking her medication. All she had to do was be open about it. She made that decision, not you."

I sat in silence for a long time debating whether I should lay all the blame on my own shoulders or accept that Yolanda truly was the only one at fault. Deciding that it really didn't matter who was to blame, I said, "I think we should come clean with the police.

In Desperation   *DK Gaston*

Tell them everything we know. It's not like we can hide from them forever and I don't want you involved any deeper than you are now." I had to stop thinking about myself for the time being and focus on Pam's welfare.

I expected her to argue, but she surprised me and said, "I'll talk to Daddy. Once he knows the truth, he'll help. I know he will."

Nodding, I regained some of my lost vigor and sat up. "So how do I do this? Just walk into police headquarters and turn myself in?"

"No," she answered. "Have your cousin Eddie, talk to the police first and arrange it."

I laughed weakly. "What? Like some kind of rich celebrity?"

"Trust me, here, Tony. It's better that way."

"Fine," I said shaking my head. "Let's go see if my cousin is in his office."

"You mean the booth at Morning Perk?"

I shrugged. "If he's not chasing ambulances, that's where he'll be."

We weren't far from the coffee shop, Pam pulled off the freeway.

In Desperation   DK Gaston
Pam

We slipped into Morning Perk without incident. The coffee shop wasn't exactly crowded but had a number of patrons in deep conversations with friends or sitting by themselves reading. In the rear, sitting in a booth, wearing a different set of clothes, as wrinkled as the last pair, was Eddie. He didn't notice us as we approached and only looked up from paperwork he was scanning after our bodies blocked some of his light.

    His gaze swiveled between us. "Yolanda, Tony? Where have you two been?" He gestured for us to sit across from him.

Sliding into the booth, Tony wasted no time. "So where are the police at with finding Yolanda?"

Eddie glowered at him like he was stupid. He wagged a finger at Tony. "They think she's dead and more importantly, the cops think you did it."

"She's not dead," Tony assured him.

Eddie's eyes lit up. "You know where she is?"

"No," I said. "But she was inside my apartment this morning."

"That's great news," Eddie said, "Did she tell you why she disappeared?"

"Ah," Tony said, "We didn't talk to her. She kind of snuck in Pam's place and then slipped out."

    The light disappeared from Eddie's eyes. "Okay two things bother me about what you just said. That bein', *snuck in* and *slipped out*. Are you sayin' she broke into your crib?" He looked directly at me.

"Broke in, is too strong. She has a key and let herself in," I explained.

Eddie's eyes narrowed. "Does she let herself in, a lot?"

"That's not the point," Tony interjected. "The point is she's alive."

"And breakin' into homes," Eddie added sarcastically.

    I glanced at the paperwork Eddie had been reading. All of it was about Yolanda. Eddie was building a time line of her life for the past couple of years. Looking up at him, pointing down at the chart, I asked, "What's this?"

He let out a heavy sigh. "I know you two may think I'm an idiot. And admittedly, there are days I can be. But I'm good at my job.

After hearing the police version of the events and knowin' my cuz and you like I do. I couldn't believe any of it. Come on, it's obvious you and Tony have a thing for each other, but betrayin' Yolanda's trust and sleepin' with one other. That's a stretch."

Tony and I shared an embarrassed look and simultaneously said, "There's nothing going on between us."

"Right," Eddie said. "No kindlin' flame there at all."

Tony turned away and looked down at the chart. "You were telling us about this."

"Yeah, I was," Eddie snickered. "I figured whatever was goin' on had more to do with Yolanda, than with you two. So I did a little digging into her life. Did you know that she's loaded?" Dollar signs seemed to replace his irises.

That tidbit of information at least confirmed some of what Milroy said. "We recently found that out."

He looked disappointed. "No surprise, huh?"

Tony and I shook our heads.

"Well this next one is a dozy and is the primary reason Tony here makes such a great suspect to the cops. "It seems that Yolanda named him as the sole benefactor on her Last Will and Testament."

"Say what?" Tony asked, gawking at his cousin in disbelief.

Eddie held up one of the pages and showed it to Tony as evidence. "If she's dead like the cops believe, you're a very rich man, cuz."

Tony straightened. "But what about her brother, DeShaun?"

Eddie cocked an eyebrow. "Who? Brother? Yolanda is an only child."

Another confirmation for Milroy. If the man was lying to us, he mixed it with several truths. Still, I was having a hard time swallowing that she might be homicidal. "Is there anything in your findings that indicate mental problems in her past?"

"Sorry, I've only been at this for a short time. I don't have much at all on her," Eddie explained. "Why? Do you think she might be nuts?" He glanced over at Tony and instantly regretted his words. "Sorry, cuz, I didn't mean to sound—"

"Don't worry about it," Tony said too quickly, deflecting the comment. "It's obvious that none of us at this table really knows who Yolanda is. Maybe she's crazy, maybe not. That fact is, she's still alive and trying her best to get me in trouble it seems."

"Did you two have a big fight?" Eddie asked.

"What?"

Eddie cleared his throat. "Maybe Yolanda finally saw what all your friends and family already suspected; that you and Pam have a thing for each other."

"That's insane," I said dismissively. "Tony and I are just friends. That's all." It felt like I'd said that a hundred times already. And it still didn't feel true. Looking at Tony's expression, I somehow knew, he was lying to himself as well. He and I did have something special going on. Could Eddie be right? It wasn't Tony's proposal that made Yolanda stop taking her meds. It was the feelings Tony and I hid.

"I would never cheat on Yolanda," Tony finally said, breaking an awkward silence.

"I know, cuz. That's why I'm investigatin' her instead of you." Eddie turned his attention to me. "Should I be lookin' into her past about mental problems? Do you know somethin' I don't?"

"We were told, Yolanda might have attacked two of her old lovers," I said.

"Really? Where did you get this info?" Eddie asked. His gaze turned suspicious. "You two went against my advice and been doin' your own investigatin', haven't you?"

There was that awkward silence again. I shouldn't have mentioned the boyfriends at all. We don't even know if what Milroy said was true or not.

Eddie opened his arms in defeat. "Come on guys, give me somethin'. How else can I help you?"

Tony shook his head. "All we have are a lot of what-ifs. We don't have anything to give you Eddie, because it's all conjecture until it can be proven."

"We do have the pictures," I said.

"What pictures?" Eddie asked.

"It's more proof of guilt if anything else," Tony explained.

"What pictures?" Eddie asked again.

I took the doctored photos out of my purse and handed them to Eddie. "These."

He scanned them, once, twice and then a third time before looking up. "You have a nice rear end," Eddie said, cocking his eyebrows up and down comically.

"That's not my butt," I told him angrily. "Those are fake."

He slipped the photos into his pocket after taking another quick glance. "I believe you, but I better be the one to hold on to them for now on."

Tony laid his hands on the table. "I want you to tell the police I'm ready to turn myself in."

"That's good, Tony. That means my partner and I don't have to worry about you resisting arrest," a gruff voice said.

Engrossed in our conversation we totally missed Detectives Madden and Dixon's approach.

Dixon twirled handcuffs around her index finger triumphantly.

In Desperation   *DK Gaston*
The Bald Man

"No, no, no," the bald man said aloud as Holman was led out of the coffee shop, his wrists cuffed behind his back.

"What is it," the voice yelled, panicked.

"Holman is under police custody. He's being taken in now."

"That was anticipated. As long as Reeb is free, there's a chance the target will eventually emerge."

That was what the bald man was afraid of. On her own, Reeb would be defenseless against the target and he wanted Pretty Pamela Reeb for himself. "Are you absolutely sure, the target wants her?"

"Of course. Why are you questioning the mission?" the voice asked.

Though the bald man has altered his orders over the years, he'd never disobeyed, not once. But his insatiable bloodlust for Pretty Pamela Reeb was too strong to ignore. For Act III to be made, she needed to stay alive, at least until he was done with her. He weighed his hatred for Yolanda against his need for Reeb and finally came up with a decision. "I can't let Holman be arrested. He's vital to the mission."

"Have you lost your mind? He's expendable," the voice shouted into the bald man's ear.

"I disagree."

Calmly, the voice said, "You're expendable too. Remember that before you do anything stupid."

Decision made, the bald man shut out the voice's words. Turning the key in the ignition, he started the engine. Buckling his belt, he laid the silenced pistol between his legs to make sure it wouldn't slip to the floor. Pressing the gas pedal all the way down, the wheels screeched as they spun and thick gray smoke rose from the tires. The car sped away. The bald man saw the police detectives, their prisoner, Pretty Pamela Reeb and some fool in a crumpled suit staring his way.

He drove half a block before making a sharp U-turn ignoring traffic. Four other cars nearly collided with his as he performed the maneuver. Once he straightened his car out, he sped back toward the coffee shop. The bald man hummed as he barreled right at the police detectives. He saw the woman cop mouthing expletives, shoving Holman out of the way and drawing her gun.

But it was too late. The bald man drove onto the sidewalk, pedestrians scattered everywhere, except for the two cops. Both pointed their weapons at the windshield. He ducked, but held the car steady as bullets pelted the glass. He felt his car scrape against the detective's car. Sparks ignited outside his passenger window as metal against metal grinded. The bald man sat upright to get his bearing.

The detectives had gotten out of the way in time and had their bodies pressed against the coffee shop's exterior wall. Holman, still in handcuffs was running frantically through the middle of the street away from the cops, which was exactly what the bald man wanted. There was no sign of Pretty Pamela Reeb or the man in the wrinkled suit. They must have run back inside the coffee shop.

Driving back into the street, the rear window was hit with bullets. The bald man laughed, did a wide U-turn ignoring all the danger. The detectives took refuge behind their car. Coming out of the sharp turn, the bald man headed directly for them. The bald man opened the driver side door, tucked his body into a ball and rolled out on the street. The detectives kept firing until the very last second before they dove out of the way as the bald man's vehicle ran into the side of the detective's car. The detective's car flipped up, rolled once to the side, then rolled again and again. It crashed into the Morning Perk's large pane window and then bucked up into the coffee shop.

On his feet, the bald man ran up to the sidewalk. Laying flat on his stomach, the male cop glanced his way with a stunned expression. His hand was empty. The cop must have dropped his gun when he had dived to the ground. The bald man didn't waste his bullets, and instead kicked the cop hard in the face. The whites of his eyes showed and then the lids closed.

People from the coffee shop were filing out, blocking a clear shot for the female cop. She shoved them aside, shouting to get out of the way. The bald man didn't suffer the concern for innocent lives. He fired indiscriminately into the crowd, hitting a woman in the shoulder. Firing again, he shot a man in the leg. They got the message and scattered out of the way. A small gap opened up. Not something the cop could safely shoot through, but perfect for the bald man who didn't care. He had the advantage.

His pistol cuffed once, twice and then a third time. The last shot hit its mark. The female cop bucked backwards as the bullet tore into her chest. Her gun went spiraling loosely into the air and clattered into the street, away from the bleeding officer. The bald man searched around, spotting Holman being stopped and then wrestled to the ground by self-proclaimed do-gooders holding him for the cops. It was hard to look like a victim wearing handcuffs. Everyone of course assumed, the person must be a bad guy.

The bald man turned to his car. Black smoke rose from the engine and two of the tires were flat. He needed another car. Running down the street, he came up on a driver who had stayed to watch the shootout. He yanked the driver's side door open, pointed his gun and ordered the driver to get out. Getting behind the wheel, the bald man did yet another U-turn, came up beside the do-gooders holding Holman and pointed his pistol.

"Get off him, now," he bellowed.

They complied. It seemed the do-gooders had gotten overzealous. Holman was battered and bruised. He was also unconscious. Waving his pistol, the bald man ordered, "Put him in the trunk"

Two men carried Holman over to the car as the trunk popped open. They stuffed him inside and then moved away. The bald man glanced back at the restaurant, spotting Pretty Pamela Reeb, kneeling beside the male cop. She glanced up toward the car. She looked as if her breath had caught inside her throat.

The bald man grinned; savoring the woman's every beautiful detail. "We'll see each other real soon," he said aloud, the second act had finally come to a close.

In Desperation   DK Gaston
Anthony

A splash of cold water woke me from a dark pit. Opening my eyes, nothing was in focus. I clinched my teeth in pain. I couldn't remember what had happened, though I recalled being arrested and being taken to Madden's car, but after that it was hazy. Wait a minute, I was running away from something—someone. A group of men grabbed me and started to hit me. They wouldn't listen when I tried to explain and hit me even harder. More water struck my face, went down my throat.

"Wake up, Holman. We need to talk," a stranger said.

The ringing in my ears prevented me from hearing the voice clearly. After a series of coughs, trying to clear throat, I asked, "Who are you?" I blinked repeatedly in an attempt to regain my vision. A hard slap across my cheek, forced my head to the side.

"I'm asking the questions," the stranger said. "But since we're going to be friends here, you can call me Bald Man."

"Bald Man?" I whispered, more to myself. The question got me another slap across the face, wrenching my head the opposite direction. The hearing in both ears was muffled.

"No more questions. You got that?"

I nodded, fearing I would get slapped again. I tried shifting, but I could barely move. I was sitting up, tightly bound to a chair.

      Glass crunched under the Bald Man's feet as he circled the chair. His warm breath wafted against the back of my ear. "What did Milroy tell you when you visited The Erikson Group?"

My heart hammered, had he been following Pam and me. I thought about playing dumb, but something told me that I would get worse than a slap if I did. "Not much really," I said honestly.

A gloved hand stretched over my shoulder with a silenced pistol. He pointed the gun at my groin. "Let's try this again," he said, so low I could barely make out his words with the ringing in my ears. "Talk, or I'll guarantee you'll never have children."

      My blurred vision cleared with an adrenaline rush through my body. My gaze transfixed on where the gun was aimed, I quickly said, "He said my fiancé was once admitted at The Erikson Group, being treated for Dissociative identity disorder."

Bald Man made a sound that might have been a laugh. He pulled back the weapon and I relaxed, only a bit. Scanning the room, I realized I was in the living room of my house. The crunching glass of the floor was the destruction that Yolanda had made. Why would he bring me back to my place? I tried to turn my head to see my captor, but he pressed the pistol against my creek and pushed my face away.

"Milroy loves playing with a person's mind. Me, I find more pleasure with cutting into a person's flesh," Bald Man said. The pistol slipped away from my skin. He said, "Stop telling me what to do?"

I asked, "What?"

More glass crashed under the weight of his foot as he moved away. "I know what I'm doing. I told you before I need Holman free."

Bald Man wasn't talking to me. He might have been arguing with someone on a cell phone, but I wasn't going to turn around to find out. The further he moved away, the more muffled his voice became. The ringing in my ears was fading and I strained to hear his side of the argument.

"I brought him here, because the police have already been through the house. But I'm hoping the target will be intelligent enough to figure out where I've taken him. That's right, I do have an actual plan."

Target? Were they discussing Yolanda? Was she the target?

"Wait a minute," Bald Man said. "I think I hear something outside the house."

I hadn't heard a thing, but that was no surprise. My hearing wasn't a hundred percent. Bald Man approached me from behind, shoved my chin into my chest and placed the muzzle of the pistol at the nape of my neck.

"Move and I'll kill you," he said. After what seemed an eternity, he let out a loud laugh. "So you've finally arrived."

Though my hearing was improving, I hadn't heard anyone enter. The way Bald Man had my head angled I couldn't see who he was talking to.

"Nothing to say? Not even a long time no see?" Bald Man asked playfully.

"Yolanda is that you?" I cried out, "Run, honey! Run!"

"Don't waste your breath, Holman. She won't run. I can see from her expression that she's tired of running."

In Desperation DK Gaston

I tried to lift my head, but Bald Man pushed it back down. "Don't worry about me, okay? Don't trade your life for mine." With the pressure of my chin I could only mutter.

Bald Man laughed. "You don't get it, do you? She's not here to help you, Holman. She's here to kill you."

"What?"

"You've cheated on her, remember? With Pretty Pamela Reeb."

"I never—"

"Too late for excuses, Holman. Too late for everything. You're either going to die by your fiancé's hand or mine. Too bad for you."

"No," I said staring catatonically at my quivering thighs. "This is insane. I didn't do anything. Why are you holding a gun to my head?"

"Because you fell in love with the wrong girl," he explained. "I loved her once too and she showed her affection by trying to kill me. After she left The Erikson Group and gave up doing contract work. I spent years trying to prove to my employers that she was a threat to the organization. Told them they needed to bring her back into the fold. When she stopped taking her meds, I knew it was only a matter of time before she screwed up. The meds kept her from remembering things. Without them, her old conditioning started to slowly kick back in, along with her memory."

Milroy had said something about her being an assassin. He said it was all in her head. Was that a lie? Was Yolanda a professional killer? But how would Bald Man know that unless he had been watching her. Milroy himself didn't discover that fact until Pam and I arrived to his office. We'd been thinking Yolanda had been setting me up to be arrested, but it was Bald Man. He has to be the one behind this.

"Yolanda," I said, "It was him, Bald Man. He's the one who sent you the pictures. He faked everything."

No answer.

Bald Man laughed. "You think she's going to believe any crap from you, Holman?"

In desperation, I blurted my thoughts, hoping she'd listen. "How does he know you went off your meds then, Yolanda? Milroy himself didn't find out about it until today. Because Bald Man has been watching you, that's how?"

Bald Man let out an audible gasp. "What are you doing, Yolanda? Don't listen to him. All Milroy wants is for you to return to The Erikson Group to be reconditioned. Don't listen to a man who's desperate to save his life." Glass crumbled as he stepped back, taking the pistol from my neck.

"Yolanda," I said jerking my head up.

I peered wild eyed at absolutely nothing.

"Fine," Bald Man yelled. If that's the way you want this to play out, then let's do it. The truth is, I'd planned to kill you anyway. No one shuns my love, stabs me in the leg and lives."

I glanced over my shoulder at Bald Man, who wasn't a man at all.

Yolanda stood in a corner of the room, near the window pointing a pistol toward the doorway that led to the kitchen. No one was there. She fired twice, plaster exploded from the wall. And then she shouted, "Yes. After all these years! She's dead! And it's all thanks to you Holman. Because you loved her, you made all of this possible."

The front door burst opened. Sergeant Maddox and two uniformed officers came rushing in, there guns pointed at Yolanda. She said, "Looks like we got ourselves some party crashers." Her pistol came up, aimed at me.

'Drop the gun," Madden shouted.

"Make me, tough guy. Oh by the way. How's the face?"

Madden automatically reached for a bruise on his jaw. "It's fine. Tell you what, Ms. Blakely, we can—"

Yolanda's face went into a rage. "Why did you call me that? She's in the kitchen, lying on the floor dead."

"You're Yolanda," I said softly. "There's no one on the floor. You only shot holes in the wall."

She seemed confused. "What the devil are you talking about, Holman?"

I swallowed hard and then said, "There is no Bald Man. He's a figment of your imagination. The Erikson Group is not an agency of assassins. It's a hospital. Try to remember."

"Lies," she yelled. "All lies."

"It's the truth," Pam said pushing her way through the crowded doorway. "You're Yolanda Blakely, my best friend. Tony's fiancé."

Yolanda looked at Pam and then at me. She lowered her arm. "Tony?"

"Put your gun down, Ms. Blakely, please," Madden said tenderly.

Yolanda's face turned into a mask of anger. "Lies," she yelled quickly raising the pistol.

The loud bang from Madden's gun roared like thunder through the house.

Yolanda crumbled to her knees, looked at me as if I had pulled the trigger. "Lies," she said before falling all the way to the floor, dead.

In Desperation
Pam

DK Gaston

The funeral for Yolanda was held a week after her death. It was quiet with only a handful of people who were mostly friends with either me or Tony. All charges against Tony had been dropped. The Erikson Group made sure that was done quietly, along with anything about the organization appearing in the news. It was all about keeping that ninety-eight percent success rate the company was so proud of.

Dr. Albert Milroy was forced to retire a day after the shooting. The reason he'd been so open, The Erikson Group was mandated to keep tabs on all former patients. Somehow, when Yolanda didn't renew her prescription, it had gone under Milroy's radar. He tried to cover it up, but after Yolanda's death, it became impossible.

Tony had a hard week, but I was there for him and he was there for me. We both lost a good friend yet sharing the experience brought us closer than either of us thought possible. We still haven't admitted our special feelings for each other. Being so soon after what happened, it didn't feel right.

Maybe it never will. I guess it doesn't really matter.

Our connection goes way beyond love.

ABOUT THE AUTHORS:

KR BANKSTON - is an escalating serial novelist, following in the famous footsteps of her idol, VC Andrews. CEO and Founder, of Kirabaco (ki-rah-buh-ko) Publishing LLC, which houses her works. She has written and published to date some 30 novels. KR's "BookOpera" series *"Thin Ice"* was voted Serial Novel of the Year in 2012 and 2013. Her other series, *"The Gianni Legacy"* has been touted as The Godfather of modern day. **Find all titles via Amazon.com**

ELIZABETH LASHAUN – resides in her hometown of Chicago with her family. As a child she wrote short stories, but then turned her attention to reading. At the encouragement of her family & book club, she completed her first novel. In 2010 Elizabeth founded Mayott Publishing and publishes her work through her company. Besides writing Elizabeth enjoys reading, traveling, and spending time with family and friends. **Elizabeth is the author of: The Love Trilogy (Inconvenient Love, Lethal Love, A Mother's Love) In His Absence. Find all titles via Amazon.com**

KEITH K. WILLIAMS – Born & raised in the gritty city of New York, Keith used writing as an outlet to ease the weight of the world he was trapped in. He's become a soldier determined to bring his unique style of fiction to the forefront of the world of literature. He's been labeled as a "Beast with a Pen" by his peers & contemporaries. Keith still resides in Brooklyn and manages to balance his time between his two loves; writing and his duties as a single father. **Keith is the Author of : Water Flows Under Doors, and Open Spaces and more. Find all titles via Amazon.com**

DK GASTON – was born in Detroit, Michigan. He served in the military as an Infantry Soldier. After leaving the Army, he earned his Bachelor's degree at Davenport University and began a career in Computer Networking. Since then, he's earned two Masters Degrees from the University of Phoenix. He is a devoted husband and father residing in Michigan. He is currently working on his next novel DK Gaston is the author of : *13: An Avery Hudson*

Adventure, Lost Hours, Darkest Hours, The Friday House, Tease, and The Promise. **Find all titles via Amazon.com**
He is a devoted husband and father residing in Michigan. He is currently working on his next novel.